DREAMLAND

DREAMLAND

by

NEWTON THORNBURG

ARBOR HOUSE
New York

Library of Congress Catalogue Card Number: 83-70475

ISBN: 0-87795-444-5

Manufactured in the United States of America
10 9 8 7 6 5 4 3 2 1

This book is printed on acid free paper. The paper in this book meets the guidelines for permanence and durability of the Committee on Production Guidelines for Book Longevity of the Council on Library Resources.

To John Larson
in memory

ONE

SIPPING hot black coffee, Crow watched the two of them from a window booth in the drive-in. Chicks out of the nest, he had thought at first, a pair of lorn adolescent lovers thumbing at the cars hurtling past them on the late-afternoon freeway. Then he saw the boy snarl something at the girl and roughly jerk her arm up into a hitchhiking stance more to his liking, and the gesture aged him, pushing him on into his twenties, already an executive type despite his long hair and scraggly beard and garish cowboy getup. The girl remained very much a kid, though, fifteen or sixteen at the most, all gangling jeans and long coppery hair. And it nettled Crow to see how she accepted her boyfriend's peevish discipline, with such a practiced resignation, as if it were already an old routine in her young life.

Finishing his coffee, Crow paid up and left. Outside, there was a sudden chill in the air and ghostly banners of fog had begun to drift in from the ocean. Too bad, he thought, that the freeway veered inland south of Ventura. Otherwise he might have had to get out the sleeping bag and stay right where he was till the morning burn-off, postpone for a few more precious hours seeing the old man again.

9

After all these years, it was not a reunion he looked forward to with any great enthusiasm.

In his rattletrap Datsun pickup, he drove on out of the restaurant's parking lot and headed up the freeway entrance ramp, telling himself that the young couple looked like trouble and that he was not going to stop for them. But for too long it had been his habit that if he had enough room and if a hitchhiker was not a one-eyed Hell's Angel armed to the teeth, he generally pulled over. And that was what he did now, motioning to the couple as he slowed to a stop on the shoulder of the freeway. The girl came running with a relieved smile, tossing her suitcase into the bed of the pickup before clambering in next to Crow. But her boyfriend took his good old time, wearily hefting a duffel bag in next to her case before he edged into the tiny cab, a sour smile twisting across his thin face.

"Boy, this is great!" the girl said. "I thought we were gonna be there for hours. I'm Reno and this is Jerry."

Jerry made a face. "Man don't want to know our goddamn names, stupid."

Crow contradicted him. "Sure, I do. And mine's Crow." He smiled at the girl.

"Crow!" she laughed. "Is that all?"

"No, there's also Orville W., but I try to keep that part a secret."

"Okay, Crow it is." She held out her hand for him to shake. "We want to go to Hollywood. You going that far?"

"Almost," he said. "Right next door."

She had warm brown eyes and a nice even face, with high cheekbones and a wide full mouth. Yet Crow judged that it would have surprised her as much as her boyfriend if anyone had told them that she would one day be quite a looker. He had pulled back onto the freeway by then and had the accelerator pressed to the floor, trying to work the old Datsun up to the speed of the traffic.

"Just hold on," he told them. "It gets a little breathtaking."

"I'll bet," the girl said.

"All this power under one hood," he went on. "I really ought to have a pilot's license."

The girl was giving him a quizzical look. "Are you somebody in

Hollywood?" she asked. "You know, like a director or somebody like that?"

Her boyfriend laughed. "Oh sure, stupid. That's why he's driving this old thing, because he's a big Hollywood director." He looked over at Crow and shook his head, inviting him to join in common ridicule of the girl, not to mention of Crow himself.

"What's the matter?" Crow asked. "You don't like my wheels?"

The kid shrugged. "A ride's a ride. I just meant—well, it ain't no Cadillac, is it?"

"Well, I like it," the girl said. "And we appreciate the ride. Don't we, Jerry?"

"Sure. A ride's a ride." He had slipped down on the seat, bracing his knees against the dashboard as he pushed his hat forward over his eyes, an urban-cowboy-type hat with a fan of orange feathers in front. His pointed boots also were fancy and colorful compared to the worn Red Wing workboots that Crow himself had on. But it was the youth's fringed buckskin jacket that Crow had the least enthusiasm for, mostly because he suspected that it was responsible for the miasma of body odor suddenly pervading the small cab. Opening the window wider, he lit a cigarette, which the girl promptly stole out of his mouth.

Lighting another, he asked if she thought she was old enough to smoke.

"Since I was twelve."

"And how old are you now?"

"Eighteen."

"You sure about that?"

She laughed. "Well, that's what we tell everyone."

"Okay. Eighteen it is."

"How about you?" she asked.

"Twice that."

"No kidding?"

"Thirty-five, actually."

"That's still a lot. It's what my mother is." The girl seemed crestfallen.

"Well, that's the way it goes," he said. "You just muddle along

11

and suddenly one day you're an old geezer."

She dragged on her cigarette, thinking about that. But then she caught his look and smiled.

"J. Christ, you ain't old. Forty's maybe old. But not thirty-five."

"That's a relief."

Crow had looked forward to this stretch of 101 south of Santa Barbara. It was hard by the ocean and the other times he had driven it the weather had been clear and the sun had lain flaked upon the water, a scattered fire dissolving in the surf as it broke beyond the beach houses and along the open stretches. But now the fog was growing heavier and the girl seemed so hungry for his attention that he seldom even bothered to look out at the ocean. Much had happened in her life during the past few weeks, she said. Her real name was Maryanne, could he imagine that, *her* a Maryanne? Jerry had started calling her Reno right off and she really dug it, because it kind of had class, didn't Crow think so? Reno, you see, was her home town. Her mother had worked in the casinos there for years, usually as a cocktail waitress. And her old man—well, the last they'd heard of him he was driving a cab in Chicago—could Crow imagine that, driving a cab in a city like Chicago? What a drag. Anyway, home was a drag too, nothing ever to do and with her mom always on her case about this or that, so when Jerry came through and hit on her right off, right there at the Taco Tico—well, she just had to go with him. It was that or die of boredom.

Throughout her monologue, Jerry sat slouched in the corner, occasionally shaking his head or making a face. Finally he told her to shut up if she knew what was good for her.

"Oh, I will, Jere," she promised. "I really will. I just wanted Crow to know how it is with us—how people really don't need a wedding ring and a house and all that junk on TV. You just need the road, that's all, the road and your thumb and you get by. You don't even have to work. Supermarkets throw away scads of food and—"

"I told you to shut up!" Jerry had raised his hand to hit her, but at Crow's look he stopped short.

"Just cool it," Crow told him. "If she wants to talk, she can talk."

But the girl was abject. Softly and fearfully she told her boyfriend that she was sorry. And she tried to nuzzle against him, only to get

12

shoved away for her trouble. Looking embarrassed, she turned back to Crow.

"What about you? Where you from?"

"Seattle," he said. "I'm between jobs right now—or at least I hope I am. Thought I'd drive down here and visit my father. He'll be sixty-eight this week. Haven't seen him in over four years."

Crow had no desire to talk about himself, but the girl was so cowed by then, so obviously desperate to have him fill the silence, that he went on and told her a little more: that he'd grown up in Los Angeles, that his parents had divorced when he was about her age, and that he himself had never married, preferring to kick around Seattle and the Northwest earning his living at everything from carpentry to entertaining.

"*Entertaining?* Really?"

"Afraid so."

"What kind?"

"A little guitar," he admitted. "A little singing."

"No kidding! What do you sing?"

"Pop. Country. Whatever needs butchering, I give it a try."

"Jesus," Jerry groused. "She'll have him singing in a minute."

Crow knew that the chances of that were nil; still, he could appreciate the kid's sense of dread. It almost made him laugh.

"Don't worry," he said, "I don't sing unless I get paid. Which has been something of a stumbling block."

By then Crow felt that the tension in the cab was beginning to ease and that Jerry had a reasonable hold on his temper, at least for the time being, while he was still Crow's passenger. So Crow idly asked the two of them what they planned to do in Hollywood, and the girl promptly told him—too much.

"Oh, it's easy to get by there. All the johns and chickenhawks and other creeps—Jerry says you can make real money off them."

Even before she got it out, he had hit her, backhanded her hard across the mouth. And her only reaction was to touch her fingers to her cut lip and look at the blood on them, almost clinically, as if she were only comparing this bloodletting with others that had taken place.

"I'm sorry, Jere," she mumbled. "I didn't mean anything."

13

They were headed inland by then and the fog was thinning, so Crow did not hesitate to pull onto the shoulder of the freeway. When he had brought the small truck to a stop he told Jerry to get out.

"If I go, so does she," the kid said. "She's with me."

"Just you," Crow told him. "Now."

The girl tried to protest, saying that Jerry was right and she couldn't leave him this way, they belonged together, she was *his*. But Crow told her to shut up. He reached over and opened the passenger door and shoved Jerry outside.

"Take only what's yours," he told him.

And Jerry did, yanking his duffel bag out of the truck bed and angrily tossing it down into the ditch.

"I'll get you!" he promised.

Crow closed the door and drove off, staying on the shoulder as the Datsun slowly gathered speed. The girl seemed more surprised than brokenhearted.

"You really can't do that, can you? I mean just dump a guy like that? Right on the road, like a dog?"

"Sure, you can," he said. "Sometimes it's easy."

*   *   *

Richard had felt lousy enough as it was, not having slept a wink the night before and already coming down from the upper Tad had given him early that afternoon, in the forlorn hope that he might finally relax and get into the mood of the party, get right down there on the oriental rug with all the other queens and simply let it happen. But that had never been his scene and never would be, no matter how desperately he might have wished otherwise, especially when he heard their final hooting derision as he beat his usual retreat. All that had been bad enough, in fact so downright negative that afterwards, tooling along the Hollywood Freeway, heading for Santa Barbara and home, he already had been in a cold sweat, with trembling hands and that sick loosening feeling in his bowels which promised yet another bout of diarrhea. And it was then, on top of all that, that the chugging suddenly began, the first cough of the supposedly super-reliable Mercedes engine gulping for fuel that apparently couldn't get through from the gas tank, at least not in adequate quantity.

Richard had gone on for almost a mile that way, chugging and slowing, being blasted by half the car horns in Southern California, until he finally took an off-ramp just before the Ventura interchange and limped along for another five or six blocks, looking for a service station whose appearance would not practically guarantee his becoming a victim of highway robbery. But not until he turned onto Lankershim did he find one, a reasonably clean-looking corner station, glassy and bright, uncluttered with broken-down cars or loafing males or other refuse. At the time it did not even cross Richard's mind that there might be a negative reason for the almost antiseptic appearance of the place. All he knew was that the station looked a more fitting harbor than most for a 450 SL owned by a Kellogg of Santa Barbara.

But right away things began to sour. The man in the brightly lit office barely looked up from his desk as Richard hopefully got out of the sports car and walked to the door. Worse, the man had a brutal beefy face with small hard pig eyes that seemed to stab right through a person, knowing all about him with only a glance.

"Yeah?" the man said.

Richard told him that he had car trouble.

"No shit."

Richard hated that word. "It just started chugging on the freeway. Do you think it could be the fuel line?"

"How the fuck would I know?" The man wearily tossed aside the magazine he had been reading, a dog-eared copy of Hustler. He looked out at Richard's car.

"That's yours, huh?"

"Yes, it's mine."

Another employee, a homely longhaired male younger even than Richard, had just come into the office from a back room. Looking out at the 450, he whistled admiringly.

"No shit? You really own that?"

"It was a gift," Richard told them.

"A gift!"

The man said it so loudly Richard almost jumped. He felt a bubbling sensation low in his bowels.

"Well, yes—my uncle is—well, never mind." He breathed deeply, trying desperately to get himself under control. He took out his wallet and produced an American Express card, the gold kind.

"But then, that's neither here nor there, is it?" he said. "The point is, the car needs to be repaired—the fuel line or the fuel pump, I don't know about those things. That's why I'm here. You fix it and I'll pay you. That's what this card is for."

The man laughed at him. "No shit. Is that how it works?"

"Meanwhile, I'd like to use your rest room. Is it locked?"

As he reached for the keys next to the door, the man gave his assistant a knowing wink.

"Which key would you like?" he asked.

"Either one," Richard said.

Both men were squealing and sputtering with laughter as he took the men's-room key and went around to the side of the building, barely making it inside and onto the stool before his bowels gave out. He flushed right away so no one would hear him and then he began to cry softly, sitting there in the chemical stench of this tiny room in an alien part of a city he loathed and feared, and yet didn't seem able to stay away from, not lately anyway. When he was finally able to get up from the toilet he scrubbed his hands thoroughly and pressed a wet paper towel against his eyes, hoping to blot out the redness and the terror he saw in them. Then he gathered himself together as much as he could and returned to the office, forcing himself once again to confront the enemy.

But this time he held up fairly well, he thought. Within a few minutes everything was arranged. The man said that the owner-mechanic did not come on duty until eight in the morning, so Richard would have to leave the car. He signed a work order, authorizing them to make whatever repairs were necessary, and he accepted the man's word that the car would "most likely" be ready for him the next afternoon. Meanwhile, Richard told him, he needed a taxi to take him up to the Sheraton Universal and both men had a good laugh at that. The older one said that Richard would have to wait at least an hour for a cab and advised him instead to take the bus, which would be along soon and could drop him at the foot of the hill, at Universal. All he would have to do is walk up to the hotel. The bus stop was two blocks down.

As Richard left the service station, the homely kid gave him a swishy "Ta-ta" and the two men had another jolly laugh at his expense. But Richard was so used to that kind of abuse that he barely thought about it. Far worse, as far as he was concerned, was the contempt he had felt directed at him that afternoon by his own kind, because he was so timid and frightened—frightened by almost everything, including this brightly lit stretch of Lankershim. He was afraid of waiting at the bus stop and he was afraid of dealing with the driver and, later, of walking up the hill to the Sheraton. All he wanted was to get back to Montecito as rapidly as possible, so he could lie in the sun by the pool again and while away whole days in his own lovely room, filled with the art and music that was his only real solace in life—except of course for Jennifer, his beautiful older sister and only sibling, home again now after a second divorce. The wonder of Jennifer was not just that she was nice to him, not just understanding as so many others were, but rather that she actually seemed to care for him, even to love him, just as he was. With mother drinking like a fish again and Uncle Henry so permanently and resolutely himself—Henry the Great, as he was called, the super-macho mover and shaker of the western world—well, that left Jennifer pretty much all by herself in the Poor Richard's Aid Society. Not that he meant to mock her—how could he, when in his heart of hearts all he had ever wanted out of life was to *be* her, to slip not only into her lovely bras and panties but into her very flesh as well, to *become* her, whole at last. And that was what he couldn't understand about so many other homosexuals, like those at the party that afternoon, who were if anything more macho than most straights, more hung up on strength and toughness and violence than a bunch of hetero marines. For such gays, cock seemed to be everything—religion, sport, food, weaponry—while he himself could relate to it only in feminine terms, as in his most persistent fantasy, in which he would pretend to be Jennifer on the occasion of her deflowering —not that he knew the actual truth of it, the when and the where and with whom. Far better to imagine it, to experience it in a hundred different settings, with a hundred different beaux.

But then enough of all that, he told himself as he reached the bus-stop corner, where two coarsely attractive young women already were waiting. Painted and dressed like whores, they soon proved the authenticity of their appearance. Catching his eye, one of them gave him a salacious wink.

"Hey, man, I dig the threads," she said. "Looks like real suede, is it?"

"I guess so."

"You *guess?*"

He looked down the street, hoping to see the bus.

"Hey, you didn't answer me," the girl said.

"Yes, the jacket's suede," he told her.

"Well, I thought so. And the loafers, what are they—real alligator?"

He didn't answer. The other girl was smiling openly at him, enjoying his obvious timidity. Trying to appear indifferent, he asked how much the bus fare was and if the driver would cash a twenty. The smiling girl snapped her gum.

"Where you from—Mars?" she asked.

"Santa Barbara."

"Same thing. Listen, you know what we do, me and Zelda here?"

He shook his head.

"We're exotic dancers. Which means we dance without clothes on. Can you believe that? A coupla sweet young kids like us?"

Richard said nothing.

"And would you believe that ain't the half of it? Tell me, Suede, you like to go twosies?"

He could not meet the relishing contempt in her painted eyes. "Not right now."

"Well, maybe later then. Maybe you could catch our act at the Club Ninety. It's in Hollywood, on Sunset."

"I'll try to remember," he said.

"You do that. It's a real fun place. When we're not dancing, we sometimes sit in the booths with the johns, and sorta mess around, you know? Without a stitch on. Tell me, Suede, wouldn't you kinda dig that? Wouldn't it make your little peepee stand up?"

The other girl was giggling and Richard again looked down the street for the bus, this time spotting one rounding a corner onto Lankershim about three blocks distant. Sighing with relief, he turned away from the girls and moved closer to the corner. And suddenly, across the intersecting street, a camera began to flash in the darkness, aimed at an old woman who at that moment was walking her dog along the sidewalk, next to the courtyard wall of an apartment building. Immediately she turned away, covering her face with one arm and pulling the tiny dog after her as she hurried between parked cars, heading across the street. At the same time two men came rushing out of the apartment building courtyard, ducking their heads and shielding themselves against the flash of the camera, though it was still aimed at the fleeing old woman—and thus at Richard and the strippers standing on the corner as she scurried past them.

Before the flashes momentarily blinded him, Richard clearly saw the two men heading for their parked cars. One was about forty, with a squarish face and neat blond hair. Carrying a white bag or pillowcase, he looked to Richard eerily like the movie star, Robert Redford. In an obvious panic to be gone, he clambered into a Ford Escort and took off—while the other man, fat, young, and bearded, had a Mercedes waiting for him, a limo with three other men inside who got out at the first sign of trouble and did not get back in until the youth was safely inside. And Richard was almost certain that they were Saudis, all four of them. Over the years, at his uncle's, he had seen enough of their swarthy, bearded stolidity—and their splendid Savile Row suits—not to recognize the look now.

But suddenly he had no more time. The bus had just hissed to a stop and the hookers were pushing past him, their bare legs flashing up the steps. Following, he found a five to pay the driver with and forgot about his change as he crouched to look out and see what was happening now on the corner. But the bus was accelerating loudly through the intersection and all he could see was a blur of darkness and reflected light.

Well anyway, he thought, it would be something to tell Jennifer about on the phone, when he called her from the Sheraton. The prospect made him smile, until he realized that the driver was glaring at him.

"You want your fucking change or not?" the man asked.

Richard took the money and stuffed it into his coat pocket. But

19

the driver was still unhappy with him.

"And would you mind sitting the fuck down? Would that be too much to ask, huh?"

In the back of the bus Richard saw the strippers laughing at him again. But this time it did not bother him at all. Soon he would be in his own motel room, alone, with a bed and a bath. And next to being at home, with Jennifer, that was about all he asked of life.

*   *   *

It had been Crow's intention only to put the girl up overnight in his father's house while he got in touch with her mother in Nevada. But Reno would not tell him her last name and had no wallet or other I.D., and she threatened that if he called the juvenile authorities or continued to try to locate her mother, she was simply going to run off and "hit the Strip" all by herself.

"No one's got to worry about me," she told him. "I'll make out. 'Cause I know the score. Jere taught me."

"Good old Jere."

"You're damn right," the girl shot back. "At least he wasn't some nosy do-gooder trying to ship me back where I don't belong."

"Sorry about that."

"Yeah, sure you are."

In point of fact, the girl had readily adjusted to the idea of not traveling with "Jere" anymore. While they were still on the freeway, she had admitted to Crow that it was a relief not having to worry all the time about getting slapped or punched, although she could understand why it happened, she said. It seemed she was always doing the wrong thing or saying something stupid. She didn't like getting hit, but she figured that she probably had it coming.

"He really had you trained," Crow said.

"How do you figure that?"

"Getting hit. No one's just 'got it coming.'"

"Yeah, well I must've."

In time the girl even admitted that she hadn't been "all that crazy" about sleeping outside and also that she'd had some doubts about Hollywood and how easy Jerry had said it would be to make it there.

"I mean, J. Christ, I didn't want to sell it or anything like that.

20

I'm not a whore, you know. But if it was just running scams on suckers—stuff like that—well, I guess I could've handled that okay. No big deal. But still, I guess I just wasn't sure what else Jere had in mind. He didn't ever go into detail about it. And whenever I'd ask—"

"He'd smack you one."

"Yeah."

So Crow had no trouble driving her on into Van Nuys, to the Valley house that his father had bought in the sixties, before the great blast-off in California real estate values. A typical thirties Spanish bungalow, it had a tile roof and beautiful interior woodwork, including arched doorways and built-in bookcases with leaded windows. Crow never did know why his father had kept the place all these years since the divorce, most of that time living alone in the six-room house. At least now the old man was renting out a basement apartment, was taking in money instead of forking it over, as Crow himself had been doing for longer than he cared to remember.

And it was the tenant of this apartment who answered the front doorbell when Crow and Reno finally arrived. For some reason, Crow had expected the tenant to be a man, a retiree like Crow's father. But this one was very much a woman, a stout, heavily made-up lady in her late forties or early fifties, with a Dolly Parton wig and a markedly proprietary attitude regarding Crow's father. When she told him that "the old man" was not in, Crow asked where he might find him.

"Just what's your business with him?" she asked.

"I'm his son."

The woman was not impressed. She looked at Reno. "And who's that?"

"A friend."

"I'll bet."

"A friend who has to take a leak," Reno put in.

"Maybe we could wait inside for him," Crow suggested.

The woman shook her head. "No, I don't think so. Listen, if you're who you say you are, why don't you just go down to the Green Mill. That's where you'll find him, lappin' it up as usual."

"How far is it?"

21

She pointed north. "Five, six blocks. Right on this street."

The prospect of living for a week or so in the same house with the woman prompted Crow to be politic. "Well, thank you very much. You've been a big help."

"Yeah," Reno chimed. "Thanks a heap."

The woman forcefully closed the door as the two of them went back out to the pickup and got in, Reno complaining that she wasn't going to be able to last.

"My teeth are floating," she said.

Crow shook his head. "Learn that from old Jere, did you?"

"Why, what's wrong with it?"

"It's unladylike. Dispels the aura."

"What *aura?*"

"Of feminine mystery," he intoned, kidding himself as much as her. "Without which a girl is just a—"

"A cunt?" Reno helped.

"There you go again."

She flounced against the door, suddenly in a pout. "You know, you ain't ever straight," she said. "Half the time I don't know whether you're laughing at me or what."

Crow was surprised. "If that's so, I apologize, Reno. I'm trying to be a friend."

"Then why laugh at me?"

"I wasn't. I was just trying to get across that a girl doesn't always have to sound so hip and tough. Especially when she's young and pretty."

"Pretty!" Reno scoffed. "Who the hell's that?"

Crow looked at her. "Who else? You."

"Bullsh——Oh, I forgot—I don't want to dispel the aura, do I?"

"That a girl."

"But who the hell wants to be pretty anyway? Rather be tough and sexy, any day of the week."

"Me too," Crow said.

Driving down this street where he had grown up, Crow felt very little sense of nostalgia, and not only because it was nighttime. Even in the dark, he could see that things bore little resemblance to what

22

he remembered from his childhood and teen years. The eucalyptus and pepper trees that once had lined both sides were gone now, lost when the street was widened to make room for two more traffic lanes between the bumper-to-bumper parked cars. The few remaining trees were mostly fan palms, incredibly tall and frail-looking, with a couple of anemic fronds growing out of the top, as if in a desperate effort to rise above the smog. Most of the bungalows had been replaced by duplexes and apartment houses already going to seed, some painted purple and orange and chartreuse instead of the almost universal white and beige favored when he was a kid.

One thing that appeared not to have changed at all over the years, however, was the Green Mill Tavern, where Crow did in fact find his father, sitting at the old wooden working-man's bar drinking a beer and watching the Dodgers on television along with six or seven other patrons, all elderly males, as was the bartender.

Crow had to tap his father on the shoulder to get his attention.

"Well, I'll be damned," the old man said. "So you made it after all."

An undemonstrative man, Orville Crow senior tried to get by with only a handshake, but Crow would not settle for that and put his arm around his father's shoulders, inflicting on him half a hug anyway. Choking and sputtering, the old man gave his drinking buddies an apologetic shrug.

"This here's my boy," he told them. "You wouldn't know it to look at him, but he's had five years of college. Can you beat it?"

Crow smiled and nodded to the other men as he casually picked up his father's glass of beer.

"Come on, let's sit over there." He gestured at the row of wooden booths along the wall, all of which were empty, even at this mid-evening hour.

Limping as he headed for the nearest booth, the old man finally took notice of Reno. "Who's she?" he asked.

"A friend. You think you could put her up for the night?"

Crow's father grunted as he sat down. "A friend, huh? Jesus, Sonny, am I gonna have to book you for contributing?"

Crow grinned at Reno. "Forgot to tell you—he's a retired Cop."

"It figures," the girl said. "And who's Sonny?"

23

"He thinks I am."

"Well, it's what you always were," his father groused. "What would you prefer—Orville?"

Reno was grinning at Crow. "Where's the john—*Sonny?*"

The old man told her. "Where it's always been."

As she went looking for the restroom, Crow sat down himself. "Glad to see you're still sweet as ever," he said to his father.

"What's there to be sweet about? Sweetness is for flower children."

It was one of the oldest sore points between them, a hearkening back to the late sixties and the time Crow had come visiting as a barefoot, bearded, pot-smoking "flower child" who incredibly (to himself now, anyway) had believed in and lived by the whole dizzy Aquarian credo, including ridding the world of police and soldiers and bankers so that the "people" could get down to the real business of life, which in essence was turning on, making love, and listening to the Beatles. After that visit, plus his failure ever to don a uniform in defense of his country, Crow had found it a slow process trying to rebuild the rapport the two of them once had enjoyed here in Van Nuys, before his mother filed for divorce and moved to Seattle with him and his sister.

"How've you been?" Crow asked.

His father called to the bartender for two more beers and a Coke. "Well, you tell me," he said. "How do I look?"

"Fine. You look just fine. Hair's a little whiter is all."

"And you look like a liar."

In point of fact, the old man's color was bad and he appeared to have put on ten or fifteen pounds, which was not good for someone his age. And then there had been the limping, from his arthritis apparently, worse now than on Crow's last visit.

"How about you?" his father asked. "Can't say you look too prosperous. Still not settling down, huh?"

"Well, I've been trying anyway, Dad. Even went into business for a while. Couple friends and I opened a bar and restaurant a few years back. Lasted about a year."

"What happened? You play your guitar for the crowd?"

Crow smiled. "Something like that."

24

"Or maybe it was the food. What'd you serve—granola?"

"And rolled oats," Crow said. "You think that could've been the problem?"

The old man had had enough. "Well, I'm sorry it didn't pan out."

Crow shrugged. "It was a long shot. A tough food town, Seattle. Too much competition."

His father then asked about Reno again, what Crow was doing traveling with a young girl like that. And Crow explained about picking her up on the freeway and that she wouldn't give him her last name, so he was unable to try to locate her mother.

"Then we call Juvenile," the old man said. "That's simple enough."

Crow shook his head. "Not tonight we don't. We put her up and we treat her nice."

His father looked confused for a moment, not sure yet that Crow was serious. And when he saw that his son was in fact very serious, he made a face and shrugged. "All right, okay—I'll be an angel."

Crow smiled at him. "That'll be the day."

Orville senior had two more beers before Crow could talk him into leaving, and by then the old man was feeling feisty. He kept patting Reno on the arm and saying that she was much too nice a girl to travel with the likes of his son and that she could do better—"Say a mature man, a retired man, with property." And he had begun to assume for some unknown reason that the girl was on his side against Crow, a party to his many old briefs against his son.

"Tell me, Reno, what do you think of a guy with five years of college and dresses like this, huh? Like a common laborer. Boots and jacket and—"

"Corduroys." Crow was the soul of helpfulness.

"Yeah, *them.* Can you beat it?" he said to Reno. "Thirty-five years old, a college graduate—you think he'd ever wear a suit? No siree. Lives like a bum, so he's gotta dress like a bum. Can you figure it?"

"Sure. Why not?"

The old man had not bothered to hear her. "And what's he drivin', huh? Lemme guess—a ten-year-old Jeep, right? Man

25

wouldn't be caught dead in a Buick. Would you, Sonny?"

"No way."

Crow patiently sat there and let the old man work out his phony hostilities against him, and then he finally helped him out to his car and drove him home, with Reno following in the truck.

The apartment tenant, who now gave them her name—Mrs. Emma Elderberry—continued to display an unusual interest in her landlord's affairs. Up from the basement, where she said her own "sainted" mother was already fast asleep, she promptly took charge of readying the guest room for Reno and the old man's office couch for Crow.

When Crow went to say goodnight to the girl, she appeared troubled by something and closed the bedroom door behind him.

"What's the matter?" he asked.

"Well, it just doesn't seem right," she said, "taking your room like this."

"The old man's office is fine," he told her. "It's got a nice big couch."

"Well, I still don't like it."

"It's no problem, Reno. Honest."

She gave him a wistful smile. "You know, it wouldn't have to be like this. I mean, you in there alone. And me in here alone."

"Oh, yes it would."

"Why? Am I that ugly?"

"No, but you're that young."

She looked both puzzled and disgusted. "J. Christ, I'll be *seventeen* this summer!"

"Right. Which makes you a minor, temporarily in my care."

"That all you think about is rules?"

"Goodnight, Reno." He kissed her on the forehead and scooted for the door, hoping to get outside before she could retaliate. But he failed.

"Goodnight, *Sonny*," she said.

In the kitchen Mrs. Elderberry was busy serving coffee and doughnuts to his father. There was a cup set out for Crow too, so he sat down at the table. The old man asked if Reno liked her room and Crow told him that she was very happy with it, which for some reason elicited a snort from Mrs. Elderberry.

"Why shouldn't she like it?" she observed.

By then Crow already was almost as irritated by the woman as he was curious about her.

"Good doughnuts," he said. "Tell me, Mrs. Elderberry, what makes you such a generous tenant?"

"Not a case of generous," she snapped. "It's my job."

Orville senior nodded sleepily. "That's right. Emma keeps house here and cooks, in return for room and board. For both her and her old lady."

"Don't call her that," she scolded. "You know I don't like it."

"Well, what in hell else is she but an old lady? Just like I'm an old man."

Mrs. Elderberry untied her apron and hung it up in a measured show of pique. Saying goodnight, she went on down to her apartment in the basement. Alone finally, the two men sat at the table smoking and drinking coffee, neither saying anything for a time. Crow tried not to watch his father's hands, which by turns mauled each other and worried his coffee cup and shakily stroked at his clothes and the gray stubble of beard on his face. Their restlessness was such that Crow wondered if there was a physiological reason for it rather than some casual nervousness of the moment. Uneasy himself, he rushed to fill the silence.

"Well, how's the private-eye business going? They keeping you busy?"

"Oh sure. All I can handle. At least all I *want* to handle."

"Well, that's good to hear."

The old man made a face. "And it's also bullshit."

Since his retirement from the police department eight years before, he had worked as a part-time consultant and occasional operative with a P-I company in West Hollywood. But even when Crow had been here the last time, four years before, his father had complained about the paucity of jobs the company sent his way. And now, with the old man nearing seventy and obviously not in the best of health, Crow would have been surprised if the company used him at all.

"Oh well," he said, "you've still got all this gorgeous sunshine

27

every day. What better place to loaf?"

He had felt stupid saying it and his father's sudden look of disgust made him feel even stupider.

"What do you take me for—a beach boy? I'm a man, goddamn it! And I want to do a man's work."

Crow nodded understanding. "I know. I was just trying—"

"To make me feel better—yeah, I know. But it don't work." He nodded towards the basement. "*She* tries the same thing. All the time. Only it don't work for her either. I may be old, but goddamn it, I ain't so old I don't know when I've been put out to pasture."

Crow sipped at the steaming coffee. "No jobs come in at all, then?"

The old man shrugged. "Oh, now and then something turns up. But it's usually a fluke. And from left field too. Always from left field."

*   *   *

Gardner Costello knew that it was not good, letting himself get so excited this early in the game. But the girl was doing such a fine job that it all seemed incredibly real to him, so real he could almost forget the careful coaching he had given her, including the exact words he wanted her to use. He could feel his heart already pounding hard as he sat there on the edge of the bunk looking down at her lovely young face and long black hair spread out over the pillow. As he'd instructed, she had the blankets pulled up to her chin, which made her so much more exciting to him than if she had been lying there nude, as she would be eventually anyway, all in the fullness of time.

"I just can't sleep, Daddy," she said.

"Maybe it's because Mommy's away."

For a moment then the girl lost it, thrusting her tongue out of the corner of her mouth as she tried to think of the next line.

"Relax," he prompted.

"Oh yeah—I can't relax, Daddy. Why don't you rub me?"

"Where?"

"My tummy. Okay?"

"Sure. Why not?" Reaching under the covers, he touched the silken skin below her breasts and let his hand slide down to her navel,

28

which he then began to circle in a gradually widening arc.

"Oh, that feels so good, Daddy," the girl exulted. "Do it all over, okay?"

Costello was not unaware what a silly figure he must have cut for the hooker: a soft balding man of fifty-five, with a Van Dyke and a pot belly, playing this pathetic little game of incest. At the same time he could not deny the hold it had on him, the unbelievable difference it made in his sexual response. And the weird thing was he'd never even had a daughter, or a son either for that matter. It was just something that was there, like a racial memory. And what did it hurt anyway? He got off on it. The girl earned a bonus. And his wife, safe at home in Ojai, never would have dreamed.

Outside he could hear the bells on the moored sailboats clattering in the light sea breeze, a delicate counterpoint to the brassy wail of a siren somewhere in Venice. Pleasantly, he could feel the slight roll of the boat as it took the chop coming in past the breakwater. But more important now, he felt her nipples beginning to harden under his touch, a response which somehow authenticated the whole charade for him.

"It's too late, baby," he told her. "You should have stopped me."

"But why, Daddy?"

"This is why." He took her hand and guided it under his bathrobe.

"Oh, you're so *big,*" she said.

"But we have to make it go away, baby," he told her. "And there's only one way."

Very slowly then, and almost reluctantly—because he hated for it to end—he joined her in the bunk, resting back against the bulkhead as she bent to her task, lying nude on top of the covers now, giving him his full money's worth there in the soft light from the galley. In time he could feel his heart begin to sprint even faster and finally there were a few moments when he thought he was surely going to die, but then it all was abruptly over and done and he was left sitting there like the old fool he was, naked and shivering and pathetic, dreading the moment when he would have to meet the girl's eyes again.

Miraculously, it was then that he felt the boat tremble and heard the light step above and aft, on the cockpit deck. Throwing a robe

29

on, he opened the louvered teak door between the bow stateroom and the main cabin and saw the shadowed figure of a young woman in a trench coat standing out on the deck. As she began to knock on the cabin's sliding glass door, Costello glanced down at the hooker, who was smiling.

"Who is it, the wife?"

"No, but you stay here anyway, all right?"

"For a few minutes, sure. But time is money, remember."

"How could I forget?"

Bending down, Costello went up the three stairs to the main cabin and proceeded back between the helm and galley to the lounge, where he unlocked the door and slid it open. To his right, and under his hand now, a loaded thirty-eight revolver rested on the second shelf of a built-in bookcase.

"What can I do for you?" he asked.

"I'm Barbara Queen."

Strangely, for a few moments the name meant nothing to him. "How'd you get through the gate?" he asked. "It's supposed to be locked."

"My father's Paul Queen."

That name registered. Taking his hand off the gun, he moved to the side and asked her to come in. He closed the door behind her.

"Cold out there, isn't it? But then April's always cold."

"I live in Colorado," she said. "To me, this is balmy."

"Yes, I suppose so. Why don't you have a seat?"

Though his boat was a thirty-six footer, a twin-screw cruiser that slept six, there was still so little room in the lounge that he was relieved as she sat down now. With more distance between them, he was able to see her more clearly: a woman in her mid-twenties, masculine-looking, with hard, dark eyes. As far as he could tell, she wore no makeup at all.

"I'm still interested in the gate," he said to her. "With what we pay for moorage here at the marina, we like to think people can't just walk in."

She smiled slightly. "Oh, the gate really isn't that high, you know. But never mind about that. I'm here on an errand for my father."

Her breezy manner left him speechless for a few seconds, during which she produced a rolled-up manila envelope from her raincoat.

"Photographs," she said, handing the envelope to him. "My father had them delivered to me. And from what little I understand, it's important to him or to the government or to somebody anyway that they I.D. the three people in the photos."

Costello had unclasped the envelope and now he took out the pictures: a half dozen five-by-seven glossies of a stylish, slightly built young man and two very sexy, very rough-looking girls standing on a street corner, apparently waiting for a bus that was approaching in the background. Four of the prints were grainy blowups: two of the male and one of each female. On the outside of the envelope someone had scrawled: *Corner of Lankershim and Beck 8 P.M.*

"What's this got to do with me?" he asked.

She smiled again. "Well, I don't really know. From what my father said, I gathered that you used to be a 'company' man too. You were in his section or something like that."

"Young lady, I'm *retired,*" he said.

"I know. So's he. He's got a place east of the Air Academy, up on a hill in the pines. And he just sits there on his deck staring out into space—got a view all the way down the front range to the Spanish Peaks in New Mexico. God only knows what he's thinking about, or involved in. All I know is some fellow ex-spook of his came by where I'm staying here—visiting friends—and gave me these photos and told me to bring them to you."

Costello had to make an effort to keep from shouting. "Miss Queen, I am *not* an investigator."

She gave a blithe shrug and stood up, preparing to leave. "Well, I wouldn't know about that. The man said you were the one to contact, that's all I know. He said that my father felt he could trust in your discretion."

"Discretion about *what?*"

"I really don't know. I have the feeling though that the people in the photographs must have seen something important. And the company must want to debrief them. Something like that."

"Then why doesn't the company handle it? Why a bunch of retirees, huh? Can you explain that to me?"

"Afraid not." She took another, smaller envelope out of her coat pocket and placed it on the bookcase next to her. "There's five hundred inside. For your time. And also the name of the motel where you're to report—with the names and addresses of the people in the photos. From what this man said, they want it all—names and addresses—by tomorrow night."

"Tomorrow night! You must be joking."

Again the shrug. "Well, it's up to you. If you don't want to do it, I'll just call my father and tell him."

Costello had the feeling that the girl knew exactly what his response would be to this seemingly innocent threat. To cover his embarrassment, his sense of humiliation, he turned away from her and reached for his liquor on the counter that divided the lounge from the galley. He asked if she wanted a drink and she said no, that she had to leave. Still turned away from her, he poured some scotch into one of his heavy-bottomed marine glasses and took a drink as he went through the charade of still being undecided, still mulling over the problem.

"I don't know," he fretted. "I'm pressed for time as it is. And to find all three of them in one day—"

"Well, I'll just take the stuff back with me, then," she said. "No problem. I'll just call my father and tell him."

As she reached for the envelope, he placed his hand on it. "No, it'll be all right," he told her. "I'll give it a try."

"Fine. It's out of my hands, then."

Like a sales executive, she flashed a phony smile and reached for his hand. Then she was gone, sliding open the door and skipping up onto the dock with the casual agility of a boy. As he stood in the cockpit, watching her move up the dock into the fog and darkness, Costello felt a biting sense of outrage. He had been taken to the cleaners and he knew it. Yet what else could he have done? Let her call her old man back in Colorado and tell him that Gardner Costello finally had said no? After all these years?

As he went back into the lounge, the young hooker came up from the bow cabin, her mouth and eyes freshly painted. She was wearing a short, tight yellow polka-dot dress and a fake fur wrap.

"Who was that?" she asked. "Your *real* daughter?"

32

He ignored the question as well as the sarcasm. "Leaving now?" he asked.

"Well, mission accomplished, right?"

"What'd you say your name was? Sherry?"

"Yeah, with an *i.*"

"And I can reach you at the same number?"

"Anytime."

He took her by the shoulders as she attempted to squeeze past him in the narrow aisle. "Listen, you think you'd be available for longer dates? Say, a couple of days on the boat. We could go out to Catalina or down to San Diego."

Like Queen's daughter, she shrugged indifferently. "Well, that depends."

"It wouldn't be like working," he said. "Be more like a date."

"But I'm a working girl."

"Just think about it, okay? A free vacation on a yacht—with a couple hundred tip. How could you beat that?"

She pulled free of his hands and he followed her out onto the deck.

"Okay, I'll think about it," she said.

In her spike heels, she needed his hand as she climbed the short ladder up over the gunwale onto the dock. Then she gave him a little wave and wobbled on toward shore between the twin rows of moored boats. Following so soon after Barbara Queen, she looked to Costello like a flamingo on the trail of a bossy barnyard hen. The fog quickly swallowed her up and he went back inside, shivering as he slid the door shut and locked it. He poured himself another drink and tossed it off, hoping to find some calm. But there was none.

Godalmighty, he muttered to himself, *Paul Queen*. He certainly didn't need that kind of complication in his life right now, just when everything was beginning to look smooth ahead, with his wife finally settling into their Ojai condo without him, renouncing for good the boat and the ocean and the life he wanted to live from now on. Which had meant real freedom for him, for the first time in his life, the chance to go out after bonita and red snapper—and for that matter, a Sherri or two—whenever the spirit moved him. He had been on full retirement for two years now, living comfortably on his government pension and the income from his mother's estate. Money was not a problem. And he had a few friends too, from his LEAA liasion stint with the Los Angeles police, on loan to Justice from the company.

So things lately had been looking up for him, and he had wanted them to go on that way. He wanted no part of Paul Queen and his crowd, with their penchant for international mischief-making. Christ's sake, he'd never even been a field agent, never a real part of Queen's section. His thing had been internal communications, systems for making sure that the company's right hand knew what the left was up to—admittedly a capability not always valued in the company. Which of course was why they had lent him out to Justice and the Law Enforcement Assistance Administration in the first place. Just because Queen and his spooks had nothing but antipathy for interdepartmental communications did not mean that others shared their bias. The L.A.P.D. in fact had valued him enough to get Justice to extend his liaison assignment by a full year. So his connection with Queen had been tenuous at best, and not very recent either. Why then this odd request? There had to be dozens of retired or semiattached company men in the area, men who could have handled the assignment as well as, or better, than he could.

But then the milk was already spilt. There was no sense crying over it. Queen wanted a job of work done and he would get it—though not necessarily in the manner he thought. For Costello was not about to overlook the fact that the thing might even involve Kellogg himself up in Santa Barbara, old Henry the Great, for whom Queen had been carrying spears all his life. If Kellogg *was* involved, then one could indeed get his tit caught in a very uncomfortable wringer if he wasn't careful.

That, however, was exactly what Costello planned to be—very, very careful. Sipping a third drink now, he began to sift through the names of local cops he knew, preferably retired, someone to whom he could safely subcontract the assignment, someone to play patsy if the need arose.

Still standing at the counter, he could see the unmade V-shaped bunk down in the bow cabin and he felt a sudden stab of anger. If

34

it hadn't been for Paul Queen and his daughter, he would have been drinking not to quiet his nerves but in celebration of a very gratifying evening. And he resented the loss. Still, he knew that later, warm in bed in the dark, with the boat gently rolling, he would go over it in his mind and experience it all again, second by second, the whole dazzling reality of it. The beauty. The passion.

TWO

CROW did not lack reasons for waking early the next morning. For one thing, the studio couch was only six feet long, his height exactly, which meant that through much of the night his feet were hanging over one end or his pillow was slipping off the other, neither of which he found conducive to sleeping late. Also, while it was still dark there had been the sound of a motorcycle revving somewhere in the neighborhood, and a little later a few rash rays of sunlight had begun to spill over the mountains and down into the Valley, edging almost timidly into this room which once had been his sister's bedroom and now served as his father's office.

In any event, by six-thirty Crow was already wide awake, lying there on the too-soft couch smoking a cigarette while he absently studied the room and its artifacts of the old man's long career in law enforcement. The desk was shiny clean and ready for business, with a gold-colored pen and pencil set poised in their holders, next to a hand-grenade paperweight. Above the desk, the wall was crowded with framed photographs of his father and his many partners and fellow cops over the years, both in uniform and out. And there were yellowed newspaper clippings too: *Robbery Suspects Surrender in Shootout . . . Police Break Hollander Case . . . Three Wounded in Bank Robbery Attempt.* Crow did not have to bother to read the clippings because he already knew them in detail from his previous visits here. And he knew the citations for bravery and for years served. And finally he knew almost by touch the configuration and texture of the item centered on the wall—the old man's detective shield, its gold-plating worn almost away, pinned against a field of purple velvet.

The whole collection was expensively framed and carefully hung. And though it was undoubtedly impressive in its way, for Crow it was also pathetic, because nowhere on the walls or desk was there a photograph or any other sign at all of Crow and his mother and sister. Rather, they had been consigned to a couple of albums that lay virtually hidden on a bottom shelf in the living room, albums that even five years before had borne a heavy coating of dust. So Crow tried not to let the little things bother him, such as the old man's penchant for criticizing almost everything about him, his clothes and haircut right along with his "aimlessness," that passion for not getting tied down which his father for some reason could see only as a failure of one kind or another. Still, for the most part, Crow believed a good deal of that nagging was simply guilt speaking out, the natural result of the old man's own feelings of failure and disappointment over his performance as a husband and father. It always amazed Crow to think back to the years before the divorce—years spent in this very house—and to realize what a small part his father had played in their lives even then. The man almost never ate a meal at home, and in all those years Crow could remember only a few times when his father had been home for the evening like other men, watching television with his wife and children. In recollection, those rare evenings seemed almost like holidays to Crow, a Southern California variation of Christmas.

From what his mother, Shirley, had told Crow, she and his father had never had much of a relationship, even in the beginning. After graduating from high school in Seattle she'd had a quarrel with her parents and to punish them had moved all the way to Los Angeles, expecting only to stay a short while. But within a few days of her arrival she had become a mugging victim and found herself leaning more and more on the strong, protective presence of the detective assigned to the case. That feeling was soon thought by Shirley to be love and after a few months she let herself be talked into marriage by the detective, Crow's father, who by then was thirty-three, fourteen years her senior.

At first, pregnancy and motherhood had kept her so busy she had little time to think about her feelings or face up to what she had done. But as the years passed, she came to hate California, with its endless sunny days and the pervasive feeling of rootlessness it inspired, "like you're on a long, cheap vacation," as she once said to Crow. And there was also the smog, the infamous San Fernando Valley air pollution, even then a great brown lake of filth that burned the throat and scratched the eyes. But worst of all, his mother told him, was her growing realization of the total lack of closeness and understanding between her and Crow's father. All he knew and lived for was police work, and she had come to hate everything about it, especially hearing about it. So after only a few years of marriage, she found herself thinking of her husband as a stranger with whom she shared a house, a dour older man relentlessly involved in work that did not interest her at all. Yet it took her a dozen more years before she did anything about it, finally pulling the plug, in the parlance of her husband's fellow cops. She filed for divorce and packed up her two teenage kids and moved home to Seattle, where in time she married a comfortable Bellevue dentist who gave her most of the things she had missed in Los Angeles, including friendship and a big house and big cars and a fistful of charge plates.

So Crow realized that there was good reason for the lack of family snapshots here in the old man's office, just as in the rest of the house. His father, he knew, still felt considerable bitterness toward Crow's mother. Even five years before, he had characterized her to Crow as a "quitter and a bugout," evidently conceiving of marriage as somewhat like a tour of duty in the Marine Corps. He hadn't minded the divorce so much, he'd said to Crow. He could have lived with that. But taking his children—"my only son, my only daughter"—twelve hundred miles away, that was something a man just couldn't forgive or forget. Not ever. And Crow had sensed that a portion of that bitterness had spilled over onto him as well, simply as one of those who had left, who had bugged out. So he tried to roll with the old man's punches. He took them on his arms and shoulders and kept telling himself that the fight would soon be over and they would be friends again, or better yet, father and son.

But Crow could not forget the previous night as the two of them sat in the kitchen finishing their coffee. The old man had got in some punches then that Crow still felt, random shots that had bled him heavily inside. They had come after the usual third degree about things in Seattle. Yes, he saw his mother and "the dentist" often enough, either at their place or at his apartment. And yes, she still looked good, Mother did, more like a woman in her forties than her fifties. And did Crow really still sing in bars? Could he actually get by on so little money as that? Didn't he ever want to take hold and *be somebody*, make his mark?

As expected, Crow's answers had only caused the old man to shake his head, more in wonder than in regret.

"I just can't imagine a grown man living like that," he said. "I mean, just going with the flow the way you do. Without any goal, or any risk or danger. It must make for real good blood pressure."

Crow had played along, reminding himself that his father was not only old but slightly drunk as well. "Sure," he'd answered. "Keeps the old blood pressure nice and low."

Again his father shook his head. "Jesus, when I think of my own life, what it's like out there in the real world. War is what it's like, Sonny. A war that don't end. The few of us against all of them. And I keep asking myself, I keep wondering—what would happen if you suddenly found yourself out there—where you're hated and shot at. I wonder how you'd react."

"I'd undoubtedly run," Crow said. "I'd just pack up and take off."

His father had looked very carefully at him then, trying to see through the years and the alcohol.

"You're mocking me, I realize that," he said finally. "But I still wonder. I guess I always will."

And now, this morning, Crow himself wondered. His father's questions had hit so hard because they were the very same things Crow had been asking himself for some time now. More and more,

39

he had been reminding himself that he was thirty-five years old and had nothing to show for it except a few good friends and a few good memories. Admittedly, it had been a conscious, almost deliberate choice on his part, this style of life he had acquired over the years. Even when he had gotten his degree at the University of Washington, he had wanted no part of teaching or of business, buttoning himself into one of those three-piece-suit jobs that the old man still seemed to consider a mark of success. And of course without such a position and its concomitant steady income, Crow had never felt solvent enough to take on that other "grown-up" responsibility: marriage and the raising of a family.

Instead he had gone his own easy way, starting with a college deferment during the Vietnam years and then simply dropping out of sight for a few years, working on a cattle ranch up in B.C. and later a gillnetter fishing the Alaskan coast, quite unintentionally giving the Selective Service the time and opportunity to lose his number, somehow drop it through the cracks of their wall-to-wall computers—which apparently was exactly what they finally did. Back in Seattle, he never heard from them again, and of course never inquired. For a time he drove a logging truck and he worked on a ski patrol in the Cascades. With friends he bought and rebuilt an old fishing boat and tried to break into the tough charter market, but failed in that just as he had in his recent ill-starred flier at being a restaurateur. And always, when and where he could—sometimes for money and sometimes not—he played his guitar and sang the songs he liked, competently, though only that. For certain, no one had ever come up and offered him a recording contract. But he had gotten by. He had had his affairs, and even had lived with a few of them. He had never gone hungry. And when he wanted to—which was not all that often anymore—he had gotten high.

So, all in all, it had been an easy, pleasant life for Crow. And that, he guessed, was the reason his father's shots the previous night had struck home. Just how long could a man go on coasting as he had? And just what *would* happen—how would he react—if he ever did find himself in what the old man called the real world? He was tempted to shrug it off, to tell himself that if his luck held, he might never find out. But he knew that was no answer. Not anymore.

The phone rang at a few minutes before seven o'clock and Crow was surprised to hear his father take it in the kitchen. He had not even heard the old man get up.

"Sure, sure, this is Orville," Crow heard. "Who's this?. . .*Lee?* Well, I'll be goddamned! How long's it been? . . . Yeah, sure. I'm free all day. You wanta drop by here?" The old man said nothing for a short time, then picked it up again. "Why sure, Lee, that'd be fine. Sure. I'll meet you there in half an hour . . . Well, of course, old buddy. Naturally. Confidential's my middle name."

Having slipped into a sweatshirt and jeans, Crow padded into the kitchen just as his father was hanging up. The old man looked as if he were about to perform a jig.

"Well, how about that?" he exulted. "Just like I told you last night. From left field. When you least expect it, something comes in. But always from left field."

"Who was it?"

"Can't tell you that, Sonny."

"Privileged, eh?"

"Yessir, that it is."

"You want any company? I could be your chauffeur."

The old man took in Crow's sweatshirt and jeans. "Nope, you ain't dressed yet. Or is that what they call dressed up in Seattle?"

Crow said that he could change and be ready within a few minutes. But his father only shook his head.

"Nope, this one *is* confidential." He was standing at the sink, finishing his coffee. "And it sounds big too. Client needs names and addresses to go with a couple of photographs. And he needs 'em like yesterday."

Coming from his father, the neologism made Crow smile. "Well, good," he said. "Nice to have a friend as a client."

"Who said he was a friend?"

"You did. You called him *old buddy.*"

"And you got big ears, young man."

Having poured himself some coffee, Crow sat down at the kitchen table. "What'd you expect, that I'd bury my head under the pillow?"

"Why not? Anyway, I've got to get crackin'."

41

As the old man headed for the bathroom, his knee seemed to give out and Crow jumped up to help him, only to be pushed away for his trouble.

"It's only the goddamn arthritis!" his father got out. "Jesus God! Why does it have to flare up now?"

Mrs. Elderberry had come up from her basement apartment just in time for his outburst. Now she watched as he limped down the hall to the bathroom.

"He's going out?" she asked.

Crow nodded. "Got a job somewhere."

She was nodding. "Yes, I heard the phone. And every time it happens, he thinks his arthritis acts up."

The woman looked to Crow as if she were on her way to a church social. She was wearing hose and jewelry and a dress with lace cuffs and collar. Even from across the room, Crow could smell her perfume.

"What do you mean—*thinks?*" he asked.

"Because he's always got it. It's just when he has to go out and do something that it gets to him. Your father's a man in pain. Almost constant pain."

Crow felt stupid. He had been primed to do battle with the lady. "Yeah, I was afraid of that," he said. "His limp is pretty bad."

After watching his father hobble out to his car and drive off, Crow picked the *Times* out of the bushes and sat down at the kitchen table with it while Mrs. Elderberry prepared his breakfast, a service she insisted on performing. The news, he saw, was not very new at all. A number of Democrat senators had joined the Republicans in trying to lower taxes to former levels, evidently willing to try almost anything in order to arrest the country's continuing slide toward insolvency. Given the economic situation, the rest of the news was so predictable he barely glanced at it, all the crime and violence and the wars and rumors of wars and acts of political unrest—all the folly with which the world's citizenry had occupied itself since the last issue of the paper, twenty-four hours before. So, like any other dazed reader, he turned to the sports and entertainment sections, half expecting to ruin his breakfast by reading about some other no-talent guitarist-singer signing a new million-dollar contract.

But this day there was no such calamity and he gladly pushed the paper aside as he heard Reno coming down the hall from the bedroom. Reaching the doorway, she just stood there for a few moments stretching and yawning, her eyes puffy from what Crow could only assume had been a very profound sleep. He also noticed, as did Mrs. Elderberry, that she was wearing only a tank top and panty briefs.

"Young lady, we don't parade around this house dressed like that!"

"I don't have any pajamas," Reno told her.

"Then get dressed first. Just like I do. Is that too much to ask?"

The girl slipped in behind the table. "There, I'm all hidden," she said. "I won't corrupt anybody. What's for breakfast?"

By then, Mrs. Elderberry had her hands on her hips. "And just what would you like?"

Reno made a face, giving the matter some thought. "Oh—scrambled eggs. Bacon. Pancakes. Orange juice."

"Is that *all?*" asked Mrs. Elderberry.

Reno frowned. "How about some Rice Krispies too? While I'm waiting."

*   *   *

By noon, Richard was already home in Montecito lying nude on his bed upstairs, almost at midpoint between the two JVL speakers, which were drowning him in the luscious voices of Domingo and Caballé singing *Manon Lescaut.* God, how he loved opera, all those instruments blending with the human voice in sound so glorious it almost made him weep. Through his open window he could smell the briny sea breeze as well as the scent of lemon and jacaranda, from the trees beyond the pool. It seemed incredible to him that only two short hours before he had been on that miserable street in Los Angeles, suffering through the fumes and all the clatter while he settled up with the Neanderthals, as he often called them, all the brutish lower-class heteros of the world. He had taken a chance and phoned them early from the Sheraton about the car and—wonder of wonders—they were finished with it. A new fuel pump, the man had said. Parts and labor, four hundred and ninety dollars. Richard had considered creating a fuss and not signing the bill, but that

43

would have meant calling Uncle Henry here at home, which of course was out of the question. The old man—or at least his accountant—would see the bill soon enough as it was, and Richard would certainly hear about it then. But what else could he have done? The car would not run as it was, and he was no lousy auto mechanic. He didn't know how to fix it any more than he knew what a fair price would have been for installing a new fuel pump. After all, the car was not some junky little Toyota. The Germans built things well, not cheaply. And anyway, his uncle probably made that much money every hour of the day. He would never miss it.

Richard had hoped that Jennifer would be home when he arrived, but she was at the tennis club, according to Mrs. Kim. Richard also had hoped to take a swim and lie in the sun for a while, but he'd found Uncle Henry already ensconced out there, reading reports and answering phones and issuing orders while he had his usual working lunch of tossed salad and fish and white wine, sitting there at an umbrella table in his obscene black bikini trunks—obscene because he was so ancient, almost seventy, though Richard did have to admit that the old buzzard was in pretty good shape for his years, without an ounce of fat on the smoky mahogany of his six-foot-three-inch body. Still, it was such a wrinkled body, so old-looking, with long, stringy muscles, as if he were a bushman or something. Richard never could understand the old man's appeal to women, unless it was the money. But then that didn't explain the rich ones who were always falling all over him too, right along with the golddiggers. You just never knew what "secretary" or "traveling companion" or "dear friend" you might stumble over when you happened into the main house, as the servants—old Kim and his ever-expanding brood— referred to the wing in which Uncle Henry lived. The other wing, occupied by Richard and Jennifer and their mother (when she wasn't drying out in a sanitarium, as she was now), was of course, simply, *the wing*. Very mysterioso.

But then Richard had to admit that the place *was* Uncle Henry's, the whole lovely sprawling sexy Spanish mansion, sitting on four acres high up in the Santa Ynez foothills, with a breathtaking view of the coastline running south to Carpenteria and beyond. (In the other direction, the Eucalyptus Hill ridge effectively hid Santa Barbara and Goleta and other atrocities to the north.) In his time, Richard had been to Tahiti and Hawaii and the Côte d'Azur, but they really didn't compare with Montecito, he felt. Here, climate and topography and money had combined to fashion the only real heaven-on-earth. All one could do was pity the poor bastards who had to live in Duluth or Cleveland or L.A. It was little wonder that they went in for orgies and highway robbery. So might he, if he'd had to share their brutal, artless lives.

Bored, Richard rolled onto his elbows so he could better observe his uncle down at the pool, as the sleek old fox swiveled from salad to phone to old Kim, who stood over his master like a well-trained Doberman. As Richard watched, Kim's older son, Lon, ushered a visitor out to the royal presence, a dark burly Arab who looked oddly like one of the men Richard had seen from the bus stop the previous night—one of the three who had jumped out of their waiting Mercedes limo to help the fat bearded youth fleeing from the building. His uncle of course stood up for the man, as he did for most Arabs, and had him join him at the table. But suddenly Richard had no time for this intriguing coincidence, because he had just seen Jennifer drive in through the front gate. Leaping up, he threw on his robe and ran downstairs to meet her, cutting through the living room out onto the colonnade, as they called it, the covered causeway running back to the garage.

Coming around the corner, Jennifer gave him a quick, warm smile and he had all he could do to keep from hugging her, which she would not have liked any more than Uncle Henry, had the old man witnessed it. Richard, after all, was only her brother, and they had been apart only a couple of days.

"Back already?" she said. "How's the car?"

"Fine. All it needed was a fuel pump."

"Good."

She was wearing a sweatshirt over her tennis outfit and her blonde hair looked curly and even frizzy from her workout, a lovely effect, he thought, against her golden tan. As the two of them walked back up to the house, she waved to Uncle Henry through the bougainvillea that grew along the colonnade. Richard followed her inside and up the stairs.

"Boy, do I need a shower," she said. "But I didn't want to stay at the club. That would've meant lunch and Mary Healy would have bitched all the way through it." She gave Richard a wicked smile. "I really creamed her."

"Bad, eh?"

"Six-two, six-one."

"Surprised you worked up a sweat."

"Almost didn't."

He had followed her into her bedroom. "Guess what those thieves in L.A. charged me," he said. "To fix the car."

"You tell me." She was pulling off her sweater.

"Four-ninety."

"Four *hundred* ninety?" At his nod, Jennifer laughed. "You're kidding."

"Afraid not. But we don't have to tell uncle yet, do we?"

She gave him a look, wry and commiserating. "No, *we* don't. And incidentally, what was that you said last night about seeing Robert Redford?"

Richard shrugged. "Just a lookalike. But some nut was shooting pictures anyway. Flashbulbs in the dark."

"Of him? This Redford?"

"I don't know. There was an old lady."

"Well, as I said, little brother, I've got to shower."

"Already?"

She had placed her fingers against his chest, and now she backed him gently toward the door. "Yes—already. I'll see you soon. And listen, be a dear, would you? Tell Lady Kim I'd like a tuna salad on rye and a tall V–8. I'll have it on the patio in fifteen minutes. Okay?"

"Of course. Bye." He waved slightly, awkwardly, as she gradually closed the door on him. Going down the stairs, heading for the kitchen, he thought how great it would have been if he had been born her little sister. There wouldn't have been any closed doors then, he told himself. Why, the two of them could have gone right on talking—while she showered. And who knows? Maybe they even would have showered together. It was something to think about anyway. It was always something to think about, what might have been.

46

Most of the morning Crow had been trying to pin Reno down about what her plans were, but she was not to be pinned. She kept changing the subject and then she fled into the bathroom to soak in the tub for the better part of an hour. Afterwards she conveniently found a movie on television, *Gidget Goes Hawaiian,* which she "just had to see."

Finally, though, Crow maneuvered her out onto the front porch and sat her down on the parapet, only to have her spin away from him. Straddling the parapet, he sat down next to her, squinting against the slanting April sun.

"It's time we had a talk, Reno," he said.

"Yeah, I know—what's my mother's name and address."

"No, I've already got your answer to that."

"You bet you have."

"All I want to know is what your plans are. What you're gonna do."

She was looking out at the street and the traffic on it, the motorcycles and dune buggies and lowriders growling past. "Boy, you sure are in some hurry to get rid of me," she said.

"That's not true."

"Oh, no?"

"Look, Reno, I'm a bachelor," he explained. "And I don't even live here. This is my dad's place, not mine. I can't just say, Sure, you can stay here for good."

"Who the hell would want to?"

"That's what I'm trying to find out."

"Your old man don't exactly dig me, you know. And Mrs. E. sucks, as far as I'm concerned."

"Oh really? At breakfast, you managed to let her wait on you, I noticed."

"So what?"

"So it's not all that honest, accepting favors from people you don't like."

She gave him a look of bewilderment. "Why not?"

"Forget it. But getting back—if you don't stay here, what's the alternative?"

"Wouldn't have been any problem for Jerry. He'd just say, C'mon, let's go. And we'd hit the road."

"Good old Jere."

"Just don't worry about me!" she flared. "I said I can make it on the Strip alone, and I can. Nobody needs you. Nobody appointed you!"

She had jumped down from the porch and he quickly followed, seizing her by the arm as she started down the walk. Gently he brought her up onto the porch again and pushed her back against the wall, his hands on her shoulders.

"Look, Reno," he said, "the way I see it, when I kicked Jerry out of my truck, you became my responsibility."

"That's bullshit."

"No, it isn't. You're a minor, Reno. A *kid.*"

"Here's your kid." She gave him the finger and he caught it in his hand and pushed it down.

"All I mean is I can't let you just run off alone—especially not into the hands of some pimp on the Strip."

"It's *my* business, what happens to me."

"And mine too."

"No, it ain't."

"I made it mine. That's the way it is."

"So why the big fucking rush to get rid of me, then?"

Sighing, Crow let go of her. "Nobody's trying to get rid of you. I just want some help, that's all. Some advice. Other than hitting the road, what do you want to do with yourself? Where could you stay? For instance, have you got any relatives anywhere—any girl friends living at home—someone who might take you in?"

She was shaking her head. "No, none of that. And I don't want it either."

"What, then?"

Though he had almost shouted the words, still he was surprised to see her eyes filling with tears.

"Just what's so bad about this, huh?" she got out. "You and me. A couple days more. That would really kill you, wouldn't it?"

Crow didn't say anything for a few moments, *couldn't* say anything. He felt stupid and mean, and suddenly he wanted very much

48

to take her in his arms and give her a reassuring hug. But she was too big for that, he knew, as much woman as she was young girl. She would not have understood.

"No, Reno, it wouldn't," he said. "A couple more days, that wouldn't kill me at all."

They were going into the house when Crow's father returned, swinging into the driveway and braking sharply. As he struggled out of the car, Crow went back to help him and the old man angrily pulled his arm free. He cursed and staggered and almost fell before Crow finally got a firmer grip on him, under his shoulder and around his back. Crow then helped him up the porch stairs and into the house, with the old man raging every step of the way.

"Goddamn useless leg! Goddamn feet! And why now, huh? *Why now?*"

Mrs. Elderberry had come in from the kitchen and she helped stretch him out on the davenport. She brought him some aspirin and asked if he wanted to go to the doctor for a cortisone injection.

"Well, why the hell else would I break off in the middle of the day?" he thundered. "With a job only half done?"

"I'm sure I don't know," she said. "But I'll call the doctor anyway."

As she returned to the kitchen to phone for an appointment, the old man continued his litany of outrage.

"And nothing else worked out either. Goddamn bus driver's day off. I go to his house in Burbank and where the hell is he? He's out in the desert with his goddamn dune buggy! Won't be home till dark."

"Well, that's about par for the course, isn't it?" Crow said.

His father angrily shook his head. "You just don't understand. This job, I'm under the gun. Client wanted the names and addresses by tonight. And I can't even walk!"

Gradually Crow pieced together as much of the picture as he could. His father's client, the "Lee" who had called that morning, had given him some photographs taken the previous night on a street corner in North Hollywood. The subjects were three young people waiting for a bus, possible witnesses to some sort of incident—maybe

49

a car accident, for all Crow's father knew or cared. All that concerned him was finding out their names and addresses and delivering the information that night to a representative of his client at a Hollywood motel. That's what he had been paid to do, he said. And that was why he had tried to find the driver of the bus that had picked up the three young people—the photographs had shown the bus's number, and he already knew the street corner and the time.

"It could've been like clockwork," the old man mourned. "The girls look like hookers and the kid like some kind of Fancy Dan. I figured the driver just might remember them, especially if they were regulars."

"So in a way you were already finished for now," Crow said. "All you could do is wait for the bus driver to return home."

"No, that's not *all* I could do!"

"What else?"

His voice hoarse with pain, the old man went on and explained that he had wanted to go over to North Hollywood and work the neighborhood where the photos had been shot, see if anyone there might have known the three. It was an off-chance, he admitted, but it just might have paid off. You never knew.

"But how the hell you gonna work a goddamn neighborhood," he asked, "when you can't even goddamn walk?"

Crow thought he knew how. "I'd have someone else do it for me," he said. "Like, say, your son."

It took a good deal of persuading before Crow finally managed to bring his father around, and even then it seemed that the old man acquiesced only because he believed his son would not get anywhere.

"It's probably a dead end anyway," he grumped. "And if you don't ask the right questions, you don't get the right answers."

"Garbage in," Crow said, "garbage out."

"Whatever that means."

Nevertheless his father did give him the envelope with the photos inside and the address and time scrawled on the outside. And by one o'clock that afternoon Crow and Reno were in the Datsun pickup driving up Lankershim, past Universal Studios and its sinister black tower. Within a few minutes they found the Beck intersection and parked.

"Looks peaceful enough to me," Reno said, as they started up the sidewalk.

And Crow could only agree. It was a narrow street lined on one side with flowering evergreen trees. There were a few bungalows on the street but most of the buildings were duplexes and small apartment houses. The one on the corner, across from the bus stop, looked a good deal like a motel: a two-story, U-shaped affair with a front courtyard and a covered balcony running back and around, so that every tenant had outside access to his own apartment. Because the apartments all faced the courtyard instead of the street, Crow doubted that any of the tenants there would have seen his trio. So he decided to start on Lankershim, at a cafe and drugstore on the same corner as the bus stop.

As they crossed the street, Reno gave him a mischievous look. "Now this is more like it," she said. "Reno Jones—private eye."

Crow pretended to take the bait. "*Jones?* That's your name?"

"J. Christ, now I've done it!" she lamented. "Now he knows."

"Sure, he does." Crow gave her a look and she laughed out loud.

To cover her embarrassment, she punched him on the arm. "You're just too swift for me," she said. "Sonny Crow—private eye."

"That's me, all right."

She was smiling as they went into the coffee shop and sat down at the counter. Crow ordered coffee and Reno settled for a chocolate shake and a hamburger. The lady behind the counter seemed to be the manager as well, so Crow took his time with her, making small talk before he finally opened the manila envelope and spread the photos out for her. It was a personal injury case, he said. He was working for the victim's lawyer. The person who had taken pictures of the accident inadvertently had "snapped these three on the corner" as well. The victim desperately needed their testimony, so Crow was trying his best to find them. Did she happen to know any of them?

Well, the manager was just not positive. She'd never seen the boy, she was sure of that, but the girls did seem vaguely familiar to her. Maybe they'd come in for coffee or a meal on occasion, or maybe she'd seen them walking past the window.

"They certainly are the kind you'd look at," she sniffed. "With those short dresses and all that makeup."

"Maybe they're hookers," Reno suggested.

"Oh, I'd hate to think that," the woman said.

Next door, Crow was not able to get anywhere with the druggist on duty, a grim-looking man with a shaved head. He refused even to glance at the photographs, saying that he wanted no part of lawsuits or lawyers. Crow tried to change his story then, admitting that it wasn't exactly a personal injury case, which only caused the druggist to get up and walk away from him, much to Reno's displeasure.

"Thanks for the help, Kojak," she called after the man, as Crow towed her out of the place, reminding her on the way that he was big enough to handle his own battles.

"Yeah, I could see that," she said.

"It was hardly a battle, Reno."

"So I noticed."

All Crow could do finally was grin and shake his head—and continue the hunt. He tried a wino in the street and a barber shop one block up on Lankershim, but got only interest for his trouble, especially from the wino, who for a short time seemed to believe that he too was now a part of the investigating team. But then he absently veered off down an alley and Crow didn't see him again.

Finally, two blocks down, they came to Sid's Service Station. There appeared to be only one man on duty, a blond long-haired youth who at first glance reminded Crow uncomfortably of Reno's friend Jerry, sharing that same look of physical and mental undernourishment. But from his desk in the glassed-in office he looked up with the kind of pleasant, guileless grin that Jerry never could have managed. And when, after some casual opening conversation, Crow explained what he was after and showed him the pictures, the kid broke into an even wider grin.

"Well, I think you came to the right party, Mac," he said, picking up one of the photos. "Him, I know. A real fag. A rich one too. We had his Mercedes in here overnight—needed a fuel pump, I think.

Hell, he just picked it up a couple hours ago." The youth was thumbing through a small stack of invoices. "Yeah, here he is. Charged it on American Express."

With no hesitation at all, the kid handed Crow the bill, almost as if he were proud of its fantastic four-hundred-ninety dollar total. But it was the card imprint, plus the filled-in address, that brought out Crow's ballpen. On the manila envelope, he copied it down:

Richard C. Kellogg
1 Old Trail Lane
Montecito, CA 93108

The youth was grinning at Reno. "Yeah, he was a real fruit," he said. "Real pathetic. When he asked for a key to the john, old Ralph, the night manager, he asked him *which* key."

Crow forced a smile as the kid laughed at the memory.

"What about the girls?" Crow asked, showing him the photos. "Any chance you know them too?"

"*Any* chance? Well, hell, yes. Them, I know even better than the fag. They come in here all the time. One of 'em's got this old yellow Cadillac convertible. Beautiful thing, but the engine's shot. Always needs work."

"You got their names and addresses? Maybe on a bill somewhere?"

"Naaw, they always pay cash. The owner gives 'em a cut rate, I guess. The one girl calls herself Zelda or something like that. But listen, why not just ask the broads theirselves? All you gotta do is go over to the Club Ninety in Hollywood. It's on Sunset. That's where they take it off, if you know what I mean." He peeled an imaginary strap off his shoulder.

"They're strippers?" Crow said.

"Yeah, only they *start* stripped. I been there. They're always invitin' us, you know, tryin' to get their money back, I guess. And just between us, I'd say they ain't just strippers either, if you know what I mean." In case Crow didn't know, he spelled it out. "They're hookers, them two. They *sell* it. They always got cash."

Crow thanked him for the information and said that he'd been a big help. Smiling, the kid then turned to Reno, as if he expected an expression of gratitude from her too. But he didn't get it.

"Come on, let's split," she said to Crow.

*   *   *

Costello had felt guilty after meeting Orville Crow that morning in the shopping mall parking lot and giving him the envelope. The fact that the old man had been so happy to get the assignment—so goddamned grateful, even—that hadn't helped matters either. And Costello knew it wasn't the money that had turned on the old boy so much as the chance to be working again, out there on the pavement right along with all his one-time buddies in the L.A.P.D. Costello hadn't given him the whole five hundred dollars, of course, because that would only have aroused his suspicions—money after all wasn't that easy anymore. But even three-fifty was not to be sneezed at, not for one day's work or even two days, if the old man's luck was running against him. Still, with Orville on the job, Costello knew that he didn't have to worry about paying in advance—the job would get done anyway, and get done right. And he could not help wondering if that wasn't the main reason for his guilt feelings. If in the end it turned out that he had indeed hired someone to play the patsy for him, wouldn't it have made more sense if that someone was a crook? Christ knew there was no shortage of them under the P.I. listings in the yellow pages. There never had been and never would be. Yet, after all was said and done, who had he chosen to do the job? One of the straightest arrows he'd ever worked with.

Fortunately, when he got back to the marina and carefully read through the *Times*, he had not found one single item relating to the area in North Hollywood where the photos had been taken. So he had a good, quiet breakfast on board and then he took the boat out of the marina and cruised south past Redondo Beach to Rocky Point before turning back. He didn't bother to put even one hook in the water and for a time he killed the engines and just let the boat float while he took the sun about four kilometers out, where the smog was almost negligible. He had stretched out on the seat behind the bridge helm, eyes closed, while the boat moved with the light sea, rising and plunging and rising again, a motion that soothed and replenished him almost as much as it terrified his

54

wife. Which of course was one of the reasons he lived on the boat: it was so much cheaper and less messy than divorce.

Lying there, sun-smitten, he thought of the girl Sherri and how fine it had been with her. One way or another, he promised himself, he had to get her to come along on a cruise with him, maybe for a whole week, down to Baja or up to the Channel Islands. Why, he could be her daddy every blessed night then, or maybe her brother, her teacher. There was no end to the possibilities. Laughing at himself, he wondered if he might not even want to play her john.

Finally he moved back to the helm and started home, loving the sound of the twin Volvos as they kicked in. He never could understand the fellows in the marina who were afraid to take out their boats alone. If there was a good wind, mooring a thirty-plus footer by yourself could be a little tricky, he had to admit that. But then that was just one more thing he liked about boating: it was about the only challenge left for him—if his luck held.

Later, after tying up, he walked over to Admiralty Way and bought a *Herald Tribune.* He took it into the Deli bar and ordered a dry martini on the rocks. As he waited for the drink, he casually scanned the first section of the paper, expecting to find nothing in it that the *Times* had not already printed. But there on the bottom of page ten a short, one-column item leaped out at him:

Photographer Dies in Darkroom Fire

Freelance photographer Ron Bernstein died of burns and smoke inhalation suffered in a fire that consumed his garage studio at 451 Whimple Street in Hollywood. A fire department spokesman stated that the blaze originated in the studio darkroom at around 10 P.M., while the photographer was working there. Chemical solvents and other darkroom supplies apparently contributed to the fierceness of the blaze.

Mr. Bernstein is survived by his wife, Elaine, and two married daughters. Mrs. Bernstein said that her husband in recent years had been working on a photo history of one-time movie stars now living anonymously in the area. Funeral arrangements were not announced.

A waitress brought Costello's martini and he tossed off half of it before going back over the news story, trying to read between its lines, trying to figure what it really meant. Oh, it could have been nothing, he knew. Just coincidence. Bernstein in all likelihood was not the person who had taken the pictures of the three at the bus stop. And there was no way of knowing, of course, without digging into the matter, which Costello naturally was not about to do.

Still, it *was* a possibility. It didn't beggar belief that a Hollywood paparazzo might have been at that intersection the previous night, hoping to snap some washed-up old star out for a walk or Christ knew what—when something happened. Something the three on the corner should not have seen. But what?

Costello was so galvanized by the news story and what it might mean that he almost missed a second item, on the opposite page. Even shorter than the first one, it nevertheless was sufficient to rivet his attention.

Choreographer Succumbs in North Hollywood, read the headline, over the brief one-column story. Keith Ambling, the apparent victim of a heart attack, had been pronounced dead on arrival at St. Andrew's Hospital in Van Nuys. A fire department spokesman reported that the fifty-one-year-old victim was already unconscious when a rescue squad, responding to an anonymous telephone call, had been forced to break into his locked apartment at 11501 Beck Street in North Hollywood. The spokesman further stated that Ambling had been found in a state of "apparent voluntary bondage," and that there were signs that a party had been in progress at the time of the victim's seizure. Various illegal drugs were found on the scene. Mr. Ambling had worked as a dancer-choreographer in numerous television shows, especially during the late sixties. He was also reported to have been active in the Gay Liberation movement. He was not married. Funeral arrangements were not announced.

Costello was familiar enough with Los Angeles to know that the address in the story, 11501 Beck Street, was at the corner of Lankershim and Beck—the same location scrawled across the envelope Paul Queen's daughter had given him. And that fact made his hand tremble as he tossed off the rest of his martini and set the glass back down. He even reached for a pack of cigarettes in his shirt pocket, for the moment forgetting that he had quit the habit over a decade before. What, he wondered, could the company possibly have to do with a Valley homo's squalid end? And especially Paul Queen, who was over sixty now and retired the same as Costello, living on a mountain in Colorado? The photographer Bernstein and the kids on the corner—just who in Christendom could they have seen fleeing the apartment building? The only possibility that occurred to Costello was that it reached beyond Queen, maybe even to Henry Kellogg, which meant Aramco, the Saudis, *oil.* And that scared the hell out of him. He did not like to think of Orville Crow tracing down those three kids and innocently delivering their names and addresses to the designated Hollywood motel. What the old man might be walking into Costello really didn't know, any more than he knew what Paul Queen had planned for the three in the photographs.

If it turned out, though, that Bernstein had indeed been the photographer—well, *then* Costello knew. But that was simply too much, just too goddamn unacceptable to give it any credence at all. Why, it would have meant not only that Orville Crow was in danger but Costello himself as well—for subcontracting the job, for simply *knowing* about it—and that he couldn't accept. A sleazy sex party in the Valley, it simply could not have been that big. And yet he had to resist a powerful urge to run to the phone and try to reach old man Crow, to call him off. But resist it he did. All his life he had successfully resisted just such urges as this. It was no more or less than a talent for survival. Some people had it, and some people didn't.

When the waitress passed near his table again, he asked for another martini.

"And make it a double," he told her. "With a lime twist."

Crow had to park on a side street one block from Sunset Boulevard, and though he knew that Reno was legally not old enough to enter a nudie joint he also knew better than to ask her to stay behind and wait for him in the pickup. She was in fact so eager to see the place that she practically pulled him along the bright and busy stretch of Sunset to the corner where the Club Ninety was located.

Going inside, Crow had the same feeling he always did when entering a strip joint in the daytime, as if he'd been dumped into some cretin's wet dream. There was the usual rose-colored light and silver glitter and smoke-clouded air, with a vampy saxophone number blasting from worn-out speakers. On the stage inside a horseshoe bar, a nude girl writhed listlessly against a dangling length of golden cord. A spotlight with a rotating disc of varicolored Plexiglas turned her body yellow and blue and red for the dozen or so dispirited men who sat scattered around the bar drinking beer in solitude and gazing at the dancer with glum indifference, as if sex were the furthest thing from their minds.

"Jesus, how do you breathe in here?" Reno asked.

"You don't," Crow said. "You fantasize."

She shook her head. "Not this kid."

Grinning, Crow guided her into one of the booths that lined the walls of the room. "Try to look twenty-one," he told her. "And say you don't want anything."

"But I do. I want a beer."

"I'll get one for you later."

"Promise?"

"Cross my heart."

Her smile was like a flash of sunlight in the gloom. Behind her, three booths away, two other dancers sat smoking and chatting. Neither they nor the one on the stage looked like the girls in the photographs.

"Boy, she really gets into it, doesn't she?" Reno was watching the dancer, who was bent over now, hanging onto the golden cord and provocatively swaying her fanny back and forth.

"Yeah, she's a real artist," Crow said. Holding a folded ten-dollar bill between his fingers, he beckoned to one of the dancers in the back booth.

"Real artist, my foot," Reno scoffed. "J. Christ, I could do that. You know, I probably *could* make it in this town, just like Jerry said."

"A wise man, Jerry."

"Well, it'd be better than starving."

"Just warn me ahead of time, okay? So I don't catch you in the act."

"Why? Am I *that* ugly?"

Crow was rescued by the dancer he had signaled, who came up to the table now, very shapely and very nude, as casual as a waitress in a greasy spoon.

"What'll it be?"

"I'll have a beer," Crow said.

Reno smiled at her. "Make it two."

As the girl went over to the bar with the order, Crow told Reno how great it was, having someone he could really count on. Which only made her shrug.

"She didn't even look at me."

"No, but the bartender is."

Squinting through the rosy clouds of cigarette smoke, the man eyed Crow and Reno suspiciously. Then finally he drew the two beers and placed them on the waitress's tray. As she served the beers, the girl gave Crow the bad news.

"That'll be six bucks."

He dropped the ten onto the tray and told her to keep the change.

"I'll just do that," she said.

Before she could turn away Crow had pushed the photographs in front of her.

"These are the dancers I want to see," he said. "When do they come on?"

"Different times."

"I really have to talk to them. Some goddamn rich lawyer in a Mercedes ran over my mother, and a photographer on the scene just happened to snap these two girls. They saw it happen. They could testify."

"Nine o'clock," the dancer said.

Crow had taken out another ten. "I'd sure like to know their names and where they live."

The girl shifted her weight and her breasts jiggled. "Zelda Leggs, like in the pantyhose. And Rose Dunn. Calls herself 'The Rose.' She really dug that movie."

Crow wrote the names on the envelope. He still had not let go of the second ten. "And their addresses?"

The dancer sighed with impatience. "They live together, at

Zelda's mother's place. But don't ask me the number. All I know is it's a little green dump on Oxford Street, just off Lankershim. It's next to a Catholic church. I been there a couple times, but I don't know the number. I ain't no computer, you know."

"That's for sure," Reno said.

Crow released the second bill and thanked the girl, as she gave Reno a look of weary contempt. Taking the tray, she headed for the back booth, where the other dancer was getting up, taking a hungry last drag on a cigarette before replacing the girl on the stage, who had just exited to the weary applause of a few men at the bar. The bartender was again squinting over at Crow and Reno.

"Drink up," Crow told her. "We've got to drive back to North Hollywood and get the number on that house."

She made a face. "I guess I really don't like beer that much."

"You could've fooled me."

"Me too," she said.

"Let's go, then."

It was a minor shock, passing through the doors of the strip club out into the brilliant California sunshine and the violent clatter of the street. Reno started to walk backwards ahead of him.

"Boy, your old man's gonna be surprised," she said. "We really did it, didn't we?"

"Looks that way."

"Or should I say, *you* did it? That bit about the rich lawyer running over your mother—that was pretty cool."

"I thought so too."

"Maybe we could go in business," she laughed, forming a sign with her hands. "Crow and Reno—private investigators."

"Why not Reno and Crow?"

"Why not?" She took hold of his hand and pulled him along.

"Come on, let's move," she said. "This is fun."

THREE

WITH each interminable sweep of the second hand on his college-graduation Seiko, Marvin "Head" Teller was becoming more convinced that the motel room, though large, was not large enough for both him and Billy Boy. Unless the man they were waiting for showed up soon, Teller was afraid that he was just going to have to do something about his jumbo partner's asinine chatter, such as drop a fistful of Valium into the man's scotch or stick his Walther nine-millimeter in his ear and suggest a few moments of silence. The mental picture of this—of frightened, shaky little Marvin Teller dominating the huge blond muscleman—almost made Teller giggle as he lay back on one of the twin beds, chain-smoking and trying to control his bladder. He'd already pissed three times in the last hour and he was afraid that if he did it again, Billy Boy might catch on and laugh at him.

"What you wanta watch now?" Billy Boy asked. " 'Real People' or 'WKRP?' "

"Either one. I don't care."

"Or there's—" Billy fell silent as he tried to find his place in the television guide. When he finally found it, he read off the third choice, pronouncing it "Greatus Mercun Hee-ro."

"You want that, huh, Head?" he asked.

"You decide."

"That one is dumb, I think. The guy keeps forgettin' how to fly. Christ, you'd think if a guy knew how to fly, he'd know how to fly. He wouldn't keep forgettin' it the way this asshole does."

He was hunkered down like a baseball catcher in front of the set, his massive shoulders and thighs straining against the seams of the ridiculous gray suit that Diefenbaker had insisted he buy, so he would look "more like a businessman." Teller, on the other hand, already had plenty of cheap suits from his days with the welfare department, but he doubted that any of them, including the one he had on now, made him look the part of a businessman any more than Billy Boy did. At five-seven and one hundred-thirty pounds, with thick glasses and a big nose and his pate already balding at twenty-seven, Teller wasn't all that concerned with what he put on his back, just so it fit the occasion. And since this was to be a "business meeting," he had dressed the part.

Billy Boy sat back on the foot of his bed now, tentatively settling for "WKRP."

"I don't dig this show either," he said. "It ain't funny, you know? But I'd like to bang the blonde on it, wouldn't you, Head?"

Teller shrugged. "Naaw, I'd just like to talk with her. Have a nice little heart-to-heart about philosophy and religion."

Billy gave him a shocked look, then grinned with relief as he caught on. "Yeah, me too," he laughed. "A real heart-to-heart."

He turned back to the TV for a short time and then whirled suddenly and began to pound on the bed with his fist.

"Goddamn waiting'!" he bawled. "It's spookin' me!"

"I don't like it either."

"Suppose this asshole don't show. What then?"

"He'll show, don't worry."

"But what if I blow it, Head? It's so fuckin' complicated."

"No it ain't. You just follow my lead, that's all. Just nod and keep quiet."

"What about later, in the car?"

"Let him do the talking. And when I pull over, have him pull over. Wait till I'm out of my car and coming over. He'll be rolling down his window to talk to me."

"It's complicated," Billy said.

"No, it ain't. You'll see."

"I rather just do it my way. Right here." Billy violently smacked his fist into his open palm.

"You'll get your chance," Teller told him.

"Yeah, I guess so."

"And you'll do fine."

"Yeah, I guess I will." A surge of confidence seemed to hit him now, for no reason at all, and he nodded vigorously. "I'll come through for you, Head—don't you worry. By the time I'm through, Queenie and Diefenbaker and everyone else in the goddamn outfit is gonna know we're the number one team. Just like last night."

"I ain't worried."

"And they'll know you was smart to line me up. By the time I'm done they'll all know you was smart."

"Sure."

"But it's killin' me, this waitin'. It's really killin' me, Head."

He went over to the television again and switched channels. Then he came back to his bed and sat there for the next five minutes watching "Real People" as if the story of a water-skiing cat were the most fascinating thing he'd seen in all his twenty-three years of life. Teller still found it hard to believe how totally indifferent the huge young blond was to the events of the previous night. One would have thought the two of them had set a trashcan on fire and inadvertently roasted a mouse in the process. From what little Billy Boy had said about the incident, Teller gathered that his partner felt killing someone accidentally didn't really count for anything. You couldn't take pride in what you'd done any more than you could feel guilty about it. It was simply something that had happened, that was all. An accident. Like running over a dog.

The word had come from Diefenbaker at slightly after nine last night, over the phone. Someone "important to the future of the group" had gotten his ass in a bind, Dief said, without explaining exactly what the bind was, other than that the man had been seen

63

—and possibly photographed—leaving some place where he should not have been.

"For some reason, there was this Hollywood photographer out on the sidewalk trying to snap some old lady walking her dog—don't ask me why," he went on. "And I guess our boy just stumbled into the line of fire. Fortunately he had the presence of mind to drive around the block and follow the guy home."

Diefenbaker then gave Teller the address and said that the leadership had to have the photographer's film and had to know exactly what he saw. If the man recognized *anybody*—if he knew *any* names —he would have to be "dealt with."

"How?" Teller had asked.

"I'll leave that up to you. Just don't go overboard."

"What does that mean?"

"Just that. Don't go overboard."

"Whatever you say."

"And don't forget the film he shot. Or any developed pictures. Our man says there were other witnesses too. Bystanders."

"What's his name?" Teller asked. "Shouldn't I know who this guy of ours is?"

"No. If the photographer gives you *any* name, that's enough."

But the man did not produce. Through split lips and loosened teeth he had cried and whimpered and begged Teller to believe that he had not seen the faces of anyone fleeing the North Hollywood apartment building—he had been shooting the old lady, he insisted. *Only* the old lady.

"Look at my prints!" he begged.

And of course Teller did look at the sheet of contact prints. There were over a dozen shots of the old woman and her dog, a few as she approached the camera, shielding her face; the rest as she hurried away, pulling the mutt along after her. Not in any of them was she facing the fat young Arab and the handsome, fortyish Anglo, both of whom had been snapped running across the sidewalk, toward the row of parked cars. Some of the contacts also showed the heads of three dark, bearded men in various stages of emerging from a black limousine into the street. Finally there were the shots of the three young people waiting at the corner bus stop—shots clearly showing

64

the full and open view the three had of the men fleeing the party. And because these and the prints of the old lady were the only ones being enlarged, Teller was inclined to believe what the photographer said. Unfortunately this was not enough to save the man, who by then was so frightened that he had defecated in his pants, which infuriated Billy Boy. Raising his massive fists, the huge blond began to pound on the poor man's head and shoulders, as if he were trying to drive him into the floor. Instead he merely knocked him senseless.

Teller gathered up all the contact prints and carefully removed the blowups from the drying line. Billy Boy meanwhile had lit a cigarette and tossed the match away—into a tall cardboard box filled with waste paper and discarded film and other refuse, some of it apparently incendiary, for the entire box as well as the wall behind it burst into flame. The fire was so sudden and so fierce that before Teller knew what he was doing he was already outside, without having given a thought to the photographer lying unconscious on the floor of the blazing garage studio. But even as he stopped, preparing to turn back, Billy Boy shoved him from behind.

"C'mon, man, *run!* We gotta get out of here!"

And Teller did just that, puffing along in front of his huge colleague until they reached their car, a block away. It was not until they were out of the area and on their way home that the enormity of what they had done began to hit Teller. But instead of the expected pangs of remorse, all he felt was an odd exhilaration, as if he'd mainlined a dose of adrenaline.

When the knock finally came, Teller bounded off the bed and opened the door—on a man much older than he'd expected. Barbara Queen had said that Costello would be in his fifties, a CIA retiree and yachtsman, most likely to show up in a blue blazer with white slacks and deck shoes. But this man looked a decade older and the suit he had on was worn and shapeless and brown. In addition, he limped slightly as he shuffled into the room, warily taking in Billy Boy, who was still sitting in front of the TV.

"You're Costello?" Teller asked.

The man nodded.

"Got any I.D.?"

65

"Don't need it," the man said, handing a manila envelope to Teller. "Here's the job, so I must be your man. My report's inside."

Contention, Teller knew, would only make his job more difficult. So he smiled and reached for Costello's hand.

"Fine," he said. "I'm Marvin Teller and this is Billy Sims. You have any trouble getting the names?"

"Not much. One dead end, but the second angle paid off."

"Good."

The old man made a move as if to leave and Teller casually stepped between him and the door.

"Hey, why not stay a minute and have a drink with us," he suggested, taking a bottle of Red Label scotch off the dresser. "I thought we might have a long wait, so I bought this earlier."

Costello looked at the bottle, then at Teller. "A man offers me expensive scotch, who am I to say no?" he shrugged.

He sank gratefully into one of two green plastic chairs near the drape-covered window as Teller poured the drinks, two fingers for himself and Billy Boy and twice as much for Costello. Teller then filled each of the frosted plastic glasses with ice, which effectively concealed the amount of scotch in them.

Costello nodded his thanks and took a good slug of the whiskey, afterwards shaking his head in appreciation.

"Well now, this is a little better. It's been a long day, believe me. Especially with this old knee of mine."

"Arthritis?" Teller asked.

"And then some."

"Don't it bother you, living at the marina?"

The old man shook his head. "Not enough of a difference. I like the clean air." He took another drink. "Yeah, it was some day, all right. As you'll see in my report, the two girls are strippers or bottomless dancers or whatever the hell they're called nowadays. They work in a joint on Sunset, the Club Ninety. And they live together, with one of them's mother in North Hollywood."

Billy Boy unexpectedly looked up from the television. "What about the dude?"

"He's from Santa Barbara—Montecito actually. Rich family, of course, living in a place like that. Drives a Mercedes sportscar.

And from what I'm told, he's queer."

"And it's all in the envelope?" Teller asked.

Costello nodded. "Names, addresses, everything."

"Good." Teller picked up the bottle again and refilled his guest's glass.

"Hey, you're gonna get me drunk," the old man said, in mock complaint. But he failed to pull his glass away.

It was Teller's understanding that Costello had taken the assignment only under some pressure, so he was surprised both at the old man's pleasant attitude and at the pride he seemed to take in what he had done that day. Teller's original plan had been to tell him that the job was not finished and that they all had to drive up to a house on Mulholland, where Teller's superior would fill them in on the next step. He had anticipated that Costello would not be very happy about the development, but he was confident that with Billy Boy standing at his elbow he wouldn't have had any real trouble getting the ex-CIA man to go along. Now, however, Teller had the feeling that it would be possible simply to motivate the man, to get him to *want* to cooperate.

"Mister Costello," he said, "I was wondering if you could take on another assignment like today's. Same pay, and not such a short deadline."

The old man didn't have to think about it. "Sure. Why not? I've got the time."

"Well, good. The only hitch is we gotta drive up to Mulholland, so our chief can give you the details. He's got a place up there, above Studio City."

"No problem. It's practically on my way home."

"Fine. We can just go up Laurel Canyon and connect. But listen, I think it'd be smart to have Billy here ride with you, in case we get separated. The boss's house, it ain't easy to find."

The old man didn't even glance at Billy Boy. "No problem," he said again. "Just let me finish this drink first. Then I'm your man."

Diefenbaker had paled the night before, when Teller, delivering the photographs, explained what had happened to the photographer. The nervous, portly Harvard law graduate had had to sit down at his

67

desk finally, his blocky legs evidently having failed him.

"Didn't I tell you not to go overboard?" he yelled.

"We didn't."

"Didn't I tell you?" he repeated. *"Didn't I? Didn't I?"* Teller said nothing and Diefenbaker sank back into his chair like a deflating blimp. Hopelessly he looked up at Barbara Queen, who had spread the photographs out on his desk to study them.

"Well, what now, huh?" he bawled at her. "What in hell do we do now?"

"First, let's see what we've got here," Barbara said.

"But the man is *dead!*"

She gave him a bored look. "Just cool it, okay, Dief? Head said it was an accident."

Diefenbaker kept shaking his head. "Oh Jesus, I don't like this. I really don't like this."

"You don't have to," Barbara told him.

She had divided the photos and placed those of the three street-corner witnesses in an envelope. "Well, it's obvious the old lady didn't see our boy," she said. "And the other man we don't have to worry about—I understand he's got as much reason as our guy to keep his mouth shut."

"What about the guys in the limo?" Teller asked. "Those Turks or Mafia or whatever the hell they are?"

"They're no problem," Barbara said. Only that.

And Teller couldn't help wondering why, since the goons obviously were with the fat young man, probably waiting for him, all trimly bearded just as he was, all wearing the same kind of fancy three-piece suits with vest lapels. Were they "no problem" because the fat one himself was no problem, just an accidental participant along with the chief's man in some obviously serious misadventure? Or was he the man himself, the one to be protected? Teller did not ask, of course, because he knew Barbara Queen would not have answered him. As the group's leader she played her cards exceedingly close to the vest. Besides Diefenbaker, she was the only one who knew the identity of their backer, the rich, powerful—and anonymous—"chief."

68

At the moment, she was putting on her raincoat, getting ready to leave.

"You mind telling me what you're up to?" Diefenbaker whined at her.

"Up to?" she repeated.

"That's what I said."

"It should be obvious," she told him. "What choice do we have? We have to find out who these three witnesses are."

"For what purpose?"

She gave him a frosty smile. "What's troubling you, Dief? Did you think we'd go on forever getting ready, playing our little games, spending the chief's loot? Didn't you think he'd ever get around to calling the tune?"

"You sure this is *his* tune?" he asked. "I tell you, I want no part of any more gratuitous violence."

"Who said anything about violence?"

"Then why bother to get their names?"

"To find out what they saw, of course. Don't you think that would be prudent?"

When Diefenbaker did not answer, Teller piped up in his place. "Of course, it would be. Any goddamn fool ought to be able to see that." He waited for Barbara to jump back in with him, against their common victim. And when she didn't, he took another tack.

"Hey, the guy in the photographs—our boy—he must be important, huh? A wheel?"

Barbara shrugged. "Just another one of the chief's projects, that's all. Same as us."

Diefenbaker had steepled his hands, playing the jurist now. "And suppose they did see the chief's boy," he said. "Suppose they recognized him?"

On her way out now, Barbara stopped to give him a patronizing pat on the head. "Just don't you fret, Dief," she told him. "We'll cross that bridge when we come to it. *If* we come to it."

Before she reached the door, she motioned for Teller to come with her. "Walk me to my car, Head, would you? Nighttime in L.A. — we all know what happens then."

Snatching up his jacket and running after her, Teller tripped and almost fell—he was that eager. Though Barbara Queen was far from pretty or shapely, she nevertheless seldom failed to stir his juices, possibly because of her beautifully husky voice or maybe just because of her manner, that tough offhand attitude which let him and every other man know precisely how unattainable she was. He'd heard the rumors about her being a lesbian—having a female lover back in Colorado, where she spent almost half her time—but even that didn't matter to Teller. Whenever he fantasized about her, though, he invariably found himself on his knees, going down on her. Somehow he just couldn't imagine her allowing a man any liberty other than that.

"I'm coming!" he'd said.

In his rearview mirror, Teller watched Billy and Costello in the old man's Buick snaking up Laurel Canyon behind him, past the houses—and *under* the houses—of a good portion of the world's dreamers. Rich and successful today, one false career move and they would wind up down at the bottom again, renting an efficiency apartment on Pico and gazing longingly up at the celestial glitter here in the Hollywood hills. Teller often thought how much fun it would be to spend a couple of days in the area with a bulldozer, pushing one cliff-hanging dreamhouse after another down into all those waiting canyons. Of course, for it to be a truly successful operation, everyone would have to be at home at the time. Only then, he told himself, would movies and TV stand even an outside chance of improvement.

Not for long, though, could Teller occupy his mind with such wool-gathering. Finally he had to think about what lay ahead, and immediately he felt the old pressure in his bladder. His weakness infuriated him. Christ, he'd already pissed umpteen times in the last few hours, even though all he'd had to drink at the motel were a few ounces of scotch. Nevertheless he was determined that no matter how strong the urge became, he was not going to give in to it. There would be no pulling over, not until he reached a suitable place, and even then it wouldn't be for the purpose of relieving himself.

Soon he turned onto Mulholland Drive, with its awesome views

70

of the city in either direction, vast grids of electric light stretching out into a seeming infinity. And he worried that it might unsettle Costello and put him on his guard, being alone in a car with Billy Boy on such a remote, aerial stretch of road. Teller knew that even if Billy sensed any nervousness on the part of the old man, he still wouldn't know what to do about it, since he was about as glib as a post. At the same time, it was also true that despite his great size, Billy Boy did not seem particularly intimidating, probably because of his beach-boy handsomeness, that dreamy, vacuous, little boy look he had.

As Teller followed the narrow, twisting road, he kept watching for a turnout that would serve his purposes. His main fear was that the night racers would be out in force, those celebrated California loonies who had turned this stretch of Mulholland into a death strip rivaling Indianapolis and Darlington. An occasional Corvette or other sports car would shoot on past him, but they didn't appear to be racing and there were no gatherings of fans on the various lookouts and turnouts that dotted the snaking road. Finally, about a mile past Laurel Canyon, he came upon a perfect spot located on the outside of a sharp curve on the Valley side. Free for the moment of idling racers or parked lovers, it had no guardrail or boulders or anything else to keep a careless and unsuspecting motorist from going over the side, into the canyon below.

As he swung off the road and came to a stop in the gravel, Teller's mouth suddenly was dry and his bladder felt as if a knife were pressed against it. But he ignored these little quirks of physical weakness and opened the car door anyway, getting out as Costello's Buick pulled in next to the Volkswagen. Teller slipped on his gloves and picked up the almost-empty bottle of scotch, which he had brought with him from the motel. Trying to appear casual, he then walked around the front of his car toward the Buick, just as the power window next to the driver disappeared into the door with a soft whine.

"What's the matter?" the old man asked. "You lost?"

Teller knew he would remember the moment all his life, the touch of irritability in the tired old face as Costello looked up at him inquiringly, indifferent to the movement next to him on the car seat, the large thick hand coming up and around.

71

"Not *me,*" Teller said to him. "I ain't the one who's lost."

And it was then Billy Boy struck, taking hold of Costello's chin and pulling brutally to the left while his other hand, heeled against the back of the old man's head, pushed in the opposite direction. It was the motion of a laborer opening a pipeline valve, suddenly, with all his strength. And in the split second of life left to him, the old man made a bleating sound and his eyes popped wide and his legs thrashed under the dashboard. Then it came, a kind of butcher-block sound, and Billy let go of him, just sat there watching as Costello flopped down against the car door, like a man trying to hide.

"He better not shit his pants," Billy said.

Teller poured some scotch onto the dying man and then pressed the bottle against one of his limp hands before dropping it onto the carpeted floor. He told Billy to pull the body over to the other side, and the big man did so after opening the passenger door and getting out of the car. Reminding him to wipe off the door handles on that side, Teller got in behind the wheel and moved the car to the edge of the turnout. He had no idea what lay beyond, whether it was a sheer drop or only a steep hillside covered with chaparral. And he decided not to bother to look, for even if the dropoff appeared unsatisfactory, he knew he was not about to drive on and hunt for a better place, not with a body on his hands.

Just as he got out, a car came around the curve and its headlights washed over him as well as over Billy, who was standing next to the VW, watching him. And Teller was relieved to see Billy fail to duck out of sight until after the double beam of light had already moved past him. Had he ducked a moment sooner, the person or persons in the car would surely have seen him do so, which would only have made them suspicious. But then that was something Teller had learned to count on—his partner's slowness. It was almost a gift.

With no other headlights in sight now, Teller reached through the open window and put the car in gear again, jumping back as it moved over the edge and plunged out of sight. Stepping to the edge himself, Teller could barely see the Buick rolling and cartwheeling down the hillside into the canyon, just an occasional glint of reflected light coming off its chrome and windows. Finally, at about two hundred feet down, the shattered car stopped rolling, and Teller

72

waited for the inevitable gas explosion, that hoary staple of television crash scenes. But none came.

Billy Boy was at his side by then, laughing and slapping him on the shoulder and saying "Good job!" over and over.

"You too," Teller said, pulling him on toward the VW.

They piled into the tiny vehicle and Teller put his foot to the floorboard as they roared out of the turnout and onto Mulholland. He did not switch on the headlights until he was well past the curve, and then he suddenly became aware of a warm dampness spreading between his legs. Furious with himself, he braked sharply on the narrow shoulder of the road and jumped out of the car, scrambling down an embankment into the scrub oak, where he fought to unzip his soggy fly and get the damn thing out before it let go altogether. And then it was almost like orgasm, only so much longer, a stabbing delicious sensation of prolonged relief as he stood there canted on the mountainside in the brilliant Southern California night. Like the stars above him, the Valley below blazed in a vast geometry of light.

*　　　*　　　*

When his father left to deliver the material that Crow and Reno had gathered, Crow had gone along with him out to the car, pretending that all he wanted to do was stretch his legs. But the old man knew him better than that and made a big show of going down the porch steps without using the railing. The cortisone shot that afternoon had made a new man of him, he said, even as he limped over to the Buick. And when Crow suggested that he go along with him, his father only laughed. He was not a helpless little baby, he said. He didn't need a wet nurse. And anyway, the job he was on was "extra confidential." He was supposed to deliver the material *alone,* and not to his client but to his "client's man—"someone in a Hollywood motel."

"And that's just what you're gonna do," Crow said.

"It is."

"Kinda figured that."

Crow watched him drive off and then he went back inside, where he was presented with the startling sight of Reno helping Mrs. Elderberry with the dishes. It seemed that the girl somehow, somewhere during the day had been assaulted by the radical notion that a teenager didn't *have* to be rude to a woman like Mrs. E., juicy target though she was, with her girdles and flowered dresses and champagne blonde wig. All through dinner the girl had been pleasant both to her and to Crow's father, which was surprising enough as far as Crow was concerned. But this—actually helping clear the table and do the dishes—it was almost too much for him to accept. Yet it certainly pleased Mrs. Elderberry, so much so that afterwards she invited the girl and Crow down to her apartment in the basement to meet her mother, a tiny, withered old woman sitting in a wheelchair in a soundproofed room, intently watching a game-show blaring from a television set not five feet away from her. She was in fact so absorbed in the show that she barely acknowledged her daughter's introduction of Reno and Crow.

Mrs. Elderberry explained that her mother was quite deaf and had "osteo-something," among other complaints.

"But she's happy," she went on. "She's got her TV and I take good care of her. I just wish I could expect as much when I'm her age."

Then, in an almost desperate rush, Mrs. Elderberry told them her unhappy story. Four years before, with their children grown and scattered, she and her husband had sold the Iowa farm they had lived on for thirty-six years and had moved to California, renting an expensive garden apartment in Santa Monica. With the first "real money" in their lives, her husband had plunged into the skyrocketing gold and silver markets, investing almost all they had in futures just as the two metals peaked and began their long downward slide.

"He might as well took a gun to his head," she told them. "The poorer we got, the sicker he got. First heart trouble, then a stroke, and finally—" She shrugged helplessly and shook her head. "Well, after I buried him, I naturally had to find a cheaper place for Mama and me. Which is why we came here. And that's about it. Family works a farm all their lives and this is how you end up. In a basement in California."

Back upstairs, Crow and Reno tried to recover some of the good spirits they had felt earlier. Crow made popcorn and the two of them tried to watch television for a while but finally gave up on it. Reno then prevailed on Crow to get out his guitar and play for her, and he ran through a couple of Beatles' tunes. She begged him to sing one then, and old trooper that he was, he flexed his vocal cords and tried two verses of "Let It Be." After that, however, he insisted that she join him, even though she said she didn't know the lyrics to any of the Beatles' songs.

"Just sing along," he told her. "You'll pick it up."

At first she was so embarrassed that she did more laughing and smiling than she did singing, but then she gradually let herself go and he was surprised at what a natural rock voice she had, rangy and strong and true. And she seemed just as surprised and pleased as he was.

"Hey, that was fun!" she said. "Let's do it again!"

"Why not?"

After "Let It Be," he taught her "Yesterday," and as she sang along with him her look of pure and total joy moved him unexpectedly. She was wearing shorts and a tank top and as usual she had a hard time staying in one place, by turns sitting with him on the couch and dancing around the room and getting down on the floor. But whatever her position, that pure strong voice and joyous smile kept coming at him and he felt again—just as he had on the porch that morning—an absurd need to take the girl in his arms and hug her. And he wondered what the hell his problem was, whether it was simply a case of frustrated fatherhood or if he was suddenly developing a Lolita fixation. But even as he trotted out these explanations, he recognized their fraudulence. Yet he couldn't bring himself to consider one other possibility—the obvious one—since he after all was still old enough to be the girl's father.

So finally, over her protestations, he got up and put his guitar away. He told her that he couldn't play anymore because his fingertips had grown soft over the past few months.

"And anyway, it's getting late," he told her. "Time you went to bed."

"What about you?"

"Thought I'd wait up for my dad. He shouldn't be this late."

"You think something's happened?"

"No—I just thought I'd wait up."

She gave him a wistful look. "Can't I wait with you?"

75

It was a question he never answered, for it was then that the phone rang. Picking it up, he heard a man's voice asking if he was the son of Orville Crow. He said that he was.

"I'm Sergeant Jack Olson, with the L.A.P.D. in Van Nuys," the man said. "I'm an old friend of your dad's. He told me that you were coming here for a visit. So I took a chance on calling you."

"What is it, Sergeant?"

The man cleared his throat. "An accident up on Mulholland Drive. I just heard about it."

"My father?"

"That's what I hear."

"How bad?"

"Bad enough, I guess. It's a one-car, off the road. Word is he's trapped inside."

"Fire?"

"I don't think so. But I don't know. That's why I'm heading up there right now. I thought I'd try you first."

"Where on Mulholland?"

"About a mile west of Laurel Canyon."

"Okay, I'll be there as soon as I can, Sergeant. And thanks for calling."

Mrs. Elderberry evidently had been worried about his father too, for she was already at the top of the stairs, just waiting there as Crow hung up the phone. Picking up his jacket, he told her only that the old man had been in an accident, and then he ran out to the pickup, with Reno right on his heels.

When they reached the crash site there were already two police cars on the scene as well as an ambulance and a fire department rescue unit, and for Crow their combined emergency flashers had turned the dark mountainside into some kind of obscene, official lightshow, almost a ritual celebration of disaster. A policeman with a lighted baton was keeping the cars moving on Mulholland, though a number of gawkers—probably having arrived before the police—already had parked on the turnout and were out of their cars, ganged up along the edge, watching the drama below.

As Crow got out of his pickup, a second policeman with a baton came running over to send him on his way, but Crow explained that the victim reportedly was his father. And the cop quickly assumed the manner of a mortician, diffidently leading him and Reno over to the rescue unit, where a crewman with a walkie-talkie was winching a traylike stretcher down the steep hillside to the mangled car below and the three or four men working there, in the light of lanterns, to free his father. Crow immediately started over the side, but the officers seized him from behind and pulled him back.

"You can't do anything but get in the way," the crewman told him. "The guy's already dead."

Crow felt as if he'd been punched hard in the stomach. He rocked on his heels and blinked. "How do you know that?"

The man nodded down the hill. "Two of them are medics down there. On this rig we're all medics. They tell me he suffered a broken neck. Died instantly."

Crow leaned back against the heavy red truck. Reno, looking at him, had tears in her eyes.

"I can't figure what he was doing up here," Crow said. "His business was in Hollywood. He would've taken the freeway."

The crewman shrugged. "I don't know anything about that. I just know he's here now and we got a job to do."

An unmarked car with a portable flasher pulled onto the turnout and a plainclothesman got out, a stocky, balding man with a florid face and small, hard eyes. He had a short conversation with one of the other policemen and then he came over to Crow and introduced himself as Sergeant Olson. He said that he had just learned the bad news and that he was sorry it had taken him so long to get there.

Looking down the hill, he sadly shook his head. "What a shame. What a goddamn shame."

"You worked together?" Crow asked.

The sergeant nodded. "Oh sure. We was partners for years. Your dad practically broke me in. And when he retired, we kept in touch too. Why, just last week he told me about you coming here for a visit. He was really looking forward to it."

Crow told the sergeant that there was no reason for his father to have been on Mulholland Drive, that he'd left Van Nuys for Hollywood just before eight o'clock to deliver a report he'd been working on.

"He would've taken the freeway," Crow said, again.

"You know who his client was?"

"No."

"You know where he delivered the report?"

"A motel in Hollywood. He didn't say which one."

Sergeant Olson frowned and shrugged. "Well, I'm afraid all that just doesn't matter much. He *was* up here, driving alone, and the boys say there's an empty bottle in the car."

"What kind of bottle?"

"Scotch."

"He didn't drink whiskey."

"Oh, sure he did. At least with me he did. So all it looks like, son, is an accident. He probably fell asleep at the wheel and his car just went off the road. It happens all the time up here."

"Just like that, huh? Nothing but an accident."

Olson gave him a searching look. "You saying it could have been suicide?"

It was a possibility that had not even occurred to Crow, and it shook him. For a few moments he could not even answer the man.

"No, of course not," he got out finally.

"Well, let's not worry about all that now," the sergeant said. "There'll be an autopsy, naturally, and we'll go over his car with a fine-toothed comb. Remember, your dad's one of us. If this ain't the accident it appears, we're gonna know about it."

He gave Crow a pat on the shoulder and said that he had to leave, but would stay in touch with him. Nodding to Reno, he went back to his car and drove off. Crow peered down the hill again and saw that the officers had got one of the car's doors open. He looked at Reno and saw that she was shivering, standing there in the cold mountain air with nothing on over her tank top and shorts. As he took off his jacket and wrapped it around her, he could hear some of the commentary of the vultures gathered along the dropoff. For the most part they appeared to be young anglos, seven or eight of them with their girl friends, some of whom looked chicano. All, though, were dressed in the manner of oldtime motorcycle gangs, clotheshorses festooned in worn leather and butch jewelry and other odd vestments. And all sounded high.

"I say he's a white guy, in his forties."

"You're fulla shit. A spade, I say, about twenty-five."

"You bot' suck. I got two tokes sez he's a Mex. A ninety-year-old beaner."

They all laughed, and Crow moved away from them, to the other side of the rescue unit. Once more he looked down the mountainside to see what progress the officers were making, and it appeared that they were working the body out of the wreck and onto the traylike stretcher. Turning away, Crow again found Reno standing in front of him, tears running freely down her puckered face.

"Why are you crying?" he asked. "You barely knew him."

"I'm not crying for *him*," she said.

And finally he did what he had been wanting to do all that full, long day together. He took her in his arms and felt his own tears begin to spill into her hair as she desperately hugged him back.

"Don't worry about me," he told her. "I'm fine."

FOUR

THE previous night, when Barbara Queen had asked him to walk with her out to her car, Teller still was not sure just how serious the operation was to be—or how far he was to go. He had hurried to Barbara's side as she left the one-story garage type building that housed the group, under the cover of New Day Construction Inc., as the leadership had named it, relishing the irony of it all, the fact that construction was about the last thing the group was interested in.

When they reached her car, Barbara told Teller to get in with her and he readily complied.

"I just wanted to clear up a few things for you, away from Dief," she told him. "He's such an old woman lately. There's no sense even discussing this sort of thing around him."

Teller nodded. "So I've noticed."

"But the point is, the chief does call the shots. It's his money that pays our salaries and rents this dump. So what he says goes."

"Naturally," Teller said.

"But as far as Dief is concerned," she went on, "—well, I guess he figures our little dirty-tricks campaign was all the man wanted. We paint a few swastikas on synagogues and burn some lawn crosses in the name of bringing down the whole rotten edifice—"

"So we can build new," Teller put in.

Barbara nodded impatiently. "Yeah, well, I'm afraid the chief is not all that patient. He's got other fish to fry—bigger fish—and one of them is our boy in North Hollywood. I guess I can tell you this much about him—he was involved in some kind of fag sex party and somebody got killed. Anyway, the chief is serious about protecting him."

Teller sat there looking at her, almost hypnotized by the theatrical drone of her voice. "How serious?"

"Dead serious," she said. "And I choose the word carefully. The chief wants no loose ends at all. And anyway, asking those three what they saw—what good would it do? They might not even remember till afterwards. And then it would be too late."

"So we—" Teller didn't know quite how to put it.

"We hit them," she helped. "We eliminate them. We protect the chief's interest. And our own."

Teller's bladder by then was aching. "He said as much? The chief?"

Barbara Queen nodded. "To me, yes." Then suddenly a light edged into her eyes, a look of almost salacious mischievousness. "But even if he hadn't, just think about it, Head—what better way to wire the man in with us, with our political and financial future? We go all the way for him, in *his* cause, not ours. So what choice does he have finally but to become even tighter with us? We not only know too much, but we *did* too much—for him."

Teller was trying hard to read her expression, the wry smile and gleaming eyes. The truth, he felt, had to be in there somewhere.

"But how?" he asked. "How would we do it?"

She shrugged. "You're asking me? After all, aren't you the one who got us to admit Billy Boy to the group? You and your golden ape—I thought that was the reason, to handle the heavy stuff, if it ever came up. Isn't that what you said?"

Teller was nodding. "Yeah, I guess so."

"You guess so—well, I *know* so." Barbara Queen was not smiling now.

81

Teller swallowed hard and squeezed his legs more tightly together. "We can do it," he said. "I'm sure we can do it."

"Of course you can."

"It won't be easy."

"It doesn't have to be, just so it gets done." She was looking straight at him now, her eyes unblinking. "And remember, you won't be alone, Head. You don't have to worry about getting their names. I'll get them for you. I'll use someone outside the group."

"Okay," he had said. "Fine."

*   *   *

After returning to the motel in Hollywood, Teller carefully wiped the room down to make sure there would be no fingerprints left behind, in case old man Costello had blabbed to anyone about his destination the night before. Billy Boy meanwhile sat watching television and tossing off V-and-V's—vodka and Valium—as if he were in a contest to see how fast he could pass out. But Teller knew better than to say anything about it, these sudden desperate thirsts that Billy had, because the big man had no talent at all for handling criticism. The few times Teller had censured him for this or that reason, Billy had gone through an identical response syndrome, totally ignoring Teller at first, pretending if not deafness at least a very large indifference to what was being said. Then all of a sudden he would jump up and seize Teller by his jacket and either shake him like a wet dog or slam him rudely against a wall—which of course was reason enough for Teller to hold his peace now. But then there was also the little matter of Teller's own drug habit, the fact that he popped Valium and Quaaludes and other tranquilizers throughout the day and never even bothered anymore to try to fall asleep at night without a Seconal or two. Not for nothing had he earned the nickname "Head" in college, though at that time he had smoked most of his dope. Now he dropped it—and in sufficient quantity that he usually had an illicit supplier or two, a "connection," just as if he were a user of hard drugs instead of brand-name depressants.

It was a habit that did not worry him, though. He told himself that he was simply a drug-dependent type, highly strung and highly driven, the kind of man who needed drugs in order to function, which was the exact opposite of someone like Billy Boy, who used

82

his V-and-V's to find intoxication and oblivion. So Teller thought of his habit not as a weakness but as a sign of strength, the crutch of a cripple determined to walk, and walk far.

Barbara Queen had paid for the room in advance, so when Teller was finished, he simply left the key on the dresser and guided Billy out to his precious red Transam, which they had left parked at the motel. It angered him to have to rely on the half-stoned Billy to follow him home to his apartment in Studio City, but he didn't want to come back for the car later. And anyway it gave him something to file away in his brief against the big man, failures he could detail later for Queen and Diefenbaker, if the need arose.

In Studio City, he parked and locked the VW, then went into his apartment to check the mail and phone his answering service, which had only two calls to report, both from Diefenbaker, both urgent. It gave Teller no small feeling of pleasure to ignore them. He was just now getting up to speed, he told himself. No way was he going to check in with a gutless temporizer like old Dief. Later maybe, after the *faits* were already *accompli*. Or was it *accomplis?* Languages never had been his forte.

He did want Barbara Queen to know, however. In fact, he had a real itch to tell her what had happened to her CIA contact Costello. On the phone, she sounded as if he had gotten her out of bed, which didn't worry him at all, not with what he had to tell her. But he was barely finished when she cut him off, saying that was enough, that she didn't want to hear another word until the job was finished. Crestfallen, he hung up—and hurried into the bathroom to urinate.

Downstairs, he prodded the nodding Billy over to the passenger seat and then he took the wheel of the Transam and drove north on the Ventura Freeway. It was a cool clear evening and he was able to leave the car windows closed as he followed the wide ribbon of concrete through the electric-lit hills toward the coastline. He kept the car at a steady if boring fifty-five miles an hour, not wanting to attract any law enforcement attention of any kind during these few crucial days. Occasionally, in the glow of the dash, he would look over at the sleeping Billy Boy and it amazed him what a sweet and innocent killer he looked, with his great curly blond head propped against the car window and his cherub mouth slightly open, his whole baby face an absolutely clean slate.

He remembered when he had first heard about Billy, not quite six months before. Never a raging success with the ladies, Teller once again had resorted to dating a mouse he'd known from his days in the welfare department, a girl one of the other caseworkers had disparagingly called "the horny conscience of California." Now a parole officer, Betty Unger had told him over candlelight and house wine about the "disturbing" new case she had, a "huge and absolutely beautiful" young man who had spent almost a third of his twenty-three years behind bars of one kind or another. Orphaned as a boy, he'd been raised by a succession of inadequate foster parents in the Ozarks. At fourteen, living on a farm in Missouri, he had killed a foster father with an ax, reportedly for having kicked the boy's pet dog. At sixteen, after escaping from a reformatory, he had killed a man in a bar fight in Oklahoma City and later was sentenced to prison in Texas for assault with intent to kill, having been hired by a tavern owner's wife to do away with her husband. Out again, he moved to California and twice had been arrested on murder charges that failed to stick. Finally convicted for robbery and assault, he served a few years at Soledad and just recently had been paroled.

Betty Unger told Teller that what made Billy such a fascinating case was the paradox he presented. Because he was outwardly "so sweet and beautiful," it was almost impossible for her to believe he'd done the things he had.

"He's really a very caring person," she said. "I've had dinner with him a few times, and he's so sweet. Really. He's always opening the door for you or standing up when you come to the table. Stuff like that. He knows what he's done—he's not insane, no court has said he was, anyway. But I really don't think he appreciates the seriousness of it. Of murder, I mean. He acts as if—well, as if it weren't that big a thing. As if he'd been caught speeding. Something like that."

Teller asked her if she wasn't afraid of the man.

"Oh no, Billy's a perfect gentleman with me. Really. The way he is now, I don't think he'd hurt a flea. And he's really terribly handsome. He could be a movie star. He really could."

His only problem was work, she went on. He had to find a job that he could hold. And it wasn't easy. Men were afraid of him. And jealous of him.

Teller had to grin now as he recalled his response to all this.

"Maybe I can help you," he'd said to poor sex-starved Betty. "I just might have something for this Billy of yours."

And he did. It had required salesmanship on his part, though, a real snowjob to get the man on the payroll at New Day Construction. Diefenbaker of course had seen no need for "hoodlums and psychos" on the roster. But Barbara Queen had been more broadminded. You never know, their leader had said. To build a great machine, maybe we'll need a few nuts.

Just south of Ventura, Teller pulled off the freeway and found a small mom-and-pop motel to his liking. He paid two days in advance for the best room available, one with twin beds, a bath, and "adult TV." Virtually carrying the monstrous Billy into the room, he carefully stood him up before letting him topple like a cut tree onto the nearest bed. Teller then took a bath and shaved and popped a Seconal, which finally netted him a few hours of sleep before dawn. He got up and bathed and shaved again, and then he watched the "Today Show" on television for another hour, as Billy Boy continued to sleep. But finally he decided that it was time to get started and he got out his drug stash again and emptied a dozen Seconal capsules one by one into a plastic vial and then dissolved the contents in a few ounces of hot water. He carefully recapped the vial and then flushed the empty capsules down the toilet.

Back in the bedroom, he turned up the TV sound until Billy finally woke.

"Hey, what's up?" the big blond asked.

"Me," Teller said.

His partner slowly sat up on the tiny bed, bowing it like a hammock. "What you been doin'?" he yawned.

"Making a cocktail. For Mister Kellogg."

"You are bad news, Head. You know that?"

"We're the bad news boys."

Billy Boy laughed happily at the designation. But once he was on

85

his feet, he quickly discovered his hangover. And for the next quarter hour, as he showered and shaved and got back into the same clothes again, he kept whimpering and moaning like a run-over dog. In time, though, he was ready and the two of them went across the street to a cafe and ordered breakfast: coffee for Teller and double orders of wheatcakes, sausages, and scrambled eggs for Billy. As the big man ate, Teller went through the L.A. *Times* to see if there was any mention of Costello's death, but he found nothing. Figuring that the "accident" had happened too late for the morning edition, he tossed the paper aside and finished his coffee.

After leaving the cafe, he went into a liquor store and bought quarts of scotch and vodka and Seven-Up. In a ladies shop he bought black lace underwear and hose and lipstick and eyeliner—for himself, he told the clerk.

"Pretending to be a man is such a drag," he explained, as the scandalized woman fumbled the items into a bag.

A half hour later, with Teller again at the wheel of the Transam, the two men were driving slowly along the curving residential streets of Montecito, looking for Kellogg's house. Teller tended to think of the town as simply a part of Santa Barbara, a rich city's richest part, a kind of gentile Beverly Hills, only more rustic and beautiful, the way it ran from the ocean up into the foothills of the Santa Ynez. Great shaggy eucalyptus and live oak lined the goat-path blacktop lanes leading past some of the most beautiful estates in California, most of them set far back from the road, half hidden in the rocks and trees, not advertising the elegant pools and tennis courts and stables one could only catch glimpses of as they drove past.

It was the kind of place, Teller knew, where two Valley hot dogs in a Transam just did not belong, even if they had been law-abiding squares on a square's mission instead of engaged as they were in ultimate mischief. So Teller drove carefully along the alien streets, still not wanting to attract any attention. And finally he found himself on Old Trail Lane, a potholed blacktop curving through the deep eucalyptus shade past a half dozen estates and ending in a cul-de-sac fronted by rock walls and a huge wrought-iron gate, standing open. Beyond the gate a narrow driveway ran back past a shuttered gatehouse and climbed toward a distant Spanish-type mansion

86

that Teller could see only bits and pieces of, hidden as it was in the trees. There was no name on the gate; just the address, in wrought-iron script: *One Old Trail Lane.*

"This the place?" Billy asked.

"Yeah, but we can't park and wait for him. We'd stick out like a sore thumb."

Teller turned through the cul-de-sac and went back up the road, trying to find an inconspicuous place to pull over and watch for young Kellogg. But Old Trail Lane was a street without a single parked car, and they had to drive almost to the freeway before they found a likely place, a small park in which two children were playing on the swings, watched over by an elderly woman in a domestic's uniform. Teller pulled in and parked, facing the car away from the children, toward the road. He had the photograph of Kellogg in front of him and he knew that the youth drove a Mercedes 450SL. He reasoned that if the kid had business anywhere—in Santa Barbara or Carpinteria or even L.A.—he would have to pass the park on his way to the freeway. But even if they did see him, Teller now wasn't sure how they would make the intercept—they couldn't just run him off the road, could they? The original plan had been to park near Kellogg's house and wait for him to come out. Depending on the circumstances, Teller had planned to take the kid either when he was getting into his car or by heading him off as he came out of the driveway. From that point on, the whole thing would have been easy, forcing the fag at gunpoint into the car and driving him down to their motel in Ventura. But the physical layout of the road and the house changed everything: not only couldn't they park on the goddamned deserted Old Trail Lane, but the house was so hidden you couldn't see anyone leaving until he was on top of you. So Teller decided that he still had some thinking to do. Some *better* thinking.

"You know, Head," Billy was saying, "there's some of this I can't figure."

"Like what?"

"Like last night, hittin' the old man. I can see this dude here and the two girls, 'cause they seen something they shouldn't of. But I can't figure the old man."

"Just a matter of tying up loose ends," Teller told him. "Costello delivers the three names to us and then reads about it later, what happened to them—well, he just might put two and two together and go to the police."

"Then why use him in the first place? Why not just get the names ourself?"

"Queen's idea," he admitted. "She figured we would've had to ask a lot of different people a lot of questions. After the hits—after they heard about it or read about it—they just might remember us or my car or maybe even the license number—you never know. But this way the trail just leads back to the old man."

"Who ain't here no more!" Billy twisted his hands against each other, as if he were disconnecting two hoses.

"That's right."

"Okay, I guess I see it now. But about this one here—no muscle, you say?"

"None. Not even a bruise. I want it to look like a suicide. Two accidents, a suicide—and then the girls."

"And them—?"

Before answering, Teller lit a cigarette and blew smoke against the dash. "Well, that'll kind of be up to you, Billy. It's gotta be different from the others—say, a sex thing. Something far out. Maybe just let yourself go, you know?"

Billy's baby blue eyes had glazed. His great body shivered and he blew on his hands, as if to thaw them. "Just wing it, huh?"

"Sure. Just let yourself go. Become an animal."

"Jesus, I'm cold, Head. And thirsty. I could use a V-and-V."

"Me too. But we don't get any, not until we're finished here."

Billy shivered again. Then, giving Teller a wild, exultant look, he smashed his fist into his palm. "Boy, this is something else! We're really cookin' now, huh, Head? I say we're really cookin'!"

But even as his partner celebrated, Teller was watching a sheriff's patrol car coming down the street that intersected Old Trail Lane. Passing the park, the car slowed noticeably and the deputy at the wheel leaned forward and gave Teller and Billy Boy a long sunglassed stare. Teller waited until the car was out of sight and then he backed out and drove off, heading for the freeway.

"It's no good here," he said. "We gotta figure some other way."

They went on into Santa Barbara, driving around the lovely sun-drenched city for a time, taking in its famed courthouse and the Spanish Mission. Circling back to the oceanfront, Teller followed the long graceful curve of the beach all the way back to Montecito, and he promised himself that if everything worked out as planned, one day he just might make Santa Barbara his home. And he figured he would be able to afford it too, if what Queen hinted at was right —that in doing the chief's dirty work, they would in effect be tapping into his fortune. Teller could just see himself living in a place like young Kellogg's, with guards and everything. He would be respected and envied—and feared. It was something to think about anyway. A goal. Something to see him through all this.

Teller still found it hard to believe that he was actually going through with the operation. Considering that he was neither a violent criminal nor a wild-eyed idealogue, he couldn't help admiring the way he was holding up. It was simply a case of being tough-minded, he told himself. But then he'd always been toughminded, had to be, because he was physically so weak. Even as a child, when his father beat him, he hadn't allowed himself to cry—even though, later, he would wet the bed. And it was the same at school, where the tough Chicago Heights dagos and pollocks had tormented him without mercy year after year. Again not allowing himself to cry, he nevertheless had developed allergies and had migraine headaches and continued to wet the bed as well as his pants on occasion. And even now he had no great faith that his body could do what his head commanded. But then that was the reason he had Billy Boy with him —to fortify his will not only with sinew but with mindlessness, that rare ability to do almost anything to anybody for no good reason at all. Together, Teller assured himself, they would get the job done. Or most of it anyway. The final bit would be up to him alone.

Teller called Kellogg from a phone booth in a small Montecito shopping center. Assuming a shy little-boy manner, he told Richard that his name was Sandy Morgan and that he was passing through town and that they had a mutual friend, Donny, who had met Richard at a party and had liked him "oh, so much" and had "just insisted" that he, Sandy, look him up if he was ever in Santa Barbara.

Kellogg said that he didn't remember any Donny but then that wasn't too surprising since "one isn't always sober at parties, is one?" He then invited Sandy to come up and have lunch at his house, but Sandy begged off.

"Oh no, Richard, I just couldn't—not yet anyway. I drove past the gate a while ago and frankly it's just *too much*. I'd feel out of place. Maybe later, after we get to know each other. But for now, why don't we just have a drink together? Or maybe lunch somewhere. Donny said we were just meant—oh well, never mind about that."

Kellogg asked where he was and Teller told him. And ten minutes later the gray Mercedes swung into the shopping center parking lot and pulled up next to the Transam, in which Billy Boy sat, blond and muscular and smiling. But before Kellogg could bound out of the car after him, Teller had slipped in next to the young homo and prodded him in the ribs with his gun.

"Just don't panic, kid," he told him. "This ain't what it seems."

Then he went on to give Kellogg a scenario that he figured would allay the youth's fears and make him easier to handle. The matter involved his being on a street corner in North Hollywood two nights before, Teller explained. There had been a ruckus—people running out of an apartment building—and he, Kellogg, had seen those people. A photographer had snapped him in the act, so to speak.

Kellogg tried to interrupt, saying that he hadn't seen anything, but Teller silenced him with another prod of the gun.

"That's not our problem," he said. "We're just supposed to hold you for these other people to question—and don't ask me who they are, because I don't know. I'm just a hired hand. We go down to Ventura and wait for them, you tell them what you saw, and that's that. Okay? Shall we do it the easy way, or do you want to do it hard?"

Kellogg was trembling and there were tears in his eyes. "Anything," he got out. "Just don't hurt me."

Teller smiled at him. "Don't worry, kid. No one gets hurt. Okay, let's go. A nice, easy drive—with no speeding. You got that? Just use your head, stay calm, and you'll be all right."

As the kid nodded again, Teller gave Billy Boy the okay sign. Then

90

he drove out of the parking lot, with Billy following in the Transam, squealing tires and revving the eight-cylinder engine even though Teller had cautioned against doing just that. But they were soon on the freeway and the big man at least had the sense to follow at a safe interval for the twenty-mile drive.

The motel was a simple one-story, one-building affair, with the office in front and an even dozen units running straight back from it. Teller's room was the third from the end and there was shrubbery and a number of small flowering trees growing along the covered entrance walk, so he and Billy had a measure of privacy as they got out of the cars and shepherded young Kellogg into the room. Teller made the youth strip and get into bed, explaining that he would be easier to handle that way.

"It'll make you think twice before you make a beeline for the door."

Instructing Billy to watch over "our friend here," Teller went into the bathroom and gave his bladder some desperately needed relief. He washed his hands thoroughly and then he went out to the car and brought in the liquor and other items that he had purchased. He asked Kellogg what he'd like to drink—scotch or vodka—and the kid said that he didn't want anything.

"Oh yes, you do," Teller told him. "It's gonna be a while before our client gets here and I'd just as soon have you nice and relaxed. Again—easier to look after."

"A vodka-and-tonic, then," Kellogg said.

"Vodka and Seven-Up," Teller corrected.

The kid shrugged as Teller poured the drinks and served them, straight Seven-Up for himself and Billy and the mixed drink for their prisoner. As Kellogg sipped, he kept glancing furtively at Billy Boy, who was leaning back in a chair near the door, with his feet up on a tiny coffee table. As usual, he had his shirt open to his navel and his sleeves were rolled up high on his bulging arms.

"Are you a private eye?" Kellogg asked him.

Billy glanced at Teller and laughed. "Yeah, I guess you could say that."

"Well, you must be good at it," Kellogg said. "I imagine you know karate and all that sort of thing."

91

"You don't want to find out," Billy told him.

"No, I don't imagine I would." The kid then turned to Teller. "You know, this is all very curious. I mean, I just can't imagine why anyone would be interested in what I saw on that miserable street corner the other night. My car had broken down and I was just waiting for a bus. That's all I was doing there. I'm not some kind of spy, you know. I don't work for my uncle, if that's what you think."

"Your *uncle?*" Teller asked.

"Well, of course. Henry Kellogg. All this must have something to do with him. I'm not a fool, you know."

Teller asked who Henry Kellogg was and the youth gave him a patronizing look. "Oh, come on. I wasn't born yesterday, you know. And now that I think about it, I'm sure one of my uncle's visitors yesterday *was* on that street corner the other night—that I can tell your client anyway. He was a Saudi, of course, and he was in this limo with three of his countrymen, waiting for a fourth, who came running out of the building. A younger man. Quite fat."

"No kidding," Teller said.

Kellogg sighed in exasperation. "No, I'm not kidding. And there was one other man too, not with the Saudis. He looked like Robert Redford."

Teller smiled. "Maybe it was Robert Redford."

"You're making fun of me," the youth said.

"That's because you're not supposed to be talking. Not to us, anyway. You're supposed to be drinking."

Over the next hour Teller almost force-fed the vodka to Richard Kellogg. Each drink he made a little stronger, until finally the youth was slurring his words and kicking off his covers and inviting Billy Boy to join him in bed, which embarrassed the big man almost as much as it infuriated him. He kept looking at Teller and shaking his head.

"Goddamn fag! Why does he pick on *me*, huh? Do I look like a goddamn fag? Huh, do I? He keeps it up, I'm gonna beat his goddamn face in."

"No, you're not," Teller said, as he again got out his drug stash.

He carefully uncapped the vial of concentrated Seconal and poured it into Kellogg's glass, then added a small amount of vodka and Seven-Up. Sitting down on the edge of the youth's bed, he patiently fed him the drink, part of the time holding him up. When it was gone, the kid fell back on the pillow with a laugh.

"You're really some kind of jailer," he said. *"My* kind."

Then he passed out.

Teller put on his gloves and wiped clean the outside of the glass, then of the vial, which was unlabeled. He pressed them one at a time against the fingers of Kellogg's right hand and then placed both receptacles on the table between the two beds. He did the same thing with the bottles of vodka and Seven-Up, and afterwards he pulled the covers off Kellogg and painstakingly dressed him in the black lace brassiere and garter belt and hose. Billy Boy meanwhile could not sit still. He paced the room and kept smashing his fist into his hand. And finally, with Teller's permission, he made himself a V-and-V and quickly downed it.

"How can you even touch the creep, huh?" he asked. "Just lookin' at him makes me want to puke. I just wish you'd let me beat on him. For just five seconds, Head. That's all I want—five seconds!"

Ignoring him, Teller applied lipstick and eyeliner to the unconscious Kellogg. Then he went over to the dresser and, again using the tube of lipstick, printed across the mirror in ragged red letters:

I'M SORRY

Billy Boy appeared totally confused by this until he saw Teller press the lipstick tube into Kellogg's hand before placing it back on the dresser.

"Hey, I get it," Billy said. "It's a suicide note!"

"You're quick today, Billy. Now you do your job with the girls tonight and we'll have five nice little hits, all different. Two accidents, a suicide and a sex thing. No one will connect them."

"Right. Boy, that's smart, Head. You're really smart, you know that?"

Teller winked at him. "Naturally. I'm a college boy."

He got the bag from the ladies' shop and put the bottle of scotch in it as well as the other items he didn't want left behind, and then he gave the bag to Billy to take out to the car. Using a damp cloth, he wiped off everything that he and Billy might have touched in the room and he smudged whatever prints there were on the doorknobs. Then he went into the bathroom and vigorously scrubbed his hands. But afterwards he had to urinate once more, which resulted in his having to scrub his hands yet again before he could leave. Finally, with only a glance back at young Kellogg lying there in his black lace, still as a doll, Teller went on outside. He hung a Don't Disturb sign on the door and pulled it shut. Walking on out to the car, he felt a trifle uneasy—felt almost a sense of guilt—at not having stayed until he was sure the youth was dead. But then one couldn't cover all the bases, he told himself. And anyway, he had to admit that it was the uncovered bases that excited him most. Like the old woman desk clerk at the motel. She had got a good look at him, yet he had let her live, just like the one in the Hollywood motel, and probably for the same reason—because it excited him, the element of risk, of vulnerability. Somewhere down the road, if the police were very smart or at least very lucky, they might get on to him. And the state might even try him in a court of law. Which also excited him. He could succeed and be a big man in the group, or he could fail and be notorious in the world. Either way, he figured, he couldn't lose. He would never again be little Marvin Teller, the wimp.

"Where to now?" Billy asked, as they reached the freeway.

"Hollywood," Teller said. "The Club Ninety."

Billy shivered and blew on his hands.

*   *   *

By two in the afternoon, unable to endure his anxiety about old man Crow any longer, Gardner Costello used his marine radio to call the ex-policeman's home. A woman answered and when he asked to speak with Orville Crow, she told him in a soft country voice that Mr. Crow had been killed in an automobile accident the night before. Stunned, Costello was unable to speak for a few moments and the woman asked who he was and if he wanted to leave a message for Mr. Crow's son.

"No, nothing," he told her. "I'm just a friend. And I'm very sorry. I—"

But by then he had released the speaker button on the mike, in effect hanging up on himself. And now he turned off the radio and got up from the pilot seat. His legs suddenly were wobbly and he could feel his heart laboring in his chest. He shuffled back to the galley and poured himself a few fingers of scotch and tossed it off.

Of course it wasn't an accident, he told himself. The boys in Queen's old section were adept at arranging just such nonaccidents as this. It was nothing new or earthshaking. He was aware that what he should have been feeling was outrage; that, and of course guilt, for having sent the old man in his place. But that was not what he felt. Not yet anyway. Right now fear took precedence, as it always did. The one question in his mind was whether or not the killers knew who their victim was, that it was not him they had hit but a ringer, a patsy. And it took only a few seconds for him to conclude that if they hadn't known last night, they certainly would today, when they checked the papers for an accounting of their handiwork. It was only a matter of time. Which of course meant that he was in mortal danger at that very moment, as he drank, as he ruminated.

Moving quickly now, Costello called his wife at home in Ojai and told her that red snapper were reportedly biting well up around the Channel Islands and that he would be gone for about a week. He said he would drive out and see her when he returned.

Hanging up, he wondered ruefully if it would work at all, trying to lay down a false trail for an old fox like Queen. In any case, it was about all he could think to do. He checked his fuel and water and other supplies and found them sufficient to reach Oceanside or maybe even San Diego, if he had good weather. So he went ahead and started both engines. As they warmed up, he radioed the big news to the marina office that he was going up around Santa Barbara for a week or so and that during his absence all his calls should be routed to his wife. As he went topside then, preparing to cast off, he heard someone calling his name and he looked in terror up at the wharf, to see who it was. But there were so many tourists and other unfortunates standing along the chain link fence that for a few moments he didn't see her—the girl, Sherri—squeezing through the crowd and bouncing up and down on wedgies as she waved at him in her too-tight, too-short hooker dress. She was carrying a huge purse and a small orange suitcase, and it embarrassed Costello to

95

have to walk up to the gate and let her in, in full view of the knowing
—and undoubtedly envious—spectators lining the fence. As the two
of them started back down the dock, a kid whistled at Sherri and
some of the others laughed—at *him*, Costello figured. But finally
they were at the boat and he helped her get on board, then scurried
forward to the bow and back, casting off the lines.

Sherri laughed nervously. "What's going on?"

"You remember that cruise I mentioned? Well, you're just in time
for it."

The girl shook her head. "Not me. No way."

Costello was steadying the craft with a boathook. "Then what are
you doing here?"

"I just came to lay low for a couple days. There's this guy I know,
he's sort of down on me."

"Guy?"

"My pimp," she admitted. "He's got this idea I've been holding
out on him. Which I guess I have."

Costello told her that he had no choice in the matter, that he had
to leave immediately—with her or without her. After studying him
for a few moments, she gave an indifferent shrug.

"Well, okay then. Why not?"

Costello smiled. "My sentiments exactly."

Climbing quickly up onto the bridge, he put both screws into
reverse for a short spurt, lightly scraping the hull against one of the
dock tires as the boat started backwards. He reversed the rest of the
way on one engine and then threw both into forward gear and
started to move slowly up the waterway between the long rows of
moored boats. And suddenly Sherri came up and joined him on the
bridge seat, sat there barefooted, with her tight little dress riding up
her bare thighs. Her jet-black hair was blowing and she was either
smiling at him or squinting against the sun—he couldn't tell. Looking past her, out over the masts and flybridges in the marina, he
observed the great brown sprawl of the city, backdropped by the San
Gabriels, ethereal in the smog, a dreamland's dream of mountains.
But with Sherri there, it all suddenly seemed almost beautiful to
Costello and he was about to congratulate himself—tricking the

fates this way—when he realized what a fine target he presented to someone on the shore.

"Get below!" he snapped at the girl.

In his haste to get off the bridge, he had to push her ahead of him down the ladder to the cockpit, and there he rushed past her into the cabin, to the helm, so he could regain control of the boat. Following him inside, she gave him a look of bafflement.

"What was all that about?"

"The wheel up there," he said. "It didn't feel right."

"So where are we headed?"

"You ever been to Mexico?"

"Tijuana."

As they reached the main channel now, he gave the engines more fuel.

"Oh we can do better than that," he said. "Much better."

*   *   *

Teller was not sure why the two girls were such an easy pickup, whether it was the money he had flashed in the smokey gloom of the Club Ninety or whether it was his explanation that he would only be a spectator and that their real "date" would be with Billy Boy, sitting there in his yellow curls and bulging muscles. Whatever the reason, when the girls got off at two in the morning, they accompanied the men to the room Teller had rented in yet another Hollywood motel, this one a real sleaze palace with big-screen TV porn and a ceiling mirror and king-size waterbed and even a sunken whirlpool situated next to the bathroom. Teller paid each girl the agreed-upon hundred dollars and when they went into the bathroom together to "freshen up," he told Billy Boy to go ahead and take his pleasure *first,* because it was important that there be "jism on the scene."

"I'll just stand here and watch for a few minutes," he went on. "Then I'll go outside and wait—while you finish up."

The girls came out nude and sexy, laughing and feeling Billy's muscles as they helped him off with his clothes. Slipping into the whirlpool, the one called Rose tweaked Billy's limp cock and then tried to bury her face between his legs as he sat down on the edge of the pool. The other one then playfully pulled him into the water with them, but Teller could see that they were getting nowhere with the big man, either because of all the booze and Valium he'd had or because Teller was there, watching him. Snuggled against him, Rose apparently was still trying to stimulate him with her hand. But now she gave up with a laugh, saying that she'd found "at least one muscle that needs work." And that was all it took. Like a dolphin, Billy Boy's huge fist came leaping out of the water and caught her on the chin, knocking her back onto the apron of the whirlpool. The other girl looked puzzled for a moment, as if she couldn't understand what had happened, and then she started to scramble out of the pool, almost getting away before Billy caught her by the foot and dragged her back down into the churning water. And for a time Teller just stood there and watched as the sledgehammer fists continued to lift and plunge, over and over, turning the whirlpool into a reddening cauldron. Finally Teller caught himself and hurried on outside, shaking so badly that when he stopped to urinate between two cars, he got piss all over his hand and on his pants. But he assured himself that he was all right, still in control of himself, still able to do what he had to do. He unlocked the trunk of the Transam and got out the gallon can of gasoline he had bought earlier—for the VW, he'd told Billy, saying that he couldn't trust its gas gauge anymore. He closed the trunk and placed the can on the floor behind the driver's seat. Then he got into the car and took hold of the wheel, firmly, trying by main force to control his trembling. When that failed to work, he popped two more five-milligram Valium and chased them with a long pull on the bottle of scotch he had bought in Ventura.

As he waited, he kept his eye on the window of the room, though all he could see were the pulled drapes and the lights burning behind them. He kept the car windows open too, but he heard nothing except the sounds of the night, mostly the dull eternal roar of traffic in this most restless of cities. And suddenly, out of nowhere, he thought of his father, thought of old Nathan Teller observing him now, just as he was, wading through this abattoir of blood. He thought of him—and giggled. Square old Nathan, the world's all-time champion right-thinking, flag-waving, forever optimistic *loser*

98

—just the idea of him seeing his boy Marvin here, now, waiting for Billy Boy—all one could do was giggle. While the old man's brothers all married "in the faith" and had become rich and respected allergists and proctologists, smart old Nate took as his wife an Irish bartender's penniless daughter, and then got on with his chosen career as a would-be tycoon, jumping all his days from one dizzy get-rich-quick debacle to the next, never staying with any one of them long enough to find out if it might indeed pan out in time. It was in fact the family joke that if Nate had been the Dustin Hoffman character in *The Graduate*, he *would* have gone into plastics—for about a month. Together with his wife Mary and little Marvin, they made the perfect American nuclear family, isolated and shabby, shunned by both sides, Jews and Irish alike, each spouse as relentlessly ashamed of the other as they were of the runty malcontent who was their issue.

"You'll never amount to a tinker's damn," his father used to say to him, chagrined at both his general attitude and his poor performance in school.

Well, Nate should have been following him these last two days, Teller thought. The old loser might have learned, for once in his life, how to win.

Even in the dark Teller could see the blood on Billy's hands and arms and face as the big man finally came stumbling out of the motel room and sagged into the car.

"Go! Go!" he got out, already fumbling the bottle of scotch to his lips.

Teller pulled out of the motel parking lot and headed for Western, taking his time, glancing over at Billy as he drained the bottle and finally threw it into the back seat. Whimpering and panting, Billy dropped his face into his hands.

"Jesus, Head," he moaned. "Jesus, oh Jesus."

"What's wrong?" Teller almost giggled again, at the absurdity of the question.

"*After*," Billy said. "I did it to 'em, Head. But *after!* You understand?"

"Sure."

"Well, that ain't right, Head. That can't be right, can it?"

"Why not?"

"They was—you know—they wasn't breathin'," he whimpered. "But I fucked 'em anyway. I did it anyway, Head."

Teller looked over at him, puzzled at this sudden show of remorse. "You did what you had to do, that's all," he told him. "I said to make it look like a sex thing and that's what you did."

"If I'd been able at first—you know, when you was there—I don't know if I coulda done it finally, Head. What I done."

"It was your job, Billy. That's all. You did what you had to do. For the group."

Whimpering still, Billy Boy began to nod. "Yeah, for the group. What I had to do."

"Right."

"It was my job."

"Sure, Billy. That's all it was."

"It was my job, that's all."

"No more, no less."

"Right. My job—no more, no less."

Teller turned in at the road leading back to Griffith Park. Dark and heavily shaded in the daytime, at night it was black as a tarpit and virtually abandoned since the park was closed after eight o'clock. Almost immediately the car's headlights picked out Teller's VW parked up ahead on the left, facing out. When he'd left it there earlier, he had explained to Billy Boy only that it was "part of the plan." Incurious then, the big man was even less curious now, and probably did not even know where they were, as he continued to sit there in the passenger seat with his face in his hands.

A few hundred yards past the Volkswagen, Teller pulled over to the right-side curb, parking the Transam in an area where no slightest ray of L.A. civilization reached: no streetlights, no neon, no anything. Getting out of the car, he looked about himself in the darkness, making sure there were no muggers or winos or other prospective witnesses lurking around, and then he took out his Walther automatic and shot his partner through the open window, twice, aiming at his head. In a brief violent spasm, Billy Boy's legs tore up the dashboard and broke through the engine wall. Then abruptly he stopped moving

100

and his huge body slumped against the passenger door.

Teller got the gas can out from behind the seat and poured half its contents over the big man, then put the top back on and set the can on the seat. Stepping back a dozen feet, he lit a cigarette and tossed it into the car, which flared in the blackness like a giant jack-o'-lantern. He ran across the street and cut left through the trees, heading for the VW. He had covered about a hundred yards when the first explosion came, followed almost immediately by the second, as the car's gas tank blew. But he did not look back.

FIVE

FOR Crow, they were days of anger and frustration as much as sadness. Beginning when the traylike stretcher finally had been pulled up onto the turnout and Crow had seen the old man's battered body—and had smelled it too, reeking of whiskey—from that point on, things had kept going downhill. No matter whom he spoke with at the police department—the chief of detectives or Sergeant Olson or just old friends of his father offering their condolences— he was confronted with the same embarrassed silence the moment he suggested that there should be an investigation, that his father would not have been driving drunk on Mulholland the night of the accident. To a man, they seemed to feel that the logical explanation for it all was suicide, that it was practically *de rigeur* for a retired cop to take his own life—or at least so Crow interpreted their shuffling, mumbled responses. And Olson had not helped matters either when he called the next afternoon with the results of the autopsy.

"Cause of death was a broken neck," the sergeant reported. "And your father was legally intoxicated. Blood alcohol point-one-one."

"Which isn't very high," Crow said.

102

"High enough. And then there was one other finding. An important one."

"What's that?"

"Your father had terminal heart disease. Could have gone at any time, according to the pathologist."

Crow thanked him for calling and then poured himself a stiff drink of vodka. Normally he seldom touched hard liquor, for some reason had come to dislike the sensation of being high almost as much as he loathed hangovers. But suddenly the stuff seemed just what the doctor ordered. If his father had been that ill, then Crow had to face the possibility that the old man might indeed have taken his own life. And it was not a thought that came easy, especially when Crow cranked himself into the equation, the fact that the death had occurred now, while he was here visiting. Which of course gave rise to the even more bracing possibility that the old man had *waited* for him to come, waited for him to be here, before going through with the act.

But then Crow reminded himself that all of that was only conjecture, a series of useless and poisonous questions which for now at least, during these few crowded and dispiriting days, he decided not to keep asking himself. And the unhappy truth was that there were enough other matters to keep his blood at a rolling boil, chief among them the fact that his mother and sister would not be coming to the funeral—as usual, for quite different reasons. His mother, who preferred sweetness to light, said on the phone that she only wished she could come, but that the spring rains had been dreadful and her sinuses were "absolutely destroying" her. She was so dizzy she could barely stand up. And poor Ralph—Crow's dentist stepfather—was having a vicious hemorrhoid flareup and had to cancel most of his appointments through the rest of the week. The two of them were "just a total washout," his mother said. And of course she was sorry about it all, deeply sorry. She would have loved to be there, "to stand right there with you, Sonny." Still, he would not really be alone, she told him. She would be with him in spirit. Both she and Ralph would be thinking of him and praying for him.

His sister Caroline, on the other hand, said that she had not bothered to visit the old man when he was alive and kicking, so she certainly wasn't going to start now, when he was dead. What kind of hypocrite did he take her for anyway?

A divorced advertising copywriter living alone in Portland, Caroline over the past few years had acquired a very low regard for males, to the point now where almost any conversation with her—even over the phone—soon took on the character of a blood sport.

"A simple yes or no would have served," he told her.

"There's no such animal, Sonny."

"No kidding."

"What about the will?" she asked.

"I don't know a thing about it."

"Well, find out, for God's sake. If that house is still free and clear, we ought to do okay, the two of us. I could use a little good news for a change."

"You're all heart," he said.

"I've been taught by experts."

"So it seems."

As irritating as she was on the phone, Crow was glad he had called her, for her mentioning of the will forced him finally to face up to the subject, as well as to a number of other practical matters that had to be dealt with before there could be a funeral. From Mrs. Elderberry he learned that his father had a burial plot bought and paid for in a Glendale cemetery. She also showed Crow where the bank records were and helped him open the locked desk file where his father kept his personal papers as well as his case records. In a manila folder Crow found a copy of the will, which did in fact state that he and Caroline were to divide their father's estate, which consisted of the house, a few thousand dollars in savings, and a ten-thousand-dollar life insurance policy. For the moment, though, Crow was more relieved to find the executor's identity: the trust department of a Van Nuys branch of the United Bank of California.

With Reno riding patiently along, he drove to the bank and established a line of credit against the estate so he could then go to the funeral home and pick out a casket and set up the other arrangements for the funeral the next afternoon. On the way, the girl quizzed him.

"You still don't think it was an accident?"

"I don't know."

"You think he did it to himself?"

"For Christ's sake, Reno, how would I know?"

"Well, you don't have to bite my head off."

Crow looked over at her, this slim and coltish teenager with her messy red-blonde hair and regal symmetry. At the moment her mouth was a pout and her brown eyes looked bruised with suspicion. And Crow wondered what on earth he was going to do with her. For certain, she could not just go on living with him, like a long-lost daughter or little sister.

"I'm sorry," he said to her now. "I guess I'm so wrapped up in my own problems, I forget about yours."

"I don't have any."

"Is that a fact?"

"Nothing important. Not until I take off, anyway."

"And when will that be?"

"Right after the funeral. Don't worry."

"I'm not worried."

"Sure, you're not."

"Where will you go? Home?"

She gave him a weary glance, as if he were a hopeless case. Then, as he pulled in at the funeral home, she put her knees up on the dashboard and scooted down on the seat, evidently unenthralled by the scene before them: the blinding green carpet of grass leading up to the establishment itself, which looked like Washington's Mount Vernon—surrounded by palm trees.

"I have to go inside and make arrangements," he told her. "You want to come?"

She shook her head. "I'll wait here. I hate the smell of flowers."

"Dead ones, you mean."

"Dead *or* alive."

"What a tough guy," he said, getting out.

"You know it."

"Well, I'll see you soon, Spike."

She told him not to hurry.

*   *   *

105

His father's will included a codicil stipulating precisely the kind of funeral he wanted: a simple graveside ceremony "without eulogy or preachment." A qualified Protestant clergyman was to read the policeman's oath, the Twenty-third Psalm, and "other appropriate lines from the Book of Common Prayer." That was what his father wanted and Crow decided that was what his father would get.

Earlier in the day Crow had taken Reno shopping, in his innocence thinking they would get some sort of basic black dress and pumps for her instead of the off-label designer black jeans and Day-Glo purple velvet blouse that she eventually picked out. But then Crow was aware that he too would not be overly elegant in his gray herringbone jacket and corduroys, though he had gone so far as to buy a white shirt and dark tie, completing the ensemble with a pair of black shoes from his father's closet.

In any case, at one-thirty that afternoon, the two of them and Mrs. Elderberry stood in the shadow of the mountains on a mottled patch of lawn in the Glendale Cemetery. Along with them were the funeral crew, the "qualified Protestant clergyman," and a total of six other mourners, including two of his father's neighbors and the bartender from the Green Mill Tavern. That left only Sergeant Olson and two other policemen out of the scores his father had known and worked with during his thirty long years in the department. And Crow found that fact almost as oppressive as the cemetery itself, with its jaundiced Valley air and gasping palms and relentlessly manicured lawn. It was no place for a human soul to rest in peace, he thought, yet he didn't know what he could do about it, especially at this late date.

Mrs. Elderberry was the only one who wept and everyone seemed enormously relieved when the pastor finally bowed his head and prayed. Smiling unctuously, he then offered Crow and Reno his condolences. While most of the mourners hastened to their cars, Sergeant Olson and one other policeman came over to pay their respects. And it was this second cop who left Crow trembling where he stood. Gripping Crow's hand in both of his, he confided with a boozy breath that it was "a real sad occasion."

"Especially when they go like your pa did," the man elaborated. "But old Orv, he just wasn't one to be happy out of the saddle. No siree. And I don't figure I'll be either, when my time comes. But I guess you gotta be a cop to understand."

Even after the man was gone, Crow continued to stand there, staring numbly at his father's casket. Then finally Reno took his hand and the two of them followed Mrs. Elderberry back to the cemetery road, where they again squeezed into his pickup. Vowing to himself not to think about what the cop had said, Crow headed home through the unquiet heart of the Valley.

On the way, Mrs. Elderberry again began to cry.

"Well, I suppose my mom and me will be out in the street pretty soon," she wept, through a heavily perfumed handkerchief.

"Don't worry about it," Crow told her. "I'm not in any hurry—"

"But it ain't up to you," she cut in. "If your sister wants to sell the house, then it sells. That's all there is to it."

"In time, maybe. But not right away. Don't worry about it."

"That's easy for you to say." She buried her face in the hanky and began to sob.

Crow looked over at Reno, who rolled her eyes and reluctantly put her arm around the quaking shoulders of the older woman.

"Hey, take it easy," she advised. "Old Crow here's a marshmallow. He'll probably let you stay on at the house forever."

That was not true of course. To settle the estate, the executor would soon be putting the place up for sale. But Crow saw no reason to say this. He knew that Mrs. Elderberry was already fully acquainted with the facts of life, such as they were.

Even before they reached home, Crow knew that he was going to have to get off by himself for a while—for a few hours or maybe even a few days, if that was what it took to get the old head on straight again. He knew that Reno would probably take his departure as a rejection of one kind or another and might even pack up and head for the nearest freeway. But that would be her affair, he told himself. On his own for so long, he had developed a considerable habit of privacy, a habit only strengthened by his occasional lapses into cohabitation with various women over the years, because it was then that his normal good spirits had seemed to sour day by day into a growing and prickly irritability. Which was precisely what he was beginning to feel now, and for

107

kindred reasons, he decided, what with looking after Reno and dealing with his father and suffering in silence the perfumed ministrations of Mrs. Elderberry. More to the point, of course, was his need for time and space to deal with the death of his father and the confusion which that death inspired in him: whether it was only a sense of loss he felt, or guilt and anger as well.

In any event, he didn't even get out at the house. All he said to Reno was that he had some thinking to do and that he would see her later, and then he sped off, without even a wave good-bye. He took the long drive down Topanga Canyon to the beach and, leaving his coat and tie and shoes in the truck, he started walking north between all the million-dollar cabins and the surf, which was white-capped and strong. He started to jog after a while and then gradually he let himself out, running on down the curving beach for well over a mile, continuing long after the pain had begun to eat like a rat into his side. Then he slowed and finally stopped and turned back, jogging and walking now, letting the sweat he had worked up evaporate.

Back at the truck, he put on his coat and shoes and drove down the coast highway until he found a suitable dive, small and unprosperous-looking, with only a few cars parked in front. Inside he ordered a scotch-and-water and sat at the far end of the bar watching colored sand drain through an hourglass fashioned in a detailed female shape, with breasts and buttocks and thighs. He found some passable music on the jukebox—Willie and Carly and Barbra—and fed a few dollars into the machine, which seemed to please the bartender. As Crow continued to sit there drinking, he approached the subject of his father's death about as he went swimming in the cold waters of the sound, submerging his body a few inches at a time in the hope that his heart would not stop beating altogether. Only gradually did he let himself consider the possibility that the old man might indeed have been a suicide, that he had felt sufficiently alone and abandoned and embittered over the years to have waited *in cold blood* for his son to return, so he would then have an audience for his act, someone to inflict it on. If so, then Crow knew that there was nothing he could ever say or do or even think that would make any difference. The facts would remain just as they were, and he would have to live with them. He would have to carry that burden of guilt all the way to his own grave. And he found this almost as amazing as it was shameful, for it had never even crossed his mind all these years that he might have been shirking his duty to the old man, possibly because his mother had set him so firmly on that path. Even in their first years in Seattle, whenever he had asked about going to visit his father, her response had been adamantly negative:

"We can't afford it. And anyway, if he wanted to see you, he could come here. There's nothing to stop him."

Then later, in his twenties, the visits had gone so badly—the old man had seemed to disapprove of him so thoroughly—that the intervals in between had lengthened effortlessly, as if by geometric progression. Yet none of that changed the fact that Crow now sat in this small Southern California beach bar trying to dull the voice in his ear, this nag who kept calling him a failure both as a man and as a son. At the same time, he thought it only fair to remind himself that the facts of his father's death were not yet known, and might never be known. The coroner's office had ruled death by accident, and as far as Crow knew, that was a perfectly correct finding. Certainly it was feasible that the old man could have been given a few drinks by the person or persons he'd delivered the information to. And it didn't beggar belief that they could have pressed the bottle of scotch on him too, grateful that he'd done such a thorough job in such a short time. Further, it was conceivable that he simply decided to take the long way home—the scenic way—and had driven up into the Hollywood hills and finally onto Mulholland, wanting for a change to see *in toto* this vast electric cage where he'd spent most of his life. And finally Crow had to admit it was also possible, on that notoriously dangerous stretch of road, that his father simply had lost control of his car.

It was all possible, yes. It was conceivable. But only that. And this of course was Crow's main problem, the reason he continued to sit there at the bar yoked to his glass of scotch. If his father's death was not suicide, nor an accident, *then how and why had he died?* Could it be that there was no answer, at least none he would ever learn? That was a prospect that only whetted Crow's thirst. He continued to drink and to throw money into the jukebox, and over the course of the evening he had an occasional conversation with the bartender and whoever happened onto the stool next to his. Once, turned around, he returned the smile of a girl sitting at a table with two beach boys in cowboy hats. One of them growled that he had better watch "who da fuck" he was smiling at and Crow shrugged agreeably.

"Whatever you say," he told the beach boy. "From now on, I smile only at you."

The character naturally had to make a big macho show for the girl, getting up and spinning his chair away, presumably ready for a showdown. But in reality he was only ready for his partner to step in, pulling him back, calming him down, telling him to forget about "the dude."

"He's just drunk," he said. "Can't you see that?"

Huffing and puffing and abusing chairs, the tough guy went back to the table, and Crow returned to his drink. Normally he never got into trouble in bars. Having spent so much time in them as an entertainer, he had a fairly keen eye for the real troublemakers, those ticking bombs it never paid even to banter with, such as small unsmiling chicanos with their hands in their pockets. In this case, though, Crow had not been worried, possibly because of all the scotch he had drunk. But also the beach boys had that telltale look of narcissism about them, in their bleached razorcut hair and well-tended muscles and golden tans. It was Crow's experience that men like that usually thought twice before risking pain and disfigurement, such as the loss of a few front teeth. Then too he had turned away himself in the end, letting them know that he was not hellbent on conflict. Still, he had liked the girl's smile, and he thought about her as he continued drinking. He thought about Reno too.

Knowing how drunk he was, Crow took the canyon curves so slowly that a number of cars gave him the horn as they shot on past. He stopped at another bar in the Valley and had two more drinks before he decided to head for home. And when he got there, on the street-dark porch, he fumbled through his father's keys for what seemed like an hour before he found the one that fit the front door. Going down the hallway past Reno's room, he looked in to see if she was there, and she stirred under the covers. For some reason this made him feel unreasonably happy, and seconds later, in the bathroom mirror, he saw himself grinning as he stood over the toilet bowl.

He went on into his father's office then, stumbling out of his clothes and onto the couch, feeling absolutely fine for the first time in days, clear headed and worry-free, a man in total control of his life, a winner winning. And the feeling almost made him laugh, for in the few sober brain cells left to him he knew just how fraudulent that old sweet song was, and how ephemeral too. By morning it would be gone, in spades. But for now he was fully content to lie back and let the booze sing in his blood, let it rearrange the very atoms of reality, so that this small and formerly oppressive room now seemed a wonderland of comfort, a canopy of soft light and warm feelings gathered about him.

Then suddenly he saw her in the doorway, refracted and strange in the dazzled air. He knew it was Reno of course, and if he'd thought hard he might have recognized her robe as his own. But he was not thinking. He was just lying there in the drift, gazing out through his snug little canopy at this new ward of his, this alien child swimming through the dimness. He watched as she sat down on the edge of the couch, limned by the hallway light, her smile by Leonardo.

"Hey, you okay?" she asked.

"Beyond okay."

"You're crocked."

"Could be."

He felt her hand on his chest, light as a cat's paw.

"I thought you'd be hairy," she said.

"Not there."

"Me either."

Her voice had cracked and there were tears in her eyes, yet she was smiling still. And he did not understand. Nor did he notice that her robe had fallen open until she lifted his hands to her breasts, which were small and beautifully formed.

"See?" she said.

"Yes, I see."

Very slowly he pushed the robe off her shoulders and then she was

111

all there for him, young and trim and lovely. And he took this as only further proof that he was indeed a winner winning. Happily he gathered the girl into his arms, planting his hands on her buttocks and rolling her under him as he started to push into the wet, warm heart of her. Then abruptly he heard from them again, that tiny clique of self-righteously sober brain cells, keeping the faith and burning candles against the darkness. He heard—and pulled back. He rolled off her and sat up.

"Jesus, what am I doing?" he moaned. "I must be out of my skull."

Reno was on her elbows by then, looking baffled and stricken in the half light.

"It's like you're my daughter," he told her. "Or my little sister. I'm so drunk I forgot."

Shaking his head, he put his face in his hands and began to maul it. And he wondered why, drunk as he was, with his blood still singing, he still felt so ashamed and desolated. He did not even want to look at the girl. But finally he did so, and it was then that she hit him, hard, right in the nose. Then she was gone, darting out of the room and down the hall. In pain, he sat there on the couch for a time, feeling his nose and the trickle of blood issuing from it. And when he got up to go into the bathroom, he heard the front door opening and the screen door banging shut. But he didn't go after her, not yet anyway. Still naked and bleeding, he got a wet washcloth and tried to stanch the bloodflow as best he could without lying back down. Holding the washcloth to his nose, he somehow managed to put on a sweater, pants, and boots. He got his wallet and keys and only then did he set out after her.

He was already feeling an abrupt drop in energy, a harbinger of the hangover to come. Every nerve and muscle in his body was sending him the same simple message—to go back to bed and collapse—but he refused to listen. He willed himself out to the truck and willed the key into the ignition and then started down the street, trying desperately to expand and sharpen the fuzzy tunnel vision which the scotch had left him. He stayed close to home, knowing that Reno could not have gone far yet. And he was amazed at how busy these supposedly quiet residential streets were, even now, after two in the morning. Dune buggies and low riders and chopped hogs and other California wheeled exotica continued to prowl the streets, along with a steady flow of normal traffic, Angelenos in their Japanese compacts on the way home from work or mass murders and other pastimes. And on the corners and small business strips, the sleepless young huddled in little groups of alienation, smoking weed and passing bottles and plotting tomorrow.

He finally spotted her just two blocks from home, on the next street over. In her funeral outfit, she was standing with her back against a stucco wall, cornered there by three young men whose flamboyantly butch costumes and Mohawk haircuts branded them as punk rockers, a species Crow had always considered too timid and dilettantish to be out on the street at night. One was holding a bottle out to her as another kept trying to touch her hair, only to have her bat his hand away. Crow double-parked and got out, bringing with him the tire iron that he kept on the floor of his cab. As he came around the back of the truck and moved toward the wall, sidling between parked cars, the kid with the bottle saw him and immediately bolted, yelling to the other two, who also scattered like chickens. Reno looked at him with loathing.

"Why'd you bother?" she said. "For someone you can't stand?"

Crow groaned. "Look, will you come on? I can hardly stand up. I've had a lot to drink."

"I'm not going anywhere. Not with you."

"Yes, you are."

Clumsy as any drunk, Crow nevertheless was able to strong-arm her away from the wall and between the parked cars to the truck. He wrestled her over to the driver's side and pushed her in ahead of him, making her slide over on the seat.

"And don't try to get out," he warned. "I'll grab you by the hair. I'll pull it out."

By then she had begun to cry, out of anger more than pain, he imagined.

"I hate you," she got out. "Oh Jesus, I hate you!"

"I'm sorry what happened," he said. "Being drunk is no excuse, I know that."

She looked up at him, her face a smear of tears and resentment.

113

"I ain't your daughter," she cried. "And I ain't your goddamn sister either."

"I know that."

"Then why, huh? Why am I so untouchable?"

He could not think of an answer.

"You think I'm a virgin, is that it? You think Jerry was some kind of saint?"

"No."

"Well, what then? Is it I'm so ugly? Is that it? Is it you just can't stand me?"

He looked at her. "That's not how I remember it."

That crumpled her face and brought on still more tears. In a choking voice, she asked him the same question again.

"Then *why?* Why can't you like me?"

He had just pulled into the driveway again and parked. Turning off the headlights, he looked over at her in the darkness and tried to explain.

"*Like* you? You know I do, Reno—that and more. Which is why I came after you, and why the damned thing happened in the first place. And if I were your age . . ." He faltered then, trying to keep his head above the great numbness rising about him. But it was no use.

"Look, baby, I can't even think," he told her. "I've got to crash."

Later he would remember how she had looked at him then in the gray wash of the streetlight, her eyes suddenly opening against the tears, brightening as a smile spread upon her face.

"You called me baby," she said.

On the porch she took the keys out of his wayward hand and unlocked the front door. She helped him down the hallway to his room and even covered him after he had fallen into bed. He remembered her leaving the room and closing the door behind her. And then there was nothing until dawn visited him with a roaring headache and so sharp a thirst that he forced himself up off the couch and into the bathroom for water and aspirin and a long, voluptuous piss. Then it was back to bed again and more oblivion until Reno woke him at ten in the morning, knocking on the door and coming in with an apologetic smile, as if she knew only too well what an unspeakable act she was committing, getting him up so early. Not until she sat down beside him on the couch did he notice the newspaper in her hand.

"You awake?" she asked.

"Now I am."

"I figured you'd want to know."

"Know what?"

She unfolded the paper and laid it on his lap. "Those two strippers —weren't their names Rose and Zelda?"

Crow nodded vaguely, at the moment more concerned with the waves of nausea washing over him. "I guess so," he managed. "What about them?"

"They're dead."

SIX

HUNGOVER as he was, Crow at first did not understand the significance of what Reno had told him.

"I saw it on the tube last night," she elaborated. "The police were wheeling the bodies out and everything. But I didn't connect. I didn't hear their names. I guess I wasn't listening."

Crow sat up very slowly, not wanting his head to shatter. "They're dead?"

"Beaten to death," Reno said. "And raped."

"Oh, Christ." Crow felt his gorge rising and choked it back down. Through watering eyes he looked at the paper, the back page of the *Times'* Metro section. There he saw pictures of both girls: cropped publicity photos, they looked like. The caption read: *Rose Dunn (left) and Zelda Coffee, nude dancers killed in savage rape-murder at the Waterbed Motel in Hollywood.*

The news story followed:

NO NEW LEADS IN DOUBLE SEX KILLING

Lieutenant Ralph Dorman of the Los Angeles Police Department reported last night that the police still have no suspects in the savage rape-murder of Hollywood nude dancers, Rose Dunn, 19, and Zelda Coffee, 20, both of 616 Oxford Street in North Hollywood.

The killings apparently took place early yesterday morning in a room at the Waterbed Motel, at 1212 Rickey Place in Hollywood. The bodies were discovered by a maid at 9:30 A.M.

Both women were performers at the Club Ninety on Sunset Boulevard. Employees there reported that the women left the club at 2:30 A.M. in the company of two white males, one tall and blond, the other small and dark-complexioned. According to the desk clerk at the motel, the room was rented by a man who registered as J. J. Biggs, of Greeley, Colorado. Police report that the name and address, as well as a Colorado license number given by the man, have proved false.

Lieutenant Dorman said that the killings were among the most savage he has ever seen. According to a spokesman for the medical examiner, the women died of strangulation. They also suffered numerous broken bones and lacerations and contusions, caused by the blows of a human fist. Both women were raped and sodomized.

The story went on to give the reactions of the victims' co-workers and of Rose Dunn's mother, with whom both girls had lived. The mother said that she knew nothing of the men described by employees at the strip club. Her daughter and Zelda Coffee (who danced under the name of Zelda Leggs) were both "good girls" who worked hard and enjoyed having an occasional night out on the town. Normally both of them came straight home after the club closed. Mrs. Dunn could not think of any reason why anyone would want to kill her daughter or Zelda. They were both such beautiful girls, the mother said. Beautiful and good.

Only as he finished reading did it begin to dawn on Crow what the story might mean for him.

"Could be I was right all along," he said to Reno. "Maybe my father's death wasn't an accident after all. And not a suicide either."

"How can you be sure?"

"I can't. But I'm not a great believer in coincidences. And this one is a lulu, wouldn't you say? The old man delivers the girls' names —and dies. And a day later the girls themselves get it."

"But they died so different," Reno reminded him. "This was a sex thing."

Crow nodded. "Yeah, a very unusual way to hit someone—if that's still the word for it." He was out of bed by then, standing in his jockey shorts, trying to get his land-legs back.

"You don't look so good," Reno said.

"I don't feel so good."

He went into the bathroom and began to splash cold water on his stubbled face. "Could be just a smokescreen," he said. "The rapes in this case. And the car accident in my father's."

Reno was watching him from the doorway. "You believe that?"

"I guess I want to—because I don't want him to be a suicide. Yet I don't want him to be a murder victim either."

"Yeah, that's scary."

He came back to the door and started to close it. "Well, I've got things to do," he said. "Do you want in or out?"

"Don't be gross," she told him.

With the door closed, Crow did what he could to begin restoring himself to normal, including taking a shower, or part of one anyway. Halfway through, he suddenly remembered the third person in the photographs he and Reno had worked from—the effete-looking young man from Santa Barbara—and he jumped out of the tub without even turning off the water. Dripping wet and pulling a towel around his waist, he hurried into the kitchen, where he found Reno making coffee.

"The kid in the photograph," he said to her. "You remember his name?"

"Sure—the same as Rice Krispies. Kellogg. Richard Kellogg."

Crow wagged his head in admiration. "Boy, you are something else today, you know that? You just may have saved a life."

He already had the phone in hand and was dialing Information. And where a few seconds before he hadn't been able to remember even the youth's name, now for some reason he had no trouble at all recalling his address: One Old Trail Lane, Montecito. Fortunately, it turned out that there was a phone listed under the name of Richard Kellogg at that address—the kid's father, Crow imagined. Getting the number, he quickly dialed and a woman answered, a woman with a heavy Oriental accent.

"No, young Wichar' not here no more," Crow was told. When he asked to speak with the youth's father or mother, he was told that they were "not here no more needer."

"Gone," the woman said. "Dey gone now—you caw back rater, prease."

And with that, she hung up. As Crow did the same, Mrs. Elderberry came into the kitchen from downstairs and obviously did not like what she saw: him standing there wrapped in a towel and dripping water on the floor while Reno, in his robe, sat crosslegged on the table.

"Mrs. E., we have something of an emergency here," he said. "Would you do me a favor?"

"What emergency?"

"It's complicated—I'd rather explain later, when I have more time."

She sighed in resignation. "All right—what do you want?"

"Food," he said. "Would you make up some sandwiches to go. And maybe orange juice and a thermos of coffee. We have to get dressed and run."

"Where to?"

"Santa Barbara."

Reno was already off the table and scooting for her room.

As they ate their way north on the freeway, the girl asked him to explain what he thought was happening. "I still don't see it," she said. "What happened to your dad was so different. Not like this other thing at all."

"Well, just think about it a minute," he suggested. "The old man's given a job to identify three people in some photographs—three people who supposedly witnessed some sort of accident. When the job is finished, he delivers it—and winds up in a canyon below Mulholland Drive. A day and a half later the two girls in the photos are killed—"

119

"And raped," Reno put in.

"Right—to make their deaths look like something other than what they were. Just as my father's was. They make the one look like a sex crime and the other like an accident, instead of simple, cold-blooded murders. Hits."

"But why?"

He shrugged. "I don't really know. But it looks like someone is killing witnesses—as well as anyone who knows about those witnesses, like the old man."

Reno was sitting sideways on the truck seat, frowning at Crow over a ham sandwich. "*We* know," she said.

"Yeah, but they don't know we know."

"Who are *they?*"

"You tell me. First thing would be to find out who the hell my father's client was—his 'old buddy Lee' who called that first morning. He could tell us a lot, I figure."

"Why not go to the police?"

That of course had been Crow's own first impulse, one that had quickly died. "They wouldn't believe me. They'd think I was just another hysterical citizen. As you pointed out, the deaths *are* very different. And I don't have any proof of any kind—no photos, no suspects, nothing. It's all just theory. The police would probably string me along—at the most, sit back and take a few notes. And meanwhile this Kellogg kid would still be in danger."

"If you're right," Reno said.

"Yeah. If I'm right." He turned to look at her. "And I guess that's the problem—I'm not all that sure myself. Not yet anyway."

"What if Kellogg's dead too?"

The thought already lay like a stone in Crow's ravaged stomach. "Then I guess we'd know, wouldn't we?"

"It couldn't be just coincidence?"

"Not all four. Even the police wouldn't be able to buy odds like that—four people linked by a few lousy photographs, and all getting killed within a few days of each other."

"They'd have to step in then?"

"I can't see they'd have any other choice."

Though Crow kept the accelerator pressed to the floorboard, he

120

still couldn't get more than sixty miles an hour out of the old Datsun
—five more than the legal limit, but still slower than most other cars
on the freeway were going. For a Saturday, the traffic seemed incredibly heavy to Crow, even taking into consideration that this was
Southern California and not Washington state. Even more oppressive was the violence of it, how the drivers kept cutting in and out
on each other, horns blaring and fingers raised, in a contemporary
version of "chicken."

And Crow had little doubt that if any accidents occurred, any
spinouts or other minor mishaps, the players would quickly be spilling out of their stalled cars with pistols blazing. Or at least so he
perceived the general level of civility among his countrymen, especially here in California, in the aching eighties. The public's poten-
tial for violence seemed almost like some universal new source of
energy, an electricity one could feel in the air, much as if he were
standing under a Bonneville power line. And Crow could not help
wondering if that was what he was involved in now, one of those
spasms of senseless violence that the times kept visiting on the
random innocent. At least it gave him something else to brood
about, something other than what awaited him in Montecito: embarrassment and lame explanations or the leaden realization that he
was too late. Somehow he had no real expectation of the latter,
probably because he wasn't convinced in his own mind that the
deaths of his father and the two hookers were anything *but* a coincidence.

As he drove on, he noticed that Reno was practically chainsmok-
ing cigarettes, and for some reason this irritated him. In fact, he was
slowly coming to realize that there were a number of things about
the girl that were beginning to grate on him, this despite the boon
she had been earlier in the day, spotting the news story about the
killings and then remembering Kellogg's name. For one thing, she
always seemed to be watching him. And each time he caught her,
she would smile inscrutably and look away. Then too she seemed
incapable of sitting quietly in one position for more than three
seconds at a time. She would hum or tap her foot or jiggle her knee.
And he was getting tired of looking at her funeral outfit, the tight
black jeans and velvet blouse that he knew she considered chic and

121

sexy but which in truth looked only gaudy and tasteless.

He kept reminding himself that she was only sixteen, a high-school dropout brought up by a cocktail waitress in Reno, and that in bed the previous night—for as long as his drunken innocence had lasted—he had found her anything but unattractive. And even now he was very much aware of her coltish sexiness: her leggy young body and her brassy brown eyes, her mop of curly flyaway hair that beauty salons could only simulate at considerable expense. Still, the smoke kept billowing out of her and her foot jiggled and he continued to catch her watching him.

As the freeway swung past Ventura to the ocean, it occurred to Crow that they would soon be passing the point where he had picked her up. So much had happened since then that he found it hard to believe only four days had gone by. He looked at her and smiled.

"Remember this stretch of road?"

She squinted out at the sea. "Yeah. And no fog today. Boy, would I like to go for a swim."

"It's cold. You'd need a wetsuit."

"Not me. I love it cold. Remember, I'm from Reno."

"How could I forget?"

She had turned away from him now, to look out the other window at the green hills rising steeply from the freeway.

"I keep expecting to find your Jerry somewhere along here," he said. "Still waiting for a ride."

"Well, if you do, you can let me out."

"Is that what you want?"

"What I want doesn't count."

He reached over and took a handful of her hair, forcing her to look at him. "Yes, it does," he told her. "It counts with me."

But she was not buying. "Sure," she said.

Crow bought a local map at a service station just off the freeway and then took a back road up into the Montecito foothills. He found Old Trail Lane and went along it slowly, past the quiet estates of the quiet rich. And at its end he came to the number he wanted. Driving through a gate of cut limestone and wrought-iron he followed a private road up the hill through huge golden boulders and

122

live oaks that looked as much tortured by the sun as sustained by it. Reno whistled softly as they crested the hill and the entire estate sprawled in front of them—the house and garage and stables and poolhouse—all brilliant white under roofs of orange tile.

"J. Christ, I don't know about this," she said. "I don't know if I want to go in there."

"You don't have to."

"But I don't want to sit in the truck either."

Crow said nothing, for by then he was able to see all the cars parked along the drive and around the circle in front of the huge L-shaped house. Except for a few beautifully preserved old Lincoln and Cadillac limousines—whose chauffeurs were loafing under a cluster of palm trees—the cars were mostly Mercedes sedans and SL's and Porsches and Jaguars. As he circled in the truck, Crow saw the royal purple of funeral flags flying from a number of radio aerials, and his heart sank.

"Oh my God," he said. "We're too late."

"Why? The flags? Could be someone else."

Crow by then was thinking out loud. "If this is already the funeral reception, they must have hit the kid even before the girls."

"We don't know who died," Reno said.

"Don't we?" After parking near the garage, in the only space he could find, Crow lowered his head against the steering wheel. His hangover was suddenly back in force and he felt like vomiting.

"God, I just can't believe it," he said. "Not only my father, but all three of them on that lousy street corner. What could they have seen anyway? It doesn't make sense."

"Are we going in?" Reno asked.

"I don't know. What's the use? The day of the funeral they're not going to want to talk with some wild-eyed stranger."

"That's you?"

Crow looked at her. "They'll think so."

"We're not going in, then?"

Crow opened the truck's door. "We don't have any choice."

That made her sigh. "Just don't like rich people," she said. "They frost me."

Crow made no response as they got out and started back past the

123

driveway island, which was crowded with exotic flowering trees growing among the boulders. But Reno, at his side, was not to be discouraged.

"A friend of mine at home, she invited me along on this dumb pajama party at a rich girl's house. And the rich girl's mother really pissed me off. She acted like I was dirt, you know?"

"There are stupid rich people," he said, "same as stupid poor."

"Yeah, well, I don't mind the poor ones. But the rich, you can keep."

As they reached the stone steps in front of the house, one of two huge carved wood doors opened and a middle-aged couple emerged, the man mousey in a gray suit, barely able to keep up with the runway stride of his regal, lacquered wife.

"I'm glad that shit's over," she said, sweeping past Crow and Reno without a glance. "Never liked the little fag anyway."

But the servant who had opened the door for the couple—a young Oriental wearing a busboy's white jacket—did more than glance at Crow and the girl. His torpid gaze took disdainful inventory of the corduroys and workboots and herringbone jacket, the denim, and the velvet. And he stepped into the open doorway, blocking it.

"Sorry," he said. "Funer reception here today. Guest onry."

"The deceased is Richard Kellogg?" Crow asked.

The servant did not respond.

"Would it be possible to see his family? His father or his mother?"

A slightly older man now appeared behind the first, this one also Oriental. He asked what the problem was and Crow told him that he had just driven up from Los Angeles to see someone in Richard Kellogg's family, because he had information about the youth's death.

"What information?"

Crow didn't know where to start. "It's pretty complicated. It would take time to explain. Maybe we should come back later, after the reception."

The servant wagged his head. "Mister Kerrogg not see you then either. Everything go through Lon Kim."

"Then maybe he's the one I should see."

The older servant said something to the other in a language that

124

sounded like Japanese to Crow. Then he left and the younger one ushered Crow and Reno into a large, two-story foyer whose center-piece was a handsome dark-wood staircase curving up to the second floor. Beyond the stairs, through a row of narrow leaded windows, Crow could see a crowd of people out on the patio, some sitting at umbrella tables while others stood about, all watched over by more Oriental male servants. The young one now led Crow and Reno out of the foyer and across a large room that looked more like a museum of Western and Indian art than it did a simple living area. There were paintings and sculptures by Remington and Russell, among others, and there were totem poles and silver-inlaid saddles and handsome Navajo rugs scattered across the tiled floor. The furniture was black leather and horsehide and there were long glass cases filled with what appeared to be pre-Columbian artifacts. As they crossed, Reno gave Crow a wistful look.

"See what I mean?" she said. "This ain't the place for us."

And the servant evidently agreed, for he took them down a short hallway to a room next to the kitchen, a bare-walled affair with plastic tube furniture, a television, and a worn stack of Playboy magazines. A duty chart on the wall, above a desk, confirmed that the room was for the staff.

"You wait here," the servant said, and left.

Crow lit a cigarette. "Not exactly a royal welcome."

"Well, at least there's a TV."

Reno had already switched it on and was beginning to flip through the channels. Crow told her to turn it off.

"Why?"

"Just do it."

Complying, she sat down in a huff, with her arms folded and her legs flung out. "You treat me just like my old lady did. Like I'm a goddamn kid."

"Because sometimes you act like one."

"Bullshit."

Crow went over to the room's single window and looked out through bougainvillea at the huge patio and the guests gathered on it. Most of them were middle-aged or older, rich people in rich dark clothes, talking and smiling in small groups, the women holding

125

drinks and cigarettes and the men drinks and tiny silver plates of canapes. There was a bar but no music, and Crow did not see a moist eye in the house. As he watched, the second servant at the front door threaded his way through the crowd to a middle-aged Oriental man and spoke confidentially with him. This man, who was wearing a suit and tie, kept nodding as he listened. Then he moved deferentially to the side of a tall, lean, deeply tanned older man who appeared to be holding court where he stood near the pool, smiling and discoursing with the couples and individuals who had been admitted to his august presence. In a break between audiences, he inclined his ear to the waiting Oriental and gave an almost imperceptible nod. The Oriental then started through the crowd, toward the house.

"I think we're going to have a visitor," Crow said.

"Who?"

"Another servant."

"What are they—Japanese?"

Crow did not answer, for his eyes suddenly had locked on a young woman standing next to the older man, and hidden until now by the courtiers pressing in upon her. She was wearing a severe black dress and her thick blonde hair had been pulled back into a pitiless bun. Yet she dazzled. Of all the people there, she was the only one who looked to Crow as if she might have suffered that day. Though she appeared to be only about thirty, Crow found himself wondering if she was the old man's wife. More likely his daughter, he decided.

"What's so fascinating out there?" Reno asked.

"People."

Followed by one of the uniformed servants, the Oriental from the patio came into the room. He didn't bother to introduce himself, nor did he ask who Crow was.

"You have information about Richard Kellogg?" he inquired in unaccented English.

"Yes—but it would be best if his family heard it," Crow said. "They do live here, I take it."

"Of course—his sister and his uncle, Mister Henry Kellogg, who is my employer and whose house this is. Mister Kellogg instructed me to talk with you."

Crow nodded towards the window. "They're the ones near the

126

pool? The tall man and the blonde?"

"As you can see, they are busy now," the man said. "They have many guests. You talk to me—or to no one."

The statement was matter-of-fact, beyond argument. So Crow did not argue.

"All right. But first—how did Richard die?"

The man smiled slightly. "It seems you are the one in need of information."

"I've just come from L.A.," Crow explained. "I had reason to believe that Richard was in danger. That he might be killed. I had hoped to get here in time."

"*Killed?*" the man said.

"He wasn't killed, then?"

The Oriental shook his head. "Young Richard committed suicide. Just as it was reported in the newspapers. He was found in a motel room in Ventura, dead of a drug overdose."

Crow for some reason was not surprised to hear this. "Can you tell me why he did it?"

The man smiled again, in polite disdain. "I am Lon Kim, Mister Kellogg's personal assistant," he said. "Mister Kellogg is a very important, very busy man. He sent me in here to listen to what you had to say only because he still has a few questions about his nephew's death, and he thought you might be one of Richard's friends and have some answers for him. But it appears you too have only questions. So I think it would be best if you and your friend leave now."

"But I *do* have information," Crow insisted. "Important information."

He hurried through his story then, trying to make it as thorough and clear as he could, despite the Oriental's cold and weary gaze. When he finished, Lon Kim once more was smiling.

"Let me get this straight," he said. "Richard Kellogg and two Hollywood prostitutes are accidentally photographed in the process of viewing some sort of crime. Your father unwittingly identifies them for the criminal and all are subsequently eliminated one by one in ways that make the killings look like accidents or suicide or sex crimes, so the police won't connect them."

127

Crow was impressed. "That's right."

"And what about the photographer? How did he fare?"

The question stunned Crow. It was so obvious, so crucial, yet it was one he had never even asked himself. He felt stupid and embarrassed. And the Oriental had more for him.

"In serving Mister Kellogg, I have spent much of my life overseas, dealing with all kinds of people." His bland voice had given a peculiarly sinister shading to the words *all kinds.* "And let me say I've never seen killings such as you describe, perhaps because killing is not that easy. If a man wants to eliminate witnesses, do you really think he gets into rape and strangulation?"

The whole confrontation had come to seem unreal to Crow. He simply could not believe that this obviously intelligent man would stand there and debate the matter with him, as if it were not a matter of flesh and blood, a matter for the Kelloggs themselves to deal with.

"But just consider the odds against it," Crow heard himself say. "Four people linked by a few photographs, all dying violently within a few days of each other."

The man shrugged philosophically. "Such things happen—and against *all* odds."

"Maybe so," Crow said. "But then that's not for you to decide, is it? This is a family matter. And I think it would be best if I waited for Richard's family."

Lon Kim's response was the soul of economy. All he did was unbutton his suitcoat so that Crow could not help seeing the gun he carried in a shoulder holster. Smiling again, the Oriental went over to the desk and picked up a pencil and pad.

"You just give me a number where you can be reached," he said. "I will inform Mister Kellogg of what you've told me, and if he wants to talk further with you, I will let you know. Is that fair enough?"

"I guess it will have to be." Crow gave him the number.

Lon Kim led the way and the uniformed servant brought up the rear as the four of them went down the hallway to the living room and on into the foyer. And there, at the front door, Crow saw both uncle and niece in the process of saying good-bye to two couples and an old woman who was hanging onto Henry Kellogg's arm as if she were afraid of falling. Like her, the other women were dressed to the teeth in designer black, with fur wraps and jewelry that flashed in the slanting sunlight. And also like her, they gushed. They kissed and hugged and clucked their condolences, and the Kelloggs handled the treacly onslaught with the ease of experts, smiling and nodding and small-talking the group out through the doors and onto the broad stone porch. Kellogg himself could have passed for a model in a New Yorker executive ad, with his aquiline features and slicked-back white hair and deep tan, his lean frame swathed in a tailored gray chalk-stripe. Yet, again, it was the niece who commanded Crow's attention. And as she turned with her uncle, heading back toward the patio and their remaining guests, Crow made his move.

"Miss Kellogg!" he called. "I came here to tell you about your brother—that he didn't kill himself."

Like her uncle, she stopped and looked back to see what crazed interloper could have said such a thing. Crow tried to tell her.

"Yesterday I buried my father in L.A. The police think he was a suicide too. But I know he was killed—by the same people who killed your brother."

By then she was facing him, her momentary look of surprise giving way to an expression of profound and shocked interest. In that moment Crow for some unexplicable reason noticed that her hair, against the distant windows, had combusted into golden fire. But it was also a moment in which he caught Lon Kim's nod, just as a pair of powerful arms seized him from behind. Instinctively he lunged forward and down, twisting his body at the same time, with the result that one very surprised servant fell crashing onto the stairway balustrade before sliding off it onto the floor like a delivery of meat.

Reno was exultant. "Godalmighty, Crow! Was that ever neat!"

As he straightened up, he saw Kellogg gesturing to Lon Kim and the servant to back off.

"No need for force," the man said. "They're leaving now."

Miss Kellogg glanced at her uncle. "But I want to hear what he has to say, Henry. Don't you?"

Kellogg looked pained. "Oh come on, Jennifer—can't you see what he is? A money-sniffer, that's all. Probably one of Richard's pansy friends."

Reno was tugging on Crow's sleeve. "Come on, let's get out of here. These people ain't for real."

To Crow, though, Henry Kellogg was very much for real, the same as Lon Kim and the uniformed servant, who was on his feet by then, ready and eager to help throw Crow out of the house on his ear. And Jennifer Kellogg must have sensed this too, this moment of calm before the storm, for she stepped forward now, touching Crow's arm and heading for the porch.

"I'll only be a second," she said to her uncle. "Why don't you go on ahead?"

But Kellogg obviously was accustomed to having the last word. "Make sure he's off the grounds in two minutes," he told his servants. "And don't bother to be polite."

On the porch, Jennifer spoke in a rush. "Look, I don't know who you are or what it is you know about Richard—but I *am* curious. I just can't believe he did what he did. I saw him that morning, and he was perfectly happy. He was himself."

By way of getting to his story, Crow started to introduce himself and Reno, but Jennifer cut him off.

"No, I'm sorry—I don't have the time now. My uncle is perfectly serious. He'll have you thrown out—the Kims probably have a stopwatch on you right now."

"But I haven't told you—"

"I know—we must talk. But not now, and not here. I'll meet you later. Say, in two hours. You know where the Biltmore is?"

"I can find it."

She suddenly changed her mind, though, evidently having just made an inventory of her own. "No, it's so stuffy there. And I know so many people. Let's make it the Seaplace, in Santa Barbara, on the beach. It's new, but it's nice."

Crow nodded. "In two hours, then. The Seaplace."

Her eyes were moist and shot with anguish. Yet she smiled now, at both him and Reno, and Crow felt oddly moved.

"Yes, two hours," she said. "And please wait for me. I'll be there."

Turning, she went back inside then, without even looking at Lon Kim and the servant, who had been watching the three of them the whole time. Reno smiled at the Orientals and started to give them the finger just as Crow took her by the hand and pulled her with him down the steps and out onto the driveway. Near the garage, he pushed her into the truck and then got in himself and backed it out. As he started down the hill towards the gate, she gave a laugh and shook her head.

"So, that's your kind, eh? Princess Grace."

Crow said nothing at first. The hillside was so steep that he could see, over the trees, the ocean stretching silver and blue to the horizon. He saw that, and he saw Jennifer Kellogg too.

"I thought she was okay," he said.

Reno was lighting a cigarette. "Yeah—well, I don't like her. I don't like her at all."

*   *   *

After leaving Billy Boy aflame in the park, Teller had thought he would drive straight to New Day Construction and wait for Queen and Diefenbaker to show so he could give them the good news, let them know just how incredibly thorough and inventive he had been in tying up all the loose ends, protecting the chief's boy straight down the line. But then he began to have second thoughts, realizing that Queen and especially Diefenbaker might not look kindly upon his final masterstroke in taking out Billy Boy as well. If there was going to be any contention, he decided it would be better if he were rested and calm.

As it was, he had thrown up in his car and he was trembling so hard he could barely register in the downtown fleabag where he finally chose to hole up. To make matters worse, he had only a few 'ludes and Valium left, and no Seconal at all. So he put in an urgent call to his connection and overtipped the ancient bellboy to go out and buy him newspapers and crackers and milk and Kaopectate, as well as any downers the man could find.

The newspapers, it turned out, had little to offer in the way of relief. There was absolutely nothing in them about a fatality on Mulholland Drive, not in that day's edition nor in the previous day's. This curious omission so upset him, so loosened his bowels, that Teller found himself on the toilet for hours afterwards. And indeed, it was there he was sitting, listening to the TV in the bedroom, when he heard the first accounts of the murders of Billy Boy and the hookers. Messily wiping himself, he waddled into the bedroom just as the coverage switched from the girls to Billy, who, to the police was still just a badly burned, unidentifiable corpse. The "fire-bombed" car was said to belong to William Sims, of Glendale, an ex-convict now employed as a construction laborer. Dental records were being checked to determine if Sims was the murder victim. The police said there were no witnesses and that so far they had no leads in the "vicious killing."

Flipping to another channel's noon newscast, Teller got the hooker story in full, including footage of the bodies being wheeled out of the motel. He saw the desk clerk again and he heard himself described as a "mousey little guy" who had registered as J. J. Biggs of Greeley, Colorado. It was Barbara Queen who had thought up the name and called in the reservation, so she could give her CIA contact, Costello, the motel and room number where he was to deliver the names. But the desk clerk didn't seem to remember anything about a woman making the reservation, just as the newspapers didn't seem interested in the death of an ex-CIA agent on Mulholland Drive.

Toward the end of his first day in the fleabag, Teller managed to score a hundred "blue beauties," as his connection called ten-milligram Valium. Teller took one every two or three hours and by the end of his second day there, his diarrhea was under control and he was able to hold down the crackers and milk as well as some take-out food from McDonald's, which the doddering bellboy also had gotten for him. Many times he thought of calling the office or Barbara Queen's apartment to tell her that he was all right and that he would be coming in soon, but he let it pass until Sunday morning. Always the cool one, Barbara said very little on the phone except that it was "nice" to hear from him again and that she would expect him at the office at three.

He was so anxious to have the confrontation over with that he arrived at slightly after two o'clock, parking almost a block away. Along each side of the filthy street were similar garagelike structures, housing machine shops and warehouses and other small businesses, none of them retail. And Teller found it fairly hilarious that after being on the New Day payroll for over a year, he still didn't know what the group's political orientation was: leftist or rightist. All that was beside the point, according to Queen and Diefenbaker. The only viable position in today's world was negative, they preached to the group, writing off one-by-one all those decrepit political systems they *didn't* believe in, such as communism and social democracy. No, a serious person had no choice, they said, except to chuck it all, bring crashing down all the rotten, termite-ridden social edifices of the modern world, including American democracy. Dief just loved to explain the political spectrum as a circle, with the middle-of-the-road American at zero degrees and the liberals and conservatives on either side of him at 90 and 270 degrees respectively, with communism and fascism meeting at the 180-degree mark, without a fig's difference between them. When anyone asked where the group's position was, Dief fairly bubbled with glee in explaining that their position wasn't *on* the circle.

Thus the group's proper program was simply destruction, all those pitiful little dirty-tricks operations they had undertaken during the past year, including the cross-burnings on black-owned property and the painting of swastikas on synagogues, not to mention all the racist call-ins on talk shows by group members—anything to keep at a rolling boil the simmering pot of social and racial unrest in greater L.A. Until now, the group's one major coup had been the firebombing of a black youth center, the action carried out largely by John Dumbrosky, the group's ex-Vietnam Ranger and all-out expert in weapons, demolition, and other techniques of mayhem. The third member of the "leadership," Dumbrosky undoubtedly would be showing up with the others soon, a fact that didn't make Teller feel any more comfortable, for he was the first to admit that Dumbrosky intimidated him, just as he did almost everyone else in the group.

Teller in fact had been more than a little surprised when Barbara Queen had turned to him and Billy Boy for the job just completed, since it would have been such a natural for Dumbrosky, with all his expertise in violence. But then maybe Queenie sensed that the man was simply not gutsy enough for such an operation. As the entrepreneur of a small karate studio in Glendale, he was practically a member of the establishment, with something to lose. Or maybe he had been offered the job and had turned it down. Maybe he was chicken.

133

The thought made Teller laugh out loud as he continued to sit there in his VW watching New Day down the street. There were times when he had to admit that the group was a pretty flaky organization, basically just a melange of misfits not unlike himself and Billy Boy. Some, like Dumbrosky and Diefenbaker, had their own careers and incomes, while others, like Teller, were totally dependent on their meager New Day salaries. There were no more than a dozen members in all and most of them showed up only occasionally, when Barbara or Dief would call them in for a meeting, sometimes because a new dirty-tricks operation was in the offing, but more often simply because Diefenbaker wanted to get on his soapbox and whip up some esprit de corps, usually by cataloguing for the group the continuing disintegration of society at large. Sometimes Dumbrosky would run the group through its paces, testing its competency at breaking down and reassembling weapons such as the M16—even though they had only one such rifle.

Since few of them were roaring successes in the great outside world, the group's members had been more than willing to join an organization dedicated to that world's destruction. Like Teller, most had been recruited by Diefenbaker, through his job as a public defender for the county of Los Angeles. In Teller's case, the fat young lawyer undoubtedly had no trouble at all in recognizing him as an ideal candidate for the group. Fired by the state welfare system, and out of work for almost a year, Teller one day had been unfairly put upon by a Beverly Hills matron and her toy poodle, which she was out walking on a leash. Like Teller, the woman had stopped for a red light, was just standing there on the street corner while her obscenely overgroomed little beast barked savagely at Teller in his VW. The matron deigned to glance over at him and his pitiful vehicle just once, apparently to assure herself that the dog was not barking out of place. And though Teller hadn't intended to turn right, when the light finally changed and the lady stepped out into the boulevard, pulling the yapping dog along after her—well, before he knew what he was doing, Teller had burned rubber going around the corner, wanting only to scare the hell out of both woman and dog. Unfortunately the noisy little creature got itself under his wheels and promptly died, though Teller wasn't sure of this at the time, not having stayed around to find out. Some poodle-loving patriot in a car behind him took down his license number, however, with the result that he was soon arrested and charged with reckless driving and leaving the scene of an accident. *Accident.*

He and Diefenbaker had had a good laugh in the jail conference room over that one. But they'd had few laughs since, possibly because the ivy-leaguer had more in common with the matron than he did with Teller, though he never would have admitted it. Anyway, that had been Teller's first contact with the group and the beginning of his proselytization. Once he learned there was a salary involved, he became an immediate convert.

As he'd feared, Dumbrosky as well as Diefenbaker and Barbara Queen showed up for the Sunday debriefing. And, generous to a fault, the three of them let him do almost all the talking at the outset. While Diefenbaker sat grandly at his desk, fretting with a pencil, the redhaired and muscular Dumbrosky stood leaning back against the office wall, his arms folded peaceably in front of him. Barbara Queen, nearest to Teller, sat staring at him as if he'd just alighted from a spaceship. Babbling along, he tried to explain why he'd been so late in reporting in, telling them all about his stomach flu and diarrhea and how every time he started to call in he just couldn't quite make it, as weak and dizzy as he was.

And then too, he said, before coming in, he'd wanted to have a newspaper account of the Costello hit, to prove what he'd accomplished. But he hadn't been able to find one in either L.A. paper. However, he wanted to assure them "right here and now" that the job had been done—with the old man winding up at the bottom of a cliff on Mulholland Drive.

"We made it look like an accident," he told them. "Booze, broken neck—a perfect job. The guy was cancelled, believe me. I just can't figure why it wasn't in the papers."

Barbara Queen was smiling at him. "But it *was*, Head. A couple of days ago."

"No shit?" Teller felt a surge of relief. "Which one? Let me see it."

"Later," she told him. "First—about the others."

135

Teller couldn't help grinning. "Well, it's all over the TV. Those two hookers in the Hollywood motel—that was Billy Boy's work. What *I* had him do, that is. So it wouldn't look like a hit either. And I guess it affected him. Pushed him right over the edge, let me tell you. It was early Friday morning and he was totally out of control —downers and booze like you wouldn't believe. So I had no choice. It was him or us."

Diefenbaker by then had his face in his hands and was slowly shaking his head. Dumbrosky's look was unreadable.

"What about the boy?" Barbara Queen asked.

"A fag from Santa Barbara. Real rich. Name of Kellogg." Again Teller had to grin. "And would you believe the kid committed suicide? Well, he did. Took a drug overdose in a Ventura motel."

Barbara suddenly had gone pale. "*Kellogg,* did you say?"

"Yeah, Richard Kellogg. Lived in Montecito."

"You're joking," she said.

"Like hell I am. Why?"

Diefenbaker looked over at her too, as curious as Teller was.

"Nothing," she said. "Get on with it."

Teller threw up his hands. "Well, that's it. And I'd say it's quite a bit, wouldn't you? Five people cancelled in order to protect 'our boy,' whoever the hell he is—and each hit is different. In fact, don't even look like a hit. I'd say the chief ought to be impressed by that little piece of work, wouldn't you?"

None of them nodded. None agreed.

"Well, what's the problem—Billy Boy? I already explained that to you. He was out of control. He was a loose cannon. I had no choice."

Sighing as if in pain, Diefenbaker pushed a folded newspaper across his desk, in Teller's direction. "Your *Costello* hit," he sneered. "The reason you didn't find it in the paper is because the name wasn't Costello, as you can see."

With trembling fingers, Teller picked up the paper, Friday's edition of the *Herald Examiner,* folded open to page ten. Circled in red ink was a one-paragraph story about a retired L.A.P.D. detective killed in a single car crash on Mulholland Drive, a mile west of Laurel Canyon.

136

Teller sagged into the chair next to Diefenbaker's desk. He felt betrayed—and angry.

"Well, how was I to know, for Christ's sake? He's the one who showed up with the job."

"I did describe him for you," Barbara said.

"The cat *said* he was Costello! What was I to do, call him a liar?"

"And guess where the real Costello is," Diefenbaker forced his puffy face into a malevolent grin. "He's bye-bye, Head. Yessir, sailed away on his boat, he did. And you'd never guess what else I found out—simply by calling the deceased detective's home and asking about the job he'd been working on for me. The talkative lady who answered generously informed me that the old boy's son had taken over all his cases—isn't that neat? The lady said that the son could answer all our questions as soon as he returned from—guess where, Head—*Santa Barbara*, of all places."

"You know where that leaves us?" Barbara asked.

Diefenbaker answered for him. "It leaves us vulnerable, that's where. Vulnerable to both of them—to Costello and now to this detective's kid."

Teller wanted to rage against the three of them for being so stupid and unfair, blaming him for what was patently not his fault, only the luck of the game. But his bladder was aching and he was just now beginning to feel a sudden weakness in his bowels. He knew that he had to get out of there, and quickly, so he shrugged his shoulders and mumbled his apologies, saying that it was all just a run of bad luck, but that he was still too sick to discuss it now, that he really had to leave.

Barbara gave him a commiserating look. "So soon?"

"What else is there?" Teller asked.

"Well, wouldn't you say we had to make plans?" she said. "Considering our new vulnerability. You know, the police have already been here about Billy Boy. And they'll undoubtedly come again. Dief hears from his sources that we're on the state attorney general's list now, as a suspected subversive organization."

Teller was on his feet by then, edging toward the door. "Yeah, well, right now I'm no good to you. Or to anybody else. I gotta get back to bed."

Barbara got an attache case off her desk and brought it over to him. "There's one thing you can do for us," she said. "Take this and keep it in a safe place. It contains documents and records we don't want the feds to see. We figure they could be raiding this place soon as well as our apartments, since we're the group's leaders. Just keep it safe and don't try to open it, okay? It's locked."

Taking the case, Teller gestured good-bye, nodding in the direction of Diefenbaker and the wooden Dumbrosky, who still had not moved or said a word. As Teller reached the sidewalk, Barbara came out after him and took him by the arm, almost like a lover.

"Listen, I couldn't say anything in there," she told him. "You know how Dief feels about this whole thing. But you did a terrific job and I want you to know I know it. You did beautifully."

Incredibly, he found that his eyes had teared and that he couldn't speak. Nodding his gratitude, he pulled his arm free and practically ran on down the street toward his VW, and sanctuary.

SEVEN

BACK in his hippie days, Crow once had camped for over a week on the beaches of Santa Barbara, so he was not surprised at their sweep and dazzle. He had thought that Reno would be, though, considering that she had grown up in Nevada. But he was wrong. Barefoot and sulking, she scuffed the surf-wet sand as they wandered along the beach, killing time until the appointment with Jennifer Kellogg.

"What's wrong?" he asked. "Don't you like sand?"

"That's dumb," she informed him. "A real dumb question."

"I like dumb questions."

"That's obvious."

"So how about it?" he deadpanned. "How come you kick sand? Don't you like it?"

"Sure, I like it," she said. "I like to kick it."

Crow squinted against the lowering sun, trying not to smile. "You know what futility is, Reno?"

"Yeah, I know exactly what the fuck futility is."

"It's kicking sand."

139

"No, it's listening to you."

Pretending indignation, Crow gave her a playful shove, expecting her to shove back. But all she did was walk on, sulking still. Ahead of them the beach curved toward the distant marina and its protective great stone breakwater, on which a scattered crowd of locals and tourists strolled in the mist of the crashing sea. On the beach itself only a few sunbathers still braved the late afternoon spring air. Behind them a steady stream of cars and pedestrians poured along the beach boulevard, where Crow had parked his truck, near the Seaplace restaurant, which was a modern natural-wood affair, a building that would have looked more at home in Seattle than it did in Spanish Santa Barbara. Glancing at his watch, he told Reno that it was time to head back.

"It's been almost two hours," he said. "We don't want to miss her."

"You mean, *you* don't."

"You're not coming?" he asked.

"Why should I? It's you two who lost somebody—not me."

Crow shook his head. "What a tough guy."

"That's me, all right."

"You just gonna stay here and kick sand?"

"Why not? I got nothing to say to Princess Grace."

"The tide might come in. A great white shark might bite off your nose."

"I'll take my chances."

He took out his keys and gave them to her. "In case you want to wait in the truck," he said. "I've got no idea how long this will take."

She gave him a rueful look. "You mean how long you can make it last."

"Whatever."

Jennifer Kellogg proved unpredictable. Crow had thought she would arrive late, still dressed in funeral black, and with her yellow hair in the same severe bun. But her hair hung loose and she came on time, wearing tan slacks and a wraparound sweater as well as sunglasses so lightly tinted he could clearly see her eyes as she came out of the restaurant onto the deck, heading for his umbrella table.

140

He stood up for her, and she nodded coolly, without smiling. Crow asked her if she wanted to order anything and she said no, that she had come to hear his story, that was all. Her manner made it seem even chillier than it was out on the deck and Crow ordered an Irish coffee. Jennifer then nodded to the waitress.

"Make it two," she said.

As the girl left, Jennifer swung her fine green eyes back onto Crow and waited. He offered her a cigarette, which she declined.

"Jesus—where to start?" he said, lighting his own.

"Why not with your name?"

"Why not? Crow." He was trying not to stammer. "Orville Crow."

"For the record," she said, "I'm not Miss Kellogg, as you called me at the house. I'm Mrs. Payne. My divorce isn't final yet."

Where Crow had hurried through his story with her uncle's man, Lon Kim, he now took his time with her, making sure she understood it fully, step by step. He told her of his coming from Seattle to visit his father and of the phone call from "Lee." He detailed how he had filled in for the ailing old man, finding names and addresses to go with the photographs that the caller had given his father— photos of Jennifer's brother and of two young nude dancers in Hollywood. Crow told Jennifer of his father's "accident" and he showed her the newspaper story about the killing of the dancers.

"First thing I did after reading it was call your home," he said. "But I got some woman I could barely understand. She told me to call back later. I thought of contacting the police then, but I had no proof of anything. I was afraid I'd be wasting precious time."

"So you got in your car and drove here."

"Right. As fast as I could."

Her eyes suddenly softened. "That was good of you," she said. "I do appreciate it. And I'm sorry about my uncle, how he behaved. But you must understand—he accepts the police version of what happened. He accepts it that Richard could have killed himself. Richard was gay, you see. And for years he and his friends have given Uncle Henry nothing but trouble. So this afternoon he naturally thought that you were one of them."

"A formidable man, your uncle," Crow said.

141

"A great man, actually. Over the years he's had much to do with keeping the Arabs friendly with the U.S."

Crow could not help grinning at that. "And with friends like that—"

"I know, I know. But we don't want to get into politics now, do we?"

"No, of course not. I was just running off—forget it. Now about your brother," he said. "All I got out of your uncle's man was that Richard died of a drug overdose in a Ventura motel. And that it was suicide."

Jennifer looked about them, at the other patrons on the restaurant deck, obviously concerned that she and Crow might be overheard. Finally she nodded.

"Yes, that was the preliminary finding. And I understand the autopsy bears it out. He was found in a seedy little motel off the freeway. He was wearing a woman's undergarments. There was an empty drug bottle on the table next to him. And he had written *I'm sorry* on the mirror in lipstick—printed it actually, the police said, in large letters."

Her eyes were brimming by then and she was holding onto her glass with both hands. Crow followed her gaze out across the boulevard, toward the sun flattening on the rim of the sea.

"Did he rent the room himself?" he asked.

"They don't know. The desk clerk is an elderly woman and all she remembers is a young man signing for the room. She doesn't remember anything special about him, can't say whether or not he was Richard. She said the man paid in advance and signed the register as Manny Keehan—a pun, I imagine."

"One your brother ever used?"

"Not that I recall."

"And the handwriting?"

"The police got a sample of Richard's hand yesterday. I don't know how they compare."

"At your house, you said you saw him that morning—"

"Yes, and he seemed just like himself. Happy, even." She had looked angry for a moment, but now there was only bewilderment in her eyes. "He even joked about the repairs on his car—how much

142

they had cost. And he told me again about seeing this Robert Redford character."

Crow had no idea what she meant. *"Robert Redford?"*

She gave him a helpless look. "That's what he said—and on the phone too, when he called the night before. He said he'd seen this Robert Redford lookalike."

"Where?"

Suddenly she brightened. "Flashbulbs! I remember now! He said some nut was taking pictures!"

"The photos given to my father!" Crow too felt a growing excitement. "And this Redford character—was that who the photographer was shooting? Did Richard say?"

"I don't think so. I think all he said was that there was this lookalike and that someone was shooting pictures in the dark."

Neither of them said anything for a short time. Crow was trying to make some sense out of this new information, just as he imagined Jennifer was pondering what he had told her. He looked out over the wood railing at the fading day. A scattering of scarlet clouds marked the place where the sun had gone down, and to Crow the entire oceanfront looked suddenly and curiously empty, as if Southern Californians were so cold-blooded a race they'd had to scurry home like lizards rather than face the terror of a sunless eve.

Crow suggested that the two of them take their story to the police and Jennifer readily agreed. She said that her uncle was a friend of the police chief and he had made sure that "some of our own people" were looking into Richard's death, in cooperation with the Ventura police. However, Jennifer doubted that the officers assigned to the case would be on duty on this, a Sunday night, and anyway she had other commitments.

"Could you stay in town overnight?" she asked. "We could meet in the morning at the police station. Say, nine o'clock?"

"No problem."

Out of the blue then, Jennifer asked him where his "young friend" was.

"I assumed you were together," she explained. "That she had come with you from L.A."

For a few moments Crow just sat there staring at her, trying desperately to think of some feasible explanation for the girl's being with him, an explanation that would not automatically typecast him as a fledgling Humbert Humbert. Opening his mouth finally, he found himself a veritable fountainhead of misinformation. Reno, as she called herself, was his second cousin, he said. The poor kid had just come to stay with his father two weeks before, after losing her parents in a car accident. And now, after what had happened to the old man, the girl was "kind of strung out." Having slept very little the last few days, she at that moment was sound asleep in Crow's truck.

Jennifer shook her head. "A child losing her parents—that's got to be toughest of all."

"Yes, I imagine so."

"But then we have our losses too," she said. "It seems to be an epidemic."

As she pushed back her chair, preparing to get up, Reno came sauntering out onto the deck, looking both defiant and shy. Jennifer smiled warmly at her.

"Well, there you are," she said. "Did you have a good nap?"

"A good what?"

"Your cousin told me all you've gone through lately," Jennifer said. "I *am* sorry."

"My cousin, huh?"

"Yes, I told her about the accident," Crow broke in. "And how you came to stay with us."

The girl gave Crow a mocking look. "Yeah, it was a real bummer," she admitted.

Jennifer was on her feet by then, pulling her capelike sweater about her. "I'm sorry to run off just when you get here, but I really must. I'm late now."

"Well, when you gotta go," Reno said, "you gotta go."

Crow found himself almost elbowing the girl aside as he hurried to escort his new friend out of the restaurant. Going through the main dining room, he couldn't help noticing how much attention Jennifer attracted, the women looking at her in envy and the men with admiration or simple lust. And it was not a feeling Crow particularly enjoyed, possibly because it made him feel like a tall

Mickey Rooney trundling in the wake of one of his stunning wives. None of which was Jennifer's fault, he knew. She was not overly made-up and her clothes were if anything conservative. It was simply her looks and carriage and manner, all of it so perfect, so hypnotically right—with the result that Crow, like the other men in the restaurant, had his own moments of admiration and lust. But he ignored all that, reminding himself it was death that had brought them together, death that they were concerned with.

With Reno trailing behind, Crow walked Jennifer all the way out to her car, a gray Porsche 911. He smiled and said he would see her in the morning, and then he closed the car door and stood there watching as she drove off. Reno gave a weary sigh and he finally turned to look at her. Arms folded, she was leaning back against the fender of a parked car.

"Well, *cousin,*" she said, "what next?"

In the small, dimly lit room Teller lay naked on a foam rubber floor mattress, waiting for the girl he had just paid fifty dollars for. The decor was bargain-basement Oriental, with Pier I Import Japanese silk screen imitations depicting geishas and samurai. There were fake jade vases and a golden dragon on a pedestal as well as a cluster of motionless wind chimes. And the piped-in music was typical Jap too, bouncy and cute, not unlike the score in a fifties Doris Day epic, as she arrived breathless and virginal in the Big Apple.

When the girl finally came in, she smiled at Teller just as all Japanese whores did, with that inherent politeness and obsequiousness that made sex so much easier, at least for him. With anglo hookers the attitude was more like: "Betcha can't get it up, creep." Which he couldn't, not with them. And even though he knew the Japanese girl probably hated his guts the same as the anglos, it didn't matter at all, just so long as she nodded and bowed and smiled at him in that special way, as if he were her own true lord and master. He gave her a forty dollar tip and she bowed again and smiled. As she slipped out of her kimona he saw that her breasts were small and that she was a little short in the leg, but he couldn't have cared less, especially as she began to soap him with a sponge that she kept

145

dipping into a golden pail of steaming water. When he was fully lathered, she put the sponge away and mounted him, using her own body as the sponge now, slipping back and forth on top of him, sometimes passing her breasts over his erection and sometimes her buttocks, until finally he told her that he was ready. And then she rinsed the soap from his genitals and proceeded to fellate him with a zest that had him coming almost immediately.

Still smiling politely, she led him to a shower and scrubbed him down again before toweling him off, giving such special attention to his cock that he was soon hard again.

"Annuder forty, I do again," she told him.

Declining, he got dressed and soon was driving home in his VW, feeling really good for the first time in weeks. And it galled him that he could afford to feel this way only occasionally, usually no more than once a month. But after the week he had just spent—and especially after the meeting at New Day that afternoon—he felt he had it coming. In fact, more and more, he was beginning to feel that he had the good life coming to him *full time*. After all, wasn't it almost a law in America that if a man took special risks, he reaped special rewards?

This idea nagged at him the rest of that evening, especially as he lay in bed smoking in the dark, having already eaten and watched the television news, which had been filled with brand-new cases of murder and mayhem, his own evidently already confined to the dumpster of history. And he thought about it, the unfairness of it all. Here he was, a college graduate in his late twenties, living like some wetback in a rundown L.A. "efficiency apartment"—actually a one-time motel room with a "kitchenette" slapped into one corner and a leaky, rumbling bathroom in the other. He didn't have to wonder if the chief lived in such a dump. No, more likely the bastard had a place like that of the Kelloggs in Santa Barbara, a whole fucking estate, with swimming pools and tennis courts and guard dogs. And it really pissed Teller that he had put his life on the line for the bastard, without even knowing who he was, or who his "boy" was. Yet he, Teller, had to live like this—while they had it all. It just didn't make sense. And it reminded him forcefully of what Barbara Queen had told him before the hits, that they would be wiring themselves in tight with the chief, financially as well as politically. But now he had to ask himself: What *they?* It was he alone who had done the dirty work, he alone who deserved to be "wired in."

It was a line of thought that inevitably began to focus on the attache case, which he had hidden under his bed (as though one could ever really hide anything in a one-room dump). He couldn't help wondering if among the "important papers" in the case there wasn't something with the great man's name on it, such as a building lease. Just maybe it was all there, right under his bed: not only who the chief was, but who his "boy" was too, the bastard whose good name was worth so goddamn many lives. It intrigued Teller—made his bladder hurt, his hands tremble—the thought of how much power, how much wealth, he might find just by opening the case.

Fleetingly it also crossed his mind that the whole thing might be a setup, a Dumbrosky-rigged bomb that he was meant to trigger by opening the case. Just as Billy Boy had been a threat to him, now maybe he was a threat to them, the leadership. But it was only the remotest possibility, he assured himself. After all, Barbara Queen had given him the case, not Diefenbaker or Dumbrosky—Dief and Dumb, as the more predictable members of the group referred to them. No, Barbara had given it to him personally, and he couldn't forget—would never forget—what she had told him out on the sidewalk: that he had done a terrific job, a beautiful job. So he dismissed the idea finally, even laughed at it.

Getting the attache case out from under the bed, he placed it on the kitchenette bar and scrounged up some old keys and a paper clip and a nut-pick. Then very carefully and patiently he began to pick the lock on the cheap vinyl case. Cheap cases of course had cheap locks, *easy* locks. So it was only a matter of time, he told himself.

And when that time came, he was aware for perhaps a millisecond that he had succeeded, that the lock had clicked and the two shiny clasps had jumped open. But immediately there was a blinding flash and a force like a locomotive striking him and tossing his body up through fire and smoke and disintegrating walls.

*　　*　　*

At Sambo's, over hamburgers and fries, Reno was having great fun at Jennifer Kellogg's expense. Smiling oversweetly, she reached

147

across the booth table and gave Crow's hand a firm shake.

"Ah, there you are, my dear," she gushed. "Did you have a good nap?"

"I don't recall any handshakes," Crow said. "Or any *my dears*."

But Reno was not listening. "Your dear cousin told me all about you. And I *am* sorry, you poor dear. Just *too, too* sorry."

Crow sipped at his coffee. "Go on, enjoy yourself," he said. "The lady was just trying to be nice to you, put you at ease. But that's not to be tolerated, is it?"

Reno tilted her head and archly pushed up the corners of her mouth. "Is this the way? Have I got the smile right?"

Crow could not help grinning at the picture she presented, so much venom in so young and pretty a face.

"Not quite," he said.

The girl shrugged. "Well, what can you expect, after me losing Mom and Dad in that terrible accident. But at least I've got my cousin to take care of me, right?"

Crow was lighting a cigarette. "Right," he said.

For a while then she sat there studying him and popping french fries into her mouth. "Wouldn't you say it's about time you leveled," she said finally. "About time I found out why we're cousins all of a sudden. And why you had to knock off my parents in the bargain."

That turned a few heads in the next booth.

"A moment of confusion," Crow told her. "I wanted Jennifer to trust me. To talk freely. So I didn't want her thinking of me as a flake."

"Having me around means you're a flake?"

"The age difference, Reno—remember those little laws I told you about?" He was practically whispering now. "Well, I didn't want her thinking of me as a lawbreaker. As some kind of old lech."

"Old man Crow," she said.

"That's me."

"Tell me, do your teeth come out at night?"

"Not yet."

She leaned toward him, her eyes suddenly grave. "Most people here probably think you're twenty-eight and I'm twenty-two. You realize that?"

148

"No, I didn't."

"Well, they do."

"Is that a fact?"

"I think it is."

Crow slid out of the booth and picked up the check. "Come on, old timer," he said. "We best be moseyin' along."

Outside they walked slowly along the palm-lined boulevard toward the room Crow had rented in one of the beach motels. Originally he had intended to get each of them single rooms or at most connecting rooms, which he would have turned into singles with the twist of a lock. But Reno had said that she would not stay alone, that she would bang on his door and let all the world know that she, a poor ravaged sixteen-year-old, was carrying his baby.

"You'd do that?" he asked.

"Sure. And everybody'd believe me too—because they don't know how you are."

"And how is that?"

Her hands blocked in a square. "Absolute and total."

Anyway he had nothing to worry about, she went on. If he touched her, she would scream. She wanted no part of "old geezers." She just didn't want to be alone in "this candy-ass town."

"Why call it that?" he asked.

"Because it ain't real. It looks like a TV commercial—for Coppertone or Orange Crush."

"Where'd you hear that?"

"What do you mean, *hear* it? I just said it."

"It's the kind of thing teenagers parrot."

"Well, I ain't no parrot."

"I should've known better."

Crow bought a Bic razor and toothpaste and toothbrushes, and in their twin-bed room they lay back and watched television: reruns of "Chips" and two CBS sitcoms, all chosen by Reno. In time, Crow took a shower and slipped back into bed in his shorts. Reno then followed, loudly locking the bathroom door and running a tub that must have been filled within two inches of the top, judging by the water he heard sloshing onto the floor. When she finally came out, wearing panty briefs as well as her trusty purple velvet blouse, great

149

clouds of steam followed her into the room. She turned out the lights then and jumped under her covers, where she commenced an almost desperate struggle to get out of the blouse and panties. Peeking out finally, she had advice for him.

"Don't get your underwear in a bundle. I'm just getting comfortable, that's all."

"I'll try to control myself."

"Some tough job," she scoffed.

The irony was that the job *wasn't* easy for Crow. He had not had sex since the night before he left Seattle, a kind of bon voyage from one of three women he saw with some regularity, all fairly typical Seattle divorcees, bright, attractive career women who used him as a kind of comfort station between their various marriages and affairs, knowing that he was not exactly the marrying kind. In his way, he cared a good deal for each of them, yet he had to admit that they didn't reach him the way a Jennifer Kellogg did—or for that matter, as Reno did. God knows the kid was not womanly yet, all legs and arms and sass, a perfect Vogue teenager, only a real street kid instead of just playing at it. Yet there in the dark he could not help thinking of her hard young nude body under the covers, her small high breasts and perfect butt. And he too had to wonder about himself, whether he might not be too much of a square, too concerned about law and decency in a world where tired old men and rich kids and pretty girls could all be killed so very casually, simply because they had seen something or knew something. In such a world, his scruples in regard to Reno seemed almost quaint. So maybe the kid was right after all, he thought. Maybe he should just turn off the old brain for a time and let his body have its say.

But he didn't. In fact he would not even let himself look over at her, limned as she was by the rectangle of light that edged past the drapes into the room. All he needed was to fix on the curve of her hip and he knew he just might lose what resolve he had. Anyway, there were other matters clamoring for his attention, such as how a Robert Redford lookalike could have figured in the deaths of young Kellogg and the nude dancers, not to mention Crow's father. And then there was the photographer himself, that player so central to the scene that Crow had overlooked him entirely. Just who the man

150

was and why he had been out there on that dark street corner—
shooting whom or what—Crow had no idea, no more than he knew
who "Lee" was or how he figured in. And that of course was the core
of the problem: just how Crow was to go about getting answers to
these questions. For some reason, he felt strongly that Jennifer
Kellogg would turn out to be of considerable help to him, possibly
because she refused to believe that her brother had killed himself,
or maybe just because of who she was, with all the clout and contacts
available to a niece of Henry Kellogg. Whatever, Crow looked forward to the morning, when he would see her again and the two of
them could get to work, starting with the Santa Barbara police.

But suddenly his reverie was at an end.

"Crow—" Reno said.

"Yes?"

"How old you think Princess Grace is? About your age?"

"Younger. Late twenties, maybe."

"Close to thirty, huh?"

"Yeah. Afraid so."

"That's too bad. You guys get better looking around then, but
women just get wrinkly. And they sag."

"Poor things," Crow said.

Reno had lit a cigarette and as she dragged on it now the red coal
illumined her dark, narrowing eyes. "What about her hair?" she
asked. "You think it's natural?"

"I could find out tomorrow. Give it a yank or two."

"You know what I mean—the color. Is she a real blonde or what?"

"Probably 'or what.' But who cares?"

"I was just wondering, that's all."

"No kidding."

"I was wondering what it must be like to wake up in the morning
with someone like that, with their black roots and no eyelashes and
their boobs sliding down."

Crow could not help laughing. "Jesus, you make me glad I'm a
bachelor."

"Well, it's something to think about, isn't it? Especially if you're
a man."

"Or a sixteen-year-old girl."

"What do you mean by that?"

"Nothing at all," he said. "And what say we try to get some sleep, okay?"

In the dimness, she looked over at him. "Well, what do you *think* I'm trying to do? A guy can't just drop right off, you know."

"Yeah, I know," he said.

EIGHT

LIEUTENANT Edward Kroneburg seemed to be of two minds in regard to his visitors. Jennifer Kellogg, in a chic brown suede pant-suit, apparently struck him as royalty of one kind or another, a person whose every word and look required an almost grim attentiveness on his part. Crow and Reno, on the other hand, must have seemed mere voices to the lieutenant, incorporeal sources of sound that at most served only to distract the Santa Barbara policeman from his rapt concentration on Jennifer.

At the moment he was looking over Crow's copy of the L.A. news story about the killing of the two nude dancers in Hollywood. And as Crow expected, when the lieutenant finished, he addressed him-self to Jennifer.

"And these two victims were in the same photograph with your brother?"

"Yes," Jennifer told him. "But as Mister Crow pointed out, he doesn't have the photographs now. His father turned them back to his client, with the names and addresses, that same night. The night he was killed."

"In an automobile accident on Mulholland Drive," the lieutenant said, repeating part of what Crow had just told him.

"In a murder made to look like an accident," Crow amended.

The lieutenant glanced uncomfortably at him, as if he couldn't quite remember who Crow was. Effortlessly he returned his attention to Jennifer. "But you have no proof of that, right? And no proof of foul play in regard to your brother? No proof that the killing of these prostitutes relates in any way to the other deaths?"

Again Crow answered for her. "Are you seriously suggesting it was all just coincidence, lieutenant? Three persons in a photograph and a fourth hired to find their identities—all dying within thirty-some hours of each other—you really think that could be coincidence? The odds against it would have to be on the order of a million to one."

The lieutenant sighed wearily. A dapper man in his forties, small and dark, he looked to Crow more like a hairdresser than a cop. But for the moment at least, he deigned to look at Crow, not just glance at him.

"I don't know about odds," the lieutenant said. "I'm not a bookmaker. I do know about evidence, however. And in this case, it appears there is none. These photographs you talk about—can you show them to me? Even one of them?"

"I already told you," Crow answered. "My father turned them in."

"To an unknown client."

"That's right."

Reno, still in her funeral outfit, was suddenly on her feet, confronting not the lieutenant but Crow.

"Just what kind of bullshit is this, anyway? If the man doesn't want to believe us, why not just get the hell out of here? Who needs this shit?"

Jennifer hurriedly tried to explain away the girl's outburst. "She was with Mister Crow," she said to the lieutenant. "She saw the photographs too. She can verify everything he's told you."

Lieutenant Kroneburg was nodding sympathetically. "Yeah, I know. But you must understand, Miss Kellogg—without evidence, without a suspect, the police have nowhere to start. If Mister Crow

154

here knew who his father's client was, that at least would be something—we'd have a starting point anyway. But even then, it wouldn't be a matter for this department. It would be under L.A.P.D. jurisdiction. Our only interest is in your brother, and even then only in a consultative capacity with the Ventura department. All this other is just blue sky as far as we're concerned."

"Blue sky?" Reno said to Crow.

"Just cool it, okay?" he suggested.

She looked to the ceiling for commiseration and dropped back into her chair. The lieutenant meanwhile was assuring Jennifer that even though the department wouldn't involve itself in "Mister Crow's problem," he personally would see to it that her brother's death was fully looked into.

"No stone will be left unturned," he promised her. "As things stand now, we're confident it wasn't your brother who registered for the room—the handwriting is dissimilar. Of course, that might only mean that the register was signed by his date—you know, the person he was with. Now, if the date was—" The lieutenant briefly ran out of words. "If the *encounter* was, well, a *gay* one, as seems likely, then there would be nothing unusual in another young man registering. At the same time, there is the problem of there being no—" Again Kroneburg became flustered and had to pause. He glanced uneasily at Reno, then stumbled on. "There being no semen, as far as the lab could find. Of course your brother may have bathed afterwards. Or possibly his partner—you know—just went down—that is, had oral sex with him."

Reno groaned and made a face. "Why not just say the guy blew him?"

Crow wanted to reach over and give the girl a swat, but he resisted the urge by reminding himself that he was not her father or brother or anything else, and that if she insisted on being a bigmouth—well, that was her business. She could carry on all she wanted—on her own. It was a freedom he suddenly was quite ready to give her. At the same time, he was more than a little surprised by Jennifer's equanimity. With each new outburst from Reno, he had expected the woman to show her displeasure, if not by saying something then at least with a lifted eyebrow or even a facial tic. But there was nothing. She remained cool and unflappable, still a perfect Princess Grace.

The lieutenant meanwhile was nervously tapping a pencil against his desktop, apparently about to pick up the thread of his argument, when a young woman knocked on the partition door and opened it. Leaning in, she said that the captain wanted a word with him. Kroneburg told her that he would be through in a few minutes, but she didn't leave. Smiling in embarrassment, she silently mouthed the word *now*.

Apologizing to Jennifer and saying that he would be right back, the lieutenant got up and followed the young woman across the bullpen area and into another office, which, like his own, had large windows facing the bullpen. Inside the office an older, heavier man in shirtsleeves spoke briefly with him, while the lieutenant kept nodding. Finally the lieutenant left and retraced his steps back to his own office. Looking angry as well as embarrassed, he did not sit down at his desk.

"Uh, Miss Kellogg," he said, "I've just been informed that your brother's case is closed."

Jennifer smiled in confusion. "Closed? By whom?"

"Well, you see, the medical examiner did rule death by barbiturate overdose. And as I said before, there's no reason—no evidence —to support anything but a finding of suicide. So as far as this department is concerned, I'm afraid I can't help you. It's out of my hands."

"You mean, it's up to the Ventura police now?"

The lieutenant smiled ruefully. "No, I'm afraid not. My understanding is they've closed the case too."

"You can't be serious," Jennifer said.

"I'm afraid so."

She looked over at Crow in bewilderment. Then a kind of knowing resignation came into her eyes and she got up, followed by Crow and Reno. She reached out and the lieutenant sheepishly shook her hand.

"I don't imagine this was your decision, lieutenant," she said. "I want to thank you for helping us."

"I wish I could do more," he told her.

"I'm sure you do."

Outside, Jennifer asked Crow if she could speak with him alone for a few moments and Crow gave his keys to Reno.

"Wait for me in the truck, okay?" he said to the girl.

"Sure thing." She gave Jennifer a mocking smile. "I'll just leave you two alone."

As the girl headed down the street to where the truck was parked, Jennifer drew Crow over to the curb, away from the pedestrian flow. And Crow was surprised to see in the cool green of her eyes something besides sweetness and light. Suddenly she looked angry. She looked tough.

"I wanted to explain that little dance the police just did," she told him. "I think the chief simply got a call from my uncle, and that's that. I've seen the phenomenon before. He gets on the phone and rivers abruptly change course."

"I can't believe your uncle wouldn't want to know the truth," Crow said.

"Oh, he does. Only he thinks he already knows it. His nephew was a fag, so naturally the poor wretch would commit suicide. The idea fits in neatly with Henry's whole cosmology."

Down the street, under the palms, Crow saw Reno clamber onto the hood of the Datsun and light up a cigarette. Beyond her the handsome courthouse dazzled in the sun, a Moorish castle bedizened with exotic trees.

"But what about the kid?" he asked. "Why didn't you want her to hear this?"

"Oh, I'll get to her," Jennifer promised. "But first, I want you to know I believe you're on to something here. I can't see all this as coincidence any more than you can. So I want to work with you. I want to help find out just what did happen to my brother. And your father."

"Good," Crow said. "I'd hoped you would."

"But there is a problem."

"Reno?"

157

Jennifer looked down the street now too. The girl was still sitting on the hood of Crow's truck, puffing on a cigarette.

"I'm afraid so," she said. "I guess I'm a touch old-fashioned. I don't like being embarrassed in public by foul-mouthed kids. Especially when they think they're being cute."

For some stupid reason, Crow wanted to defend the girl. But that was not what came out. "I know what you mean, believe me. But I don't think it'll be a problem. Reno has other relatives—back in Reno, as a matter of fact. And that's where she'll have to go. I can't take care of her."

"I'm not asking you to send her away," Jennifer said. "I'm just saying that if we're going to be working together on this thing— working with the L.A. police or whoever—I'd rather she cleaned up her act. Actually I like the girl. She's got a lot of spirit. But when we're with others—as we just were—I'd appreciate not having to keep biting my tongue."

"I know the feeling."

Jennifer smiled now. "I imagine you do. Well, anyway, that's off my chest. What's our next step?"

Crow told her that he would be getting in touch with the L.A. police when he got back to Los Angeles and that if she wanted to join him—bringing along the news stories about her brother's death —it would be of help. He said that if the police there turned out to be as indifferent as those in Santa Barbara and Ventura, then the two of them would have to sit down and map out a strategy of their own. Jennifer wrote down his address and phone number and said that she would be calling him as soon as she was settled in at the Sheraton Universal.

"My uncle keeps a room there for business purposes," she explained.

"Fine," he said. "I'll wait to hear from you."

And he was relieved when she did not reach out to shake his hand as she had the lieutenant's, so brisk and businesslike. Much better the lovely smile she gave him now, touched as it was by pain, a sense of shared loss.

As she drove off in her Porsche, he walked on down the street and got into the pickup, next to Reno, who by then had abandoned the

158

hood. Even though the window was open, the air in the cab was thick with cigarette smoke.

"Boy, what a smudge pot you are," he said, starting the engine.

"I know, I know," Reno lamented. "Now Princess Jennifer, she doesn't even smoke, does she? Just why the hell can't I be more like her, huh, Crow? Why can't I be fucking perfect too?"

Crow gave her a look of wearied disgust and she laughed so infectiously he soon was laughing too.

On the drive back to Los Angeles, Crow said nothing to the girl about Jennifer joining him in trying to find out what was behind the killings, nor did he tell her that Jennifer had criticized her in any way. Instead he made the criticism his own, as in fact it was, to a degree.

"Do you really have to wise-off so much?" he asked her. "Especially when you're around grown-ups? People you don't even know?"

Reno was sitting sideways on the seat, with her drawn-up knees pressing lightly against his right arm. "Is that what she said to you on the sidewalk? Was that her big secret—to bitch about me?"

"This is *me* bitching," he said.

"Okay, then I'll answer. Yes, I have to do it. The devil makes me do it."

"He does, huh?"

"Somebody does."

"You do it out of insecurity, Reno," he told her. "You're afraid people won't like you, so you avoid the rejection by rejecting them first. By wising-off and using foul language."

"*Foul language?*"

Her laugh almost had him grinning again, in spite of himself. "That's right," he said. "Foul language."

"Like what?"

"Like when the lieutenant was talking about oral sex—"

"Oral sex!" she hooted.

"The phrase is perfectly adequate," he told her. "We knew what he meant. The poor bastard was only trying to be polite in front of you, because of your age. So what do you do? You embarrass him."

"By saying the one guy *blew* the other? Why's that worse than

159

saying they had oral sex? *Oral sex!* Boy, is that ever dumb. Sounds like dentists doing it."

Crow had no comeback for that. "Dentists doing it?" he laughed. "That's right."

"You win."

She nudged him with her knee. "You're too easy, you know that?"

"You bet I do," he said.

As soon as he got back home, Crow phoned Sergeant Olson at the Van Nuys station and made an appointment to see him the next morning. He told the sergeant that he had new information regarding his father's death, but that he'd just as soon not go into detail about it on the phone. It would keep till morning, he said, not bothering to mention Jennifer Kellogg or that she would be accompanying him at the meeting.

When he hung up, Mrs. Elderberry had a plethora of questions for him. Just what on earth was going on anyway? Why had he and Reno run off to Santa Barbara the way they had? What had happened up there? Did it have anything to do with his poor father's death? And why was he calling the police again? Did he know something now that he hadn't known before?

Fortunately she did not wait for answers. Still highly distraught over her new predicament—living in a house that might soon be up for sale—she seemed incapable of being still long enough to listen to a completed sentence. Nor did she seem able to pause in her relentless scouring of the kitchen sink.

"I been callin' up about rentals in the paper," she lamented. "And they're all so dear it just scares a body to death. Where on earth will that old lady downstairs and me stay when we leave here? With what little money I got left, they won't give me welfare. And I called my sister back home in Iowa and she says they're on their last legs too, couldn't take in a dormouse even if they wanted to. So here we are, just waitin' to be put out in the street."

Once again, Crow tried to calm the woman by pointing out that if the house had to be sold, it would not be put on the market for some time yet; and that even then, given the general economy, it probably wouldn't sell for months or maybe even a year. When that failed to reassure the woman, he told her not to worry about paying any rent, that he would continue with the same arrangement his father had had with her. This calmed her down a little, and Crow in time was able to start working on his father's files, trying to find some reference to the mysterious "Lee." There were only two file drawers: one filled with case histories and the other with personal business folders, everything from Birth Certificate to Will. With Reno hovering over his shoulder and chattering like a talk-show host, Crow soon found it impossible to concentrate on what he was doing. So he put the girl to work on the personal files, telling her to go over every scrap of paper in them, looking for a "Lee." Meanwhile he would continue to work on the case file, he told her. And when they were finished, they would switch drawers, ostensibly to give each file a double combing, though his true reason was merely to give himself a crack at the whole works, in silence.

But like most of his plans regarding Reno, it soon went awry. Reaching his father's correspondence folder, she quickly got mired down. Who, she wanted to know, was Caroline?

"My sister," Crow told her.

"Boy, what a shit. This is a Christmas card, and you know what she writes on it to your old man? *Hope you're having an OK holiday. Mine would be better if I had some extra bread. Hint, hint.—Caroline.*"

"That's my sister, all right."

"Incredible."

"Just read 'em in silence, okay? I'm trying to concentrate."

"Me too. But just one more. Who's Shirley?"

"My mother."

She gave Crow a pitying look. "Boy, you can really pick 'em."

At that he put down the folder he had been going through and looked over at her, glared at her long enough to cause her to draw up her shoulders and make a face, that of someone who had just dropped a bowl of eggs. After that, the girl managed to stifle her curiosity, or at least her expression of it, sufficiently so Crow could concentrate on the case folders. And he found out that his father's cases were largely referrals from other private investigation agencies, and that most were what the old man liked to describe as the "dingleberry beat"—divorce or other domestic affairs cases involving long hours of surveillance, sitting in a parked car. But not in any of them was there mention of "Lee"—not as a referral investigator, not as a cop, not as a client.

As he continued to work his way through the files, Crow couldn't help feeling a strong sense of unreality, involved as he was now in a personal criminal investigation. In his experience, it was the sort of thing one saw only in movies or television shows, individuals becoming caught up in the investigation of crimes or conspiracies that the police or other law enforcement agencies either were not interested in or could not solve or—most often, in these post-Watergate years—were trying to cover up. So he had always considered the phenomenon more as an entertainment device than anything else, a *plot*.

In the real world, people just didn't get involved in such matters, probably not out of fear or ignorance so much as because, if there really was a case to investigate, then the police would already be involved in it. And yet here he was, hundered over, going through his father's files, looking for a name or possibly a nickname. He kept telling himself that if the case had been a simple robbery-murder—even with the murderer uncaught and unknown—he still would not have gotten involved as he was now. For one thing, the police would have been on the case. And for another, the murderer would have been merely one of the multitude, that ever-burgeoning American underclass of murderous acquisitors for whom a human life held no more value than that of a fruit fly. The culprit's identity and capture and punishment would have been virtually meaningless, not unlike pinpointing a virus that had randomly killed a loved one. But this case—this, for Crow, was altogether different in that its murderousness was so obviously *not* casual or mindless but imaginative and efficient and, above all, *arrogant*—so inhumanly arrogant, killing off a trio of innocent young people and a sick old man on the apparent off-chance that they might have seen something, might have known something. That arrogance had kindled in Crow a small blue flame of rage, a kind of pilot light that simply was not going to burn out, at least not until it touched off something far grander than itself.

*   *   *

At five that afternoon Jennifer called him from the Sheraton and asked if he wanted to come over for cocktails and dinner.

"We still have much to discuss," she said. "Like the fact that we don't really know each other yet."

"That's true. What time?"

"Seven okay?"

"Sure."

Crow promptly abandoned the files, much to Reno's displeasure. "Boy, a call from the princess and you just jump to it."

Crow told the girl to be sensible. "Look, we talk to the L.A. police in the morning. We've got to be prepared. We have to go over everything."

"Yeah, I'll bet."

"What does that mean?"

"I take it I wasn't invited."

"For Christ sake, Reno, this is not a *date*. If you'll remember, I lost my father, and Miss Kellogg lost a brother. We have a mutual concern."

"Well, what about me? I lost my parents, didn't I?"

"Here we go again."

"Well, that's no small thing, you know, losing your mom and dad."

"Yeah, I know. Anyway, you get to hold down the fort here." Crow gave her a fatherly pat on the head, and got his hand slapped away. "I've got some shopping to do. Can't go around looking like a bum forever, can I?"

Reno called after him. "What's good enough for the rest of us ain't good enough for her, is that it?"

"If you say so."

In downtown Van Nuys, Crow cashed half of his travelers checks and bought himself a pair of dress boots and a two-hundred-dollar calfskin jacket, as well as new slacks and socks and sport shirts. He knew he would feel like an idiot showing up at her room in spanking new clothes, but he didn't see that he had much choice. If Jennifer's tastes ran to hotel restaurants, he felt he would just have to go along for now, which would require something other than the old windbreaker and corduroys. Anyway, he reflected, now that he was a virtual Sam Spade, he might as well look the part.

163

Back at the house, Reno pretended to be more interested in a game show on television than she was in his clothes, and when he said goodnight to her on his way out, she managed only an apathetic nod. He was almost out of the door before she called after him:

"You look pretty cool, you know."

He looked back at her. "That's nice of you to say, Reno."

She waved him off. "Go on. I'm watching TV."

Crow was surprised at Jennifer's choice of hotels, since he considered the Sheraton as basically a tourist mecca, a hostelry for corn farmers and Japanese touring Hollywood, and especially Universal Studios. Though there was the little matter of her uncle keeping a permanent room in the hotel, Crow nevertheless figured that her real reason for using it was a simple case of tact and graciousness: because Crow himself was so obviously not a Beverly Hills Hotel type, then she wouldn't be either, at least not while they were working together. But once he arrived at the hotel and found her room—her *suite* of rooms—he had to reconsider. For the suite was luxurious indeed, and located not in the hotel tower but on the second floor of the lanai section, which bordered the patio, a huge area forested with palms and other exotic flora.

A chicano servant girl answered the door and Crow found Jennifer already dressed and waiting for him, sitting out on her private deck sipping white wine and looking down on the almost deserted swimming pool.

"Right on time," she said. "What would you like, something stronger than this?"

"No, that'll be fine."

He sat down in a chaise next to hers and the servant promptly brought him a glass of wine. Jennifer told him that she'd made an appointment for eight o'clock in the hotel restaurant and she hoped that wouldn't be too late for him.

"Not at all," he said, relieved that she took no apparent notice of his new attire. At the same time, he couldn't help observing hers, the fact that she hadn't really dressed for the occasion, was wearing only a simple sweater and skirt. And though he knew this was as it should have been, because they were having a meeting, not a date, somehow he still felt a trifle let down.

Jennifer smiled regretfully. "I stopped off in Ventura this afternoon. Case closed, just as Lieutenant Kroneburg in Santa Barbara told us it would be."

"Everyone's so efficient," he said.

"Aren't they, though?"

She went on then and explained that she no longer thought her uncle had anything to do with the two departments closing the case. The officer in Ventura, a sergeant, had been very sardonic about it all, she told Crow.

"A real macho type," she explained. "Like my uncle, he seemed to feel that it was almost a homosexual's duty to kill himself. So why question whether or not he had?"

Crow told Jennifer then how close the sergeant's mind-set was to that of his father's old buddies in the L.A.P.D., who seemed to feel that a retired cop had almost no choice except suicide.

"Which leaves us pretty much on our own," Jennifer said.

Crow was not that sure. "It depends on tomorrow. On this old partner of my father's—Sergeant Olson. If he's blind too, then yes, I guess we'll be on our own."

In the dying light, she smiled slightly, a shy thoughtful smile that Crow found so lovely he forgot what else he was about to say.

"Maybe that won't be so bad," she put in. "Something to do for a change. Something real. I feel it's already helping me deal with Richard's death. Keeping me from thinking—"

Her eyes had teared and she looked down at the pool again, where a pair of elderly tourists were gingerly testing the water with their toes.

For a while Crow tried to make small talk with her, and then at eight the two of them made their way over to the high-rise part of the hotel, where the restaurant was. And Crow discovered that the place had not one decor but four, including the wooden deck of a clipper ship, where he and Jennifer wound up. He ordered a chardonnay and they drank and talked about the case again as they waited for their trout amandine. And only gradually did they begin to talk about themselves. Crow did not want any part of a heavy-handed confessional, so he told her about his father's "mystifying" disappointment in him, because Crow was a college graduate and yet had never held down a "three-piece-suit job" in his life.

"Actually, I know quite a lot about business," he deadpanned. "I've started three of them in the last five or six years. And shut them down too."

Jennifer made a face, dismissing his tale of failure. "Anybody can be a success in business. I think it's mostly a matter of luck and having a high boredom threshold."

"You could be right. If I'd only been dumber, I might have made it."

His smile was ironic; hers wasn't. She asked him then about women, whether or not he'd ever been married, and he said no, that the right girl hadn't asked him yet.

"Consider yourself lucky," she said.

"That's right—I keep forgetting you're Mrs. Payne."

"So do I. Somehow it's so easy."

"Bad as all that?"

"A fairly typical Santa Barbara marriage," she told him. "David is a stockbroker. Or at least he has a desk at a brokerage house. But his real occupation was entertaining himself. Tennis, golf, drugs, women—he worked quite hard at it actually, even though he didn't have any real money of his own. I guess my uncle just made him feel so unwelcome that he went off the deep end. Which was pretty much the story of my first marriage too. All either one of them wanted was to be close to the money. Which meant getting close to Uncle Henry. And I'm afraid that wasn't in the cards."

Crow was finding it nice and cozy, sitting there on the clipper ship deck, killing the last of the wine. Next to them were great hawsers and pulleys and above them burned a ship's lantern, all of it undeniably campy, but warm and comfortable nevertheless. They finished eating and ordered coffee and brandy and Jennifer slowly added to her story, one in which her uncle figured more importantly than anyone else. Her father, Henry's brother, had died of a burst appendix when Jennifer was just a child, and her mother had been boozing and drying out ever since. So her care and feeding, as well as Richard's, had fallen on Uncle Henry, or at least upon his hirelings, since

166

he had been overseas much of the time, until his retirement five years before.

Jennifer said that when she was young she was never quite sure what the old man did. She remembered being told that he was a member of the foreign service, a diplomat who specialized in Mideast affairs. Then, for a time, he had been an executive in Aramco, the Arabian–American oil company. And finally he had been some sort of consultant to the house of Saud. It was in this role that he had done his most important work, Jennifer said, by helping to keep the Saudis in the western camp. And of course he had helped himself too, she admitted. Over the years, with Saudi advice, he had invested his money wisely and was "fairly comfortable" now.

Crow had to smile at that. "*Fairly* comfortable?"

Jennifer smiled too. "By Saudi standards."

"I see. Tell me then. If he was in the Mideast all that time, how come he surrounds himself with Orientals?"

"They're Koreans," she said. "He was in intelligence during the Korean war and there was this couple—the Kims—who served him so well that he managed to bring them over later, with their children."

"The servants at the house—they're all one family?"

Jennifer nodded. "Plus a few relatives they've brought over themselves. The family's so large now that most of them have other jobs in the area. On special occasions though, they help out."

Crow almost let the subject die there—it really was not all that important, he knew—yet he couldn't help himself finally. Some questions had a life of their own.

"Do they all pack guns?" he asked. "Or just the one named Lon Kim?"

Jennifer was not smiling now. "Some of the others too, I would imagine. I guess politically, over the years, my uncle has made enemies. And then too he's always been afraid of kidnapping, even though we're all grown up now." At that, she shook her head. "There I go, talking about Richard as if he were still alive."

From that point on, their conversation narrowed to the matter at hand: what they had to do and how they would go about it if the

L.A.P.D. joined the Santa Barbara and Ventura departments in washing their hands of the case. Crow told Jennifer that he had already started with the files, but as yet hadn't found any reference to "Lee." If he continued not to find anything, he said they would have to go to the street corner where the photos were shot and start knocking on doors and asking questions. They would check again at the strip joint and spread a few dollars around, buy some more answers, and they would have to go through all the newspapers, issue by issue and column by column, starting at least a week before his father's death. They might even check on hospital emergency room records as well as police records—certainly Sergeant Olson would cooperate to that extent, Crow said. And somehow, some way, they would find out who the photographer was and what had happened on that street corner, maybe even learn the identity of the Robert Redford lookalike.

"Somehow we'll get answers," he said. "After all, no one's paying us for it. We can afford to really dig."

Jennifer gave him a slightly mocking smile. "That sounds dangerously cynical," she said. "Coming from you."

"I'm not supposed to be cynical?"

"Well, you don't come across that way."

"It's a pose," he said. "A hangover from my days as a boy scout."

"I don't think so."

Crow had not planned this turn of conversation, but he saw in it just the opening he needed—to make a clean breast of things. He had known the truth would have to come out sooner or later, and had naturally opted for the second. This opening, though, was simply too large. Too perfect.

"Oh, I do my share of lying," he said.

She was still smiling. "Is that a fact?"

"And stupid, unnecessary lies at that," he went on. "Like the one about Reno. She's not really my cousin."

"I didn't think she was."

"And she didn't just lose her parents in a car accident."

"I didn't think she had."

"Oh no? Why not?"

Jennifer shrugged. "Her attitude. She doesn't act like she's lost

168

someone. More like she's *found* someone."

Crow pretended that the shot had gone straight over his head. "Well, don't you wonder why—why the stupid lie?"

"I figure you had your reasons."

"The main one was you," he said. "I wanted you to believe what I had to tell you. And I guess I was afraid you might not, if I came across as a flake."

"You mean because you had a teenager in tow?"

"That particular teenager, yes."

Jennifer shook her head. "I would have figured—as I do now—that it was your business."

"You mind if I tell you the truth of it?"

"Not if you want to."

"Well, I do."

Briefly then Crow told her about picking Reno up on the highway and kicking "old Jere" out. He explained that the girl had no I.D. and refused even to tell him her real name, so he could not contact her mother in Reno.

"She gave us a choice—let her stay or send her on to Sunset Boulevard."

"You did the right thing," Jennifer said.

"She's just one more lost kid. Thinks of me as a big brother, I guess. And that's how I treat her." This last he gave no emphasis at all, and he saw in the light of the ship's lantern that he didn't have to.

Jennifer smiled reflectively. "Well, the important thing is, the girl was with you the day you subbed for your father. She saw the photographs. Her testimony will be important."

"Right." Crow was beginning to feel an immense sense of relief, as if he'd just pulled a thorn out of his foot.

When they were finished he walked her back to her lanai suite and at the door she touched his shoulder and gave him her cheek, not so much to kiss as to brush near it, in the Beverly Hills fashion. So it was really no more intimate than a handshake, yet he went happily back to his pickup truck, still breathing the clean, clear scent of her and feeling her hair soft against his face.

NINE

UNLIKE the lieutenant in Santa Barbara, Sergeant Jack Olson only had a desk in the corner of the detective's bullpen. The building itself, the Van Nuys police station, was modern and sprawling, with carpeting and floor-to-ceiling windows that looked out on a small tree-lined courtyard dominated by a golden cigar-store Indian. Or at least so the statue appeared to Crow, sitting with Jennifer and Reno around the crowded perimeter of the sergeant's desk. Having already been there over an hour, Crow was about to stand up and stretch when the detectives from Hollywood finally arrived. Their names were Humboldt and Reed, and they were about as dissimilar as partners could get, Humboldt being young, white, and well-groomed, while his colleague was coal-black, middle-aged, and flamboyantly sloppy. Both, like the pink-skinned Olson, were detective sergeants.

From the outset, when Crow and the girls first got there, Olson had seemed interested only in what Crow had to tell him about the two dancer-hookers. The deaths of Crow's father and of Jennifer's brother were simply nonevents for him—an accident within his jurisdiction and a suicide without—this despite their being linked to the same photographs and the same scene as the hookers were. Like Lieutenant Kroneburg in Santa Barbara, Olson kept coming back to the fact that there *were* no photographs, that there *were* no suspects, no motive, not even a client, at least not until Crow could produce them. Meanwhile, the two hookers were very definitely an open case and Olson wanted the Hollywood detectives working on it to drive over and listen to Crow's story and probably take a signed statement. To that end, he had called them almost an hour earlier.

In the interim, he had listened to Crow and Jennifer and Reno, nodding and sighing as he made little lists and diagrams on a legal pad: this alleged event leading to that one, and so on. And finally he began to deal one by one with the questions Crow had raised. The first, the identity of the client "Lee," he tossed out to the bullpen at large, banging on his desk and asking in a foghorn voice if "any of you fine gents" knew of a Lee, first name or last, now in the department or retired. And all they came up with were two young motorcycle officers, one whose family name was Lee, the other having it as a first name. There was also a James E. Lee, now retired and living in the Ozarks. Olson checked with personnel downtown and learned that the man had been dead for over a year. He then asked the same officer in personnel to "crank up" the computer and send him a list of all Lees, first name or last, who had worked in the department during the sixties and early seventies, and to underscore those who might have worked with retired detective Sergeant Orville W. Crow. Olson gave them Crow's father's badge number, and then he turned to the next item on his list, the corner of Lankershim and Beck.

Shaking his bald, beefy head, the sergeant perused three sheets of case reports for the day in question, and he said that there was nothing relating to the area of that particular street corner.

"No murders, no muggings, no rapes. Not even a traffic violation. But to be safe, let's look at the day before the picture-taking. And the day after."

Going through the added sheets, he kept wagging his head. "Still *nada*. There was a burglary about four blocks down Lankershim and a disturbance at a gay bar even further away." He looked up at Crow then. "So what could these three have seen that was so important? So important it doesn't even make our sheet?"

"I don't know," Crow said. "I only know they're all dead now. And my father too."

"I know, I know," Olson sighed. "It is incredible. You and the girl here say the photos existed, so I believe you. But even if I had 'em right here in my hands, it still wouldn't make a case. I've got to be honest with you. For them to be hit as witnesses, there'd have to be a crime, something for them to witness—don't you see? But there wasn't anything. You don't have a suspect, or a motive. And their deaths are all different—an accident, a suicide, a sex killing."

"What about the photographer?" Crow asked. "Anything in there about a photographer having an accident? Or committing suicide?"

Olson was shaking his head even before he returned to the sheets. "Not that I know of," he said. "Anyway, the cases aren't catalogued as to occupation. And this don't cover all of L.A. To really find out you'd have to go down to Central and sit in front of the computer there for about a week, watching the display, case by case."

"Isn't it cross-referenced?" Crow asked. "Couldn't we just punch in occupation and date and the right cases would come spitting out?"

"Naw, I don't think so. Anyway, who's to say this alleged photographer of yours wasn't on the other side? Maybe he ordered the—"

"The *alleged* hits, yeah."

Reno by then was groaning softly and rolling her eyes, probably as much from having sat in one place for an hour as out of simple frustration, not feeling free this day to say whatever popped into her pretty head. Jennifer, on the other hand, sat still and elegant, content to let Crow do most of the talking.

"All I meant," Sergeant Olson said, "was there are different ways to view this thing of yours. And the reason for that is you really got no case. But that about the hookers, now that's different."

It was then that the two Hollywood detectives, Humboldt and Reed, came on the scene. And they quickly demonstrated that though they may have looked like opposites, in every other way they

172

could have been each other's clone. From the outset, they both looked at Jennifer and Reno as if the two girls had been caught in a vice raid, especially after Crow had introduced Reno as a "family friend." And whenever Crow said anything, they would throw at him the same yawning looks of contempt and amusement, as if he were beyond any question the girls' john, a jerk caught in his underwear. They listened to his story of the photographs—and the subbing for his father—as if they'd heard it all before. And when Sergeant Olson stepped in, explaining about Crow's father's "accident" and Richard's "suicide," the two officers then began to look at Crow as if he were a sexual psychopath as well as a john, the fiftieth such creep they had interrogated that day. The fat one, Reed, scratched absently at a patch of hairy black skin showing above his belt, where his too-small shirt had come unbuttoned. His partner meanwhile kept running his tongue back and forth over his teeth, as if he'd just eaten peanut butter.

"Look," he said to Crow, "we ain't interested in traffic accidents or suicides, especially up in Santa Barbara. We're here about Zelda Leggs and Rose Dunn. Now, you say you took your father's place and ran down the girls' names and addresses for this guy named Lee. You don't know who the cat is, yet you call him old. Why is that?"

"I said he probably was old. My father called him 'old buddy' on the phone."

"*Old buddy,* huh?" the black one wheezed. "Tell me, any chance your old man's from Greeley, Colorado?"

Crow had not forgotten the news story: the name and address given by the little man who registered for the motel room in which the hookers were killed.

"Are you serious?" he asked the sergeant.

"Hell, I'm always serious. Ain't I, Jimmy?"

"You bet he is," his partner said. "He's always serious."

Sergeant Olson was shaking his head again. "Come on, you guys —I didn't call you in on this so you could harrass these people. If you'll remember, Orville Crow died a couple of days before your hookers bought it. And as you can see, his son here is not small and mousey, and not a blond giant either."

173

The Hollywood detectives didn't seem to hear him. "For the record, Crow, where were you Thursday night and Friday morning?" Reed asked.

"In my father's house. In bed."

"With Miss Reno here?"

Crow asked the sergeant if he'd like to get his face punched, and the heavy black man turned to his partner with a look of mock amazement and fear.

"Did you hear that, Jimmy?" he asked. "Did you hear this police officer getting threatened with bodily harm?"

"I sure did," Humboldt said.

Reno meanwhile was giving Crow an appreciative nod. "That's telling him," she said.

Sergeant Olson sighed and suggested that they all "simmer down a bit."

"We seem to be missing the point here," he went on. "Which is that Mister Crow and Miss Reno just might be able to *help* you guys. Whoever this Lee was, and whatever the reason he hired Orville Crow to do a little digging for him, the fact remains that it was these two who did the actual digging, these two who went to the Club Ninety and found out the hookers' names and addresses and turned them over to the old man." Olson threw out his hands to the other detectives. "So it's in your court, gentlemen. Aren't there any relevant questions you want to ask these two? Do you want to take down a statement? What?"

Neither man seemed at all impressed by Olson's challenge. They were looking at him now as if he too might be something of a john. The one named Humboldt gave his teeth a good tonguing and turned back to Crow.

"Anybody in the house with you that night?" he asked.

And so it went. The two detectives kept asking questions, most of them hostile, and they even took a few notes. Finally they had Crow make a statement to a stenographer and sign it, and then they got up and left, again leering at Jennifer and Reno. When they were out of sight, Sergeant Olson apologized for them, saying that they were not among L.A.'s finest.

174

"The job does strange things to people," he said. "Especially partners. Sometimes they get on a wavelength all their own. And *everybody* becomes the enemy. I've seen it dozens of times."

Jennifer had gotten up. She thanked the sergeant for his help and then asked Crow to accompany her to the front door. Telling the sergeant that he would be back, Crow went along with her. He commented on what a wasted morning it had been and she agreed but said that perhaps it was just as well.

"After all, we don't want them taking our jobs."

Nearing the entrance, she told him why she'd asked him to see her out. An old friend of hers from college was married to a city councilman and Jennifer was having dinner with them that evening, at Scandia. Would he care to join them?

"Of course you'd have to wear a coat and tie," she said, smiling. "But it could be worth it—the councilman just might be able to help us. I'm sure he knows a lot of people in the state's attorney's office."

Crow wanted very much to see her that evening, but not with "old friends" at a celebrity hangout, and especially not with a city councilman. So he told her that he couldn't make it, that Olson had promised to work with him that afternoon on finding out who "Lee" was and that their search might spill over into the evening.

"Anyway I don't have any ties," he told her. "And I wouldn't know where to get any."

"It *is* a problem," she smiled. He said that he would call her in the morning and then she went on out to the parking lot while he returned to the detectives' bullpen on the second floor. Olson had in fact promised that he would spend the afternoon with Crow, trying to identify his father's client. So Crow made an appointment to see him later, at two o'clock. He told the sergeant that he had to take Reno home and also had some personal business to take care of.

Outside, crossing the tree-lined courtyard, he and Reno walked past two well-dressed men—one redheaded and the other quite fat—sitting on a park bench, sharing a bag of peanuts. And Crow was mildly surprised when the two men failed to look up, even at Reno in her shorts and tanktop. Crow asked her if she was hungry.

"You could say that."

"What would you like?"

"Chili dogs, onion rings, and beer."

"You keep forgetting you don't like beer."

"Okay then—Doctor Pepper."

"And how about a stomach pump?" he asked, as they got into the pickup.

"There he goes, putting me down again," she sighed. "What did the princess eat last night—rose petals and honey?"

"Okay," Crow said. "Chili dogs, it is."

*   *   *

That first afternoon had been perfect. The sea had been calm as a lake and the Dramamine had worked beautifully on Sherri, allowing her to lie out on the bow in the sun without feeling seasick at all. Looking down on her from the bridge, where he was piloting the boat, Gardner Costello could not help feeling that he just might be snatching a marvelous vacation from the jaws of flight. And when the girl finally shed even her bikini, though calling up to him not to get any ideas, he felt more optimistic than ever about the whole thing. He shouted to her a couple of times that she might be getting a sunburn, but she dismissed the idea with a wave of her hand. So he settled back and went with the gentle roll of the sea. Now and then he would give her curvaceous young body a long and hungry look, reminding himself of the pleasures that lay ahead for him. But most of the time he kept his eyes on the water and the coastline and the boat's instrument panel.

With the ocean so calm and the wind behind him, Costello decided to go for San Diego that first night instead of Oceanside. And after a couple of hours he set the automatic pilot and went below to make lunch for the two of them. He had a hard time talking the girl in off the bow, but finally she came in, grousing a bit as she adjusted her bikini, saying how much she loved it out there, "going up and down, up and down—and not getting paid for it!"

She laughed out loud, and Costello for the first time found himself wondering about her: who she was and where she came from and what kind of life she'd had. But when he asked her about herself, she shrugged and said that "no one cares about that crap."

"I do," he insisted. "That's why I asked."

"Fuck it," she said. "Fuck the past."

She ate her own ham sandwich and half of his, joking that it was hungry work, lying out in the sun. She chugged down a light beer, went to the toilet, and hurried back out onto the bow. Feeling somewhat abandoned, Costello finished his own beer and returned to the wheel, this time at the cabin helm.

Just before dark he turned into Mission Bay in San Diego and tied up at a marina there. He took on over one hundred and eighty gallons of gasoline and bought groceries and other items, including Noxzema and Dramamine, at a store a few blocks away. He half expected to find Sherri gone when he returned, but she was already beginning to suffer from sunburn and apparently did not feel like doing anything on her own. She didn't eat a bite of the small supper he made, concentrating instead on vodka-and-Tang, an orange drink he kept aboard for his wife, who still had a sweet tooth even though she wore dentures. Sheri mixed the two at a ratio of one-to-one, with the result that she was soon slurring her words and stumbling about the cabin, crying about her sunburn and "this fucking tub of yours."

Finally he helped her forward and put her to bed in the bow cabin. He undressed her and rubbed Noxzema over most of her body and when she was sound asleep he brought himself to orgasm against her buttocks. He cleaned her off without her knowing anything had happened and then he got a few hours of sleep himself.

He cast off while it was still dark and had them out into the ocean and even past Cabrillo Point before the girl woke. Those few early hours at the wheel before hearing her first ferocious moans were the last relatively peaceful moments he would know for the next four days, as he worked down the Baja coast toward Cape San Lucas and Mazatlan. The sea had gotten rougher and the Dramamine no longer worked for her. Doubled over with cramps, she would come moaning out of the cabin and stagger into the head, there to cry and retch and sometimes even vomit, if she was lucky. She would come back and prop herself in the doorway, naked, her skin a raw vermil-ion. And then she would proceed to scream at him for as long as she could, a few precious seconds of fury and recrimination before her seasickness and sunburn would force her back to the bunk, there to

177

curl up and cry and moan as the endless miles of ocean fell slowly behind them.

While he was still in American waters he used the radio phone to call the Mexican consulate in San Diego. He told the woman who answered that he was aware he should have registered his boat with them in person but that circumstances had not permitted, so he was doing it now, en route to Mazatlan. He gave her his passport number, the boat's Coast Guard number, its name—*Mako*—and its itinerary and "passenger list." He was uneasy about this, leaving a possible trail that Queen's people could follow, but he figured it was not likely they would check with the consulate and anyway he had no desire to sail into Mazatlan without a registered boat. That too could lead to complications.

So Costello had his share of worries. And the girl only added to them, raging at him whenever her strength permitted: "Take me back, you bastard! *Ashore!* I have to go ashore! I'll kill you, you cocksucker! I'll kill you soon as we land!" And then of course there was *them*—Queen, possibly Kellogg, maybe the goddamn company itself. Most of the time—piloting, dozing, drinking—the same endless questions trooped across Costello's mind: What in the name of Jesus Christ could have happened on that damned street corner? What was so big that they had to hit *everyone* who touched it, in any way, a secondhand investigator the same as an eyewitness? The first day out he had heard a radio account of the sex killing of two hookers and he wondered if they could have been the girls in the photographs, who definitely had had a whorish look about them. If they were the same ones, then the thing was even bigger than he had thought, for the guilty party to go to such lengths, covering the hits as other than what they were. It made him wonder about the male youth in the photograph, what his fate might have been.

But most of all, Costello worried about his own fate and the choices he had made, fleeing by boat and bringing the girl along with him instead of just taking off alone, by cab and bus. Certainly a boat was an easier thing to find than a man alone in a big city, holed up in some roach house. But he had panicked—he could admit it to himself now. After hearing about old Crow, he simply had had to get out of Marina del Rey that very afternoon, as fast as he could, and the boat had seemed such an easy answer, such a natural one. Now, when it was too late, he regretted using it. He thought of turning back and sometimes he even considered scuttling the boat, taking a dinghy into one of the Baja fishing villages and living undercover as an antiquated beach bum.

But he kept going. He put into Rosario and then Santo Domingo, taking on fuel and other supplies—at least he still had plenty of cash on hand, he consoled himself.

In each place Sherri packed her suitcase and prepared to leave, then thought better of it when she saw the town. She knew of Mazatlan and he had told her more, specifically that a pretty girl like herself could get rich in no time. So she had come back aboard each time, sullenly tossing her suitcase into the cabin and sidling past him as if he had a social disease.

Finally, on the fifth day, he reached Cape San Lucas and headed across the Gulf of California toward Mazatlan. As evening fell he throttled the engines down to trolling speed and Sherri came up from the bow cabin to ask him what was going on.

"We'll be there tomorrow," he said.

"So?"

"So you haven't done me one time. You realize that? Not once on the whole trip."

She looked at him as if he were insane. "You're fucking crazy."

He shook his head. "No, it's something I really want. Just like the last time. The same in every detail. And if you won't do it, we'll just sit out here. I love to fish. I'll fish all day tomorrow, just sitting here."

Sherri's eyes had teared in anger. Her face, like her body, was still red and splotchy, even though most of the burned skin had peeled away. "Christ, I hate you!" she said.

He told her to get ready and in time she turned and went back into the cabin. While she was gone he brushed his teeth and dabbed after-shave on his face and neck. He opened a beer and drank it as he waited. And then finally he heard her voice, calling wearily from beyond the louvered door.

"Daddy? Would you come in here, please?"

*   *   *

After dropping Reno at his house, with instructions to help Mrs. Elderberry in any way she could, he drove on to his father's bank and made arrangements for drawing on his estate if the need arose over the next week or so of investigating—he was determined not to let Jennifer pay more than her share of the tab, no matter what it eventually came to. He got the executor to okay a personal check of his drawn on a Seattle bank, where he still had about twenty-four hundred dollars on deposit. The executor then told him that he had been in touch with Crow's sister and he would have to put the house on the market during the coming week, unless Crow was interested in buying out her equity. Crow of course had no interest in holding on to the place, nor did he have the means of doing so even if he had wanted to. So he told the man to go ahead with the sale, though with the proviso that the tenant-housekeeper be given one hundred and twenty days to vacate.

"She was more than a housekeeper to my father," he explained. "He would have wanted her to have the time."

The executor agreed and even wrote out a memorandum to that effect. And Crow went on back to the police station. He had no idea what Sergeant Olson had in mind regarding further investigation into the identity of his father's last client. And it turned out that the sergeant didn't have any ideas either. Crow was sitting next to the man's desk when he returned from lunch at two, redolent of peppermint and gin. Olson suggested that he and Crow "get away from this fishbowl" and Crow went along with him out to his unmarked car.

The sergeant's color by then was more scarlet than pink and he was breathing heavily, just sitting behind the wheel and driving. Crow asked where they were headed and the sergeant said they might as well have a look at "that corner of yours"—Beck and Lankershim. On the way, he again commented on the behavior of Humbolt and Reed.

"Godalmighty, Reed's been in the department probably longer than me, and yet he acts like he did this morning. So unprofessional. It's just a goddamn shame. But it's true of everything nowadays, you know? Waiters don't wait worth a damn, mechanics can't fix your car, mothers don't know how to mother. We're just fucked up. No two ways about it."

He looked over at Crow and said that he couldn't call him Orville because that was his father's name. Would "Sonny" be all right? He remembered Orville calling him that.

Crow endured the name from his family, but he figured that was enough. "Why not just call me Crow?" he suggested.

Olson shrugged. "Okay, if that's what you want. Sonny just sounds more friendly, if you know what I mean."

Crow saw no reason to be a hard case. "Sonny will do fine," he said.

The sergeant beamed. "Good. Well, if we're on our toes this afternoon, Sonny, we just might get something done. People don't know it, but pure and simple thinking is the biggest part of this job by far. You want to run down a felon, you got to think like a felon. Believe me."

Olson found a parking space on Beck, about a half block from Lankershim. The two men got out and walked back to the corner where Richard Kellogg and the hookers had been photographed. Putting himself in Kellogg's place, Crow looked across the street, toward the "camera," and all he saw were parked cars and the U-shaped apartment building with the courtyard in front. In the brilliant sunshine it was a handsome enough scene, might even have been a street corner in Santa Barbara. But then, as one turned, looking down Lankershim, the bright day disappeared in the smog and everything seemed dull and hard, a creature of the traffic ceaselessly rolling past.

Olson was lighting a cigarette. "See, what'd I tell you? Peaceful as a New England town."

"Not entirely," Crow said.

Across Lankershim an old man was being harrassed by three young boys. They had taken his cane and were playing "keepaway" with it, tossing it from one to the other while he shuffled between them, flapping his arms and crying. Finally one of them took the cane and sailed it like a skip-stone down the sidewalk and into a gutter. Olson's hand stroked the air in a gesture of dismissal and contempt.

"Aw, that kind of stuff goes on all the time. You just can't get involved. All you can do is let it eat away at you."

"Maybe if you got involved, it wouldn't eat so much."

181

"Could be." Again Olson gestured, this time with his cigarette. "Anyway, this whole area, like I said—there wasn't one damn police incident on the night in question. None the night before, none the night after."

"Why don't we try the apartment building? Knock on some doors and ask about that night?"

Olson laughed. "Are you kidding? We don't even know what to ask about."

"Why not just ask if anything happened that night?"

But Olson was definitely not about to be trapped into any purposeful labor. He said the department frowned on "random interrogation." He had to have a case number, he said. He had to have an explicit reason to go knocking on doors and asking questions. When Crow then asked the sergeant what they were doing there, Olson said "Waiting."

"Too bad your dad ain't here to tell you," he went on. " 'Cause he'd tell you the same thing. Waiting is the most important part of this job. You got to wait a case out—wait till it's ready. Then sometimes it just drops into your lap. Like a rotten apple."

Crow wanted to ask what had happened to "thinking" as the most important part of the job, but he didn't. He just settled back and went along, and the next stop on the sergeant's itinerary was up on Mulholland Drive, on the turnout where Crow's father had died. He got out of the car with Olson and followed him to the edge of the dropoff. He followed his stubby finger as the detective pointed back in the direction of the curve.

"You see how he could've come around that bend. It's dark and he's feeling no pain, and he just goes straight into the turnout. Before he knows what's happened, he's airborne. Happens all the time up here."

Crow asked him if Mulholland was a route *he* would have taken home to Van Nuys from Hollywood.

"Sometimes you can't stand the freeways anymore," the sergeant said. "You just have to get off and piddle along, even if it's out of the way. Even if it takes you three times as long."

Crow pretended to accept that. "All right, maybe that's what happened. But I still don't see what any of this has to do with finding out who his 'old buddy Lee' was."

"All in due time, Sonny," the sergeant said. "All in due time."

*   *   *

Two hours later, in the gaudy gloom of the Club Ninety in Hollywood, Sergeant Olson was already sucking the booze off the ice cubes in his third martini. Somehow he had forgotten all about having a case number to work on, the killing of the hookers still being a Hollywood Division case, as far as Crow knew. But then the sergeant wasn't really doing any investigating. He was drinking. And blubbering.

Did Crow know that he, Olson, had killed a kid about five years back? Well, he had—a fourteen-year-old spade stickup artist that he and his partner were waiting for, in a liquor store stakeout. And when they came out of the back the kid just started firing, "like a goddamn Dillinger." So Olson and his partner "blew him right out of his sneakers." It was a righteous shooting, though, Olson insisted. The review board took less than thirty minutes to pass on it, but did Crow think it ended there? Did Crow really believe that you can take a shotgun and blow a kid in two and not have it affect your life?

Well, it had sure affected his life, he said. Actually it was the proverbial straw. He and his wife were already sleeping in separate bedrooms by that time and his twenty-year-old daughter had become a Moonie, an honest-to-God follower of "that Korean crook." And she was his only kid too, his wife having miscarried three times, could Crow believe that? *Three* times.

He ordered another round of martinis and asked Crow if he knew what it was like to lose an only daughter to a bunch of "latter day zombies." And the really bitching part of it, he said, was that his wife for some reason blamed him for what the daughter had done.

"If I'd been more this or more that, then the girl would still be with us. Can you believe that? It ain't bad enough I got high blood pressure and can't sleep and have to deal with winners like Humboldt and Reed all the time—no, she's gotta lay this on my ass too. I tell you, your old man had the right idea. One of these days I'm going up on Mulholland and take a drive of my own. Who needs this shit, huh, Sonny? Just who needs it?"

Crow at that point was close to leaving the sergeant alone with his gin and sorrows, but he hadn't forgotten that Olson so far was his main connection with the police. And Crow was still convinced that it would be through the police—or even *within* the ranks of the police—that the mysterious Lee would be found. So he stayed right there in the booth with the sergeant and pretended a solemn interest in the man's long and unhappy litany. To make the job easier, Crow drank right along with him and concentrated his attention on the two dancers performing together on the stage, listlessly simulating a sex act. They both had lovely bodies and he felt more than a slight stirring of sexual interest. He also could not help overhearing two other dancers sitting in the next booth, waiting to go on.

"You're real nice-looking, Dawn," the one said. "And you dance up a storm. But to make it these days, baby, you gotta sell it. You gotta lay back and spread 'em. There's no other way."

"Yeah, I suppose so," the other answered.

The first was nodding sagely. "Yeah, these days no one gives a shit about art. No one."

*   *   *

It was after eight o'clock when Crow finally pulled into the driveway of his father's bungalow. Even in the failing light he could see that the lawn had been mowed, and he grinned at the thought of Reno out pushing the ancient unpowered lawnmower about the yard. Going inside, he found her in the living room watching a sixties beach movie on television.

"Hey, somebody mowed the grass," he said. "You notice that?"

She yawned. "What time is it anyway? I thought maybe you ran off with the princess and got married."

"Haven't seen her since this morning. As I was saying—about the grass."

She got up from the couch, smiling mischievously. "I did more than cut your old grass," she said.

"Is that a fact?"

She took him by the hand and led him down the hallway, toward his room. "Yes, that is a fact. And incidentally, you smell like a brewery."

"For good reason."

In the room, she turned on the light and went over to his father's desk, sat on it, facing him.

"Did you find anything out about your Mister Lee this afternoon?" she asked.

"Nary a thing."

She was smiling in spite of herself now, fairly bursting with her secret, whatever it was. "Well, that's all right," she said. "It doesn't matter. Because *I* did."

Reaching up, she took one of the framed pictures off the wall, a color photograph of a tall, goateed man standing on an ocean dock, humorously pretending to be holding out at arm's length an enormous skipjack tuna, which actually was supported by a line running out of the top of the picture. Like all the framed photos on the wall, Crow had already carefully looked at it—or so he thought until Reno slowly turned it around now and held it up for him to see. Unlike the ones he himself had turned over, which were sealed with a gray framing paper, this one was open, so that one could see the back of the photograph—so that one could read it:

> *Mazatlan, Sinaloa, Mex.*
> *25 May 1973*

> *Who sez us spooks can't catch*
> *the big ones?!*

> *"Leaa"*

"Goddamn, Reno! You little genius!" In his excitement Crow lifted her off the desk and spun her around, holding her under the buttocks. She laughed happily and he started to kiss her on the cheek, but she would not have any of that and kissed him on the mouth. Trying to cover a slight sense of alarm, of caution, he gingerly put her down and picked up the framed photo again.

"What a weird spelling of Lee," he said. "And why the quotes?"

Then it hit him and he quickly pounced on the top file drawer, throwing it open and riffling through the folders until he came to the one marked *L.E.A.A.*—for *Law Enforcement Assistance Administration,* a one-time federal program under the Justice Department, as Crow understood it, Washington experts helping local police departments develop state-of-the-art procedures. In the folder were a number of L.A.P.D. memos dealing with "interdepartmental communications," a few signed by Crow's father, but most by Gardner J. Costello, of the Law Enforcement Assistance Administration.

"That's it!" he said to Reno. "Lee is Gardner J. Costello! We've got the bastard! Thanks to you, we've got him!"

Reno humbly blew on her fingernails and shined them against her top. "Aw, any brilliant girl could've done it," she said. "And don't forget about the grass."

"How could I?"

"Mrs. E. really kept an eye on me. I guess she was afraid I might miss a blade."

Crow wanted to start tracking the man down immediately, but the hour was late and he knew that Reno wanted attention, had it coming. So he put the folder with the photograph on top of the desk and weighted both of them with his father's hand-grenade paperweight. Taking hold of the back of Reno's neck, he playfully guided her out of the room and down the hall, ahead of him.

"Listen, we've got some celebrating to do," he said. "How would you like to make us some coffee."

"*That's* celebrating?"

"You got any better ideas?"

"I sure have," she said. "Just follow me."

In the kitchen, the girl went over to the refrigerator and got out a bottle of domestic champagne.

"How about some bubbly?" she asked. "I found it up above, in a cabinet. When someone leaves you alone for eight hours at a crack, you can find all kinds of things."

"So it appears."

She handed him the bottle to open. "And don't argue with me. Remember, you really owe me now."

"I'm not arguing."

She dumped a bag of nacho cheese chips into a bowl and got a carton of onion dip out of the refrigerator. Crow popped the plastic cork, barely making a sound.

186

"I don't know about this stuff," he said. "Especially on top of vodka."

"Just pretend I'm Jennifer. You'll manage."

"Will you get off her case, please? I don't want to hear another word about the lady tonight. You think you could manage that?"

"With pleasure." Reno gathered up her chips and dip and a couple of glasses and went into the living room. Crow followed with the bottle.

"Well, what's up?" he asked. "We gonna sit here and get fat and drunk?"

Reno smiled cockily. "Yep. And we're gonna dance too."

"Not this cat."

"Oh, yes you will." She turned off the lights and the television and found a rock station on the radio, at the moment playing something that sounded like World War III.

"You expect me to dance to that?" He was sitting on the sofa, pouring out their drinks.

Reno drank off half her glass and put it back down on the coffee table. "Wow. Sure. That's A.C.D.C., and they really move."

"Not me, they don't."

"Watch."

Smiling, she began to move with sinuous abandon, stretching her already too-tight shorts and tanktop to their limits. In the dimness —in the reflected light from the kitchen—her long arms and legs flashed like sabers, and Crow found himself drinking the champagne almost as she had, as if it were water. When the number ended she came over to him and took his hand.

"Come on, you can do that, can't you?"

"Not a chance. When I dance, I like to hold the girl."

Reno cocked her head. "Well, okay then. That sounds all right." Returning to the radio, she dialed until she found something slow, Simon and Garfunkel's "Bridge Over Troubled Water."

"Will this do?" she asked, taking another drink.

"Just fine," he said.

He drained his glass and got up. Reno was a tall girl, only a few inches shorter than Crow, so she was able to meet his eyes as he held her chastely out in front of him. Almost immediately, though, she

187

shook her head in mock disgust and pulled herself in tightly against him, pressing her face against his neck and cheek. And as they danced, his right hand inevitably found the gap between her top and shorts, the slick warm skin.

The music changed and he refilled their glasses and they drank. Then they were dancing again. She raised her face to him and he kissed her on the forehead, but again she would not settle for half measures and brought her lips up to his. By then he had a full erection and she was not at all bashful about pressing herself against it.

"You don't really dislike me," she said.

"That's for sure."

"Then why can't we?"

He tried to play the innocent. "Why can't we what?"

Her lips brushed against his and pulled away. "You know what."

"I've already told you."

"Well, we could at least neck, couldn't we? Just come close? They wouldn't throw you in jail for that, would they?"

Crow knew that he should have said no, should have backed away once more, but he was beginning to feel like a pantywaist in regard to the girl, like some sort of pathetic moralizing eunuch. And anyway the champagne was already doing its pleasant work: her pelvis felt like a steel bar against his erection and his rib cage blazed under the pressure of her small firm breasts. So he let his left hand join the other at the small of her back. He let them slide down under her panties, flat against her buttocks, whose hard, silken fullness only confirmed him in his madness. Her mouth opened in momentary shock and he kissed her that way, sucking in her tongue. He lifted her off her feet and carried her to the sofa.

"Sure—one time," he said. "What could it hurt?"

He pulled off her shorts and panties and then got out of his own clothes as she slipped her top off.

"Oh God, I didn't think you ever would," she said.

"Me either."

Taking her there on the sofa, he found it almost different in *kind* from the sex he was used to, the competent, varied, and even athletic coupling he enjoyed with his women in Seattle. The difference, he guessed, was passion and innocence. Reno, for all her tough-guy ways, obviously had not had much experience, and her cataclysmic response stimulated a kindred one in him, so that he too felt almost consumed by the thing. He could not hold her tightly enough, could not kiss her as deeply as he wanted, could not thrust beyond the maddening limits of their flesh. And when she came, and cried, he kissed away her tears. And he heard the familiar command.

"Don't move. Stay right there."

"Don't worry," he said. "I ain't going anywhere."

As he continued to lie there holding her in his arms, he could feel her tears welling up again and he asked her what was wrong.

"Nothing."

"Sure there is."

"Nothing you can help."

"Try me."

For a time she did not respond, just lay there in his arms. Finally she shivered.

"You really want to know?"

"Of course."

"Okay then—I'm really sunk now, that's what's wrong."

"Why say that?"

"You don't know?"

"That's why I'm asking."

She hugged him more tightly and burrowed her face into his neck. "Because I love you," she got out. "Because I really love you, don't you know that?"

The word *love* had been like ice water for Crow, a bucket of it dumped right on his head. Abruptly sobered, or at least able to will himself to think soberly, he wondered what he could possibly do to limit the pain he would inevitably inflict on the girl if what she'd said was true. For certain, he would not let himself just pull away from her and resume his eunuch's role, go back to his room and have her go to hers. There had to be a better way than that.

And in time he thought he'd found it. He whispered to her that he was not keen on getting "caught like this" by Mrs. Elderberry coming upstairs for one last cleanliness inspection of the kitchen.

189

"Your bed is bigger than mine," he told her. "Let's go there."

"Really?"

"Of course. Come on."

He took her by the hand and led her into her room and closed the door behind them. He pulled down the covers and lifted her onto his body before gently placing her on the bed and making love again, more slowly this time, gradually bringing them both to a climax that felt as if it would break his back as well as hers.

Later, lying next to her, he asked if she didn't think it was a little strange, a normal thirty-five-year-old man like himself never having married.

"Doesn't it make you wonder?" he asked her.

"Wonder what?"

"Why I never got involved. I mean, can you imagine how many girls a man can have by the time he reaches my age? And some of them almost as sexy as you."

"Am I really sexy?" She hugged him tightly.

"You're not listening," he told her. "I'm trying to explain something. Think of all those other girls and the fact that I've never let myself get tied down. Doesn't that tell you something about me?"

"What?"

"That I'm a lousy bet."

She was lying with her head on his chest. "Don't talk," she said. "Okay?"

"It's something you ought to hear, Reno."

"Not now."

Doggedly he continued. "Any girl who ever said she loved me— she wound up changing her mind."

But Reno wasn't listening to his words. "I can hear your heart," she said.

TEN

CROW woke at first light and carefully got out of bed, not wanting to wake Reno. He went down the hall to his room and ruffled the bedclothes on his couch, feeling like a perfect jackass as he did so. But he figured that Mrs. Elderberry already was carrying enough of the world's problems on her broad back without adding his and Reno's morals to the load. He put on a pot of coffee and then shaved and showered and dressed. Back in the kitchen, he got out the L.A. and Valley phone books and tried to find a listing for a Gardner Costello, but there was none. He drank his coffee and waited until the wall clock read seven-thirty, then he called Jennifer at the Sheraton and gave her the good news about having found Lee's identity.

"Actually Reno did it," he explained. "She looked right where I'd looked, only she wasn't blind. His name is Gardner Costello. No address as yet."

Jennifer said nothing for a few moments. Then: "I've heard the name somewhere—I'm sure I have. Maybe through my uncle. In his work, he deals with hundreds of people, in and out of the government. You want me to call him?"

Crow was not sure why he said no, but he did. "Oh, I think we can find the man ourselves," he said. "I still haven't checked Orange County information or Ventura. There are plenty of ways yet."

"But not the police?"

"Not now," Crow said. "Not yet." After yesterday's memorable experiences with Olson and the Hollywood detectives, Crow wanted no part of the police. Giving them the name, he felt, would have been tantamount to sealing it in a bottle and dropping it into the sea. And anyway he was already too personally involved in the case to back off and return to Seattle, there to wait meekly for further developments.

"I've got an idea," Jennifer said. "You know the dinner date I had last night, with my friend and her city councilman husband? Well, I wouldn't be surprised if the councilman could get the address for us. I know he'd try."

"I'll bet he would," Crow said.

Jennifer laughed. "What do you mean by that?"

"Nothing. Sure, go ahead and try the man. Meanwhile I'll keep on the phone company. And if that doesn't work, I'll call Police Science or some other law enforcement journal and say I'm Costello and haven't been receiving their magazine—what address have they been sending it to?"

"It might work," she said.

"We'll see."

He made a date to pick her up at nine-thirty, after breakfast. By then, he said, they hopefully would have Costello's address and could try to make contact with him.

"And who knows? We might even get some answers." He didn't bother to tell Jennifer that Reno would probably be coming with them, nor that she had just come into the kitchen and had sat down on his lap, half naked and half asleep, kissing him and running her hand inside his shirt, obviously expecting to pick up where they had left off. Hanging up, he walked her back to her room and told her to get dressed.

"What happened last night, Reno, that's got to be *our* secret," he said. "We don't let Mrs. Elderberry or anyone else know anything about it. It's just between us. Understand?"

Though she still looked half asleep, she managed a nod. "Sure, I understand. It's just between us."

She started to hug him and he took her by the wrists and held her off. "Sure, you do," he said.

"Well, I do."

He told her to get dressed. "You can come with us today, if you want."

She popped her cheek with her finger. "Lucky me."

"Right." He kissed her on the forehead and swatted her butt. "Get moving."

Back in the kitchen, he picked up the phone again and began checking with Information in Orange County and Ventura. It was like falling off a log.

Well, the Ventura operator said, she did have a Mrs. Gardner Costello in Ojai—would he want to try that number? Yes, he would. The woman who answered said that she was indeed Mrs. Gardner Costello, but that her husband was not there. Crow told her that his business with her husband was somewhat urgent and she said that Costello could usually be found on his boat in Marina del Rey, but that he was out fishing at the moment. She gave him the slip number on Mindanao Road and wished him luck. He thanked her and hung up. It was not yet eight o'clock.

*   *   *

On the drive over to the Sheraton, Crow had a lot more to think about than Reno and the problems she presented, yet it was she who occupied his mind. He still could hardly believe that he had done what he had, that he could have let himself be so weak and stupid. It was not as though he hadn't known how the girl thought she felt about him, and yet he'd gone ahead anyway, like all the other users in the world. And the worst part of it was how he had carried on, like a goddamn kid himself, seemingly every bit as moonstruck and passionate as she was. So how was he supposed to convince her now, in the cool and smoggy light of day, that last night had not been real at all but just a casual foray into fantasy land, into dreamland. He was afraid that no matter what he said, no matter how vigorously he might lay claim to his former eunuchhood, she was not going to believe him. For if ever there was a case where deeds spoke more loudly than words, this undoubtedly was it. So he could understand her not believing his words. He could understand—but he couldn't accept it. Somehow, some way, he had to get through to her.

Even now, as he drove, she had cuddled against him, resting her head on his shoulder and letting her hair blow across his face. Gently, but firmly, he pushed her away.

"You're forgetting what I told you," he said.

"Yeah, it's *our* secret—I remember. But we're alone now."

"I mean, you're forgetting what I said last night."

"What's that?"

"That what happened was just a one-shot. That I'm a lousy bet. That when a girl gets lovey with me, I run for cover. I can't help it, Reno. It's the way I am."

"You didn't run last night."

"No, I never do—not at night. But when daylight hits, I'm gone."

He looked over and found her studying him with her head canted, as if he were an abstract painting.

"I know what your problem is—it's Princess Jennifer," she said. "You're worried she might find out you ain't so noble after all."

Crow nodded. "It's true, I don't want her to know what happened, Reno—but not for that reason. Only because of what we're involved in—this whole investigation—and I need her trust."

"What bullshit."

"Believe what you want."

"Tell me, if she was the one you'd balled last night, would you be giving her this same kind of shit?"

"I don't know," he said.

And he saw that that had hurt her, which in turn caused his gut to clench. If the girl had hauled off and punched him, he would have been grateful. But she did not. Instead she just sat there fighting tears.

"What a bastard you are," she said finally. "Even Jere was better than you. At least he didn't come on like some kind of big brother."

Crow nodded grimly. "That's what I've been trying to tell you."

"Well, just don't worry—I won't be kissing you anymore or touching you or anything else. Especially not around your fucking Jennifer. Will that do?"

"That will do fine," he said.

An hour later the three of them, in Jennifer's car, were driving slowly along the perimeter road at Marina del Rey, past the high-rise condos of the retired rich and the indebted young, with the marina itself stretching out behind, blue and gaudy, the masts of its sailboats looking to Crow like a burned-out evergreen forest, an almost endless field of spars. Jennifer had come down to Los Angeles in a Mercedes sedan rather than in her Porsche, so the three of them had plenty of room, especially Reno in the back seat. Squirming and sighing, she vented her unhappiness on the electric windows, push-buttoning them up and down, until Crow asked her to stop.

"Whatever you say," she told him. "Wouldn't want to fuck up one of Jennifer's cars."

Jennifer made no response. Even earlier, when the girl had made a crack about the older woman's stylish white jumpsuit, saying that a janitor in her high school had a similar outfit, Jennifer had smiled and let it pass. And Crow did not have to wonder why. Like him, she undoubtedly had little time for anything except the man they were getting nearer to now, the man who might have been responsible for the death of her own brother. On the way, she had asked Crow if it worried him, confronting the man unarmed.

"If he's guilty, there's no telling what he might do," she said.

But Crow did not think the case was that simple. He found it hard to believe that a retired federal law enforcement officer by himself could have been responsible for so much carnage. For one thing, on the evening of his death, Crow's father had said that he wasn't delivering the job to his client but to his "client's man"—proof as far as Crow was concerned that Costello was not the only one involved, that they were in fact dealing with a conspiracy of some kind.

They came to Mindanao Road and took it a short distance before parking and getting out. The dock number was G–3400 and they found it immediately, the first one jutting into the Mindanao branch of the marina. There was a low, locked chain link fence with a

195

gangway beyond it leading down to the dock itself, which was about fifty yards long, with a dozen or so boats moored on each side, a few of them genuine yachts, the others mostly sailboats under thirty feet. Asking the girls to wait for him, Crow climbed over the fence and walked out on the dock until he found the slip number Costello's wife had given him. As he'd expected, the slip was empty. The only persons around were a young couple getting ready to go out on a small sloop. He asked them if they knew Costello or where he might be and they said that they were new at the marina and were barely acquainted with anybody yet. The man suggested that Crow check at the office and pointed to it, a small building at the end of the branch, backdropped by the high-rises on Admiralty Way. Thanking them, Crow went back up the dock and rejoined the girls.

"Had to make sure he wasn't there," he told them.

"We'll find him," Jennifer said.

Crow led them around the corner to the office, which was cramped and glassy, presided over by a California version of Mona Lisa, sleepy-eyed and slightly smiling, grooving on some constantly amusing private joke. When Crow asked about Costello—where he might have gone on his boat—the woman told him that the marina wasn't exactly a navy yard and that the tenants rarely kept her posted about their comings and goings.

"Free country, you know. That sort of thing."

"Maybe you saw him leave," Crow said.

But she was not listening. Her cryptic smile widened. "Weird thing about this, though, is your boy Costello did call in when he left. Like I give a shit that he's going out fishing. Weird."

"Did he say *where* he was going?"

"Yeah, Santa Barbara. It was sure a big load off my chest to hear that. How about you?"

"Yeah, us too," Crow said. He asked her if any of the other tenants were friends of Costello and might know when he'd be back.

The girl wagged her head in amusement. "Boy, you really got a thing for this guy, huh?"

At that point, Jennifer stepped forward with a twenty-dollar bill in her hand.

"We sure do," she said. "Why not take advantage of that fact?"

196

                    *   *   *

The tenant that Mona Lisa put them onto had the slip next to
Costello's. His name was Mort Greenberg and he ran a taco stand
on the oceanwalk in Venice. It was a place that Reno had seen only
in movies and on television, and it definitely caught her fancy.

"Wow, it's just like on 'Chips,'" she said. "I keep expecting Erik
Estrada to come skating by."

The day was brilliant and clear, free of the misty sea air that
usually clung to the Southern California coast in late spring and
summer. Beyond the palm-lined greensward a light surf pawed at the
beach, which like the oceanwalk itself was crowded with the detritus
of a continent: the flamboyant and the crazy, the lost and the
beautiful. In bikinis and uniforms and junk-shop costumery they
floated by on roller skates and dope and dreams. And Reno drank
it all in. She seemed especially enthralled by a utility building mural
depicting the walk itself: the painting for some reason a take-off on
Botticelli's *Birth of Venus*, with Venus roller-skating and the scallop
shell in hot pursuit.

Turning from the painting, Reno looked down the oceanwalk and
out at the beach. "You know, this really ain't so bad," she said.
"When Crow dumps me, this is where I'm coming."

Crow shook his head. "Little Miss Paranoia," he said.

"That's me, all right."

The look she gave him made him wish for sunglasses. Tell me
about last night, the fearless brown eyes said. Tell me your lies.

Rattled, Crow steered both girls toward a bench along the walk.

"Wait for me, okay?" he said. "I'm gonna come on to this guy
as Costello's nephew. Maybe he'll open up."

"If he knows anything," Jennifer put in.

"Yeah—*if.*"

Crow went over to the taco stand and waited until there were no
other customers before asking the man behind the counter if he was
Greenberg. The man said he was, and Crow explained then about
going to the marina and being referred to him by the office girl there.
He told Greenberg that he was Costello's nephew and hadn't seen
him in over ten years and really didn't know if he should bother to
wait for him to return. Did Greenberg think Costello was the kind

of guy who might help someone down on his luck?"

"Well Jesus, Mac, how would I know that?"

"The girl said you were friends."

Greenberg laughed. "Sometimes we exchange three or four words about our boats. And that's it. I really don't know the guy."

"He was a cop, right?"

"Yeah. CIA, I've heard. Something like that."

"He's supposed to be fishing up around Santa Barbara—the Channel Islands, I would imagine. You know how long he usually fishes? How long he'll be gone?"

Greenberg was already shaking his head. "No, I don't know. And anyway he wasn't going in that direction. About five days ago the wife and me was off Oceanside and I saw him steaming past, with a naked young broad on the bow—would you believe that? A man his age? He could've been heading for Mexico, for all I know."

"That far, huh?"

"How do I know? And why the fuck am I telling you all this anyway?" Greenberg gestured in exasperation. "I got a fucking business to run."

Crow thanked him and ordered tacos and Cokes, which mollified Greenberg sufficiently for Crow to risk another question.

"I'm not sure how to ask this, but would you say my uncle's straight? Ever any signs he might be mixed up with criminals?"

Not answering, Greenberg kept working on Crow's order and finally set it in front of him. "Four-eighty, mister. And you already got your money's worth."

Crow gave him a ten and told him to keep the change, which Greenberg readily did.

"Clean as a hound's tooth, your uncle," he said, ringing up the sale. "Except for that broad on his bow."

Crow thanked him and carried the order across the walk to where the girls were sitting. He passed out the food and told them that he had not gotten much, except that Costello had sailed south instead of north. But Jennifer did not seem to hear him. She was holding her taco out in front of her as if it were a dead rat.

"If you don't want it," Reno said, "I'll eat it."

"Be my guest."

As Reno took the extra taco, Crow told Jennifer that the girl was on a diet. "Eleven thousand calories a day," he explained. "No more, no less."

Jennifer smiled. "Well, it seems to be working just fine."

Reno didn't return her smile. Instead she was giving Crow the fierce brown eyes again, a long, level look that in the end made him turn away. Later, he promised himself. Later he would deal with the girl.

"Come on," Crow said. "Let's eat up and go."

Reno promptly got to her feet, Coke in one hand and a taco in the other, her first having already disappeared. Crow asked her if she was going to eat and walk at the same time.

"I can handle it," she said.

"What a girl," Crow kidded, as the three of them started back up the broad promenade.

Reno did not take kindly to his kidding. "Yeah? Well let me tell you something else this *girl* knows. Something I bet neither of you grown-ups even noticed."

"What's that?" Crow asked.

"We're being followed," she said.

"Is that a fact?"

"It sure as hell is."

Crow looked back over his shoulder.

"Don't bother—they're gone now. Two guys, one of them a real fatso. They were watching us at the marina, in a car. And till a few minutes ago, they were watching us from that empty bench over there. While you jawed with the taco man, Fatso must've pigged down five bags of peanuts."

"It's probably just a coincidence," Jennifer said. "The marina and here are both tourist stops."

Reno shook her head. "They weren't tourists. They were wearing business suits."

"Tourists can wear suits," Crow told her.

Reno tossed her cup and napkin into a refuse can. "Okay, they were tourists, then."

"Or businessmen ogling the skaters," Crow said.

"Whatever."

199

*   *   *

When Mazatlan first came into view—the tourist hotels like white beads on an old leather necklace—Costello had wondered what he would find waiting for him there: asylum or the company, solitude or death. But he kept moving landward and finally reached Creston Island harbor, which was about as good as a saltwater anchorage gets. Located on the east side of the Mazatlan peninsula and protected by a breakwater, it was smooth as a lake and had a number of public and private docks for boat service or going ashore by dinghy.

Once he had anchored, though, Costello made no move to go ashore, and Sherri naturally did not take kindly to this.

"Goddamn, we're here now! What the hell we waiting for?"

"Harbor patrol or customs," he said. "One or the other, they'll be here soon enough."

She had been drinking beer from one of his heavy-bottomed tumblers, and at his answer she tossed the glass out into the water. "I just can't believe what a wimp you are," she bawled. "You really take the cake, you know that?"

Ignoring her, he sat down at the galley table and wrote a short note to his wife, saying that he couldn't satisfactorily explain why he had fled to Mexico because he himself didn't know what was going on, except that people were getting killed and that the matter probably involved some renegade element in the company. If anything happened to him, she was to contact headquarters at Langley and tell them Paul Queen, in Colorado Springs, was behind it. Barbara Queen, his daughter, had been Costello's unwitting contact, getting him into the whole mess.

He broke off then, as he heard a small diesel engine chugging toward the *Mako*. He folded the unfinished letter and put it in his shirt pocket, then he went out onto the stern deck to meet whoever was drawing near. The boat, he saw, was a typical harbor patrol craft, a white thirty-footer with a long cockpit and a stubby bow bearing the single word *POLICIA*. Incredibly, the pilot edged the boat toward his *with* the wind, which resulted in a collision that almost knocked Costello and Sherri overboard. Fortunately the police boat, like his own, was fiberglass, so no lasting damage had been done—

200

an oversight which the mate tried to rectify by digging his boathook into a teak runner on the *Mako*. But then he and the pilot both seemed much more interested in Sherri than they were in a safe tie-up, and they kept ogling her as Costello belayed their line and then frantically set about adjusting his fenders to protect the boat from further mauling.

The "mate," it turned out, was the man in charge, and his interest in Sherri persisted to such a degree that he almost fell between the boats in coming aboard. Apologizing for his clumsiness—or at least so Costello interpreted the man's peasant Spanish—the officer tipped his cap to Sherri and grinned at Costello.

"*Vuestra esposa?*" he asked. Your wife?

Costello shook his head. "No, just a friend," he said, in his own stilted, company Spanish. He introduced himself and Sherri, and the policeman smiled and bowed.

"Sargento Costa achoor service," he announced in labored English.

Costello smiled and invited the sergeant into the cabin, where he handed him his passport, with a hundred-dollar bill folded inside. The sergeant casually pocketed the bill and Costello then proceeded to detail for the policeman what he wanted for his money. He showed him his rifle and thirty-eight revolver and said that he kept them on the boat for protection only, not to smuggle them into Mexico. He showed him what wine and liquor he had aboard and said that that too would stay right where it was. It was not for sale. Finally he told the sergeant that he would require a favor from customs. The girl Sherri didn't have a passport or even a driver's license, so getting a tourist card for her might be difficult. He would need a favor.

The sergeant shrugged eloquently. It was no problem. All he had to do was show the *aduanero* his passport, "wis ze gratuity." Everything would be *correcto*. And that was exactly what Costello did. He followed the police boat into the customs dock and tipped two little boys who helped him tie up. Sergeant Costa had a few words with the customs inspector, who then came aboard and checked out the boat, giving special attention to Costello's passport. He exchanged four hundred dollars more for pesos at the official rate and then he

201

made out a tourist card for Sherri, who took the card and a fistful of pesos and promptly debarked, without a word or even a glance at Costello. By the time she reached the head of the dock she already had a john in tow, a dark little man who eagerly hailed a taxi for the two of them.

With his passport stamped and everything in order, Costello took the boat out into the harbor again and anchored. He cleaned his guns and reloaded them, and then he took a shower and changed his clothes. He made himself a sandwich of ham and stale rye bread and sat out on the stern deck eating it and drinking a lukewarm Heineken. He felt enormously tired, and yet he didn't see how he could simply forget about everything and go to bed. He had to remain awake. He had to be ready. But of course he also had to sleep. Every man had to sleep eventually. The trick was to wake again. Sitting there drinking in the cabin's shade, feeling the gentle rise and fall of the boat in this alien harbor, Costello felt more alone and vulnerable than he ever had before.

If Reno was impressed by Jennifer's hotel suite, she didn't show it. Maintaining a frosty silence, she peered into the two bedrooms and walked through the kitchenette and finally went out onto the terrace, where she stood looking down at the pool. Jennifer asked her if she'd like to go for a swim and Reno shook her head.

"I haven't got a suit," she said.

"You could use one of mine."

The girl looked at the older woman's figure. "It'd be too big."

"A tie bikini," Jennifer said. "You can draw it as tight as you need to."

Shrugging, Reno followed Jennifer into one of the bedrooms and when they came out a few minutes later the girl was wearing the bikini, a black one. And as she'd predicted, it did look too large for her.

"Anybody laughs and I take it off," she said.

"No one's laughing," Crow told her. "You look fine."

"Yeah, sure." Without even a glance at Crow, the girl walked past him and headed for the door.

When she was gone, Jennifer gave Crow a commiserating look.

"She seems unhappy about something. What is it—me?"

"No—me."

"Well, let's hope it passes. Meanwhile, I think there's some iced tea in the fridge. You want a glass?"

"Sure."

Jennifer brought the drinks out onto the terrace and the two of them sat there like parents watching their daughter as Reno dived into the pool down below and came up adjusting her bikini top. And though they continued to watch her, it was other, more pressing, matters that they talked about.

If and when they got to Costello, just what would they do, Jennifer wondered. How could they get him to talk? And even if they did, how could they be sure he was telling them the truth?

They were questions that Crow already had asked himself. "I'm not worried about getting the man to talk," he said. "Chances are he either killed my father or set him up. So if I have to lean on him —so be it. And as far as what he tells us, I think we'll recognize the truth when we hear it."

Jennifer then brought up the subject of the two men Reno had seen at the marina and on the oceanwalk. "If they really were following us," she said, "I've got an idea who they might be working for."

"Who?"

"My uncle. I'm afraid he still thinks of me as his little girl. He wants me in Santa Barbara. In fact, he wants me right there with him, at home. And when I'm not there, he has me call every day. Even when I went abroad with my ex-husbands, he'd have one of the Kims go with us, as a kind of combination chaperone and bodyguard."

"And your husbands put up with that?"

"Without a peep. Uncle paid the bills, you see. He still does."

"But you're not overseas here."

"No, but he was quite upset at my seeing you Sunday, after the reception. And then coming down here. I wouldn't put it past him to hire a couple of private investigators to keep tabs on us."

Crow thought about it. "I don't know. Chances are, Reno was just seeing things. But even if she was right, there could be another explanation. The two men could just as easily be working for Cos-tello—checking on our progress for now, and putting themselves in a position to protect their man, if they have to."

"Then shouldn't we be worried about that?" Jennifer asked. "Shouldn't you be carrying a gun?"

That was another question Crow had been asking himself—with-out getting a satisfactory answer.

"In the first place, it's illegal," he told her. "I don't have a permit. And I don't even know how to use one of the damn things. A rifle or shotgun, yes—I've done my share of hunting. But a handgun?" He shook his head. "Anyway, I guess we really don't know yet that Costello did anything wrong. Could be he was simply a patsy in this thing too, same as my father."

"Well, *somebody* did something wrong," Jennifer said.

She then commented on how odd it was that the city councilman had not gotten back to her. He'd told her on the phone that if Costello had worked for the L.A.P.D.—which of course he had—then the councilman would have no trouble finding his address for her. He would call her back in half an hour, he'd said. But he had not called. Lucky that Crow had phoned Ventura information, Jen-nifer observed.

Crow again told her about the photograph in his father's study, with the Mazatlan address on the back.

"That could well be where he is now," he said. "Remember, Greenberg at the taco stand said he saw Costello heading south. Maybe I ought to fly down and check it out."

Jennifer gave him a wry smile and jumped up. "Boy, are we stupid!" she said. "You know, we don't have to wonder if he's there. We can ask."

"Ask who?"

He had followed her inside, where she was already picking up the phone.

"Customs, of course," she said. In quick succession she got opera-tor assistance, then Mazatlan Information, and finally the customs office. For no more than a minute she spoke with someone there, in fluent Spanish, finishing with words that even he knew: *Muchas gracias, señor.*

204

Smiling triumphantly, she put down the phone. "He's there, all right! Señor Gardner Costello in his little yacht, the *Mako*, anchored at Creston Island harbor. I know the place. We've cruised the Mexican coast a number of times."

Crow was smiling too. "Okay then, let's keep moving. You make a couple of plane reservations and I'll get Reno out of the pool."

At first, Crow couldn't pick her out from the terrace, but that was because he was looking for a solitary swimmer and at the moment she was anything but solitary, was in fact sitting on the edge of the pool next to one deeply tanned young man while another stood in front of her, in the pool, playfully flicking water on her. She was smiling and Crow felt a kind of pain, a rush of something, hot and angry. It was not jealousy, however—he quickly reassured himself of that. Rather, a big brother's violated sense of protectiveness. Something like that.

He tried to signal for her to come back up, but she wasn't looking. So he left the suite and went down to get her. By the time he reached the pool, the boy sitting next to her had his hand on her shoulder and the one in the water was pushing his wet head between her knees and panting, apparently in the belief that he was a Labrador retriever. Crow told her that they had to leave, and she groaned. She also introduced him.

"My Uncle Orville," she said. "He's a killjoy."

On the way back Crow told her that he didn't think much of her definition of joy and she said she had to find it where she could.

"It's pretty hard for a girl," she went on. "Some guys love you up at night and then tell you to get lost soon as it's day."

"No one told you to get lost."

"Didn't they?"

Going up the stairs, Crow told her that they had located Costello in Mazatlan and that he and Jennifer were going to fly down and find out what they could.

"I'll have to stop by the house. And we'll have to drop you off too," he said.

"I don't get to go, huh?"

"You don't have any I.D. We couldn't get you a tourist card even if we wanted to."

"Which you don't."

"It could be dangerous, Reno. You could get hurt."

"And the princess? You don't care if she gets hurt?"

"She's an adult. And anyway this is her thing as much as mine. Remember, it was her brother—"

"Yeah, I know, I know. Hey, what if I gave you my real name—could I get a card then? Would you take me with?"

"I already know your name," he said. "You're Reno."

They were walking down the corridor and he had reached out to give her a playful nudge. But she only pulled farther away, unwilling to give him a thing.

Knowing that Jennifer might be on the telephone, he had taken the room key with him. And he used it now to let himself and Reno in. As he'd expected, Jennifer was still on the phone. But she was in her bedroom this time, and talking not with an airline reservation clerk but with someone else, someone close. Crow considered going out onto the terrace in order not to overhear her, but the conversation obviously was about him. So, while Reno went into the second bedroom to change, he stayed right where he was.

"I assure you, darling, he's straight in every sense of the word. No, he's not using me. It's just as he tried to tell us at the house—he's not satisfied that his father met with an accident. And I'm not satisfied about Richard either." Jennifer broke then, listening, and Crow lit a cigarette. When she spoke again, her voice was uncharacteristically tight and hesitant.

"Yes, Henry dear, I know what the councilman told you. All we wanted was the man's address. Because . . . no, I'm not getting in over my head. All we want to do is ask him a few questions, find out why . . . Yes, I do know what I'm doing . . . I know that, dear, yes . . . No, please, don't do that. I'll be all right, darling. I promise . . . No, please don't . . . Yes, I promise . . . Yes . . . Good-bye."

After she had hung up, Crow heard her go into her own private bathroom. He heard water running. Reno, who hadn't bothered to close her door, now came out of the second bedroom, dressed.

"Wonder who that was," she said. "Sounded like a boyfriend, wouldn't you say, Crow? Could be you've got competition."

"You're not supposed to listen to other people's conversations," he told her, absently, for he was still deeply puzzled at what he had overheard. *Dear* and *darling*—not how one usually addressed an uncle.

"Oh, really?" Reno was in the kitchenette, hanging the bikini on a towel rack. "And just what were *you* doing?" she asked.

Crow did not respond, for Jennifer appeared in the bedroom doorway now, with a smile that did not reach her eyes.

"I got us seats on Mexicana," she said. "Takeoff's in about ninety minutes. You think we can make it?"

"Sure."

"Just give me a minute to change and pack."

"You've got it."

As the door closed, Reno went over to the terrace and looked down at the pool. "I've always wanted to go to Mexico," she said.

ELEVEN

CROW was already aboard the Mexicana 727, sitting with Jennifer in their first-class seats and looking out through the tiny window next to her at the concourse gate when he saw the two men. They obviously had run the length of the concourse, trying to make it to the plane in time. The fat one was red-faced and open-mouthed, doubling over in exhaustion, while the other—trim and athletic, with short-cropped red hair—did not even look winded. Though they were both wearing business suits, as Reno had said, they were at the moment anything but businesslike: angrily thrusting money at an airline clerk and waving their arms, trying to push past her toward the boarding ramp, which apparently had just been closed, as had the aircraft's door.

Crow pointed the men out to Jennifer and she asked how he could be sure they were the ones Reno had seen.

"Because I've seen them before myself," he said. "They were outside the Van Nuys police station yesterday. And I remember, even then they struck me as a little odd, the way they looked away

208

when Reno and I passed. You'll recall she was wearing shorts and a tanktop."

Jennifer smiled. "I see your point." Then suddenly she was angrily shaking her head. "Goddamn him, having me followed by these lousy spooks of his. What does he think I am anyway—a subversive?"

Crow wondered if he had heard her right. "You mind explaining that?" he asked.

"Oh, it's nothing. I'm just mad, that's all."

"You said *spooks*," he reminded her.

She gave him a rueful smile. "I know, and I shouldn't have. It's really nothing. As I've told you, my uncle once worked for the government—"

"CIA?" Crow asked.

"I really can't say."

"Or won't say?"

"It doesn't really matter here, does it? How could it relate to our problem?"

"I guess it couldn't," he admitted.

"Except for our tails. Oh well, we've lost them for now anyway."

"It would seem so."

When the plane reached cruising altitude, a stewardess brought them the margaritas they had ordered. Jennifer went at hers with unexpected gusto and soon ordered another, which also quickly began to disappear. As she drank, in silence, she kept looking out the window at the sea and the dun-colored coast far below. Crow finally asked her if she didn't like to fly, and she said no, it wasn't that.

"What then?"

"My uncle. What you must have overheard when I was on the phone with him. It's not easy to explain."

"There's nothing to explain," he said.

"Yes, there is. I can imagine how it must have sounded. Like we're a couple of weirdos." She looked up at Crow now, her lovely eyes grave and intense. "*Incestuous* weirdos. Which I assure you is not the case."

"I never thought—"

209

But she touched her fingers to his mouth. "No, I don't imagine you did. But I want to explain anyway. It's just one of those things that develop in childhood and you can't change it. He was like my father, always, and as far back as I can remember he'd call me *darling* and *sweetheart* and all those nice things. And smart aleck that I was I started calling him by the same words, which I guess he thought was pretty cute of me. And it just became a habit, that's all. To change it now would seem—I don't know—a gratuitous cruelty."

"I can understand that," Crow said. "But really, I didn't think a thing of it."

"You must have."

"Well, I've got this little problem about you. And I've had it since we first met. Whatever you say or do, I just don't seem to question it. For some reason, I figure it must be right."

Her solemn gaze softened, and she smiled. She took hold of his arm and touched her forehead to his shoulder.

"Did I mention how much I like being with you?" she said.

He kissed her lightly on the head and she straightened up, smiling still.

"Me too," he said.

The flight to Mazatlan lasted little more than an hour, which did not give Crow much time to think about anything for very long. He did have time, however, to remember Reno as he hurried into the house and packed a few changes of underwear and shirts, along with his swimming trunks and a razor and toothbrush.

"Traveling light, eh?" she'd said, standing in the doorway.

"Yeah, this shouldn't take over a day or two."

"You want me gone when you come back?"

He gave her a despairing look. "If you aren't here, I'll hunt you down. Remember that."

"Sure."

In the bedroom doorway he took her chin in his hand and forced her to look at him. "I mean it, Reno. I'll be back soon, and I want you here—unless you decide to go home to your mother."

"Fat chance," she said. "I'll be here."

He kissed her on the cheek and she made no move to return the kiss. He said "So long" and she said nothing. And when he and Jennifer drove away in the Mercedes, he waved at her standing behind the closed screen door. But she did not wave back. And it gnawed at him now, the idea that she might not be there when he returned. How else could he take her unwillingness to say "So long," or to wave?

But suddenly now he caught himself, warned himself that this was not the time to think of anything but what lay ahead for him and Jennifer: the confrontation with Costello. For once in his life he just might be, in his father's words, "playing for keeps." And he couldn't help wondering—just as the old man had—if he'd be able to cut it, or if as usual he'd just take the reasonable way out, tell himself that he was in over his head and swim straight for shore?

Except for the shanties at the edge of the city, Mazatlan looked pretty much like California to Crow: the same parched ground and palm trees and Spanish architecture. And what with Jennifer's command of the language—she seemed to speak it as well as the natives—they sailed through customs and the Avis desk without a hitch, renting an Olds Cutlass which she drove, since she was familiar with the city. She said that they could have tried a hotel downtown, which would have put them closer to the Creston Island harbor, but that the beach hotels all had purified water and she personally didn't want to chance a bout of Montezuma's fabled revenge.

Cutting across the city to the ocean boulevard proved something of an adventure, as Jennifer made her way through the demolition derby traffic, trying especially hard to avoid attacking taxis and small motorized rickshaws that she called "pneumonias."

"Actually the name is *pulmonias*," she explained. "But everyone calls them pneumonias—I guess because they're a bit cold and windy, especially along the ocean."

A mile or so north on the beach drive she pulled in at one of the sprawling oceanfront hotels and they rented connecting rooms, each with double beds—all that was available—again using Jennifer's omnipresent Gold American Express card. Crow himself had only a Master Charge card, but he was keeping a careful account of their

211

expenditures and planned to pay his full share when the thing was over.

Their rooms each had terraces overlooking the ocean and the narrow beach which was lined with palm trees and thatched-roof *cabañas*—actually sun-shades—which looked like so many giant mushrooms under the setting sun. Jennifer, who seemingly had the habit of changing clothes with each change in the day's activities, now went into her room and shed the pants suit she had worn on the plane in favor of a handsome, silky dress. Crow smiled his approval and, tongue-in-cheek, asked if she wanted him to change his shirt or socks.

"No, you look just fine."

"You look okay too," he said.

"Then, let's go. I'm famished."

But when they reached the restaurant downstairs, which was not all that crowded in this between-seasons week, Jennifer seemed more thirsty than hungry, again ordering margaritas while Crow made do with one of his favorite beers, Dos Equis, cheap in Seattle, though not so cheap here in the country where it was made. He and Jennifer endured some strolling guitarists for a few minutes and then they settled back in their corner booth, both of them keenly aware that they were not out for a simple evening of enjoyment. On a local map which Crow had picked up at the desk, Jennifer showed him where the Creston Island harbor was—on the inland side of the peninsula on which the city itself was located. The harbor had been formed by breakwaters, one of which connected the island to the city. There appeared to be a number of docks and marinas along the shore, which Crow was relieved to see.

"If he's anchored in the harbor instead of moored somewhere on shore, we'll need a boat in the morning," he said. "Something we can rent, not charter. We won't want anyone with us."

"What if he sees us coming."

"The man doesn't know us. He won't know who we are."

"Let's hope you're right."

"We'll come in from his bow. Chances are, he'll be in the galley or out back. Maybe we'll surprise him."

Jennifer smiled. "No matter how we arrive, I think we'll surprise him."

"No doubt about that."

Jennifer said nothing more for a time then, just sat there worrying her swizzle stick and looking over at Crow occasionally, with a slight, embarrassed smile, as if she'd been caught wearing jeans and a sweatshirt. When he asked her what was wrong, she shrugged and said that it was nothing she could put her finger on.

"I guess maybe I feel a little guilty about all this," she went on. "I mean, taking off on a kind of wild goose chase just a few days after Richard's death."

"But Richard is the reason you're doing it," he said.

"Is he?"

"You tell me."

She drained the last of her margarita and signaled the waiter for another. "I'm not sure. I think part of the reason is I just didn't want to be at home, where everything reminded me of him. Jesus, I'm going to miss him." Her eyes suddenly had filled. "He may have been gay, but he was a beautiful kid, Crow. He really was. And a lot closer to me, I think, than if he'd been straight. In many ways, he was like a kid sister, only without the competition."

The waiter brought her drink and she promptly sipped it down from the brim. Wiping her eyes on a napkin, she told Crow not to worry about her, that she would be all right. She was just feeling "dopey and blue," that was all.

"It's only to be expected," he said. "In my case it's more anger than grief, because my father was old and we weren't all that close. In fifteen years, I only saw him four times."

"Well, don't worry about me," she said again. "Tomorrow I'll be fine. I promise. I'll be your strong right arm."

"Let's hope we don't need one."

"I'll buy that."

When their abalone steaks were served, Jennifer barely touched hers, preferring instead to nurse her last margarita through much of the meal. And she told Crow that another reason for her mood was her uncle, that she hadn't wanted to be around the house during these days after the funeral because she knew that it would have been "business as usual."

"Henry almost never said anything about Richard's homosexuality. But he didn't have to. He just treated Richard most of the time like he wasn't even there. He almost never called him by name. And if Richard said something to him, he'd usually just ignore the kid, pretend he hadn't even heard him. I guess it's Henry's one weakness —the weakness of others. He has no patience with it. No sympathy. Like my mother's drinking. He seldom mentions it. Or her. His world is one of winners. And if you lose—well, you're out of it. You don't exist for him."

It was an indictment that obviously gave Jennifer no pleasure. When the waiter came again she ordered double brandies for both of them and Crow reluctantly nodded his agreement to the waiter. He was not keen on mixing brandy and beer but figured that he should at least appear to be going the distance with her. She had begun to slur her words and even took one of his cigarettes and had him light it for her—the first smoke he'd ever seen her have. She spoke wryly of her ex-husbands' unrequited love for Uncle Henry's power and money, recounting how one of them had gone so far as to throw his coat under the wheel of Henry's Rolls when it was stuck in the mud at the polo field. By way of showing his gratitude, Henry had called the poor fool "Sir Walter" for months afterward. Nor was Jennifer very complimentary about the general level of social life in Santa Barbara, describing it as a town of "old money and diseased livers." The men made it a habit of "getting up their fifth martinis if nothing else," she said, judging by her own experience and the testament of her women friends.

High as she was, Jennifer was oblivious to the irony in her critique, the pot once again calling the kettle black. But Crow said nothing. When she was ready to leave, he put his arm around her and guided her out of the restaurant, trying to make his support look like intimacy instead of what it was. In the elevator she asked him if he knew that her uncle used to be in the CIA.

"Yep, one of their top boys," she went on. "A revolution here, an overthrow there—you'd think the old man would quit, wouldn't you?"

214

"Hasn't he?"

She shook her head. "No way. And yet he's got time to put a tail on little old me. Can you figure that?"

"No, I can't."

"Me either.

Upstairs, she sighed and fell back on one of the beds in her room. "Oh Christ, am I bombed!" she said. "I don't ever get this bombed."

"Why tonight then?"

"Why tonight, he asks."

"So I did."

Now she laughed. "Because of you, dear Crow."

"What about me?"

"That's what I keep wondering. What about you?"

Smiling, Crow sat down next to her. "You're not making a lot of sense, you know that?"

"I suspected as much."

"What say we get you to bed?" Standing again, he took her by the hand and pulled her to her feet. He started her toward the bathroom. "You go in there and do what you have to do, and I'll turn down your bed. I'll tuck you in and even close the door between us."

"You sure this is what you want, Crow?" she said. And for a moment his heart leaped.

"Now that you ask—no."

But she turned and put her hands on his shoulders. "Well, I am." She pushed him back toward the door. "And I'll tuck myself in, if you don't mind."

"Just trying to be of help."

She let him kiss her on the lips, and then her hands came up again, ushering him on through the door.

"I trust I don't have to lock this," she said.

"Not on my account."

"Fine, then. Goodnight."

True to her word, she didn't lock the door. But as far as Crow was concerned, it might as well have been chained shut. No matter how much he wanted her, he wanted even more *not* to be rejected by

215

her. That, he knew, would have put quick death to whatever was growing between them. He didn't mind an old lover handing him his dick—women after all occasionally *did* have actual headaches— but he definitely disliked having the poor thing handed to him by someone new. From that point on, for him, the relationship was subtly altered, and not for the better. So he was not a great one for unilateral seductions. If the thing was going to happen, he believed, it was going to happen. And the heavy breathing would be on both sides.

So he undressed and showered. Then, putting on his pants again —because he hadn't packed a robe—he went out onto the terrace. To his right, the hotel-lined beach curved like a sickle of diamonds toward a distant point, and he wondered how many other men, in all those sparkling rooms, were as unlucky as he, to have such a desirable woman just an unlocked door away. To console himself, he thought of the day ahead and the danger it might hold for both of them, especially if they didn't have their minds on the business at hand.

Lighting a cigarette, he reflected on what Jennifer had said about her uncle being an old CIA hand, still involving himself in international mischief. There was definitely no shortage of such mischief being carried out around the globe, and somebody had to be behind it. So why not Henry Kellogg? The man certainly fit the part, Crow had to admit. At the same time, he couldn't see that it related in any way to him or to his and Jennifer's problem—unless of course she happened to persuade the old man to enlist the CIA itself in their quest. That would be the day, Crow told himself. The celebrated day when hell finally froze over.

Later, as he was about to fall asleep, the door between their rooms opened and Jennifer came into his room, hugging a handsome tartan robe tightly about her. Smiling slightly, she sat down on the edge of his bed.

"I can't sleep," she said. "Can you?"

"Not a wink."

"You think we're being too puritanical?"

"Probably."

"You suppose there's anything we could do about it?"

216

"I suppose so."

"Like what?"

"We could count sheep."

"Not me."

"Well, maybe we could make love," he said.

She pretended to give the matter some serious thought. "Yes, I suppose we could."

"We'd really sleep then."

"You think so?"

"Sure."

"That'd be nice," she said. Then, as slowly and artfully as a stripper, she edged her robe off one shoulder and let it slip from her body, which in the dimness was as excitingly beautiful as anything he'd ever seen.

"Christ, you're gorgeous," he told her.

She was slowly pulling the covers off him. And as she finished, her smile turned a touch wicked.

"You're not so bad yourself," she said.

As usual, Crow woke early. Leaving Jennifer asleep, he went into his room and put on his swimming trunks and a shirt to serve as a beach robe. He went downstairs and out to the pool, only to find it closed. There was a bilingual sign giving the hours it was open, but since six A.M. was not one of them he went on out to the freshly raked beach and waded into the ocean. The surf was light and the water warm, which was disappointing to a man who loved to swim in the Sound. But he made the most of it, diving under the breakers and swimming hard and steadily until he was about a quarter mile out. Treading water then, and body surfing, he slowly made his way back toward the beach. And he thought about Jennifer and their lovemaking, which had been damned fine, considering that she had not been overly sober at the time. It had in fact been vigorous and expert and oral—and not "like dentists doing it" either, he mused —the two of them playing along that torturous edge for what seemed like hours, time after time pulling back only at the very last second, until finally there was no more pulling left. And later, both of them half asleep, a pair of slow and languid missionaries. Yes, it

217

had been good. The earth may not have moved and there may have been no tears, but it had been good. After all, they were not children. Sex was not some new and marvelous country to explore so much as an old neighborhood to wander in—but the best of all neighborhoods, the one you never tired of.

As for what it meant, their having had sex together, Crow had no idea. It was true, what he'd told Reno about his being a lousy bet and fleeing like a vampire before the morning light. But the reason for this often was economic. Like any normal man, he'd never found it hard to fall in love, especially when he was in the arms of a lovely woman. Unfortunately those "loves" had never seemed quite so strong as his aversion to committing himself to a lifetime of bread-winning in order to support the woman and their issue. Certainly he wanted no part of a working-wife family, with its concomitant neglected children and exhausted bed-partner and all the rest. He had too many friends, male and female, caught in that vicious treadmill for him to want to give it a try.

But now if the woman in question happened to be a Santa Barbara heiress—he had to admit that might put things in a different light. The problem of breadwinning would disappear as if by magic. And suddenly Crow was laughing out loud as he swam, for he had just pictured himself throwing his old herringbone jacket under the wheel of Henry Kellogg's Rolls. And he thought, what a jerk he was, having romantic ideas about a girl simply because she had slept with him. Here they were, two reasonably young, reasonably attractive (*unreasonably,* in her case) grown-ups traveling together, drinking together, sharing connecting rooms in a Mexican seaside hotel—how else should they have wound up, except in bed? And what finally did it mean, other than that having breakfast together soon they would each be a trifle less relaxed than they otherwise might have been?

So he decided to put his mind on more pressing matters, such as what Costello was doing at that very moment. Was the man up and around yet? Did he have even the slightest premonition that he would soon be having visitors? Crow thought not. No, he figured that Costello was probably sleeping like a baby.

*   *   *

But he was not. Through the whole long cool night, Gardner Costello had not slept more than two hours, and even that hadn't been in one stretch. He had started out in the stateroom under the main cabin, figuring that if anyone came aboard he would hear them better than if he'd been in the bow stateroom. But lying there in the cramped bunk under the low ceiling, he'd felt like a rat in a trap, even with his police special under his pillow and the twenty-five-aught-six leaning against the ladder to the cabin. So he had got out a sleeping bag and took it along with a pillow and the thirty-eight up onto the command bridge. There was enough room under the control panel so he could put the pillow there, under cover, with the rest of him stretched out across the narrow floor. Naturally, there was nothing comfortable about it, especially considering how high up he was, where every slightest movement of the boat was magnified. But then that was one of the reasons he had chosen to be there, so he could feel as well as hear anyone trying to come aboard. And just as important, if anyone did come aboard, he would be in a position to surprise them, "to get the drop" on them, so to speak.

Ironically, it was that kind of phrase—that kind of thought—that made it so difficult to sleep. How incredible it all was! How stupid and bizarre and, yes, frightening! Why in God's name had they involved him in it?—they being the company, Queen, Kellogg—*whoever.* It was so goddamned unfair, so downright infuriating, that he was constantly choking back tears and zipping himself out of the sleeping bag so he could hang out over the side in the dark to urinate. He would have to cut back on the Heineken, he told himself. Either that or cut back on the terror.

Lying awake did have one advantage, however. He was finally able to think the whole thing through, especially this wild and stupid flight of his. More than ever, he realized that leaving by boat had been a total and disastrous mistake. Because the boat was so easily traceable, he knew it eventually would lead them to him as surely as if he were writing home with a return address. And it was a mistake one couldn't simply undo. He still couldn't bring himself to scuttle the damn thing, nor could he hope to sell it here in Mexico for anything like it was worth. No, his best shot, he decided, was to keep moving, to cruise down to Panama and go through the canal and come back up the east coast past Yucatan and on to Florida. There, in Tampa-St. Pete, he figured he ought to be able to find a buyer, even if only at wholesale. Then, free of the boat and heavy on cash, he could go to any large city and lose himself for however long was necessary.

To make such a trip, though, he would need another crew member or two—he could not go on forever sleeping as little as he had the past week. So after breakfast he planned to go ashore and start looking for some young latter-day California hippies who could be expected to leap at the chance for a free cruise to Florida. He still called them *hippies* only because he couldn't think of a serviceable modern word for what they really were: more like hippie descendants, wanderers still, but more clean-cut and practical than their forebears, though probably just as fond of drugs and indolence. You could find them by the hundreds in Big Sur and Santa Barbara and Venice, so he figured there had to be at least a few of them here in Mazatlan, and probably a lot more than a few. If nothing else, they could at least keep the wheel on a heading, give him time to catch a few winks now and then.

He had the money for such a trip and of course he had the motivation. (Survival was one hell of a motivation.) So he was not particularly dispirited at having spent another all but sleepless night. At least he had something to show for it. A plan. A way out. And he would take it.

At first light, he unzipped the sleeping bag again and cranked his aching body up onto his feet. To his left a long low breakwater divided the sea and sky. In front of him, Creston Island rose up out of the dark water like a mountaintop, mantled in sun instead of snow. At its summit, the lighthouse rose higher yet, and along its base were sport-fishing docks and other piers. Around him, in the harbor itself there were about a dozen other anchored boats, none of them very close. Feeling stiff and unrested, he holstered his thirty-eight and climbed down to the deck and went into the cabin. He used the toilet and washed and shaved, leaving on the same clothes he had worn yesterday and through the night. He touched inside his shirt pocket to make sure the letter was still there, the unfinished letter to his wife, which he was not even sure now that he would complete and send. Queen and his company cohorts were probably already monitoring her mail, not to mention maintaining a tap on her phone. He still liked the idea of naming them on paper, getting at least a posthumous revenge against the murdering bastards if they did happen to find him. But that of course could not take precedence over survival. Above all, he had to be careful. So for now he would just hold onto the letter, maybe send it from Tampa later, on his way out of the city.

He made coffee and then cooked up a breakfast of pancakes and sausages. But he had to go to the toilet again before he could sit down to eat, and then he went once more before finishing breakfast. It didn't alarm him because he was prone to diarrhea: it was just a matter of tension and poor diet, and he'd certainly had a sufficiency of both during the past week. His one consolation was that the toilet worked electrically, was not one of those horrible portable types that one had to keep emptying and cleaning. Still it was irritating, not being able to finish his pancakes when they were hot, and having to sit there in the lockerlike dimensions of the head, with the door closed—because in order to sit down one *had* to close it—all of which meant that he was unable to keep an eye out for anyone approaching the boat. At least he still had his gun with him, lying right there on the floor between his feet. And, oddly, it was just as he was thinking this, taking comfort in the fact that his gun was within reach, when he heard and felt something strike the stern of the *Mako*. Immediately the boat dipped slightly, out of rhythm with the waves, and his bowels gave way again. His mouth turned powdery and his hand shook violently as he quietly pushed the door bolt closed and picked up his gun. It crossed his mind that he was going to behave just like all those other pitiful victims, from Holocaust Jews to Seven-Eleven clerks, holding back and hoping for the best until it was too damned late to do anything but die.

There were two voices, both male, one high and shaky, the other calm, strong.

"Where is he? Jesus Christ, where is he?"

"All right, Costello—come on out!"

Costello heard the door to the bow stateroom being flung open; he heard heavy steps inches away from him, on the ladder down to the other stateroom. Whoever the man was, Costello could have shot him through the flimsy wall of the head, but then he too would have died within the next few seconds, shot by the other man. So he continued to sit there. And finally one of them knocked on the head door.

"Okay, Costello. Time to get off the throne."

The other laughed nervously. "Careful. He may have a gun."

And somehow Costello managed to speak. "Let me wipe myself, all right?"

"Definitely."

Again the other laughed.

When Costello finally unbolted the door and opened it, neither man was visible in the opening. Costello pushed his gun out with his foot, and then an arm swung into the opening and took him by the shirt and pulled him roughly out into the aisle. He found himself facing a square-faced, red-haired man of about thirty-five, lean and very strong. The man dragged him back into the salon and threw him down into one of the easy chairs there. The second man then hove into view behind the first, corpulent and wheezing, his chubby face laced with panic. Both men wore suits.

"You're a real cute ass, aren't you?" the redhead was saying. "Take money for a job and then send someone else to do it."

Costello's heart was sprinting and his throat felt as if it were about to combust. The only moisture in him had found his eyes. "I don't know what this is about. Honest. Jesus Christ, tell me."

The fat man kept looking out the windows. His terror seemed almost the equal of Costello's.

"Come on, hurry!" he cried to the redhead.

"When I'm fucking ready," the other said. "Tell me, cute one, you aware that the old man you hired got himself killed doing your job?"

Costello again insisted that he didn't know what any of this was about. "A girl who said she was Paul Queen's daughter came by the boat and begged me to do a job for her, and as a favor I said yes. But later I found I couldn't do it and so I hired someone else—that's all I did, for God's sake! I don't know anything else! Honest, I don't!"

222

The redhead brutally shoved his forty-five into Costello's face, splitting his lip and breaking off a tooth. And both Costello and the fat man whimpered.

But the redhead was enjoying himself. "Well, let me tell you a few things then, cocksucker. The old cop you hired, his kid is after you too—did you know that? No doubt for setting up the old man. So what do *we* do? Why, we let the fucker lead us straight to you, that's what. Which means now we can *interrogate* him and you both. Ain't that neat? We'll just *interrogate* you now and hang around until him and his cunt show up, and then we *interrogate* them too. What do you think of that, old man? Tell me, you ready to be *interrogated?*"

Costello opened his mouth to say once more that he knew nothing, but before he could emit a sound the redhead had hit him again, this time with a karate half-fist straight into the bridge of his nose. There was a momentary stab of pain, then a kind of starburst in darkness, a lovely arching of fiery fragments that drifted slowly down, going out one at a time until finally there was only the one left, orange-colored, like a flare at sea. Then it too disappeared.

As Crow had anticipated, Jennifer was uneasy with him when she finally awoke. Sounding brittle and embarrassed, she fled into her bathroom and softly called out for him to have breakfast sent up if he wanted any—all she required was coffee and orange juice, she said. Ravenous himself, Crow phoned room service and ordered scrambled eggs and bacon and toast as well as coffee and juice. He showered and shaved and dressed—and waited. And when Jennifer finally appeared in the doorway, she looked as fresh and sharp as ever, if a little sportier, in slacks and sweater, ready for the day's adventures. But when she spoke, he could still hear the change in her, the brittleness, as if she had contracted some odd neurological disease during the course of the night.

"Well, that was really some performance, wasn't it?" she said. "I don't know when I've drunk so much. I guess I really let myself go, didn't I?"

Crow couldn't help smiling. "No more than I did."

Looking rattled, she turned away from him and peered out at the ocean. "I didn't mean here. I meant down in the restaurant. I hope I didn't embarrass you."

"You didn't. Not down there. And not up here either."

"Yes—*here*." She shook her head in bewilderment. "I'm afraid there's no explaining that. The important thing, I guess, is just to pretend it never happened."

"Why?"

"Because it shouldn't have happened. I didn't want it to. And I'm sorry it did. Working together won't quite be the same now."

"No, I guess not."

She looked directly at him. "But it should be. What happened last night really didn't mean anything. You know that, don't you?"

"Sure."

"I was exhausted, and I'd had too much to drink. And—"

"Me too," he said, deadpan. "Otherwise it wouldn't have happened. No way."

"Well, let's just pretend it didn't, then. Let's just forget about it."

"Why not? It's not as if we don't have other matters to worry about."

She looked surprised, almost disappointed. "Exactly," she said.

"Maybe later, when all this is over—"

"Yes, we can talk about it then."

"Deal with it."

"Right."

Fortunately, the room service boy arrived with breakfast at that moment. But Jennifer, apparently already forgetting her order of only coffee and orange juice, sat down with Crow and helped him eat the toast and eggs and bacon. Swimming had left him so hungry that he almost felt like crying as he watched *his* food disappearing into her mouth. He tried not to think about it, though. And he tried not to think about what else she had taken into that same lovely mouth not too many hours before. But in neither case was he successful. All in all, it was not one of the more enjoyable breakfasts of his life.

When they reached the harbor road, Crow drove slowly past the buildings and docks of the various sport-fishing establishments.

There were signs advertising *Star Fleet* and *Fishing Safari* and *Flota Faro*. Though most of the boats already had gone out, there were still a number of tourists milling around, most of them dogged by Mexican kids hoping to make a few pesos running errands or acting as guides or maybe just begging, for all Crow knew.

One of the smaller docks advertised boats for rent, and it was there he parked the car. He suggested to Jennifer that she remain outside while he rented the boat, in case they ran into trouble later.

"That way, they'll be looking for a man alone," he said.

She asked him about the cost—didn't he want her to charge it? —and he told her no, that he had cash. Inside he gave his name as John Orville and he found the manager's English to be almost as bad as his own Spanish, which made for difficult communication. In time, though, they managed to agree on a boat and a price, and Crow paid the man in advance. Including a two-hundred-dollar deposit on the boat and life jackets, Crow unburdened himself of almost thirty thousand pesos in cash. The manager's boy then took Crow out to the dock and showed him how to operate the craft, though Crow already knew, since it was a simple eighteen-foot runabout with an inboard-outdrive setup and up-front controls.

Not until the boy started to throw off the lines did Crow finally reach up and give Jennifer a hand down into the boat. Till then the kid undoubtedly had thought her a spectator, a waver-goodbye. But the change did not seem to bother him and he himself waved as they sped off into the harbor.

Crow by then was feeling something quite rare in his life: the excitement of fear. He had known it hunting moose and working with cattle in British Columbia, and he certainly had felt it once on Puget Sound when a killer whale swam inquisitive circles around him and the dinghy he was rowing ashore from his charter boat. His fear now was not quite that acute, however, possibly because he really didn't expect any violence from Costello, still figured him as some sort of middleman in the affair. The phone call to his father, the postcard from here in Mazatlan, the tone of the memos—none of it suggested a sick or dangerous sort of man.

Still, there *were* four people dead—four that Crow knew about.

He wouldn't have minded having a gun with him, but he hadn't wanted to chance bringing one by plane and he had no idea how to go about getting one in Mexico, not without courting more trouble than he already had.

He looked at Jennifer and she gave him a plucky smile.

"See it yet?" he asked.

She shook her head.

They were making their way around the outer perimeter of the anchored boats, some of which were tied up to harbor buoys. There were more sailing yachts than power boats, so it didn't take them long to spot the *Mako,* a thirty-six foot Uniflite anchored off to the side, farther from shore than any of the other boats. Costello, he decided, had wanted his privacy.

Like the current, the wind was coming in from the west, so the boats had all swung around on their anchors and were facing back out to sea. And as Crow had told Jennifer at dinner the previous evening, that was the direction they would take, coming in by the *Mako's* bow, since he figured that Costello would most likely be out on the stern deck—the *cockpit,* as the purists called it—eating or fishing or just sitting there in the morning sun, trying to work the night's chill out of his body.

Crow throttled down and the boat slipped slowly through the water toward the yacht. They went past its anchor line and started around the side of it, coasting now, throttle all the way back. Quietly Crow reached out and up for the teak cockpit runner, to bring his boat to a stop—too late seeing the second dinghy—not the *Mako's,* which was still in place, hanging on the stern—but another, in the water, tied to the boat's swim platform. And then suddenly there was a forty-five automatic not a foot away, pointed right at Crow's forehead. Beyond it the pale blue eyes of the redheaded man had a look of triumph.

"Just like clockwork," he said. "Come on aboard, assholes."

In the cabin doorway behind him, the fat man stood gulping air and wiping at his sweaty face. For a few seconds Crow felt the blood draining out of his head and his legs going soft, but then he caught himself. Terror was no answer. It would only hasten what he feared. Shouting this in his mind, he tied the runabout to the *Mako* and climbed aboard, stepping first on the swim platform. Then he put his hand out to Jennifer and helped her aboard too. Despite her California tan, she looked ashen. At their feet, strewn across the deck, were blankets, pillows, sheets. The redhead was waving his gun at Crow and Jennifer.

"In the cabin," he said. *"Now."*

The fat man went ahead of them, moving backwards. His mouth was working soundlessly, as if he were trying to speak or smile, but couldn't manage either. His chubby hands darted about him, like a marionette's.

"This is all so unfortunate," he got out finally, looking from Crow to Jennifer and back. "So stupid. It's like a freeway accident. One car gets out of line, and then it's just one after another. There's no sense to it."

The redhead told him to shut up. "Jesus Christ, you sound like some old cunt," he said.

Crow could see all the way into the bow stateroom, but there was no sign of Costello. He wondered if the man was below, in the stateroom there, or already overboard, dead.

"What do you want with us?" he asked.

Jabbing with his forty-five, the redhead pushed Crow and Jennifer down into the dinette, making them sit across from each other over a plate of half-eaten pancakes and sausages.

"Answers," he said to Crow. "And the first wrong one, I'm gonna blow off one of her arms."

Jennifer buried her face in her hands. But she made no sound.

"Sure," Crow said. "Just ask."

The redhead laughed at him. *"Sure, just ask.* Like you ain't a bit scared, huh, asshole? Not even with a forty-five jammed in your ear?"

"So ask him!" the fat one cried. "Why drag it out?"

"You got a point, Dief. Okay, Mister Crow. First, we wanta know why you're such a fucking enigma—can you tell us that?"

"I don't know what you mean."

"What I mean, sweetheart, is we been dogging you for some time now, watching you playing footsie with the police. And we can't figure why. Your old man dives off a cliff—what made you think it wasn't an accident?"

227

"When I saw it in the newspaper, about the girls getting killed."

"What girls?"

"The ones in the photographs."

"Your old man showed you the pictures?"

Crow nodded. "He was sick. I helped him run down the names."

The redhead grinned. "So that's it! We been wondering about that."

"Okay then, let's go!" the fat one urged.

The redhead ignored him. "Be very careful on this one," he advised Crow. "You try to con me and I'll do just what I said. Now, what about the police—both in L.A. and Ventura? They working on your old man's case, or the Kellogg kid's?"

Crow shook his head. "Again, that's why we're here."

"Okay then—another biggie. Give me the photographer's name. Tell me what happened to him."

"I don't know anything about a photographer."

With his left hand, the redhead punched Crow just in front of his ear and Crow momentarily sagged against the window. Both Jennifer and the fat man cried out at the blow, but the redhead continued, unperturbed.

"Who does know his name? The police, would you say?"

Again Crow shook his head. "No, just you bastards, I would say."

The redhead laughed. "Still cocky, are you? Well, we'll see what we can do about that. But first we want to know about Costello. He gave your old man a job to do. Now think carefully—who gave Costello the job in the first place?"

"I don't know."

Again the man's fist slammed into the side of Crow's face.

"Wrong answer," he said. "Now think again—who could have given Costello that job?"

"I don't know," Crow said again, flinching this time.

"Me and Dief, do you think? How about the two of us?"

Crow took a deep, ragged breath, trying not to pass out. The pain in his jaw was building. "I don't think you understand," he said. "This woman and I are civilians. I lost a father. She lost a brother. And we're just looking for answers, that's all. All we've found out is that Costello gave my father the job. And that's why we came here —to ask him why."

The fat man edged around the redhead and backed toward the door. His hands were outstretched, imploring. "Come on, John, that's enough! We've got to get out of here! It's just like I told you —they don't know anything! And what difference does it make anyway? Just do it and let's get out of here!"

The redhead reluctantly agreed. "All right. You get the gas can and douse that shit on the deck while I take care of Ken and Barbie here. And remember to open the boat's gas cap, for Christ sake!" Switching the forty-five into his left hand, he picked up a loaded flare gun, which Crow had not seen until that moment. And as he brought it up, he completed the picture—the caricature—of himself as a two-gun desperado. With the flare gun, he motioned for Jennifer to get up.

"Costello's in the bedroom downstairs. You wanted to talk with him, right? Well, now's your chance."

As Jennifer fearfully sidled past him toward the ladder leading to the stateroom below, the redhead raised his foot and shoved her into the opening. And at that moment, while his foot was still lifted, the fat man must have stepped off the *Mako* into their small boat—for the yacht suddenly dipped, only slightly, but enough to pitch the redhead, standing on one foot, out over the same opening that Jennifer had just fallen into. Instinctively he reached out with his left hand, the one holding the forty-five, to brace himself against the bulkhead and push off, to regain his balance. But in that moment of vulnerability Crow struck, tackling the man from behind and driving him face-down into the aisle, the flare gun caught under him. And as he struggled to turn, heaving back against Crow with all his considerable strength, Crow began to punch him in the back of the neck, over and over, until the man suddenly screamed and a brilliant orange-white fire radiated up and around his shoulders and head, like a terrible halo. The flare's fire quickly concentrated into a stream enveloping his face and pouring forward into the bow stateroom, turning it into a magnesium inferno. And Crow shoved the man into it, like a log into a furnace, sliding him and the flare on down the aisle and through the opening.

Then Crow turned and pulled Jennifer back up the ladder, out of his way, so he could go down and get Costello. But she held him back, yelling that the man was already dead. He followed her out onto the stern deck then and through the scattered bedding, which still had not been soaked with gasoline. The fat man apparently had been in their skiff, getting the gas can, when Crow overpowered the redhead. And he immediately had taken off. Still only a few hundred feet away, he was sitting in the stern of the small boat, steering its tiny outboard motor as he looked back at Crow and Jennifer in bug-eyed terror. Ignoring him, they scrambled over the side and into their runabout. And while Jennifer pulled the line free, he started the boat and pushed the throttle forward gradually, trying not to flood the small engine. Within seconds, though, they were at full speed and heading for the harbor entrance—opposite from the direction the fat man had taken in the other small boat. Crow would have dearly loved to follow him to shore and intercept him, pound it out of his already puffy lips—whatever truth there was in the man. But that would have risked involving the Mexican police, with the likely outcome that all three of them would be tied in with the *Mako* and the bodies in it. As it was, Crow had no idea whether he and Jennifer could make it or not, get away from the burning boat without having been seen from shore or from another boat. At that very moment, he knew, binoculars might be trained on them, someone might be lifting a phone and dialing the police.

Jennifer was kneeling next to him on the seat, looking back at the *Mako.*

"God, it's really burning now," she said.

Crow turned to look back at it, and at that moment the *Mako's* gas tank blew, engulfing the boat in a roiling orange cloud that sent debris sailing in every direction. And when the smoke cleared, there was no boat anymore, just a smudgy blaze that sank slowly into the placid water of the harbor.

"The redhead was gonna blow it as they pulled away," he said. "With the flare gun."

By then, they had gone past the breakwater and Crow had veered right, heading up the other side of Creston Island. And for the first time Jennifer seemed to take notice of the fact that they were out in the ocean.

"What are we doing here?" she asked. "Where are we headed?"

"The hotel. And then home."

She lowered her head against his shoulder and held him tightly. "I'm for that," she said. "Oh boy, am I for that."

TWELVE

CROW had no idea whether the boat had enough gas to take them all the way to their hotel. The gauge read half-full when they left the harbor and it fell steadily after that, as they punched their way north through swells of two and three feet—moderate by oceanic standards—but a decided challenge for the small craft. To keep from riding parallel with the swells, Crow tacked like a sailor, angling in toward the shore for a time and then turning back out to sea.

When they finally came abreast of the hotel, he switched on the power-tilt, which slanted up the outdrive. Then he began the run for shore, trying to ride the light surf. There were a few swimmers out in the water and he honked the boat's horn to warn them out of the way, undoubtedly confirming their impression of him as a late-morning drunk, but someone to stay clear of nevertheless. Still riding the surf, he managed to get the boat into shallow water before he and Jennifer had to jump out and pull it the rest of the way up onto dry sand. And there Jennifer took over, with her easy command of the language, explaining to the lifeguard that Crow had fallen while in the boat and had hurt himself. The lifeguard glanced at

Crow's swollen cheek as Jennifer went on to explain that they were hotel guests and that they were going to contact the rental company and someone would come for the boat. The sunbathers and the early drinkers in the cabanas, like the guests at poolside and in the lobby, all gave the two of them a curious look as they hurried into the hotel and went upstairs to their rooms. There, Crow inspected the damage —his swollen cheek and the flash burns on his arms—and he judged that, though he undoubtedly could have used medical attention, he would survive without it. He changed his shirt and packed his few things, then phoned down to the desk and told the clerk to get their bill ready and to call a taxi for them. He got out some hotel stationery and wrote a terse note to Avis, telling them where the car was and that he and Miss Kellogg regretted not being able to return it properly. He scrawled *Avis* across an envelope, put the note and the car keys inside, and placed it on the dresser, next to a ten-dollar tip for the maid.

Jennifer by then was ready and they went down to the desk and checked out. Jennifer signed the bill and assured the clerk that everything had been just fine. They took the first of two waiting taxis and found its driver to be the comedian Bill Dana's long-lost character, José Jimenez. That was the name on the man's license card and he not only looked like Dana, but sounded like him as well. And under different circumstances—lighter ones—Crow might have chanced mentioning the Dana coincidence to him, probably for the ten-thousandth time during the man's career. But the circumstances were *not* different.

Crow and Jennifer were both agreed that they couldn't take a chance on a Mexicana flight, considering that they might have been seen leaving the *Mako,* a pair of gringos in obvious flight. If they'd been reported to the police, then it followed that couples answering their description might be detained and questioned before being permitted to board any scheduled flights to the United States. With this in mind, Crow had Jennifer tell the driver in Spanish that they wanted to charter a plane, and did the man know of any private charter pilots who didn't require advance notice, somebody who would be ready and able to take off at the drop of a charge plate, so to speak.

233

"Oh choor," José told her. "Choor, I know chust choor man."

The man turned out to be a broker, a Mexican who kept a current listing on freelance pilots who had brought in charters and were waiting around to pick up return parties. José, according to Jennifer, had made the man sound like a fairly shady operator. But when they met him he seemed open and businesslike. He put in a call to a pilot and within twenty minutes they were in the hands of "Doc" Stannard, a heavyset man in his fifties who smelled of whiskey and kept blinking his eyes. He made soft, little groaning sounds, and occasionally he would start to whistle or hum a tune, then abruptly abandon it, as if the sound had shocked him. So Crow was surprised when the man led them out onto the tarmac and showed them not a battered two-seater biplane but a new and handsome six-seater Beechcraft turboprop. He wanted forty-five hundred dollars for the trip, however, which gave even Jennifer a moment's pause—long enough for Crow to jump in and bargain the man down to thirty-two hundred, which was still an outlandish amount as far as Crow was concerned, but something he was prepared to live with.

"I'll lose money at that price," Doc Stannard said. "But not as much as flying home alone."

While he went in and settled up with the broker, Crow and Jennifer climbed aboard the silvery twin-engine craft, which on the inside looked to Crow more like a yacht than it did an airplane, with its plush leather seats and hardwood trim.

"I guess this will do," Crow said.

Jennifer had sat back, eyes closed, mouth set. "Can't he hurry? Can't he see we have to get out of here?"

Crow took hold of her hand. "Let's hope he doesn't," he told her.

Once they were airborne, Crow felt an enormous weight slip from him, because he had a very real fear of Mexican jails and justice, especially during the current economic and political travail that the country was experiencing. And while Jennifer undoubtedly shared his relief at being under way, he soon learned that there was little else she felt good about. It was only after they were at cruising altitude and well out over the Gulf of California that she began to let it all out of her. She trembled and wept and quietly raged at herself and at him, wiping at her tears as if they were scalding her.

"I've had it!" she said. "I've just had it! I don't want any part of this goddamn crusade anymore! Do you realize we came within an inch of getting killed? That it was just dumb luck we got out of there alive."

"I know that."

"And the redhead, that maniac—you have any idea how many more like him there are? Against *us*, I mean?"

"No idea at all," he admitted.

"In fact, we still don't even know who or what we're up against. It would be suicidal to go on."

"We found out we were right," he said.

"Oh sure. And what good will that do us? Would you want to go to the L.A. police and tell them what happened down here? Would you like to return here and explain to the local gendarmes about Costello and the redhead? I'm sure they'd all believe everything we told them."

Crow couldn't help smiling. "Yeah, I can just see Capitan José Jimenez smiling politely as we explained."

Jennifer looked at him in shock and anger. "You can joke about it? You think it's funny that we just about lost our lives?"

"Of course not."

"Then why act like it? I think it's time we faced reality. Richard and your father are dead, and it doesn't really matter how they died. Finding the truth won't bring them back. And anyway, we're not the ones to find it. We're not detectives or CIA agents. Why, you don't even carry a gun. We're alive right now because we were lucky. And I don't intend to go on betting my life that we'll stay lucky. And you shouldn't either."

Crow asked her if she would be going straight back to Santa Barbara after they landed, and she nodded. She also reached across the narrow aisle and took his hand.

"And please don't think this means I don't want to keep seeing you, because I do. But not this way. Not as fellow 'detectives.' But as—"

She didn't seem able to find the right word, so Crow tried to help her.

"Friends?"

She smiled wryly. "At least that."

Crow leaned across the aisle and kissed her, first on her forehead, then on her lips as she bent toward him. They were sitting in the second pair of seats, facing the first pair, which were located on either side of the cockpit door. At that distance, and with the sound of the engines, Crow was reasonably sure that the pilot had not been able to overhear their conversation. Nevertheless, to check it out, he went up to the cockpit and asked Stannard if he could sit in the co-pilot's seat for a while.

"Long as you don't try to fly her," Stannard said.

Crow found the seat more than comfortable, much like the pilot's seat in a trawler, a place seemingly designed expressly for him.

"It's a beautiful plane," he said.

Stannard nodded. "A King Air. Actually it's my company's plane. I got this little plumbing supply outfit in Burbank and bought the thing because we sell pretty much all over the Southwest. Just for the hell of it, I learned to fly it. And now I like to fly so damn much I squeezed out my pilot and spend more time up here than behind a desk. To make the thing pay, I do a little charter work. Which is why I happened to be in Mazatlan. Took two fellas down there last night." Stannard wagged his head at the memory. "Boy, were they in an all-fired hurry."

It crossed Crow's mind that the two men could have been *his* two, but he considered it so remote a possibility that he almost said nothing. "A fat guy and a redhead?" he asked, finally.

Stannard looked over at him. "How'd you know that?"

"Just a wild guess. We met them in Mazatlan. In fact, they're the ones who told us about chartering a plane. Gave us the idea."

"Must've had important business down there. Every five minutes the fat one wanted to know our E.T.A."

Crow casually asked Stannard if he happened to remember their names, and the pilot gave him another look, this one newly appraising, ironic.

"Yep—Smith and Jones. Paid in cash. And just what is all this? Drug investigation or something like that?"

"Something like that," Crow said.

236

Earlier Stannard had showed him the liquor cabinet and told him that he and Jennifer were welcome to "partake" if they wanted to. So Crow now turned in his seat and called back to Jennifer without raising his voice, asking what she'd like. But she was unable to hear him. Satisfied, he got up and went back to her, stopping on the way to make two vodka tonics.

"It's great up there," he said, giving Jennifer her drink. "When I grow up, I want to be a jet pilot."

"I gather he can't hear us," she said.

Crow shook his head. "Wouldn't matter if he could, though. He seems straight enough. You know who his last passengers were?"

"Who?"

"Fatso and Red."

Jennifer seemed to sag into her seat. "You're kidding."

"No, I'm not."

"Did he get their names?"

"Smith and Jones."

"It's just as well. I don't even want to know who they were."

"One thing we did find out about them, though—they obviously weren't working for your uncle. Not unless you two are a lot less friendly than you thought."

She gave him a withering look, but said nothing. Crow, thinking out loud more than anything else, said that he still wondered why the redhead had asked him who he thought had given the job to Costello.

"Chances are *he* gave it to him. So why ask? Especially considering that he planned on killing us anyway. It doesn't make sense."

Still Jennifer said nothing. But Crow was not to be discouraged. His head was so filled with speculations and questions that he had a real need to get them out, to verbalize them. Answers could come later, if ever.

In their small boat, racing back to their hotel, he had asked Jennifer about Costello, how Red and Fatso had killed him, and she'd said that he had been shot. Now he asked her *where* the man had been shot.

"In the head. I barely looked. He was such a mess."

"Was he in the bunk?"

237

She looked at Crow in exasperation. "Do we *have* to go over all that again now? Is it *so* important?"

"If I'm to go on alone, yes. I have to know everything you know."

"Yes, he was in the bunk. "He—" And suddenly she had a look of rueful astonishment. "My God, I almost forgot about this." She took a folded sheet of paper out of her pocket and handed it to Crow. "This was sticking out of his shirt pocket. Everything was happening so fast I forgot about it. What does it say?"

Crow had already unfolded it and was reading, avidly:

Dearest Betty,

There's no way I can satisfactorily explain to you why I'm mailing this note from Mazatlan. Let me just say that this has not been a pleasure cruise. I don't know what is going on except that people I knew and worked with were getting killed. So I fled.

All I can figure is that the danger to me comes from some renegade element in the company. If anything happens to me, please contact headquarters at Langley and tell them that Paul Queen, in Colorado Springs, was behind it. Queen's daughter Barbara was my contact, the one who unwittingly got me into the whole mess.

And that was that. The letter was undated, unsigned, and probably unfinished. After hurriedly reading through it, Crow read it aloud to Jennifer, who for some reason didn't seem either as bewildered by it, or as excited, as Crow was.

"Paul Queen," she said. "Where have I heard that name?"

"Someone your uncle knows?" Crow suggested.

The idea seemed to upset her. "Why always bring his name into this thing? He's got nothing to do with it."

Crow shrugged. "The CIA. Those initials just keep popping up."

Jennifer shook her head and laughed, not very happily. "Crow, I don't think you understand about the 'company,' as they call it. If someone in your family happens to be in it, you might know that. But that's all you'd know. They don't talk shop around the house."

"Meaning?"

238

"Meaning I wouldn't have ever heard about a Paul Queen from my uncle."

"My mistake," Crow said. "I guess I just got the wrong idea. You know—when you first heard Costello's name."

Jennifer evidently had forgotten about that, for she looked flustered now. "Well, I was wrong then," she said. "I was reaching."

"It doesn't matter. The important thing is we've got this letter." He was folding it and putting it into his shirt pocket. "We've got a name now. And a place. We don't have to just limp home and try to forget about it all. Pretend it never happened."

"*You* don't," she said.

"That's right—I keep forgetting. I'm alone now."

She reached across the aisle and took his hand again. "No, you're not alone. You just lost your 'street partner,' that's all. Anything else —well, you just ask."

Her smile in the sunlit cabin was full and flawless, yet it failed to annul the fear in her eyes. Crow raised her hand to his lips, and then the two of them settled back into their seats. Up front, Doc Stannard was contentedly smoking a cigarette as he surveyed the ranks of instruments in front of him.

Turning his head, Crow looked down through the window next to him at the sere, sun-withered barrens far below, and it made him think of home and how much better it would have been to look down and see lakes and forests, the everlasting *ever green* of the Northwest. Someday soon, he promised himself. When all this was over.

Crow had wondered how it would be, the parting with Jennifer. But when the time came, as she pulled up in front of his father's house in the Mercedes, Reno unintentionally saw to it that the parting could be only perfunctory. Standing out in the front yard, the girl was overseeing the loading of some furniture—Mrs. Elderberry's, as it turned out—into a small van. Even though she barely glanced his way, Crow for some stupid reason felt inhibited by her presence—as was Jennifer, it seemed. And all the two of them managed was an almost formal peck on the lips, not unlike a pair of communist diplomats greeting each other. Nor did Reno come over to welcome him as Crow got out of the car and Jennifer drove off. Instead, she just stood there watching him, not missing a thing.

"Boy, look at you," she said. "What the hell happened?"

"A burro stepped on me."

"On your *face?*"

"Where else?"

Reno had turned and was walking ahead of him, toward the house. "Come on. You don't want to just stand there and let the whole world see what you look like, do you?"

Crow asked her what was going on.

"Mrs. E. found another place a couple of blocks from here. Some old lady who needs caring for, same as her mother. They can live there rent-free."

It was good news and normally Crow would have said as much. But he had just run into something like the "wall" of the long-distance runner. Too much had happened to him over too short a period for him to deal with and the result was a sudden and debilitating exhaustion, a numbness of mind and spirit and body. All he wanted to do was drag himself back to his room and fall into bed and never get up. But somehow he managed to deal with Reno and her sullen hostility as well as with Mrs. Elderberry and her problems. He gave the woman two hundred dollars to help cover her moving expenses, and with Reno sitting in the back of his pickup truck, he drove Mrs. E. and her mother over to their new place. Then he bought two six-packs of beer on the way home and sat down with Reno at the kitchen table and told her in detail what had happened in Mazatlan. He let her read Costello's note to his wife. And when she was finished, she asked him what was wrong, why he was so "wiped out."

"It's nothing," he told her. "I'm just trying to figure out how I can sleep and drink beer at the same time."

The girl didn't seem at all frightened by his tale of what had happened on Costello's boat, and when he told her that he would be going on alone to Colorado Springs, she even managed a smile.

"You mean Jennifer isn't going?"

"Nor anyone else, except me."

"Well, what do you know? The princess turned chicken, did she?"

Crow gave her a weary look. "You weren't there. You don't know."

"Going back to Santa Barbara and play tennis, huh?"

Crow took a drink of beer. "Someone once said, Reno, that getting shot at wonderfully concentrates the mind."

"Churchill," she said.

"Sometimes you amaze me, you know that?"

"Why? You think I'm a total zero, is that it?"

"Not at all. It's just that I remember my own high school teachers, and that was not the sort of thing they imparted to us."

"Us either. I probably picked it up on TV."

"Probably."

"Still, I ain't the dumbo you think, Crow. Our school shrink said my I.Q. was one-forty and that I should've been making straight A's. What do you think of that?"

"I'm impressed." He could see that she didn't know whether to believe him or not.

"Yeah, well, I bet the princess runs about one-oh-one."

"She speaks Spanish like a native."

"So does everyone else in L.A." Making a face, Reno finished her beer and crumpled the can. "The fact remains she bugged out and now you're gonna try to go it alone."

"I can manage," he said.

"You wouldn't have to go it alone, you know." She was sitting directly across the small table from him, trying to get him to meet her solemn, fearless gaze.

"It's out of the question," he told her.

"Why?"

"You looking to have your mind 'wonderfully concentrated,' are you?"

"I'll just stay at the motel there. You'll need me to identify your body. And if you're worried about anything else—don't be. I'm not interested in you that way anymore. And besides, I feel my period coming on."

Crow could not help grinning. "What a sales pitch," he said. "How can I resist?"

241

"Another thing. With Mrs. E. gone, what do you expect me to do—stay here alone? No way. I'll probably just head for the Strip or Venice."

"That's blackmail, Reno."

"Take me along, and I'll do just what you say. I promise. You really need someone—"

"To identify the body. Yeah, I know."

The level brown eyes still had not blinked. "Well, how about it, Crow?"

What could he do finally but shrug? "Yeah—why not?"

He had barely got it out before she was around the table and onto his lap, hugging him and then jumping up, apologizing.

"Sorry, I forgot. No more of that, I promise. But Jesus, Crow—*Jesus!*" She spun around in her sudden joy, clamped her hands to the sides of her head. "Hey, can we go by air? Can we fly?"

The thought of bringing her back down to earth held no appeal for him. "Sure," he said. "It's the only way to go."

In the mail that afternoon there was a letter from his father's insurance company, saying that it had his beneficiary check ready for him and would he please come into the office so they could "finalize" the policy. He also got a phone call from the bank executor, who told him that his sister had phoned twice from Portland and wanted to get the house on the market immediately. She wanted "no more foot-dragging," the executor reported. Crow said that he would be happy to sign the papers as soon as he could, but that he had to fly to Colorado in the morning and would be away for a couple of days. Anyway, he said, he couldn't see what the great hurry was, considering that the Los Angeles real estate market was not exactly bullish.

He tried unsuccessfully to find Barbara Queen's number in the local directories. He called Information then and got a Glendale number that he immediately dialed. But it rang and rang, and he was just about to hang up when a woman answered and generously volunteered the information that Barbara Queen "just a day ago" had returned to her family's home in Colorado Springs. Crow then called Information in Colorado and got Paul Queen's number, which meant that he was in the phone book and would therefore be no trouble to locate.

After that, Crow made reservations on a morning United flight to Colorado. He also let Reno drive the Datsun out for food, and was not totally surprised when she brought home enough pizza and salad for six people. He had her pack what clothes she had and he himself packed for about a week's stay, using a suitcase large enough to accommodate not only his clothes but an old portable typewriter and case his father had owned—and inside of which he secreted the old man's thirty-eight caliber Police Special, with an ankle holster and two boxes of shells, figuring that there was enough steel in the old typewriter to hide the gun from even the prying eye of the airport's X-ray machines.

With all that out of the way, he went back to his beer, carrying two cans with him into the bathroom as he prepared to take a long, hot bath. He inspected his still swollen and discolored cheek and the burns on his arms and concluded that he could still get by without any medical attention. He regretted not having been able to put icepacks on his face right after the incident, for that at least would have held down the swelling. On the other hand, he had to admit that he looked a touch sinister as he was, and it occurred to him that this just might come in handy when he confronted Paul Queen and "company" in Colorado Springs.

Other than that random fancy, he spent very little time speculating on Queen and the CIA: just who the man was and how he figured—along with that most secret and privileged of government agencies—in his father's death. In *all* the deaths. Crow didn't speculate because he wouldn't have known where to begin. Even after Mazatlan, he still figured he knew almost nothing. Which of course was the reason he was going on to Colorado Springs—in order to learn, in order to *know*. And then too there was that irreducible measure of rage he still felt at the killing of his father. In Mexico, he'd told Jennifer that he and the old man had never been very close, which was true. But it was also true that they were flesh and blood, that in their fumbling and embarrassed way, they had loved each other. So Crow did not lack for reasons to go on to Colorado, nor did he lack the will. If he was short of anything, it was expertise: how

243

to go about doing what he had to do without getting himself or Reno killed. This time, he knew, he could not just bumble into the enemy camp and hope for the best. He had to have a strategy: a reasoned plan of attack.

At the moment, though, he needed a good night's sleep more than anything else. And to that end he gave Reno a kiss on the cheek and slumped off to bed in his father's office at about nine-thirty. He had no idea what time the girl turned in or even if she came into his room to check on him later, to see if he actually was *that* tired, because he fell asleep almost the second his head hit the pillow. His beer-distended bladder woke him at about three and, after relieving himself, he did look in on her—to see if she was asleep, he told himself. Yet when that was how he found her—deeply, beautifully, asleep—he felt an odd touch of disappointment. And he wondered about this as he padded back to his room. Had he reached the point where he felt ill-used by life if he didn't have one of them or the other—Reno or Jennifer—each and every night? It was odd how quickly one adjusted to plenitude.

In any case, he and Reno were dressed and fed and ready to leave for the airport by eight in the morning. And it was then that Jennifer called from Santa Barbara with the news that she would be going to Colorado Springs after all, but on a later flight.

"That's great news," Crow told her. "What changed your mind?"

"I'll tell you when I get there," she said. "And I'll make the hotel reservation, all right? The Broadmoor's nice."

Crow told her that Reno was going with him and Jennifer said that was fine, as long as he didn't think the girl would be in any danger.

"None of us will be," he said. "We'll play it careful this time."

"By all means. But aren't you in a hurry right now?"

"As a matter of fact, yes," he laughed. "A big hurry. We'll talk tonight."

Reno was waiting for him on the porch, sitting back against the pediment studying her exhaled cigarette. Suitcase in hand, he closed and locked the door.

"That was Jennifer," he said. "She's meeting us there."

"Yeah, I heard."

Reno picked up her bag and followed him toward the truck.

"You're taking it like a trooper," he said.

She shrugged. "Why not? Maybe this time she won't be so lucky."

Crow gave her a look that unfortunately only made the girl laugh.

"Hell, I didn't mean it, Crow," she said. "Maybe if they just mussed up her hair a little."

Against all his better instincts, Crow found himself laughing too.

The only time Reno showed any fear during the flight was at takeoff, when she squeezed his hand so hard, so long, that it began to turn white. After that, about all he saw of her was the back of her head as she stared out the window at Malibu and then the mountains and the Mojave. But he didn't mind, since the plane trip seemed to have brought her out of the sullen funk she'd been in since his return from Mexico.

"Man, how little it all is!" she exhulted. "How neat! This must be the way God sees us. No wonder he doesn't do anything."

Crow had had to take the No Smoking section in order to get her a window seat, but the deprivation didn't seem to bother her, such was her fascination with the ground thirty thousand feet below. Once she asked him what his last words would be if the wing fell off, and his answer—"Ma-ma!"—obviously didn't lift him in her eyes.

"Not me," she said. "I'd just way Wow! all the way down."

"Well, you're a tough guy."

"And what are you?"

"Not so tough."

"Who says?"

"A middle-aged, not-so-tough guy."

For his trouble, he got a knuckle in the ribs. "Don't try to con me. Guys like that don't have lumpy faces. And they don't travel with girls like me."

"You've got a point there."

"You bet I do."

Crow settled back then and tried to think about other things, such as whether or not he would find both Paul Queen and his daughter

Barbara in Colorado Springs. That, he figured, would simplify matters a good deal. If the girl had been an unwitting contact, as Costello's letter stated, it followed that she was not one of them—whoever *they* were—yet might be in a position to know about them. The only question was, could she be made to talk? If not to the police, then to Crow or Jennifer? There was no way of knowing, of course. Not yet anyway.

When lunch was served, over Utah, Reno was not amused.

"Hey, Crow," she whispered. "What is this stuff anyway? Veal *what?* Why can't they just give us a hamburger or a chilidog?"

"Beats me."

"It tastes like an eraser."

Crow laughed. "That's a taste I forgot."

Eraser or not, Reno made short work of the food and was back at the window in time for the Grand Canyon, whose appearance the pilot had just announced on the intercom. Once again she took a firm grip on Crow's hand.

"Oh wow, look at that, Crow! What a view!"

All he could see was her arm and her lissome back, her rust-colored hair curling thickly down over her trusty purple velvet blouse.

"Sure is," he said. "It's just great."

Five years before, Crow and two male friends had forsaken the better fishing and better camping of their own Cascades for a try at the Colorado Rockies. After six days of waiting in line at campsites and tangling their fishing lines with those of other tourists, they made their way down to Colorado Springs to see the sights and sample the nightlife. And Crow had seen the Broadmoor on that occasion, in fact had joined his friends in trying to pick up girls in the ornate splendor of one of its bars. So he knew it for what it was: a huge and luxurious resort hotel resembling a high Renaissance castle and its surrounding village, definitely not the sort of place one would choose as a convenient base of operations for the kind of mission Crow and Jennifer were on. He would have preferred a simple motel where he could have parked the car right at the door to his room. Yet when Jennifer had mentioned the Broadmoor on the telephone, saying that she would make the reservations for them, the name had sailed right past his head. He would ask at the car rental desk, he thought at the time, forgetting that he already knew where and what the Broadmoor was.

So as they approached it on Lake Avenue, Reno had but one more reason to gape. Her first flight in an airplane, the landings in Denver and the Springs, the sight of snowcapped Pike's Peak and the front range, and now this Italianate castle looming in front of them—it all had been more than enough to widen even her cynical young eyes.

"J. Christ, Crow," she said, "you sure they'll let us in?"

"Of course they will. We rich people always dress casually."

But as he pulled under the massive portico and got out of the car, he didn't like the way the liveried doorman looked at the two of them—as if Reno were a hooker and Crow her john, a lowlife trying to bring disrepute on so fine an establishment. The bellmen, swarming over their two bags, seemed to have no such prejudice, however, probably because they knew lowlifes to be better tippers.

Going into the huge and beautiful lobby, Reno gave Crow a light elbow in the ribs.

"What're we doing here?" she asked.

"Jennifer," he explained. "I don't think she's ever heard of Holiday Inn."

"Well, I never stayed in one of *them* either," the girl said.

At the moment, the male desk clerk was taking in her velvet blouse, her jeans, her age, all with mounting dismay. She seemed to fill him with the most poignant of pains. But when Crow mentioned his name, the man recovered.

"Ah, yes," he said. "Miss Kellogg called in your reservation. If you'll just sign here please."

Crow registered Reno as Renata Crow (sister), which brought an almost audible sigh of relief from the desk clerk. He gave the bellman the key and they were off—to a sixth-floor two-bedroom suite with a fine view of Cheyenne Mountain, in the bowels of which the North American Air Defense Command maintained its vigilance against a Russian air strike. In the corner of the plushly furnished sitting room, there was a made-up cot, which drew a knowing glance from Reno.

"Guess who sleeps there," she said, as the bellman exited.

247

"You'll manage," Crow told her.

"Well, at least I can keep track of everybody. Like who's sleeping where."

"The girl with the one-track mind."

Reno made a dive onto the sofa, then rolled off it onto the floor. "Boy, what a day," she said. "Renata Crow, world traveler. What's next?"

"We bum around. And then we buy you some clothes."

"Really?"

"Yes—really."

"Heaven," she said. "I've died and gone to heaven."

Colorado Springs was not an easy place to judge. On the one hand, there was the glorious sunshine and sparkling mountain air; on the other, one's lips quickly began to peel and there did not seem to be enough water in all the world to drink. There was Pike's Peak and the whole awesome front range to delight the eye; but there were also the low treeless hills east of the city, a vast rolling grid of chockablock housing and sprawling shopping centers.

But then it was not important to Crow, what the town was really like. At the moment he and Reno were in his rented Ford Mustang and he had an address—from the phone book—as well as a map purchased at a service station. And he wasn't overly surprised to discover that his quarry lived in an area about as far from the Broadmoor as one could get without leaving the county—not just on the opposite side of the sprawling city but six miles into the country as well, in a high pine-covered exurb called Black Forest, a place of five- and ten-acre "ranches," some of them old run-down house-trailer-type places strewn with sheds and junked cars, while others were genuine estates: large new rustic homes with horse barns and paddocks and fancy board fencing. And almost every one of them had a magnificent view down out of the trees and across the barrens to the city below and the front range running south to infinity, dotted with exquisite little landmarks such as the Air Force Academy and even the Broadmoor, a good twenty miles distant.

There was a blacktop running through the area and the roads radiating from it were almost all gravel lanes twisting back through

248

the pines, whose shade evidently was responsible for the snow that still covered the ground in places. When Crow found the road he was looking for—Tashoda Lane—he followed it back for about a half mile, passing only three other places before he came to a dead end —and the number he wanted, 13086, which had been carved into the rustic wooden gate. The driveway leading back from the gate curved upwards so steeply that he couldn't see what was at its end, on the top of the hill.

"Rotten luck," he said, stopping the car. "All I wanted today was a look. Just to be sure it's there."

"Well, let's drive on up and see."

"Not on your life. No more blundering into trouble if we can help it." He backed the car around and started down the road toward the blacktop. "I'll go up tomorrow, alone. With you and Jennifer on the outside, for insurance." This was about all he'd been able to come up with in the way of strategy.

"What are you gonna say to them?" Reno asked. " 'Hey, did you people kill my old man?' "

Crow grinned and shook his head. The girl did have an unnerving talent for going straight to the heart of a problem, if with a certain want of tact.

"I don't know what I'll say," he told her. "I'll just have to wing it."

"Alone, huh?"

"That's right."

"I don't like it," she said.

"Well, them's the breaks."

On the way back to the Broadmoor, Crow stopped at a shopping center and bought Reno a pair of designer jeans, some checked tailored shirts that she didn't like at all but which looked smashing on her, and finally a tan suede jacket that made her stare at him as if he'd lost his senses.

"This costs a hundred and fifty bucks," she whispered.

"So what? It looks great on you."

For the briefest moment, her eyes filmed and she turned away from him and went over to a distant mirror to check herself out. When she came back, all she could manage was a shrug, as if the jacket was now a matter of total indifference to her.

"Why not wear the new stuff?" he said. "Carry the old in a bag."

"Could I?"

"Of course."

While he settled up with the clerk, Reno peeled off the tags and went back to the mirrors for another session. And Crow wondered if she saw herself as he did: in many ways more than ever the teenage Vogue model, with her long, leggy body and glorious hair and pert face—yet finally not really like them at all, because of her eyes, the vulnerability in them, the old pains and new, desperate hopes. And it was precisely that, the look in her eyes, that touched Crow the most and made him glow too as he watched her in front of the mirrors.

In the car she hugged him and kissed his sore cheek and said that he was "the best" and that she would do just what he said from that moment on. He smiled and almost told her that it was nothing, that buying the clothes had given him as much pleasure as it had her. But then he caught himself in time, and shrugged.

"I was just trying to make you a little more presentable," he said, and immediately hated himself for saying it. But he had to bring her down, didn't he? Had to bring them *both* down—to reality. And reality wasn't him and a sixteen-year-old girl. It was a lesson she was just going to have to learn.

And for the rest of that evening, Reno acted as if she had indeed learned it. They stopped to eat at a Denny's and throughout the meal she barely glanced at him. She went at her burger and fries and milkshake without enthusiasm and any attempt he made at conversation—whether about the "case" or the dry air or the Broadmoor—quickly died. He told her that she looked great in her new clothes, but even that got him nowhere.

"Well, at least I'll be more *presentable* for Jennifer," she said.

When Jennifer arrived, at slightly after nine o'clock that night, Crow was relieved to see that she was once again the cool and self-assured woman he had known before the incident in Mazatlan. The fearfulness and agitation she had exhibited on the flight back to Los Angeles were not in evidence now as she swept into the suite in front of a bellman limping under the weight of four pieces of matched leather luggage. She naturally was wearing an outfit he had not seen before, but Crow barely noticed it in his pleasure at seeing her smile again. She kissed him on the cheek—his good one—and told Reno how nice it was to see her again.

"Especially looking so stylish," she added. "What a beautiful shirt."

"Crow bought me some new stuff," Reno told her. "To make me more *presentable.*"

Jennifer did not miss the edge in the girl's tone. She smiled at her. "Well, we can all use a few new things now and then."

"So I've noticed."

Jennifer let the missile slip right past her. "Well, I've got to freshen up," she said, heading for one of the two bathrooms.

Crow told her that he was going to call down for drinks, and was there anything she wanted.

"Just something cool," she said, as the door closed behind her.

Crow turned to Reno. "What about you? You want a Coke or something?"

"How about some warm milk?"

"Coke, it is."

For the next ten minutes or so Crow and Reno sat watching the president's ex-wife on television as she cut a wide swath through the wine country of Northern California. Then, just as room service arrived, Jennifer emerged from the bathroom wearing pajamas and a long black velvet robe. Crow tipped the boy and started mixing the drinks. Reno went over and got her Coke, then dropped sullenly back onto the sofa. When Crow gave Jennifer her vodka tonic, she smiled and asked if it might not be a good idea to turn off the TV and talk.

"I'd like to hear what plans you've made," she went on. "We should discuss them."

"We should watch TV," Reno said. "That's what we should do."

"Aren't you worried about tomorrow?" Jennifer asked. "Don't you want things to go off as well as possible?"

The girl gave her a bored glance. "It's this show I'm worried about. I don't want *it* to go off."

"You can go in there and close the door," Crow said, indicating the smaller of the two bedrooms. "It's got a TV, and anyway I've decided I'm the one who'll sleep out here on the couch, not you."

"That should be convenient." But finally Reno did go over and turn off the television. Then she went on into the bedroom, without a glance at either Crow or Jennifer.

Jennifer said goodnight to her, but the girl did not respond. The door went shut and the two adults were left standing there, looking at each other.

"She'll be all right," Crow said. "She's just mad at me for what I said about her new clothes."

"Making her presentable?"

That's what I said, all right."

"Well, it *was* a little tactless."

Sitting down again, Crow sighed. "At the time, it seemed necessary. She'd misinterpreted it, me buying her clothes."

"I can imagine."

"She was happy about it," Crow said. "And I couldn't let her have that, could I?"

Jennifer's smile was sympathetic. "Of course not." She took a drink of her vodka tonic. "You haven't asked why I'm here. What changed my mind."

"I was about to."

"Well, the answer is—I don't know. Or at least it's not easy to explain. I just didn't seem able to come down. One moment we're in Mazatlan, almost getting killed by Richard's killers. And the next thing I know, I'm home—and everything is just as it always was. For Uncle Henry and the Kims, it's strictly business as usual. Everything back to normal. No one even mentioned Richard. It was as if he'd never lived."

"Even if we find the truth," Crow said, "that might not change anything at home. For your uncle and the Kims anyway."

"You're probably right. But then that was only part of my reason. The main thing, I guess, was you. I just didn't like the thought of you coming here alone and—well, God knows what could happen."

Crow asked how her uncle had taken it, her leaving again, and she said that she hadn't told him about being in Mazatlan or what had happened there, so he had come to the conclusion that her and Crow's "investigation" had degenerated into an affair.

"And I didn't try to disabuse him of the notion," she said. "Even now I guess he figures I just ran off with you somewhere, for the weekend."

Crow smiled. "An intriguing idea. Be a shame to prove him wrong."

Jennifer smiled too, though not without a touch of irony. "But that's not why I called. And that's not why I'm here."

"I know that."

"Good."

Crow felt as if he'd stepped out of a cool dark bar into hot sunshine. It took a few moments to adjust. "The important thing is you *did* call," he said. "Because the plan really calls for a grown-up on the outside—I would've worried, having Reno do it alone."

"Plan?" Jennifer asked.

"Yes—I think I know how we should go about it. You and Reno will be on the outside—in town somewhere—when I go in. And you'll phone Queen's place while I'm there, so they'll *know* someone is on the outside, able to contact the police, able to nail them in case they try anything."

Jennifer was nodding. "Yes, that sounds fine. A lot better than just going straight at them. But tomorrow? Are you sure we should move that soon? Shouldn't we fine-tune the plan? Shouldn't we wait?"

Crow told her that there was no way of knowing who would be at Queen's house, and when. "We could wait around for days and have every step mapped out," he said. "And when we go to make our move—no one's there. We simply don't have enough facts to go on. Enough intelligence. So I figure we might as well just take a deep breath tomorrow and jump in."

Jennifer looked uneasy. "And sink or swim."

Crow shrugged. "Well, as I said, you and Reno will be on the outside, as backup. And anyway, I'm not going to take on Paul Queen. The object is his daughter, to somehow separate her from him, try to get the truth out of her."

Jennifer was sitting curled up on the sofa, glass in hand, one side of her in shadow and the other limned by the light from a lamp on the Empire end table. Her yellow hair shimmered against the burgundy wallpaper behind her, and she was looking at him in a way that made him wonder if this might not be his night too, just like the one in Mazatlan. It would be risky, he knew, with Reno in the other room. She might come in on them or hear them, and then suddenly he decided that that might not be such a bad development after all. Somewhere, sometime, the girl was going to have to learn that they were of different generations, and that whatever physical attraction there might have been between them, it was not enough to overcome all the negative factors, such as age and education and experience. And he had the feeling that the moment Reno saw this, she would see him too, just as he was—warts and all—and maybe have herself a good sixteen-year-old laugh.

In any case, he thought it worth a try. On the eve of battle, a man had it coming, didn't he, all the good things he could get? So, after making a drink for himself, he sat down next to Jennifer on the sofa. He sipped at his vodka for a short time, before placing the glass on the coffee table in front of them. Then he put his arm behind her, on the sofa. He kissed her hair and her forehead, her eyes. And she leaned toward him, smiling slightly, turning her mouth up to his as his hand moved under her robe. When their lips parted, her smile came again, but wry now, commiserating.

"Would you believe I have a headache?" she asked.

THIRTEEN

THE condemned man did not eat a hearty breakfast, Crow reflected, as he choked down a bear-claw with his black coffee. Nor did Jennifer do any better, eating only half of her grapefruit and not even touching her toast as they breakfasted in the brilliant morning light pouring through the windows of a coffee shop located about a mile from the Broadmoor. Jennifer naturally had wanted to breakfast at the hotel on linen and bone china, but Crow had suggested that they didn't have an hour to kill waiting for eggs Benedict and hot croissants to be properly served and savored. Of the three of them, only Reno had an appetite, and even she seemed less interested in her eggs and bacon than she was in the noisy urban cowboy crowd scattered among the plastic booths and at the counter. In his mind, Crow once again went over the telephone conversation he'd had earlier up in their room.

"Hello. I'l like to speak with Barbara Queen, please."

"This is she."

He'd had a momentary impulse to hang up then, having already found out what he wanted most to know—that she was actually there, in the Black Forest house. But there was also the problem of getting in to see her when he finally drove up that steep hill through the pines. And suddenly he heard himself taking an approach he'd already considered—and rejected.

"My name is Richard Moore, Miss Queen. I'm the nephew of a Betty Costello in Ojai, California. And it seems that her husband Gardner Costello disappeared a week or so ago and the only contact she's had from him since then was a postcard from Mexico saying he was on some sort of job for you."

"Really?" The woman's voice was bland.

Crow tried to sound embarrassed, even amused. "I know it's probably just one of these little domestic things—a middle-aged guy takes a vacation, and, well, you know. But I did promise my aunt that I'd try to see you. I was coming to Colorado anyway, on business."

"What business is that?" Barbara Queen asked.

"Real estate."

"I see. And we can't handle the matter by phone?"

"I'd rather not, if you don't mind. I'll only take a few minutes of your time."

"You know where I live?"

"I have the address."

"We're out in Black Forest."

"I'll find it. Ten-thirty all right?"

"That'll be fine."

After he'd hung up, Jennifer and even Reno went at him, saying that he shouldn't have mentioned Costello, that he'd put the enemy on guard now.

"An impulse," he told them. "It seemed right at the time, and I think it still does. If she runs, we'll know she was a part of it too, not just an unwitting contact. And if she does see me—well, then maybe I won't be all alone up there. Maybe I'll have an ally."

Mistake or not, he was glad now for what he'd done, finally taking the bull by the horns—or the heifer, at least. He was not an expert, not a James Bond. He was just going to have to feel his way through this thing, he told himself, make it up as he went along. And though this seemed a realistic approach, it did nothing to ease the knot in

256

his stomach or make the breakfast roll in front of him look any more digestible.

He lit a cigarette. "Well, ladies, are you ready?"

Reno nodded and Jennifer sighed. "I guess you could call it that," she said.

"Then let's go."

A half hour later Jennifer left her car in the parking lot of a small log-built restaurant in Black Forest and got into the Mustang with Reno and Crow, who then drove to Tashoda Lane and followed it back to the wooden gate again and turned around.

"I just wanted you to know where the place is," he said. "In case you do have to call in the police."

Jennifer looked worried. "And that's where you'll be? Up on top of that hill, in a place you haven't even seen yet? Why, they could have an army up there waiting for you."

"An *army!*" Reno said. "Why in hell would they need an army, against one man?"

"I'm just saying he doesn't know *what's* up there."

"Barbara Queen is," Crow said.

"Plus her father and God knows who else."

"Which is the reason for you two," Crow reminded her. "Remember—you call Queen's at eleven sharp, and you ask for me. If I can't come—"

Jennifer finished it for him. "Then I tell them I'm calling in the police. And if you do come to the phone and say you're okay, that's not enough. You're not okay unless you call me Ethel."

"Right."

She gave him a rueful look. "And why *Ethel* instead of some other name—some pretty name, like Elizabeth—I can't imagine."

"A quirk," Crow laughed. "Ethel I figure we won't forget."

He looked back at Reno then, expecting—or at least hoping for—a smile. But she was grimly serious. And a wink from him only made her turn away and gaze out the car window toward the distant Air Force Academy, whose chapel looked to Crow like a squadron of missiles poised against the dark green thrust of the mountains.

When they reached the restaurant parking lot again, Jennifer got out, but not Reno. Waiting, Crow again looked back at her.

"Well?" he said.

"Well, what?"

"Time to get out."

"Why? We don't need two people to make one lousy phone call."

Crow groaned. "Reno, I'm not letting you go up there with me. So get out. *Now.*"

Her eyes flashed at him, begged. "I wouldn't have to go *in* with you. I could just stay in the car."

"No way."

"You keep saying how safe it all is. So what could happen?"

Jennifer, already out of the car, leaned back into the door opening. "Come on, Reno," she scolded. "You're holding us up."

"Butt out!" Reno told her.

Crow asked the girl if he was going to have to remove her by force and she said, yes, she was afraid so. He tried to be reasonable then, patient.

"Reno, there's nothing you can accomplish up there. Alone, I just have to worry about my own ass—no one else's."

"I'll take care of my own ass," the girl said.

Jennifer looked at Crow and shrugged. "Let her go, then. It's her choice. It's almost ten-thirty."

"Yeah, so it is." Crow had an idea. "I'll tell you what. She can drop me off up there and then drive back here. After you phone, if everything's okay, she can come back up and get me."

Reno was enthusiastic. "Sure. That sounds great."

"Well, that way at least they'll *see* you're not alone," Jennifer said to Crow.

"Right." Crow then needlessly asked Jennifer again if she had the phone number and she nodded. She reached into the car and squeezed his arm.

"You be careful," she said.

"You too. Don't worry. We'll be all right."

As they drove off, Reno tumbled into the front seat, next to him.

"Thanks, Crow," she said. "I sure didn't want to wait back there with her."

"Yeah, that would've been rough."

"Don't be mad at me, okay?"

Crow looked at her, dumbstruck that at a time like this the girl's one fear was that he would be "mad" at her.

"When I get out of the car, you take off," he said.

"Right."

"Maybe you ought to have my gun."

She looked at him. "Hell, no. What would I do with a gun?"

Turning off on Tashoda Lane, Crow wondered the same thing about himself: what *he* would do with the gun? At the moment, it felt like boulder in his boot, something that very definitely did not belong there. Just as he himself didn't belong here, he thought, when he came to the gate at the end of the dirt road. Turning in, he pressed the accelerator and started up the steep, curving drive through the pines.

"You scared?" Reno asked.

"Sure."

She smiled at him. "Me too. But I'm glad I'm with you."

He looked at her and shook his head. "You're too much," he said. "You know that?"

If she answered, he was not aware of it, for suddenly the house stretched out in front of them, all glass and redwood and moss rock, built right into the crest of the hill, so that while both its floors opened to the south and west, only one ranchlike level rose above the ground on the other sides. And it was to the north side that the gravel driveway led—to a formal entranceway before continuing in a circle past the garage and back down the hill. There was no lawn anywhere, just the pines and the boulders and barren ground with patches of snow showing here and there.

"Nice place," Reno said. "A little small for Jennifer, maybe."

Crow went around the circle before pulling up at the entrance, so that the car was already pointed downhill. In front of them, snowcapped and prodigious, Pike's Peak appeared to be about a block away instead of the twenty-five miles Crow knew it to be. He opened the car door and got out.

"All right, you slip over and take off now," he said.

Reno suddenly had a look of desperation. "You sure?"

"Yes, I'm sure! Now get out of here!" Crow closed the door and motioned for the girl to go on, and finally she did so, giving him an anguished little wave. As the car headed down the driveway, the front door of the house opened and a tall, light-skinned Negress came out onto the stone-and-redwood porch. She was not wearing a maid's uniform and her manner was casual, even indifferent. Unsmiling, she asked if he was Mr. Moore.

"Yes, I am," he said. "Are you Barbara Queen?"

The question evidently struck the woman as ridiculous. "No, I am not Barbara Queen. Barbara Queen is waiting out in back for you."

As he started into the house, Crow looked down the hill and saw that the car was gone now. Reno was safe. As for himself, he felt a sudden sense of relief and reassurance the moment he stepped inside, because everything was so open and handsome, so *unsinister*. Here, on the top floor, the south and west walls of the L-shaped structure were mostly glass, with a number of sliding glass doors letting onto a broad redwood deck that looked out over a flagstone patio bordered by huge boulders and tall pines whose limbs had been trimmed up to a height of thirty feet and more, obviously in order not to block the view, which was spectacular. Inside, the decor conformed tastefully with the redwood and moss-rock construction, including a massive fireplace that Crow could see in the front room of the house. There he also saw the back of someone with long gray hair sitting in a wheelchair, watching television. At that distance, Crow could not determine if the person was male or female. And before he was able to find out, he had to follow the young black woman down an open, curving staircase to the lower level and into a large game room, located right under the living room, at the south end of the house. Here there was another fireplace, plus a wetbar and a handsome antique pool table. Through the sliding glass doors Crow saw another young woman, in old jeans and a sweatshirt, out on the patio painting a picnic table. She was small and wiry, with short dark hair and a strong, almost masculine face.

The black woman slid the patio door open for Crow and then gestured expansively, like a circus ringmaster.

"There she is, in the flesh," she said. "Barbara Queen."

Miss Queen gave Crow a rueful smile. "Don't pay any attention to that bitch," she advised. "Kitty thinks she's free."

The Negress laughed. "You need me, just call."

As Kitty disappeared, Barbara Queen explained. "She doesn't work here, Mister Moore—she's my friend. My *very* good friend."

Crow took the explanation at its face value: as a gratuitous statement of sexual preference. But as to why Barbara Queen felt the need for any such statement, Crow could only guess. And his feeling was that the woman simply liked to shock people, especially males. But in this instance, Crow reflected, Barbara Queen was in for a shock or two of her own.

"Well, it's good to have close friends," he said. "Incidentally, my real name isn't Moore—it's Orville Crow. I guess you could say I'm here under false pretenses."

"Oh, really?" She didn't seem at all alarmed to hear this.

"Yes. But the reason I'm here does have to do with a job you gave to Gardner Costello."

Miss Queen cocked her head in thought. "Gardner Costello, you say? I'm afraid I don't know anyone by that name. Oh, I guess I might have heard the name somewhere, sometime—I don't know. Possibly through my father. He used to work for the government, and he knew an awful lot of people."

"But you personally don't know the man?"

"No. So I can't see what any of this has to do with me. I'm an actress, Mister Crow. I don't 'give out' jobs to people."

"Well, it's as I told you on the phone. This Costello claims that the job—the assignment—was given to him by you."

She gave him a mocking smile. "All right, I'll play along. Just what kind of 'assignment' was it that I gave to Mister Costello?"

"Supposedly, it was delivered by you in a manila envelope," Crow said. "Inside were photographs of three young people, taken on a street corner in North Hollywood."

"Sounds intriguing."

"Oh, it is. And it gets even better. Costello, you see, was supposed to find out who they were, get their names and addresses and deliver it all to a certain motel room in Hollywood. Only he didn't do it— he farmed the job out to my father, an ex-cop."

"So now I've hired your father," she said.

"That's right. And after he did the job and delivered it—*he was killed*, Miss Queen. Then, one by one, the three young people in the photographs were killed too. When I found out that Costello had given the job to my father, I traced the man to Mazatlan in Mexico. Only someone else beat me to him—a pair of goons who killed him, and almost killed me too."

As he was telling her this, Barbara Queen put down her paintbrush and leaned back against an unpainted part of the picnic table. Her look was unreadable.

"Are you serious about all this?" she asked.

Crow said that he was, and the woman sadly shook her head.

"Then all I can say is that I'm sorry for you. But it still has absolutely nothing to do with me. I still can't even figure why you're telling me about it."

"The same, simple reason," Crow explained. "Maybe you can tell me why Costello would write a note from Mazatlan, saying that he was on the run, that a lot of people were getting killed and he wasn't sure why, except that it had to do with the job that Paul Queen's daughter Barbara had given him to do—and which he'd subcontracted to my father."

Finally Barbara Queen's expression began to change. Looking exasperated and even angry, she got out a cigarette and lit it, then walked away from Crow, moving past a luxurious sunken spa over to the boulders edging the patio. For a time she just stood there smoking her cigarette and looking out at Pike's Peak and the rest of the front range. Then she turned and came back to him, her anger miraculously gone now, replaced by a look of amused resignation.

She spread out her hands and shrugged. "I already told you I was an actress. So what can I say? All right, I *did* deliver an envelope to this Costello character, I'll admit that. But I didn't know what was in it—and I don't know now. I don't have the foggiest. Somebody just came to my apartment in Glendale and asked me to deliver it."

"*Somebody.*"

She made a face, a grimace of disgust, and nodded toward the second-floor deck, behind Crow.

"Yeah. Probably some colleague of that old fascist up there," she said.

262

Crow turned and looked up just as Kitty appeared, pushing the patient in the wheelchair out onto the deck—a man, Crow saw now, an old man with a stubble of white beard and an eyepatch. The only thing about him that seemed alive was the other eye, which at the moment was fixed on Crow. Kitty went back into the house and immediately came out with someone else—Reno. She was leading the girl by the hand.

"Hey, Barb!" the Negress called down. "Look what I found! Ain't she something?"

"Just behave yourself," Barbara laughed.

Reno had already pulled her hand free, and now she looked down at Crow and shrugged. "I came back a little early."

"So I see."

"She invited me in. What else could I do?"

"You okay?" he asked.

"Sure."

Kitty gave Crow a look, more amusement than outrage. "What you think, Jack—I'm gonna molest your little sister?"

"Not at all." He turned back to Barbara Queen. "Now, what were you saying about the man up there?"

"My father—Paul Queen," she said.

Crow tried not to show his surprise and puzzlement. *"That's* Paul Queen?"

"Yep—in the flesh." She looked up at the old man again and raised her voice so he could hear. *"And I called him a fascist! Which is just what you are, isn't that so, Daddy? A messy old fascist!"*

The white-haired man's one eye now was trained on her like a laser, but Barbara was totally indifferent. Casually she turned back to Crow. "He's an ex-CIA hand. Supposedly retired five years ago. Only he didn't really retire until he had a stroke last year. Before that it was strictly busy-busy, if you know what I mean. Him and the rest of the die-hards, they just hate to think of a revolution-in-progress somewhere in the world without them having a hand in it—an unhelping hand, most of the time."

Crow glanced uneasily up at Paul Queen. "Are you saying he had somebody give you the envelope for Costello?"

She sniffed with disdain. "No way. How could he get anyone to

263

do anything for him? You can see what he's like. He can't move, he can't talk, he can't even eat by himself—in fact, he can't do anything but glare at his no-good leftist dyke daughter. We go the rounds all the time. I talk and he glares. I think if he had his way, Kitty and me both would wind up splattered on the rocks down below."

Crow looked up at the deck again and saw that Kitty had walked off with Reno, was pointing out the view to her from the west deck. The girl's presence made Crow feel doubly vulnerable, and it angered him that he had been so foolish as to let her come with him. He should have known that she wouldn't have driven back to be with Jennifer, leaving him here to face the Queens alone. That simply wasn't her style. He turned back to Barbara Queen.

"Okay, you and your father don't get along," he said. "I can see that. And I can see that he probably wasn't the one who had you deliver the job to Costello. But who did, then? Who *was* behind it?"

"I really don't know."

"Five people dead so far—and you don't know?"

"Well, for one thing, I didn't know about any five people being dead."

"You know now. So who do you think was behind it?"

Barbara Queen smiled slightly and shook her head, as if his persistence only amused her. "You won't accept it, huh? That I just don't know?"

"I don't want to."

"You want me to lie? You want me to make something up?"

"Not at all." He kept staring at her, and finally her smile went wry and she shook her head, as though in defeat.

"Well, I can tell you this," she said. "The man who brought the job to me is nothing. A servant. Like a lot of other people—including the old fascist up there. Anyway, this delivery boy—this gook—if I had to guess, I'd say he was probably working for a man in California, ex-CIA, the same as my father. Except this man turned his contacts into a fortune, into millions and millions. And he ain't sitting in no wheelchair either. What he sits on is more like a throne, and he pulls strings here, and he pulls strings there—and people die. People like your old man and Costello."

"This man have a name?" Crow asked.

"Sure—Henry Kellogg. Lives in Santa Barbara, in a kind of fortress. With dozens of Korean servants who will do anything he asks. *Anything.*"

Crow said nothing for a few seconds, not sure that he could trust his voice. Finally he spoke: "Why would this man have *you* deliver the job to Costello?"

Barbara Queen sighed and shook her head. "I really don't know. I suppose in the past he would have used the old fascist—"

She cocked her head in the direction of her father. "Who in turn probably would have assigned one of his ex-assistants. I think it's compulsive with these ancient spooks—they lay down false trails the way the rest of us lay each other." The witticism seemed to please her and she grinned again. "And that's all I can give you, Mister Crow. Honest. Because that's all I know."

For a moment Crow considered mentioning Richard Kellogg to her, the fact that if she had her villain right, then among the killings the man had ordered was that of his very own nephew. But Crow held back, probably because there was not one thing about Barbara Queen that inspired trust. He had to admit, though, that her fantastic charge against Kellogg held a certain appeal. The man did after all fit the role to a T. His guilt would have answered so many questions so neatly. Yet Crow could not really believe it, not yet anyway. Jennifer couldn't have been that naive, he told himself. She couldn't have been that blind.

"You saw the photographs you delivered?" Crow asked.

Barbara Queen shrugged coyly, admitting culpability. "Yeah, I had a peek."

"The three on the corner—why would Kellogg want them dead?"

"How do I know? He probably never even saw the shots. And one of them showed this fat young Arab—a Saudi, I figured—running from the building. The three on the corner undoubtedly saw him too —and shouldn't have. Kellogg probably just heard that one of the boss's kids was in trouble—that is, one of the fucking royal family —and so he sent out the word to clean it up."

Crow told her that his father had shown him the photographs and that there hadn't been any like she described. But Barbara Queen had an answer for that too.

"Costello probably deleted it. All I know is the Arab was there when I saw them. A fat little guy making a beeline for a limo filled with other Arabs—all waiting for him."

"There wasn't someone else running too?" Crow asked. "Someone who looked like Robert Redford?"

Barbara gave him an amused look. "Not even one who looked like Paul Newman."

Crow felt numbed by all this. To cover his confusion, he looked up at the deck and saw Reno still on the west side with Kitty, still trying her best to fend off the black woman's attentions. And Paul Queen of course had not moved either. His eye at the moment was fixed on Crow, boring into him. Crow casually reached down and picked up a flagstone chip. And almost as an act of absentmindedness, he tossed it underhand up at the old man, who did not move a centimeter, even as the chip struck his shoulder and clattered onto the deck. Instead of outraging his daughter, the test had amused her.

"You're not a very trusting guy, are you, Crow?" she laughed.

"No reason to be."

"Of course not. But that's it, I'm afraid. I've told you all I can. And all I'm going to."

"And you really think this Kellogg was behind it all?"

She shrugged. "Why? Are you going there next? Straight into the lion's den?"

"Maybe."

"Then take an army. You'll need it."

"Not necessarily. You see, I'm no danger to anyone. I don't have the police behind me. To them, the killings were all accidents or suicides or what-have-you. So I can't really do anyone any real harm. All I can do is find the truth."

"There's always revenge," Barbara said.

"Not for me, I'm afraid. I'm not the type."

She gave him an ironic smile. "Well, that's good to know—in case I ever cross you."

Crow said nothing for a few moments, wondering about her words, her look. "Just one last thing," he said. "Do you live here or in L.A.?"

"Both, really. I've got an apartment out there, in Glendale, because that's where my work is. As I said before, I'm an actress." She struck a comic pose for him. "Heavies are my bag. Barbara Queen —villainess."

"But you also live here."

"I come home a lot, that's all. I have to check on the old fascist. Then too, there's Kitty." She smiled and waved at her in the distance, playing some kind of game with Crow, with herself, with everybody. "She takes care of him, you see. And takes care of me too, when I'm here."

"Well, that's good to know," Crow said. "I'm happy for you both."

Even as he turned to leave, the phone in the game room began to ring. As Barbara Queen hurried in to answer it, Crow followed her.

"That may be for me," he told her.

"We'll see." She picked up the phone and said hello. After a few seconds, she spoke again. "No, I'm afraid there's no Mister Moore here. There is a Crow, however. An Orville Crow."

Crow reached for the phone.

"It's me, Ethel," he said to Jennifer. "Everything's fine."

She told him that Reno hadn't returned yet and that she had been "going crazy." Was everything really all right?

"Yes, Ethel," he reassured her. "Reno's here with me and everything's fine. We'll be leaving soon."

Barbara was smiling when he hung up. "My, my—not only lacking in trust but exceedingly cautious too. Just what did you expect here?"

"Who knows?"

"Sorry we were such a disappointment." She had followed him up the curving staircase to the main floor, where Reno and Kitty had just come in off the deck.

"Time to go," he announced.

"You know," Reno said, "on a clear day they can see all the way to New Mexico."

"It's true," Kitty confirmed. "We can see the Spanish Peaks, in the Sangre de Cristos, over a hundred miles away.

"Is that a fact?" Crow said.

267

"Yes, it is," Barbara put in. "Your sister should join us some evening in the whirlpool out front, especially when the west is blood red. The peaks stand out like firm young breasts."

"Oh, don't they, though!" Kitty laughed.

Crow thanked Barbara Queen for seeing him and then he and Reno left. As they drove down the hill, the girl let out a sigh of relief.

"Boy, what a creepy bunch," she said. "Especially the old man in the wheelchair."

"The women weren't exactly girl scouts either."

"You can say that again."

Crow looked at her. "You know, I'm pissed at you. You had no business coming back up there. No business going inside."

Reno gave him a defiant look. "Well, you were there alone. I thought—"

"I know what you thought. And I appreciate it. I really do. But you could've been hurt, for Christ's sake. We told you what happened in Mexico."

"Well, we're both okay, aren't we? So what's the beef?"

"No beef." He couldn't help smiling at her now. "Like I said before, you are too much, Reno. Just too much."

The girl tried to look cool and indifferent, but finally she couldn't hold back her smile either. "Just don't forget it," she said.

"I won't. Listen, what did Kitty say to you? What did you talk about?"

"She asked if I'd ever had sex with a woman."

"That's all?"

"With *two* women."

"Sounds like a lady with broad interests."

Reno missed the pun. "She did say one other thing."

"What's that?"

"That watching you and Barbara Queen together was like watching a cat play with a mouse."

"And which one was the cat?"

"Not you."

"She was probably right."

"Why? You didn't get anything out of her?"

"No, I got a good deal—probably all of it lies."

"You want to tell me?"

"Later. With Jennifer."

"Why not now?"

"Just because."

Reno sighed in disgust. "I wonder if you ever try that number with *her*. 'Just because.' That really cuts it, you know? It just really cuts it all to hell."

"Right now," Crow said, "it's the best I can do."

Once she heard Barbara Queen's charge against her uncle, Crow had no idea how Jennifer would react, and he didn't want to find out in public. Nor was he keen on the idea of letting her drive all the way back to the hotel in a state of shock and outrage. So when they reached the restaurant parking lot, he put her off too, saying that all he had gotten was lies and that it would be better to discuss it later, in their rooms at the hotel.

"There's nothing you can tell me now?" she asked.

Crow shrugged. "Well, Barbara Queen is innocent of everything, of course—or so she'd have us believe. And her father, he's a mute quadriplegic in a wheelchair."

"He's *paralyzed?*"

Crow nodded. "A stroke victim. And the rest—well it's pretty involved."

"I've got the time," Jennifer said.

"And I'll tell you at the hotel. I just want to get it all straight in my own mind."

"Whatever you say." Jennifer headed for her car.

"Reno can ride back with you and tell you about her new girl friend," he said.

But the girl balked. "I'm okay here." She was still sitting next to Crow in the Mustang.

"You go with her—I've got some thinking to do."

"Which you can't do with me around?"

He reached over and opened her door. "Please?"

"Sure. Why not?" Getting out, Reno slammed the door shut and went over to Jennifer's car and got in.

As Crow followed them on the winding blacktop out of the forest and across the broad sloping prairie toward the city, he went over what Barbara Queen had told him, hoping to make up his mind about it—whether any part of it was even remotely feasible—before he recounted it to Jennifer. Playing devil's advocate, he tried point by point to make a case for what Barbara Queen had alleged. First, there was the undeniable fact that Henry Kellogg and his Koreans on that first day had behaved in a most unusual way toward Crow, considering his mission—that he had come to warn young Kellogg that his life was in danger, and failing that, to give his family reason to believe the youth was not a suicide. But Henry Kellogg had not wanted to hear any such message. And then a day later it was he— according to Jennifer—who had interceded with the police and got them to drop the case.

Then there was the CIA tie-in, the fact that wherever one turned, the "company" logo kept popping up. Gardner Costello was a retired company man, just as were Paul Queen and Kellogg himself. And then there was the little matter of Jennifer's reaction when she first heard the two men's names, saying that she thought she had heard of them somewhere before. Where else but at home, in the course of her uncle's business day? And probably even more important was Barbara Queen's assertion that among the photos she'd taken to Costello was one showing an Arab—a Saudi—running from the building. If one of them had indeed got himself into a bind, who would be more likely than Henry Kellogg to come charging to the man's rescue?

And finally there was the simple matter of Barbara Queen's word: why would she lie? What would she have to gain by it? There was no need to absolve her father, since the man could barely participate in life, let alone some murderous conspiracy carried out in another state as well as in a foreign country. And as for her own possible guilt, in Crow's eyes her quirky, capricious personality absolved her almost as unequivocally as Costello's note had. Crow simply could not imagine a lesbian bigmouth like her involved in such dangerous and convoluted mischief. Then too she had no way of knowing that Jennifer, a Kellogg, was working with him. To believe she was intentionally misleading him, he would have had to believe that she was involved with Fatso and Red, the killers not just of Costello but

270

probably also of his father and the three in the photographs. For Crow, it beggared belief that a cold-blooded hitman like Red could have worked for—or even *with*—a flake like Barbara Queen.

Why else then would she have lied about Henry Kellogg? Crow didn't know. And for that matter, he didn't know that she *had* lied. In fact he was afraid he still didn't know much of anything—except that whatever relationship he had with Jennifer was about to be put to the test.

When they reached their rooms, Crow had hoped that he could be alone with Jennifer long enough at least to cushion the shock of what he had to tell her. But instead it was she who had to use the bathroom and Reno who joined Crow at the windows, where he stood looking down at the pond which the hotel grandly called Cheyenne Lake.

"Something's the matter, isn't it?" Reno said, taking his cigarette pack out of his pocket and flipping up a pair.

Crow lit the cigarettes. "You could say that."

"I just did."

"Incidentally, you were okay out there," he said. "But I still don't know why you did it—unless you figure somebody's got to look after me."

"Well, considering what you were up against—a man in a wheel-chair and two lesbians."

Laughing, Crow sat down in one of the two chairs facing the sofa.

"You still haven't told me what's wrong," Reno said.

"Something about Jennifer's uncle." Crow did not realize that Jennifer had just come into the room.

"What's this about my uncle?" she asked.

Crow tried to cover his surprise, his discomfort. "It's complicated. Why don't you sit down?"

"I don't mind standing."

"Come on, indulge me. Just sit down and relax, okay?"

"If it's so damned important, all right, I'll sit." She sat down on the sofa's edge, like a kid about to be reprimanded. "Now, tell me."

"Well, as I said out in Black Forest, Paul Queen turned out to be an old man in a wheelchair. A stroke victim. Can't move or even

271

talk. And his daughter presents herself as a sort of corrupt *naif*, totally innocent. A lesbian flake who wants to be an actress, and spends part of her time in L.A. She calls the old man a fascist, but says it wasn't one of *his* old CIA underlings who dropped off the package for her to deliver to Costello." Crow dragged on his cigarette and put it out. "It was a Korean, she said."

"So—?"

Crow took a deep breath. "A Korean servant—of Henry Kellogg."

Jennifer didn't respond immediately. She looked incredulous. *"And you believed her?"*

"I wouldn't trust Barbara Queen as far as I could throw her."

Jennifer supplied his next word: *"But—!"*

Crow shrugged. "Well, you've got to wonder why she'd choose your uncle's name out of the blue. She didn't mention Richard. She apparently doesn't know anything about you—that you're working with me. And there are all those CIA connections—Costello, Queen—names that you admitted rang a bell."

Jennifer got up and went over to the windows. She put a hand to her forehead. She let the hand fall. She kept shaking her head. She seemed unable to stop moving.

"And you actually believe such shit? *You actually believe it?"*

"Not at all. I'm just telling you what the woman told me, Jennifer. And that we can't just reject it out of hand."

She turned to face him. *"And why the hell not?"*

Crow was on his feet now too. "Because it answers so goddamn many questions, that's why. She mentioned another photo that was in the envelope when it was given to her—a picture of some young Saudi fleeing the building that Richard and the girls were looking at."

Jennifer by then was in tears. "So what are you saying? That Henry Kellogg had his own nephew killed in order to protect some lousy Arab?"

Crow shook his head. "Barbara Queen figures he never even knew who was on the corner. They were witnesses, that's all."

"To what?!"

"Who knows?"

"And your father and Costello?"

"I guess it was a case of hit the witnesses as well as everyone who knew about them."

Leaving the windows, Jennifer had walked back across the room, only to turn around and retrace her steps.

"I just can't believe this of you, Crow," she said. "We go to all the trouble of finding Costello, and almost get killed doing it. And then we come all the way out here, and what do we end up with? Why, Henry Kellogg, of course. It's so easy, isn't it, to believe the worst of our superiors?"

"Oh bullshit, Jennifer!" It was Reno, climbing from the floor onto the sofa. "Crow's just telling you what he found out, that's all. And anyway, you wouldn't be screaming so loud if you didn't half believe it yourself."

Jennifer turned on her almost with a sense of relief. "You just shut your nasty little mouth, all right? This doesn't concern you."

Crow told her not to talk to the girl that way, and Jennifer sneered at him.

"Oh, that offends you, does it? It's okay to make criminal accusations against one of the greatest men in this country—but one just can't call a slut a slut, is that it?"

Crow reached out to stop her as she swept past him. "Hey, will you take it easy, for Christ's sake! This is something to discuss, that's all."

"Like hell it is!"

In a rage, she pulled her arm free and ran on into her bedroom, slamming the door behind her. Crow heard her fall onto the bed, and then there was silence.

Reno shook her head. "Jesus, when it comes to her uncle, she kinda loses her cool, doesn't she?"

"She does."

"And this is what the big secret was, huh? What you didn't want to talk about in Black Forest?"

Crow was feeling rotten. "Yeah, that's it. And I sure did a beautiful job of telling her, didn't I? The man's like a father to her. I should've known how she'd react. How else could she?"

"Yeah, you do everything wrong, Crow. You're such a bastard."

He was in no mood for the girl's ironies, even well-intentioned ones. Like a father peeking in on a sleeping child, he went over to Jennifer's door and opened it a crack, to see how she was. She screamed at him to shut it.

"What now?" Reno asked.

"Beats me."

"How about some food? I'm starved."

Crow thought about it. He knew that for the time being at least Jennifer would have nothing to do with either of them. And the truth was, he was hungry himself. So he told her through the door that he and Reno were going downstairs for lunch and did she want him to order anything for her.

"Just leave me alone," she said.

He asked if she was all right and she told him to go to hell.

"Well, she sounds better anyway," he said to Reno, who gave him a pitying look.

*   *   *

Though it was after two o'clock, the luncheon crowd was still fairly heavy in the glassed-in Garden Room, with its live indoor trees and other tropical flora. The two of them had ordered burgers and fries, with a chef's salad. And though Reno went at her food with zest, she also demonstrated considerable interest in the elegant crowd chattering away at the glass-topped tables.

For his own part, Crow couldn't think about much of anything except Jennifer lying alone in her room upstairs. Under the circumstances, he didn't know what else he could have done except tell her, as he had, of Barbara Queen's charges. Yet somehow he still felt guilty for what he had done, or maybe just because of *how* he'd done it—straight out, almost as if he himself believed the charges. Which was not the case. He didn't know what to believe, and he was beginning to wonder if he ever would.

Reno went on about what a weird couple Kitty and Barbara Queen were.

"And I don't mean just because they're lesbians," the girl said. "It was—oh, I don't know—"

"Because they flaunted it?"

"Yeah. Like they had to make sure we knew."

"I got the feeling a lot of that was for the old man," Crow said.

"I think Barbara Queen enjoys making him suffer. Rubbing it in—when he can't do a thing about it except listen to it all, and see it all."

Drinking the last of her Coke, Reno took an ice cube into her mouth. "Anyway, Kitty and I really hit it off. My hair is 'just fabulous,' did you know that?"

"I did."

"She dug my presentable new jacket, too."

Crow sighed. "You ever gonna let me off the hook on that one?"

"We'll see." The girl took another mouthful of ice and then suddenly her eyes widened. "Hey, there was one other thing I forgot to tell you. There was this flower pot on the deck and someone had been using it as a wastebasket. You know what was in it?"

"No, what?"

"Little bags of Planters peanuts. *Empty* bags."

Crow had been about to light a cigarette. But suddenly he forgot all about it. "You're not kidding me?" he said.

"No way. Those little bags of peanuts just like the fat guy in Venice kept pigging down."

In his excitement, Crow almost jumped up and ran out of the restaurant. Then, remembering that he still didn't have the check, he signaled for the waitress. "Reno," he said, "one way or another you do keep saving my ass, don't you?"

The girl looked surprised as well as pleased. "This is important?"

"You bet it is. It means Barbara Queen is definitely a liar."

"So Jennifer's uncle is off the hook?"

"Right."

"Me and my big mouth," she said.

Minutes later, with Reno trailing indifferently behind, Crow hurried down the corridor to their suite of rooms. He unlocked the door and went on into the sitting room, where he saw that the door to Jennifer's bedroom now stood ajar. And he heard her clearly, heard her not crying but talking on the telephone in a thin, urgent voice:

"Yes, I'm serious, darling. That's what we're doing out here—still working on the 'case,' as he calls it—not having some stupid fling. And I'm telling you that's what this Barbara Queen woman told him

275

—that you're behind it all, Henry. That one of the Kims gave her the job to deliver to Costello, and he farmed it out to Crow's father . . ."

For Crow, it was a virtual clone of the scene in the Sheraton Hotel in Los Angeles. And he felt as uncomfortable now as he had then —and just as disinclined to walk away. As her voice broke off and she began to listen, Crow motioned to Reno behind him to be quiet and not to close the door. Then Jennifer went on:

"I just wanted to warn you, dear, that's all. Of course I know it's not true. But I wanted you to be aware of it, so you could—oh, I don't know—*protect* yourself. He's like a dog with a bone. He won't let go. He really won't . . . I realize that, darling. Yes, I know it's absurd. But I wanted you to be aware of it anyway . . . Yes, I'm all right. No, he's not like that. I'll be fine. I just wanted you to know . . . Yes, darling. Yes, I will. But I wanted to call anyway, to let you know . . . Yes, Henry. Yes, dear . . . I will. Good-bye."

After she had hung up, Crow gently pushed the bedroom door open all the way. And he just stood there until, turning, she saw him. Her eyes flared and her hand flew to her mouth. Then abruptly she was herself again: steel and Chanel.

"You gave me no choice," she said. "I had to warn him. If I'd had the chance, I would have warned Richard and your father and the hookers too."

Crow stared at her with pain and rage. "Very noble," he told her. "Except for one little thing."

"What?"

"That if your uncle is the one, then you just put a contract on my head."

Jennifer's eyes blazed. *"But he's not the one!"*

Crow nodded. "Yeah, I know that now too—or at least I think I do. But it's a little late, isn't it?"

"What do you mean, you know it too?"

In a flat, emotionless voice Crow told her what Reno had remembered seeing at Queen's place, and he said it might mean that Fatso was there, which in turn would mean that Barbara Queen was a liar.

Jennifer looked triumphant. "Well, there you are! It proves I was right—that I had good reason to do what I did."

"Sure, it does," Crow said. "And you keep telling yourself that, okay?"

He had already turned away from her and was heading out of the suite—with Reno, naturally, not far behind.

For Crow, the rest of that day was an agony of postponement and indecision. Learning that Fatso might be with Barbara Queen had fired his resolve to push ahead with the investigation, find once and for all the answers that had to be lying out there in the pine woods somewhere. But the breach with Jennifer seemed to have put everything on hold. He expected her to pack up and leave while he and Reno were gone from the hotel, yet he couldn't be sure that she would do so. And he was not about to proceed with things until he knew definitely whether or not she would still be with him. This, to him, was as much a matter of principle as it was of safety. After all she had done—and spent—he was not about to write her off out of hand. Nor was he so egotistical that he couldn't see what her phone call had been: not so much a betrayal of him as an act of loyalty to her uncle, her own flesh and blood. Yet even this admission did nothing to lessen Crow's anger. No matter what clean, innocent face he tried to put upon her action, the fact remained that in calling her uncle, she could have been—indeed, still might have been—putting his life at risk. Just because Fatso might be in Colorado Springs didn't mean that he, like Barbara Queen herself, wasn't on the payroll of Henry Kellogg. Barbara wouldn't have been the first employee to badmouth the boss.

In any case, Crow had decided not to proceed with the investigation, at least for the time being. So, at loose ends, he drove Reno around the plush Broadmoor area and in time followed a winding road that led up Cheyenne Mountain past the local zoo and on up to a granite tower called the Will Rogers Shrine of the Sun. Crow parked off to the side, facing the car toward the view, which was truly breathtaking. They could see not only Broadmoor below and the red-rock forest of monoliths called the Garden of the Gods, but also the entire city and the plains east and north of it, including—on the horizon—the dark green smear that was Black Forest.

For a time the two of them sat there in the car saying nothing,

277

Reno evidently feeling just as uncommunicative as Crow did. She lit a cigarette and when he took it from her, she lit another, smiling at this turning of the tables.

"I suppose she'll be gone when we get back," he said.

"Could be."

"Won't exactly break your heart, I guess."

The girl shrugged. "Oh, I don't know. Jennifer's okay."

"Since when?"

"Why kick her when she's down? I guess she really digs that screwy old uncle of hers."

"So it seems."

"But she digs you too."

"Is that a fact?"

"Don't we all?"

Totally ignoring the view, Reno had scooted down on the seat, with her knees as usual braced against the dashboard. In her new jacket and jeans, and with her rumpled hair and lazy brown eyes, she looked coolly stylish. And coolly desirable.

"Did you two make love yet?" she asked.

"Oh sure. We had so much free time down in Mexico."

"Does that mean you didn't?"

"What are you, a reporter?"

"I guess that's off-limits, huh? You and Jennifer."

Crow made a groaning sound. "Here we are, on the heels of a bunch of murderers, and you want to talk about romance."

"Not romance—*sex*. Did you do it?"

Irritated at being grilled by her, he almost said yes, that they had "done it," but there was something in the girl's eyes—an anticipation of pain, almost a resigned acceptance of it—that tied his tongue, and finally forked it.

"No," he told her. "We were too busy getting shot at."

It was not much of a disclaimer, he knew. Yet it touched off a smile that was simply too much for him, too fine a payoff for a lousy little lie. Trying to make amends, he moved closer to her and kissed her on the shoulder. He edged his hand behind her, accidentally slipping it under her shirt and onto her bare back, which was ridged like a dancer's.

278

She took a drag on her cigarette. "Aren't you forgetting something?"

"What?"

"That this isn't the time for romance. Murderers and all that."

He took the cigarette out of her mouth and tossed it onto the gravel parkway. "No, I didn't forget. I just want to kiss you, that's all. And maybe tell you what a neat young lady you are."

She smiled again. "Well okay, then. One kiss. And you tell me that."

He did as he was told, and slightly more, taking her in his arms and kissing her on the mouth, chastely at first, then more and more deeply. His hand found her breast and hers closed on his mounded fly.

"You're a very neat, very sexy young woman," he said.

Then suddenly there was a giggle, and another. Looking up, Crow saw two small blond boys standing about three feet away from the car, holding hands as they stared up at him and Reno. The taller one was no more than five years old, and they were both dressed alike, in ski suits and cowboy boots.

"We thaw you," the older one said.

"You kithed her," said the other.

Crow grinned at them. "Tho I did," he admitted.

Reno was looking down at the boys, resting her chin on the car door, in the open window. "What are your names?" she asked.

"Mark and Doug," they answered, in unison.

"Well, Mark and Doug—how would you like me to kiss *you?*"

Giggling again, the brothers scampered toward their parents, who had been watching them from the sidewalk that led to the tower. Reno turned and looked over at Crow, and her smile ebbed as she too seemed to sense that the interruption—innocent and funny as it was—nevertheless was enough to bring them back down, to kill the moment of carelessness. As she had just reminded him, this was not the time for romance. Everything was still up in the air. Nothing had been solved. Nothing had changed. Except that at the moment he was feeling exceedingly stupid and frivolous, not unlike a kid caught shoplifting a candy bar.

To cover his embarrassment, he talked about Jennifer and her

279

phone call to her uncle. He went over the reasons Kellogg could not have been behind the killings, probably trying to convince himself as much as Reno. And he theorized about Barbara Queen and Fatso, trying one scenario after another in a vain attempt to explain all that had happened. Reno listened and smoked, blowing tiny rings into the cool, thin air. And eventually Crow started the car and they went down off the mountain. They drove about the city for a time and stopped at a drive-in for Cokes and tacos. Then Crow went north on Academy Boulevard and turned onto the road to Black Forest. When they reached Tashoda Lane, he followed it slowly back through the trees and pulled in at the third house along its powdery, half-mile length: an unfinished cement-block affair, roofless and abandoned. Crow drove around behind it and parked, hidden from the dead-end dirt road, whose traffic at that point would have been confined almost exclusively to persons going to and from Queen's place.

Getting out, Crow saw a gas meter behind the structure, and this surprised him, considering how few and far-between the houses in the area were. He had taken his father's thirty-eight out of the glove compartment and he carried it at the ready as he led Reno back through the ponderosa pines. The ground underfoot was spongy and needle-covered, and they came to a run-down barbed-wire fence at about a hundred yards north of the unfinished house. Holding the wires apart so Reno could pass through, he quietly told her that they were probably entering Queen's property, since his place was the next in line after the cement-block house.

They moved on a short distance and suddenly Crow was able to see through the trees a high boulder-strewn hill rising sharply ahead. Above its crest, the front peak of the house stood like a glass teepee against the sky. Crow pointed it out to Reno, and she asked if they were going to climb the hill so they could observe the entire house. Even as he answered her, saying that he hadn't decided yet, he saw a glass door slide open up above and a male figure came waddling out onto the upper deck of Queen's house.

"Fatso!" Reno said.

"None other."

For ten or fifteen seconds the fat man stood there on the deck in a terrycloth robe, holding onto the railing and breathing deeply. Then he lit a cigarette and waddled back into the house.

"Jesus Christ," Crow said. "It's like the man was waiting for us to show up."

"Maybe he comes out regularly all day long."

"Like a cuckoo, huh?"

Reno laughed. "Well, is there anything else you wanted to see?"

"No, that'll do for now, thank you."

When they got back to the hotel, Crow expected to find Jennifer gone and a farewell letter waiting for him. Instead the lady herself was there, in silk pajamas and robe, watching TV from one of the easy chairs in the sitting room. She had a drink in her hand and on the table next to her there was a silver tray holding a half-full fifth of vodka, an empty bottle of tonic, and an ice bucket as well as a half-eaten serving of prawns and cole slaw. Instead of turning to look at Crow and Reno as they entered, she tossed back her head and observed them upside down.

"Well, there they are in the flesh—Sam Spade and sidekick."

"She's smashed," Reno said.

Jennifer laughed. "*Observant* sidekick," she amended.

"Thought you might be gone by now," Crow said.

"No such luck," she said. "Come and watch Merv with me. He's having an ass-kissing contest with Liberace."

Reno expressed Crow's own response: "Yuk!"

Jennifer had righted her head by then. She looked at them with contempt. "Oh, of course. I keep forgetting—you two have more important things on your minds. Bigger fish to fry. Like 'Let's play detective,' and 'Let's play house.' Tell me, Reno, how many times has His Holiness here got into your pants? Ten, twenty?"

"Why don't you just be quiet and finish that bottle," Crow suggested.

Jennifer's eyes widened, as if in happy surprise. "What's this? His Holiness running out of patience? Can this be?"

Crow sat down on the sofa. "You know, you don't handle your booze so good."

She drained her glass and laughed. "Sure I do. It goes right down."

Reno had gone into the bathroom and closed the door.

"How was it with her this afternoon?" Jennifer asked. "I'll bet your little 'cousin' has been able to teach you some new moves, huh?"

"No, but she could teach you about a few things," he said. "Like guts and loyalty."

"*Loyalty!* I thought that's what our problem was—that I am loyal."

"To your uncle maybe. But what about your brother?"

She threw the ice in her glass at him. "You bastard," she cried. "Sanctimonious bastard." Clumsily, she tried to make another drink, and then it seemed to dawn on her that the tonic was gone. She picked up the empty bottle and showed it to Crow.

"Call down for another, okay?"

"Call yourself."

"Do it."

Since she already had enough vodka, in fact far too much, he knew it didn't make much sense to argue with her about the tonic. But her imperious manner put him off.

"I think not," he said.

Smiling, she mocked him. *"I think not."* She got to her feet and wobbled over to the phone, dropping into the chair next to it like an old woman. Crow was amazed at her lack of motor control; the alcohol had not affected her speech anywhere near as much. And she proved this as she called down to room service and ordered more ice and tonic. But when she got up, she teetered and fell against the table, almost knocking over a lamp before Crow jumped up and caught her. He started to walk her to her bedroom, but she pulled free and fell full-length onto the sofa. Reno had come out of the bathroom by then and she helped Crow get her to her feet. As they guided her on into the bedroom, she clung more to Reno than to Crow.

"Don't trust him," she said to the girl. "He's like all the rest. Only worse. 'Cause he *seems* different. But he isn't. Believe me, kid—he really isn't."

They got her into bed and Crow pulled the heavy curtains shut. As he closed the bedroom door behind them, Reno gave him a wicked smile.

"Is she right?" she asked. "*Are* you worse than the rest?"

"You heard the lady."

Crow had room service bring them up some food in addition to the ice and tonic that Jennifer had ordered. After they ate, he and Reno spent the evening watching television—or at least Reno did. Crow only looked at the thing—saw the motion pictures, heard the sound—but none of it got through to him. His mind was on the house in Black Forest and the four odd characters who inhabited it. The next day, with or without Jennifer, he was going to do—or at least *begin* to do—whatever was required in order to learn the truth about the four: how and why they figured in all the deaths. And the more he thought about it now, the more convinced he was that none of it would lead back to Henry Kellogg. Not that Crow would have minded if it did. Even when he first saw the man, holding court out by the pool, Crow hadn't liked him. And of course later, when the sonofabitch had tried to have him thrown out on his ear—that hadn't added to the man's appeal. Nevertheless, it just didn't make sense that in his zeal to protect some young Saudi's reputation Kellogg would have had his own nephew killed. Nor was it plausible that the killers would have carried out the assignment unaware that one of those they were hitting was the top man's nephew. So Crow had come to accept it that Barbara Queen's story had been nothing more than a fiction, a red herring, something to divert him from the true target of his investigation—perhaps Barbara herself.

But it was useless, Crow reflected, to go on speculating as to what the truth might be. Much more important now was the matter of *how* he would go about securing that truth. And he had come to the conclusion that Fatso was the one to concentrate on, the one to separate from the others, the one to lean on. Everything about the man suggested softness and pliability, the likelihood that he would have a low pain threshold and a highly developed sense of self-preservation. And getting him alone would not be too difficult, Crow judged. He had noticed that the mailboxes and newspaper holders were all on the blacktop, which meant that once or twice a day someone at Queen's place had to drive down Tashoda Lane to Black Forest Road to pick up the mail or the newspaper. Or they might have to take the blacktop all the way to the grocery store, which was located across from the log-cabin restaurant. If Barbara alone ran the errand—or if she took Kitty along with her—Crow would simply drive up to the house and confront the fat bastard alone, make preparations to welcome the other two when they returned. If, on the other hand, Fatso himself ran the errand, Crow would simply follow him to his destination, take him into "custody" and interrogate him, use him to get Barbara and Kitty in his power—long enough anyway to get their versions of the truth. Then, comparing their stories, maybe he would be able to come away with what he was after: the whole truth. As for bringing them to justice, he still had no illusions about that. It would be his word against theirs. And there remained the little matter of the two deaths in Mazatlan. He wanted no part of trying to straighten all that out in a Mexican court.

So in effect he would be playing the role of an investigative reporter, not that of a freelance avenger. And he was painfully aware that it was not enough, certainly not all he would have liked. But it would do, especially since he didn't see what other choices he had. Not for a second did he consider taking the law into his own hands, meting out justice of his own. He hoped he had many years left to live, and he had no inclination to live them as a murderer.

After ten o'clock there seemed to be nothing on TV that Reno liked and she got ready for bed. She took a bath and then came back into the sitting room wearing her usual "pajamas"—a tanktop and panties.

"What do we do tomorrow?" she asked.

"You do nothing," he said. "At the most, you wait for me in the car."

"What'll you be up to?"

"I'm gonna waylay Fatso. Ask him some questions."

"And Jennifer?"

Crow shrugged. "I don't know. You tell me."

The girl smiled suddenly. "You know, it was funny with those two little boys today. If they hadn't giggled, they might've seen something they shouldn't have."

Crow had no trouble seeing the direction of the girl's conversation. And it was a direction he didn't want to take, especially with Jennifer in the other room.

"Oh, I don't know," he said. "Old guys like me, we don't get that carried away."

"That's for sure."

"You tired?" he asked. "Ready for bed?"

"Not particularly."

"Well, I am. So I guess I'm just gonna have to kiss you goodnight." He took her by the shoulders and pecked her on the cheek.

"You afraid of me?" she asked.

"Not that I'm aware of. Why?"

"Out there in the open today, you really kissed me. But not here. You afraid what might happen?"

"I'm afraid of tomorrow, that's all. I'm afraid of getting killed. So right now all I want is to go to bed and lie there and worry. Okay?"

"Sure. I know all about that." She gave him a sudden kiss on the mouth, tongue and all, and then scurried off to her bedroom, looking back over her shoulder to catch his reaction. He shook his head and grinned. And she seemed pleased with herself, even happy, as she closed the door.

When Crow woke at about two in the morning, it didn't take him long to realize that the sound was coming from the main bathroom, which could be entered either from the sitting room or from Jennifer's room. Reasonably certain what the sound was, he wearily got out of bed and knocked on the door before he entered the bathroom. Inside, he found her on the floor in front of the toilet stool, hugging it like a lover. There was vomit on her pajamas and on the floor and even in the bowl itself.

"Not feeling so hot, huh?" he said.

Jennifer shuddered and looked up at him with queasy scorn. Nevertheless she let him help her to her feet, and she let him hold her from behind as she retched again, doubling over the toilet, trying to get the last bit of sickness out of her. Finally Crow asked her if she was finished, and she nodded.

"Okay, let's clean you up, then," he said.

He helped her off with her pajamas and used a wet washcloth to clean her face and hands. He gave her a glass of water to rinse out her mouth and she followed it with mouthwash.

"Ready for bed again?" he asked.

"I hope so," she got out.

He helped her across the carpeted floor and into bed. And she reached up and took his hand as he started to pull away.

"Stay a while, okay?" she asked. "I feel terrible."

"Sure. Anything else I can do? Anything you want? Aspirin?"

"No. Just stay here with me a while, okay?" She was still holding onto his hand. "I feel like such a jerk. Such a pitiful jerk. Not only do I call Henry on us, but I get drunk on top of it. And now this."

"Forget it," he told her. "We've all got our problems. And I understand about your uncle, believe me. He's always been there. You owe him, and you love him."

Her hand tightened on his. "Only like a father."

"I know that."

"I'm like the stupid sunflowers in our garden. As he moves, I move. I—"

Softly she began to cry. And Crow, bending over her, patted her shoulder. "Hey, it's gonna be all right," he said. "Don't worry about it."

But she couldn't stop. Yet she tried to speak as she cried, getting the words out in little gasps and pieces. "Stay with me, Crow. Okay? Till I'm asleep."

"Sure." Like Reno, Crow let his underwear serve as pajamas, had on only a pair of jockey shorts. So getting under the covers, out of the cool night air, held its own appeal for him, without his being offered the world as well. Yet he gathered it to him. She nuzzled in against his neck and he felt her leg edge across his body.

"Just this," she said. "Let's sleep like this."

"Sure," he told her. But he couldn't help responding to the silken body twined with his. His cock worked out of his shorts and he

286

accepted it that before the night was over he would get what he wanted. But then, without even knowing what had happened, he suddenly was gone and there was nothing, not even dreams, until he slowly became aware of the nimbus of morning light edging in behind the heavy window curtains. Leaving Jennifer asleep, he got up and went into the sitting room, puzzled by the fact that the door was open, as well as the one to Reno's room. He went inside and found her bed empty. He looked into her bathroom, but she was not there either. And then he noticed that her small cardboard suitcase was gone, along with all her clothes—all except those he had bought for her, which lay in a heap on the bedroom floor.

FOURTEEN

THE first thing Jennifer noticed when she came into the sitting room was that her jacket was missing.

"My chamois," she said. "Oh no, did she take that too?"

Crow had just found Jennifer's open purse on the floor and he handed it to her now. Indifferently she rummaged through it, finally opening the wallet inside and checking that too.

"She might have taken a hundred or two," she said. "I'm not sure."

"Not sure? How much did you have?"

"Six or seven in cash. Could've been eight."

"How much is there now?"

"Five and change. But I've spent some of it, of course."

"How much?"

She waved the matter away. "I don't care about the money. But my jacket—I've never seen one with that cut before. It was my favorite."

"What'd it cost?"

"Six hundred. But it's not that."

288

"Yeah, I know—it's the cut."

"Well, it is."

Neither of them had mentioned yet the fact that they had just slept together, lain in each other's arms through the long cool hours of the mountain night. It was almost as if it were an embarrassment, to both of them.

Crow told her now that he had no idea what time Reno had left, that it could have been as early as two-thirty in the morning or as late as six.

"Chances are, she's hitchhiking. So I'm gonna take a spin on the freeway, check it in both directions for five miles or so, see if I can find her." He was hurriedly getting dressed. "And either way—with her or without—I'll be back to pick you up. We'll get something to eat—and then we'll move on Black Forest."

Jennifer was holding a damp cloth to the back of her neck. Her eyes were red and full of pain and her hair was in disarray. Yet she somehow managed to look elegant too, standing there in her velvet robe. "We *move* on them, huh?" she said. "Just like an army. All two of us."

"You won't be in any danger," he told her. "I've got it worked out."

She was shaking her head at him in disbelief. "You forgetting Mazatlan already? How our best-laid plans just about got us killed?"

Crow was confused. "I thought we'd already been over that. I thought you'd changed your mind."

"Not really."

"Well, if you feel that way, what are you doing here? Why'd you bother to stay on?"

She shrugged and sank down on the sofa. "I guess I just didn't want to leave you. And I didn't know how to back out. And then after yesterday, I figured I had to stay for Henry's sake, so I could keep him posted, warn him in case Barbara Queen interested you in something more serious than slander."

"Such as?"

"It doesn't matter."

Crow was dressed now, ready to leave. "Why? You don't feel that way now?"

She shook her head. "No, I don't. There's nothing like a hangover and bright sunshine to help you see things as they are. More than ever, I know that Barbara Queen is simply a liar. And I've also come to realize that Henry Kellogg doesn't need me to protect his good name. So—"

Crow cut her off. "So we'll talk at breakfast. I'll be back soon—with or without your coat."

And he left her that way, stylishly disheveled, sagging back against the sofa. Later he would remember her expression—rueful, resigned, indulgent—the way one might look at the family cretin. But all Crow had on his mind then was getting to his car and reaching the freeway as soon as he could, hoping that he might find Reno and pick her up before she got a ride. It sickened him to think of her thumbing her way back to California, betting her life with each vehicle that stopped for her, trusting that its driver would not be one of that growing multitude of psychopaths crowding every freeway and dirt path in the country.

But he didn't find her. He drove south of the city for over ten miles and then crossed the median to the other lane of the freeway and headed back. He went through the city and continued north until he passed the Air Force Academy, with Black Forest lying a few miles to the east, and still there was no sign of her. Turning back again, he drove to the police station downtown and asked if there was any report of an accident involving a teenage girl. He gave them Reno's description, and the sergeant on duty made a few calls and then told him that he had "drawed a blank." The sergeant also said that Crow would have to wait forty-eight hours before filing a missing person's report. But Crow of course had no intention of filing any such thing, knowing the response he would get when he informed the police that he was not a relative of the girl and didn't even know her name or address. He already had enough troubles, he figured, without inviting more.

So he headed back to the Broadmoor. And on the way, the idea crossed his mind that Reno's leaving might not be the worst thing that had ever happened to him. He hated to think of her hitchhiking and he knew that he was going to miss her a good deal, but the fact remained that somewhere, sometime, the girl was going to have to get on with her own life—and get out of his. And it just might be true, he told himself, that there was no time like the present. For one thing, he hadn't been keen on the idea of taking her with them out to Black Forest again, since he was determined that this was going to be a day of action, not conversation, and the girl might have gotten hurt. Then too it was probably a good thing that she had left now, without their having had sex again. He knew how she *thought* she felt about him, and he himself sometimes felt half in love with her. But since the thing was so obviously impossible, so doomed from the start, he couldn't help feeling that it might be a damned good thing for both of them that it end now, this way, with her running out on him.

Still, on the way back to the hotel, he drove slowly and kept an eye out for her. But she was not to be seen. He was afraid that she was gone.

Ironically, when he reached the hotel, he found that the same was true of Jennifer. He was crossing the lobby toward the elevators when one of the desk clerks beckoned to him.

"From Miss Kellogg," the man said, handing him a sealed envelope. Inside, Crow found a note written on hotel stationery:

Dear Crow,

Sorry to take off so abruptly this way, but I had to catch an 8:30 flight to L.A. I hate to leave you in the lurch but I really have no stomach for any more affairs like the one in Creston Harbor. Nor am I very keen on the idea of helping you try to prove that my uncle is a monster.

Even more important, I figured that if you were all on your own, you'd realize the futility of what you're trying to do, and give it up.

I think of you as much more than a friend. And I look forward to being with you again—in Santa Barbara.

Love,
Jennifer

As he finished reading the note, the desk clerk drily informed him that he didn't have to check out.

"Miss Kellogg paid for the suite through the end of the week," the man explained.

"Is that a fact?" Crow said.

"Yes, it is."

"I'd like a copy of the bill, please."

The desk clerk assumed an expression of effete bewilderment. "For what purpose?"

"My own purpose."

"I see. Well yes, I suppose so." The clerk got the bill out of a drawer and took it away, apparently to be photocopied. When he returned, he handed Crow the copy without looking at him, pretending total interest in a co-worker's telephone conversation.

"Thanks a lot," Crow said to him. "I like to keep a record of what I steal."

By the time he left the hotel again, Crow was beginning to feel a sense of relief at being on his own finally, able to concentrate all his energies—his curiosity as much as his rage—on the matter at hand. He hadn't forgotten how much help the girls had been so far, but he couldn't help feeling that from this point on he would do better alone, without having to worry about their safety or their problems. There were times during the last few days, in fact, when the murder of his father and the others had come to seem almost like an abstract concern of his, little more than a hobby. He'd felt somewhat like a fighter who had to dance and make small talk between rounds. And though he didn't blame the girls for this—and especially not Reno, since the investigation wasn't in any way her fight—still he couldn't deny the new sense of purpose and concentration he felt as he sped north on the freeway.

Near the Academy intersection he pulled into a shopping center and bought cigarettes and beer and snack foods and some other items he figured he might need in the hours or days ahead: a blanket, a hunting knife and sheath, a two-inch roll of adhesive tape, and a box of thirty-eight caliber shells. Then he proceeded on the road out to Black Forest and turned onto Tashoda Lane. He pulled in at the abandoned cement-block house, parking behind it just as he had with Reno the previous afternoon. Only now he positioned the car so he had a clear view of the dirt road through the windshield as he sat and waited—a wait that might last one hour or twenty-four, for all he knew. The only thing he was sure of was that eventually Barbara Queen or Fatso was going to have to come driving past him on an errand of one kind or another. And then he would make his move.

It was around noon when he got there, and he spent the first hour just sitting in the car, smoking an occasional cigarette. Later, he exchanged the old bullets in his thirty-eight for new ones and returned the gun to his ankle holster. He ate a packaged ham sandwich and drank a can of beer, and every half hour or so he would get out of the car and stretch his legs for a few minutes. And by three o'clock he had a much better understanding of why his father had called such duty the "dingleberry beat." Though Crow himself as yet didn't have hemorrhoids, he could well imagine how years of stake-outs might change that fact. At the same time, he felt none of the boredom implicit in the term, and for the obvious reason that he was not waiting for a client's wife to leave a motel assignation, but rather —what? Was it death he was waiting for? Or only conflict, revelation, satisfaction? The latter, he told himself. Surely, the latter.

It was after four when the first person from Queen's place came driving past. Only it was the woman, Kitty, probably on her way to get the mail. So Crow stayed where he was and a few minutes later the car went past again, this time heading back to the house. Crow was well aware by then that Barbara Queen or Fatso—or both— might have left during the morning, before he arrived on the scene. And he was beginning to accept the fact that even if they were there, still up at the house, whole days might pass before one of them or the other went out on an errand. He had known this all along, of course, but had pushed it to the back of his mind, telling himself that it was more likely than not that one of them would leave their citadel sometime during the afternoon or evening. He had expected to be at least that lucky.

But now he was not so sure. The sun was sliding toward the mountains and he knew that the moment it disappeared, the air would turn sharply colder. It was a prospect that did not appeal to him, spending a long May night at over seven thousand feet, with only the car and a blanket to keep him from freezing to death. He had enough experience in the Cascades to know what a fatal combination thin air and even mildly cold temperatures posed. A number that would only cause discomfort at sea level here would have one stiff as a board by morning. But even as he accepted it now that he could not stay where he was much past nightfall, he found it just as impossible to accept another night of frustration and postponement. Yet he didn't know what else he could do. Certainly he couldn't just drive on up the road and "move in." He didn't need Jennifer to remind him that if the two of them didn't constitute an army, neither did he alone.

So he continued to wait. He ate another sandwich and had another can of beer. He watched the sun's rays turn almost horizontal, filtering like brass bars through the pines, lighting an occasional squirrel, scrawny black little things, more like tree rats than squirrels as he knew them. And then the sun was gone and the cold hit like a sudden wind. Crow was out of his car at the time, moving about the area, waiting, thinking. And he was there an hour later in the growing darkness when a bank of floodlights suddenly came on high up in the trees, accompanied by an outdoor stereo blasting a heavy-metal rock number so loud it seemed to come from right above his head, as if the sky had split and the apocalypse was upon him. Forgetting the road, he made his way through the trees and past the barbed-wire fence to the base of the hill on top of which was Queen's house. In the light of the half-moon, the hill didn't appear difficult to climb, despite its rocky face.

Before he started, though, Crow tried to figure out what might be waiting for him up there. Why, he wondered, had the lights and stereo suddenly come on? Considering how cold it already was— probably close to the freezing point—he doubted that the women or Fatso would have come out onto the patio for more than a few seconds. If it hadn't been for the stereo, he might have been able to hear if any of them were outside, know for sure what he was getting into without first climbing to the top of the hill and having a look. But the music thundered on.

An added concern of his was whether or not they had any dogs on the premises. He hadn't seen one the previous day, nor any sign of one, yet he knew it was possible that there could have been one or more somewhere in the house—sleeping then, but out watching over their mistresses now. Where the women and Fatso would not sense his coming, especially if they were drinking, a dog certainly would. But he decided finally that he had no choice except to go with his own observation—that there were only people on the hill.

He took the gun out of his boot and put it in the right-side pocket of his leather jacket. The hunting knife and sheath hung from his belt, on the other side. And he had the adhesive tape in another pocket, something with which to bind the three of them, so he could handle them by himself. He could have been better-armed, he knew —an Uzi submachine gun would have been nice to have—yet he didn't feel unprepared as he made his way up the hill, around and over the boulders that seemed to hold the promontory in place. The closer he got to the top, the louder the music became, music that sounded like a sawmill operated by Valkyries. In the din he listened for the sound of a dog barking, but he heard none. And then suddenly he was at the top, peering between boulders—and what he saw was the whirlpool spa and the heads of the two women, barely visible in the steam, which billowed against the house, floodlit and spectral. He looked for a sign of Fatso, but the man apparently was in the house, either alone or with Paul Queen.

Concentrating on the women then, Crow saw the shotgun lying next to their robes on the pool's apron. For a few moments he watched as they sported in the steam, laughing, kissing, fondling each other. Briefly Kitty rose up out of the water and presented her breasts to the avid mouth of Barbara Queen. And it was then Crow slipped over the top of a boulder and walked quickly toward them, gun in hand. Neither of them even saw him until he was upon them, pocketing his own gun and picking up the shotgun, a double-barreled sixteen gauge. Through the steam, he motioned with the gun.

"Get out. One at a time."

Barbara Queen came first, covering her meager breasts with her hands and looking at him with loathing more than fear. He told her to put on her robe and clasp her hands behind her head, and she complied.

"What the fuck do *you* want?" she asked.

Telling her to shut up, he motioned for Kitty to come out of the whirlpool. And she did so with a sullen cockiness, sticking out her high, fine breasts and raking him with her eyes. When she had her robe on and her hands behind her head, he motioned with the shotgun for the women to start for the house, which was brightly lit, both upstairs and down. Crow could see that there was no one in the game room; nevertheless, he stopped the women just outside the door.

"Play it smart, and no one gets hurt," he told them.

"Where's your young friend?" Barbara asked. "Or are you all on your own this time?"

"I'll ask the questions," he said.

"We're freezing!"

"Me too," Crow said. "But first, where's the fat man?"

"Upstairs. In the kitchen."

Crow leveled the shotgun at her. "It'd be stupid to try jerking me around."

"That's where he is, for Christ's sake! He's baking a fucking cake!"

Crow slid the glass door open and motioned them in ahead of him. Closing the door behind him, he asked the women if there was a place where he could keep the fat man for the time being.

"You could lock him in the wine cellar," Kitty said, and Barbara gave her a searing look.

"Where is it?" Crow asked.

"Down the hall."

"Lead on."

They went out of the game room and past the open stairway and turned into the west wing of the house. Just past a utility room, they came to a heavy wooden door. Opening it, Crow reached in and turned on the light in the small dank windowless room. He asked where the key was and Kitty told him that it was hanging next to the light switch. After he found it, he again motioned with the shotgun, this time for the women to enter the cellar.

"White bastard!" Kitty said.

Barbara Queen laughed at her. "What did you expect, dumbo?"

Crow couldn't believe how cool the two of them still were—no different from yesterday, in daylight, not under a gun—and he had to wonder if they knew something he did not: such as that a CIA hit squad was waiting for him upstairs. He checked to make sure that the lock was not operable from the inside, then he stepped back out and closed the door and locked it. His heart was beating hard by now and the pressure in his bladder made him dearly wish that he had not drunk any beer. To make sure of his weapon, he broke it down and checked the shells inside, then closed it again and started back. When he was only halfway up the open stairway he could see the old man, Paul Queen, in the living room, once again sitting in his wheelchair, watching television. As Crow reached the top, he noticed the old man straining to turn his head, evidently having heard him. But Crow turned quickly in the other direction, passing the front door and moving down the other wing, past the dining room and toward the kitchen from which the steady whirring sound of a food processer emanated.

And then he saw him, the fat man, aproned and sweaty and flour-dusted, happy as a cat in a birdcage. As he turned, switching off the processer, he suddenly saw Crow standing there, holding the gun on him, and he jumped back in such fright that he almost fell down. Eyes bugged, holding his heart, he bleated at Crow:

"How did you get in here? What do you want?"

"Answers," Crow said.

Holding his hands in the air, gulping and nodding, the fat man toddled toward Crow.

"Yes, answers!" he cried. "I'll tell you everything I can! The whole truth! I really will! Just don't hurt me! Please!"

"I'm not here to hurt you," Crow told him. "But then I'm not here to listen to a bunch of lies either. I want it straight."

"Oh, you've got it! You've got it!" The man practically ran into the gun in his eagerness to comply.

Crow had to prod him with it. "Cool it, for Christ's sake!"

"Yes, yes. Of course." Fatso was wiping his hands on his apron now, bowing and shuffling like a comic Oriental waiter.

Crow told him to lead the way down to the wine cellar, that he had to check on the women before he could begin his interrogation.

The women had seemed almost too cooperative, Crow thought. He wondered if they had an extra key or some other surprise waiting for him.

"You've got them already?" Fatso squealed. "That's where they are?"

"That's where I left them."

"Congratulations. You do good work."

Crow told him to shut up. They had gone down the stairs, again stimulating in the old man what must have been a rage of curiosity. But Crow continued to ignore him. When they reached the wine cellar, he tossed the keys to Fatso and told him to unlock the door and then to get down on his knees and touch his head to the floor. If the women were going to emerge with flying bottles or any other weapons, he wanted to have the advantages of distance and a clear shot. But as it turned out, they didn't even come out. They remained inside, almost as docile now as the man.

"Okay, lock them up again," he said.

As the fat man did so, Crow asked him his name.

"Diefenbaker," he was told. "Calvin Diefenbaker. People call me Dief."

"All right, Dief—stay on your knees and crawl toward me." Crow had backed up to a second stairway located at the nexus of the building, a stairway that probably led to the garage. He sat down on the second step and told Diefenbaker to prostrate himself, with his hands behind his head.

"Okay, first question," Crow said. "Who killed the retired policeman, Orville Crow? Who pushed him off Mulholland Drive in his own car?"

"Teller and Billy Boy Sims," he was told.

"Who are they? The redhead one of them?"

Diefenbaker shook his head.

"So, who *are* they, then? They work for you?"

"For Barbara Queen, yes, they did. But they're dead now."

"You sure about that?"

"Oh yes. I can prove it."

And they did the hookers too? As well as the kid in Santa Barbara?"

Diefenbaker was trying to nod, which was not easy for a fat man lying on his stomach. "Yes—all of them," he said.

Over the next few minutes, Crow learned that Diefenbaker was a lawyer, a public defender for Los Angeles County. He got his address and found out that the group he worked for was called New Day Construction Company and that Barbara Queen was in charge of it. John Dumbrosky—the redheaded man in Mazatlan—was second in command. The group's purpose originally was simply "dirty tricks," the fomenting of civil unrest through such acts as desecrating synagogues and burning crosses on black-owned properties—"little things like that."

Crow put the shotgun right against Diefenbaker's head then and the man whimpered.

"Later I ask Barbara Queen these same questions, Dief. So I wouldn't try to snow me."

"I'm not! I'm not!" he cried.

"Okay then, let's move on from 'dirty tricks.' Let's talk about the photographs Barbara Queen delivered to Costello. What was that about? And keep in mind, there's a great deal I already know."

Haltingly, so short of breath he could hardly speak, Diefenbaker led him through the story. A young state senator, Richard Schoonover, and some rich young Arab had had a simultaneous "date" with a male prostitute, an ex-Hollywood choreographer who was some sort of expert in sadomasochism and bondage, and had a simulated dungeon in his North Hollywood apartment.

"He had racks and chains and all that kind of exotic junk. And he had a lot of speed and amyl nitrite and whatever else anybody needed."

Crow told him to get on with it.

"Well, the choreographer, I guess, experienced a little too much excitement and had a heart attack. Schoonover and the Arab thought he was dying—which he was—so they called the fire department and then they both took off. On the street in front of the apartment, some goddamn fool was taking pictures—apparently of some old lady and her dog. But he also snapped the senator and the Arab—as well as the three kids on the corner, who were observing it all."

Diefenbaker had to stop for a few moments, trying to catch his breath, and Crow told him to relax, that nothing was going to happen to him.

"Okay, okay, I'll try," the man gulped. "Well, Senator Schoonover followed the photographer home and then he called the man who owns him and told him about the problem. Now this was a very big man he called—in fact, the same man who owns us too—New Day Construction. He pays the bills and doesn't really ask for much in return."

"Henry Kellogg?" Crow asked.

The fat man laughed. "Heavens, no, he's just a smokescreen of Barbara's. I guess she's always hated Kellogg because he had so much power over her father. Actually the two of them—Kellogg and her old man—are just a couple of old CIA hands who happen to believe in the same things—everything we at New Day *don't* believe in. So she runs him across the stage every now and then—a convenient red herring."

"All right then—if not him, who?"

"You'll never believe it."

"Try me."

"The Hollywood producer, Ted Matson."

Diefenbaker had been right—Crow found it very hard to believe that Matson could have been the man behind it all. One of the most successful TV and film producers ever, Matson was also a national political figure, a staunch backer of liberal and leftist causes both at home and abroad. Not only rich and famous, he was a card-carrying member of the jet set, the "beautiful people."

"And you're saying *he* ordered the murders?" Crow said.

Diefenbaker shook his head. "Not at all. Oh, Barbara might say that, but I know better. All Matson wanted us to do was track down who the witnesses were and find out what they saw."

"To protect his boy, huh?"

"Yes."

"Senator Schoonover—not the Arab."

"Right."

"This Schoonover, he's somebody big in California?"

Diefenbaker shook his head. "Naw! He's just a lightweight. But a comer maybe—you never know. He—"

"Looks like Robert Redford?"

Diefenbaker didn't answer for a few moments. Then he nodded. "Yeah, I guess he kind of does. I never thought about it before."

"It doesn't matter. Get on with it. If Matson didn't order the killings, who did?"

Diefenbaker moaned and shook his head. "Until I came here I figured that nobody did. I figured they just happened because of Teller—the guy we sent to the photographer's to get the pictures. His full name was Marvin Teller and it turned out he was a lot more psycho than we thought—both him and Sims, his ex-con boy. As I said before, they both worked for us. For New Day. And for a time I thought Teller just took it on himself to hit everybody—"

"Including the photographer."

"The photographer was first, yes. I just couldn't keep up with it all. I couldn't even believe it was happening."

"You said you *used* to think it was all this Teller's doing—until you came here. What changed your mind?"

Again Diefenbaker had to catch his breath. For a time he just lay there on the carpet, breathing heavily, saying nothing. Then he began to shake his head. "You've got to protect me," he said. "You can't let her—"

Crow prodded him again. "All I *have* to do is pull this trigger."

Diefenbaker whimpered again and nodded vigorously. "Well, let me just tell you this—in the office down the hall Barbara showed me a kind of photo album. And in it are all the original snapshots—of Senator Schoonover and the Arab and the kids on the corner. Even the old woman and her dog. And there's also the press clippings of all the hits, starting with the photographer and then your father and the hookers and the kid in Santa Barbara."

"So?"

"So I asked her what she was doing with it and she smiled and said it was her ticket to Ted Matson's checkbook. 'We're gonna be big,' she told me."

301

"You're saying she ordered the killings in order to blackmail Matson."

Diefenbaker made a kind of shrugging motion. "Not *ordered*. I think she just sensed the—what would you call it?—the *inclination* of Teller. And went along with it. Used it."

"And this Teller and Sims—how did they die?"

"Teller shot Sims in his car in Griffith Park and set it afire. Then Dumbrosky—the redhead—he gave Teller a briefcase not to be opened. But of course Teller opened it anyway. It was a bomb."

"Teller and Sims—they in the photo album too?"

"Not their pictures, but as news items, yes. Everybody's in it. Everybody so far." Diefenbaker suddenly let go of the back of his neck and rolled over. He pressed his hands to the sides of his head. "This whole thing is killing me," he sniveled. "It's like a nightmare that won't end. A dreamworld. Teller, I could understand—he and his Billy Boy lived in a kind of fugue state, dreaming their way through life. But now Barbara—and *you*. The dream just goes on. It never stops."

Crow told him that there were two things he still had questions about. The first was how they had known about him, known that he would lead them to Costello, and the fat man explained how he had called Crow's home and how the housekeeper had offered that "Mister Crow's son" was now taking over all his cases, in fact had already gone up to Santa Barbara, "to investigate something."

"It was just a gamble," Diefenbaker said. "Barbara figured you were probably in touch with Costello and would lead us to him."

"Which I did."

"Yes. And what was the other question?"

"The kid up in Santa Barbara—did you know he was Henry Kellogg's nephew?"

Apparently feeling safer now, Diefenbaker sat up and scooted back against the opposite wall. He looked dumbfounded.

"Kellogg! Christ, now I remember Teller using that name when he finally reported—and how Barbara reacted. But it didn't connect. I never thought it was *that* Kellogg."

"You telling me it was just a coincidence?"

The fat man held out his hands, like a beggar. "It had to be."

Crow didn't know whether to believe him or not, even though everything else he'd said had the ring of truth.

"And the Arab that came running out of the building with the senator—he didn't figure in anywhere? He had no part in the case?"

Diefenbaker shook his head. "None at all, except in Barbara's head, when you showed up. She undoubtedly thought of him, an Arab, as a convenient tool for diverting suspicion onto Kellogg."

It was Crow's turn to shake his head. "Hard to believe."

"Because it's all a dream," Diefenbaker explained. "We live in a dream world."

"Well, my bladder's for real," Crow told him. He motioned him into the bathroom down the hall and made him kneel on all fours in the tub while he, Crow, took a long and much needed beer piss. By then he was feeling almost exultant at the way things were working out. With what he'd found out, and if he could get the photo album Diefenbaker had told him about, he began to believe that he wouldn't have to settle for just learning the truth himself but now could go after the lovely maiden herself: Justice. Diefenbaker, he believed, could be made to turn state's evidence—against not only Barbara Queen but the big fish himself, Ted Matson. It would be a long and complicated trial, and just the thought of being a part of it, being tied down in L.A. for Christ knew how long—the prospect was not very appealing. But then what choice did Crow have? Too many people had died for him just to walk away now.

"Okay, get up," he said to Diefenbaker. "We go get the ladies now. And where is this photo album you've been telling me about?"

"In Barbara's office. Next to the wine cellar."

The more Crow learned about the conspiracy, the more he wondered at its total lack of a moral center, some sort of philosophic or political motivation to help explain all the carnage that had taken place. So as he herded the three of them into Barbara Queen's office he was almost relieved to see on the walls of the room at least a pictorial statement of political belief. There were ancient posters of Mao and Che Guevara and Malcolm X as well as an artistic rendering of the Stalinist slogan: *You can't make a revolution with silk gloves.* There was a potpourri of photographic memorabilia of Viet-

303

nam, including pictures of the My Lai massacre and defoliated forests and Colonel Loan caught in the celebrated moment of executing his prisoner. There was also a huge, almost abstract rendering of two women locked in sexual embrace.

As a political statement, it all would have struck Crow as being merely hackneyed and unfocused, were it not for Diefenbaker's charge that Barbara Queen had either initiated the killings or at the very least had permitted them to take place—for money. And that made her little walls of idealistic propaganda seem not just pathetic but offensive too, not unlike the grimly self-righteous expression of Colonel Loan himself.

Barbara Queen and Kitty had said almost nothing when Crow unlocked the wine cellar door and herded them, along with Diefenbaker, into the office, which was about twelve feet by twelve, most of it taken up by a huge flat desk and a black leather sofa that sat facing each other. Crow had the women sit down on the sofa and then he stood over Diefenbaker as the fat man got the photo album out of one of the desk drawers. Taking the album, he told Diefenbaker to sit down next to the desk, in a straight-backed chair there. He thought it important to keep them all divided: the women on one side and him on the other, with the fat man in between.

Crow then sat down at the desk, still holding the shotgun out in front of him. Without taking his eyes off the women for more than a second at a time, he riffled through the album with his left hand, feeling a kind of shock at seeing again the old photos of Richard and the hookers. But it was the other pictures that gripped his attention, the ones he'd never seen before: Senator Schoonover and the Arab running toward the camera; the old lady and her dog fleeing from it; the Arab getting into a limousine, with three of his countrymen standing guard. And then there were the news clippings, those terrible, negligible little items about death and violence, no different from the thousands of other such stories that crowded the pages of the world's newspapers day after day, *ad infinitum*.

"I don't know what you think you're going to do with that," Barbara Queen said to him. "It means nothing. And it's not mine. I've never seen it before."

She and Kitty were sitting close together, both in their hooded, terrycloth robes. While the light-skinned Negress merely seemed filled with hatred Barbara merely looked haughty and condescending. Crow did not doubt that if the shotgun still had been in her control, he would have been dead for some time now.

"And as for this fat ass here," Barbara went on, indicating Diefenbaker, "how could you or a judge or anybody else believe a word he says. He recently killed a man down in Mexico—didn't you, Dief?"

The fat man would not even look at her.

"Oh, I don't know," Crow said. "I find it pretty convincing, what he had to say about you and New Day Construction and the famous Ted Matson." Crow reached for the phone on the desk and pulled it in front of him. He looked at Diefenbaker. "And I think the police or the FBI would find it convincing too. You could make a deal, you know. Turn state's evidence."

The fat man was sitting forward on the tiny chair, shaking his head and rubbing his hands. "No, I couldn't do that," he said. "Anyway, I thought you just came here for the truth. Nothing else. That's what you said."

"Only because I didn't think anything else was possible," Crow told him. "Someone like you—on the inside of it all, but not a part of it, even against it—I didn't know you existed. If you turned state's evidence, they'd let you walk. I know they would. Even the Mexican thing—the redhead did it all. I'll testify to that."

Diefenbaker was still shaking his head. "No, Ted Matson would beat us. He'd hire the best—for her too."

Barbara had taken a pack of cigarettes off the desk and now was lighting one. "You bet your ass he would," she laughed.

Crow looked at her, at the dark scornful eyes in the narrow, almost aquiline face. "You're a real prize, aren't you?" he said. "A rich man's leftist. If you can't make a revolution, you'll at least make some money."

"Up yours," she said, blowing smoke at him.

"And all the lives involved—all the people you had killed—it really doesn't bother you at all, does it?"

She looked at him with loathing and amusement. "What lives?" she asked. "What killings?"

"You'll find out." He picked up the phone then, preparing to dial the operator and ask her to connect him with the police. But even before his left index finger found the correct hole on the dial, Barbara Queen had turned and nodded to her lover.

"Okay, do it," he heard. "And don't worry—he's chicken."

Where the tiny automatic had come from, he had no idea—he could have missed it when he'd checked their robes out by the pool, or maybe she'd picked it up in the wine cellar, or just now, from between the cushions of the sofa. Whatever its source, Crow found it oddly mesmerizing as it rose in Kitty's olive hand, so compact and deadly. And just as his other forefinger had begun its terrible contraction, the fat man was off his chair and lunging for the gun, apparently to push it down. But before he reached it, Kitty had swung it on him and pulled the trigger, filling the room with brief thunder. And immediately blood began to bloom on the white bib of Diefenbaker's apron. Wall-eyed, he covered the chest wound with one of his chubby hands, almost as if he were ashamed of it. Then he dropped to his knees, his free hand grasping an in-and-out basket and pulling it with him as he fell, knocking off the desk an ashtray, a stapler, and an ornate kerosene lamp, which shattered on the floor, spilling its fuel. In the microsecond Crow saw all this, he also saw the tiny silver automatic swinging again in his direction. Only this time he didn't wait to pull the trigger—and Kitty was tossed up and over the sofa, a ragdoll with most of its head missing, spouting a soft sleet of blood.

In the smoke, in the terrible silence, Barbara Queen followed Kitty down onto the floor and for a few seconds she seemed to be trying to find a way to hold her, to hug her. And when she couldn't, she began to scream and scream. Then abruptly the piercing sound stopped, along with Crow's heart, as he saw the woman reach for her dead lover's gun. In some cool, faraway part of his mind he wondered what it was: a suicide pact or only hatred, some savage and irresistible lust on her part to try to kill him at any cost? If it was the first, then she quickly got her way—for even as she was raising the gun, he cut loose with the shotgun's other barrel and almost tore her in two.

The room by then was filled with smoke, from both the shotgun and the kerosene Barbara Queen's cigarette had ignited on the rug.

Flames had already spread to the wastebasket and were beginning to crawl up onto the drapes as well as onto the mounded figure of Diefenbaker lying on the floor. Crow quickly pulled him back behind the desk, out of the flames. But the man had no pulse and his eyes were lifeless; the bullet evidently had rent his heart. As for the women, the shotgun hadn't left much to check. Dropping the gun into the fire, Crow picked up the photo album and hurried out of the small office.

For only a moment he considered trying to find a fire extinguisher. Then he realized that the fire might well be a godsend, something to cover up the terrible—and virtually unexplainable—events of the last few minutes. What police department, he wondered—in fact, what jury—would ever believe his story of how the killings had taken place? And even if in the end the fire didn't totally obscure the fact that the victims had been shot, still there might be so little evidence left that the police would never be able to build a case, against him or anyone else. In any event, he decided that it would be better not only not to extinguish the fire, but to help it along.

So he moved quickly up the stairs and into the living room, where he snatched a pair of afghans off the sofa and tossed them, along with the photo album, onto the lap of Paul Queen, who was still sitting in his wheelchair in front of the TV. Crow checked to make sure that the old man was firmly strapped into the chair. Then, as he swung it around and started out of the room, he noticed that the fireplace, unlike the one in the game room below, had phony iron logs. He'd hoped there would be a gas range in the kitchen. But now he didn't even have to look there, he realized, as he stopped the wheelchair and went over to the fireplace. Turning the petcock, he heard the gas and smelled it too as it jetted into the room. Soon it would reach the stairway and begin its slow descent toward the fire, not unlike a serpent seeking warmth.

Meanwhile Crow rapidly pushed the old man to the front door and on outside. His original intention had been to push the wheel-chair halfway around the circular gravel driveway and to leave the old man there for the firemen to find later—while he, Crow, ran back through the woods to where his car was parked. But it occurred to him now that when the house blew, Queen might be hit by falling debris. So he decided to push him all the way down the driveway —or more accurately, to *brake* him, to hold onto the wheelchair and keep it from careening on its own down the curving, moonlit drive into the pine trees on either side or into the gate at the bottom. The hill was so steep and the roadbed so rough that Crow had all he could do to keep the wheelchair under control. And all the way, he was painfully aware that he hadn't as yet said one word to the man about the shots he undoubtedly had heard, or even about what they were doing now, rattling down the long hill together in the darkness. In the end, he decided that there was really nothing he could say about the shootings, nothing that would make them other than what they were, nothing that wouldn't in some way incriminate him, if only to a man who couldn't speak.

So he said nothing, not until they reached the gravel road at the bottom.

"I'm gonna leave you here, Mister Queen," he told him. "The fire trucks will spot you. Your house is gonna blow any minute."

Facing the old man, he tucked the afghans in tightly about him, and for just a moment he met his eye glaring at him in the night light. Taking the photo album, he backed away from him for a few feet and then turned and started to run down the road. And he couldn't help thinking that a number of firefighters would probably never forget what they were soon about to see: a one-eyed paralyzed old man sitting in a wheelchair in the middle of a dead-end dirt road, over a hundred yards from his house blazing up on the hill. For certain, it was a sight that Crow would not forget.

Just as he reached his car behind the cement-block building, he saw the flash in his peripheral vision, an orange-white sun rising for a split second above the hill back in the trees. And then came the thunderclap and finally the fire itself, scattered and small at first, then burgeoning higher and higher. Crow didn't want to be seen driving out on Tashoda Lane as the fire trucks and police cars came heading in, so he waited in his rented Mustang. And within a few minutes the official vehicles came roaring past, sirens blaring and flashing lights illuminating the great clouds of dust they had kicked up. They were followed by a number of unofficial cars, as the curious and the idle gathered to watch what was undoubtedly turning into a very impressive fire.

Not until there was a break in their coming did Crow leave. He drove slowly down to Black Forest Road, and he stayed at the speed limit as he took the highway back to the city. Every now and then as the road curved east or west he was able to see off to his side in the darkness, far away, a soft orange glow. And it occurred to him that if he hadn't known what it was, he might have thought it beautiful.

FIFTEEN

ON the flight back to Los Angeles, Crow remembered Sergeant Olson's tale of the fourteen-year-old "spade stickup artist" he had shotgunned in self-defense. And Crow had to wonder if in time he too would become a hypertensive, alcoholic insomniac—or maybe even worse, considering that his offense was double that of Olson. He kept reminding himself that he'd had no choice in the matter, that in both cases he too had shot only in self-defense. But somehow it made no difference. His hand continued to shake as he sat there clutching a vodka martini, and squinted out the tiny window at the sun splintering off the jet's slender silver wing.

After leaving Black Forest and returning to the hotel, he had not slept a wink, in fact hadn't even tried to sleep. All he had wanted was not to think about Barbara Queen and Kitty as he'd left them, not just shot, but mangled, destroyed. Over and over he saw the young Negress taking the first load, bouncing up and over the leather couch, with her arms and legs flying. And it did no good to ask himself *why*—why the two of them virtually had committed suicide, why they for some incredible reason had thought he wouldn't defend himself. It was monstrous. It was absurd. But above all it was sickening, the knowledge that he had killed, and in *that* way.

He finished the martini and promptly ordered another, much to the displeasure of the *Watchtower-*reading young woman who sat next to him, with her knees locked tightly together and her elbow tucked in, a good six inches from the armrest between them. And Crow could only wonder if the woman had the gift of extrasensory perception, some special antenna able to pick up the negative "vibes" that he figured a killer must give off.

He found it a bitter irony that in getting themselves killed, Barbara Queen and Diefenbaker had effectively prevented him from going to the police or the FBI with what he now had: virtual proof of the conspiracy, including the names of the conspirators. It would have been no small pleasure for him to take the photo album in and dump it in front of Olson and the two Hollywood cops, those supersleuths who knew a troublemaking john when they saw one. But without Diefenbaker as state's evidence, Crow knew that the album itself wouldn't be enough to sustain a case. And anyway all the conspirators—all the killers—were themselves dead now. As for Ted Matson and Senator Schoonover, Crow had to admit that their guilt was problematic at best. No politically ambitious district attorney would prosecute so weak a case against such powerful men.

If the weakness of the case had been his only problem, Crow still might have done something, such as send the album anonymously to the police, with a cover letter from, say, "a former employee of New Day Construction." Expressing remorse at this past association, he would have gone on to explain the meaning of the album: the chain of guilt running from Ted Maston down through Barbara Queen and Diefenbaker to the killers themselves: Teller and Sims and Dumbrosky. But Crow was afraid that such a move at this time would only alert the police to what had happened in Mazatlan and Black Forest, give them a case against Crow himself more than anybody else. Even desultory detective work would surely turn up the fact that he had been in both places at the time of the deaths. So it seemed by far the better part of valor to keep it all a secret, even from Jennifer. And he saw no reason why this would be particularly difficult, especially after reading the morning Colorado Springs paper, which had bannered the story:

Three Deaths in Mystery
Black Forest Fire

Reading on, Crow had learned that fire companies from the Springs as well as from Black Forest had answered the alarm and that there had been almost nothing left of the house when they arrived. A gas explosion was thought to have been the cause of the fire, which had spread into the pine woods south of the house. A Black Forest Fire Department spokesman reported that the three bodies found in what had been a downstairs room were all burned beyond recognition. There was no mention of gunshot wounds or of finding any guns, yet both the police and the arson squad were investigating— because of the "mystery element," the story explained, "the fact that the owner of the house, Paul Queen, was found sitting out in the road in his wheelchair waiting upon the arrival of the fire trucks. A seventy-two-year-old stroke victim, Mr. Queen is reported to be unable to speak or move his limbs."

There were two news photos on the front page: one of the old man sitting in his wheelchair, watching the fire as it consumed the remains of his house; the other of the lonely gravel road down below, with an X marking the spot where he had been found. (The firemen evidently had taken him back up the hill.) Together, the pictures provided pungent illustration of the fire's most intriguing aspect— not how it had started or how the three had died, but how and why Queen had gotten where he was. Given that enigma and the public interest it would arouse, Crow didn't doubt that the bodies would soon be identified and their wounds specified and the guns recovered. But because none of this had been done at the outset, he could only conclude that the house was totally destroyed, a pile of char in which any evidence pointing to him would be gone, burned.

In fact, short of Jennifer or Reno reporting him, he saw little chance of his ever being linked to the deaths. And as far as that went, he didn't think it likely that the authorities would ever connect the Black Forest killings with those in Los Angeles and Mazatlan. To do that, the police would have had to know what he knew. And they did not.

So in effect Crow was returning home a victor. Without even seeking it, he had gotten revenge upon his father's murderers. And if the cost of that revenge was to be bad dreams and a sense of guilt —well, so be it. For dead certain, he was not going to go to the police and confess just so he could feel better about himself and sleep his usual eight hours a night. Barbara Queen had already deprived too many innocent people of their lives for him now to let her ghost deprive him of his liberty. That small final victory would not be hers.

Out the window of the jet he could see, far below, the beige carpet of the Nevada desert, already parched in May. Turning from it, he signaled the stewardess for another drink.

As soon as he was home in Van Nuys, in his father's house, he called Jennifer on the phone, determined to tell her all that he could without revealing his involvement in the killings and the fire. Which meant, of course, that he had to lie to her.

"I found out what we wanted to know," he said. "Richard wasn't a suicide. My father's death wasn't an accident. And Henry Kellogg had nothing to do with any of it."

He went on then and told her how he had waited for Barbara Queen or Fatso to drive past, and finally had followed the latter to the Black Forest grocery store. "Waylaying" the man there, he then had driven him back to the cement-block house, where the fat one had spilled his guts. Crow briefly told her everything that Diefenbaker had told him, and then he added that the man had agreed to turn state's evidence. But first, he wanted to go back up to Queen's house alone to get a scrapbook kept by Barbara Queen—a photo album containing the incriminating photographs and the news clippings of the killings. He'd promised Crow that he would bring the album to him at the Broadmoor.

"But he didn't come," Crow said. "And in the newspaper this morning I read that Queen's house burned to the ground last night and that three bodies had been found in it. But not Paul Queen. Him they found sitting in his wheelchair, out in the road. No one can figure how he got there."

Jennifer at first made no response. And when she finally spoke, her voice was soft and full of doubt. "Is that the truth, Crow?"

"What do you think? I'm a murderer and an arsonist?"

"No. I just—"

"I don't know what happened, Jennifer. As I said, Diefenbaker was supposed to meet me at the Broadmoor. With the proof—this photo album scrapbook of Barbara Queen's. Naturally, I haven't told anybody about any of this."

"Except me."

"Yes—except you."

"And Reno—she's not with you?"

"No, she's still gone."

He told her then that he had added up all their expenses, including the charter flight from Mazatlan, and his share came to twenty-one hundred dollars.

"I'll send you a money order tomorrow," he said. "After I cash my father's life-insurance check."

"You don't have to do that," she told him.

"Sure I do."

"All right, then."

She didn't ask when he would be coming up to Santa Barbara, and Crow was relieved that she hadn't. He still wanted very much to see her again, but for some reason he wasn't in any hurry. What he needed now, he figured, was time alone.

About an hour after he called her, he got a phone call from the executor at his father's bank, and it seemed that there was a realtor interested in buying the house for ninety thousand dollars cash—about twenty-five under market. Crow's sister had already okayed the sale, was in fact "very eager" to close.

Considering that there would be no broker's commission to pay and that there was no guarantee how long it might take to get full value for the house, Crow saw no reason not to concur with his sister's wishes.

"Sure," he told the executor. "Dump it."

The banker also told him that his sister wanted the furniture sold and that he was going to bring a couple of used-furniture buyers around to make an offer and that it would be a good idea for Crow to segregate what he himself wanted to keep—"personal items and so forth."

The way Crow was feeling, it was a chore that almost didn't get done. But finally he got a couple of empty boxes together and filled them with the framed photographs and clippings and other memorabilia hanging on the office wall. He also tossed in some other personal items he found in the old man's desk and files. Free then, he went straight into the kitchen and made himself a pitcher of martinis and sat through the evening and most of the night watching television and drinking. On his way back from the bathroom once, he stopped and looked into the guest bedroom, trying to remember just how Reno looked. But for some maddening reason, her features would not form. And finally all he could do was grin, accept the fact that even now, after she was gone, the girl was still able to thwart him.

Early that morning, before his flight out of Colorado Springs, he had called the police to check on her again, to find out if there had been any report yet of a girl matching her description being in an accident or having been picked up for one reason or another. But there was still nothing on her, so he went on to the airport alone, confident that she was hitching her way back to California. He still disliked the idea of her being on the road by herself, but he was relieved that she hadn't been in an accident and wasn't involved in any way with the police. He was also immensely grateful that she hadn't been with him out at Queen's place, hadn't had to witness what happened there, and didn't even have to know about it. So more than ever, he was glad that she had run when she had. Not only was he free of her now, but he didn't have to worry about her either, at least not in the special way he would have if she'd been there with him, a party to what he himself could only characterize as a slaughter. He might have bad dreams from now on, but at least Reno would not be part of them.

Considering all this, he would have thought he'd feel some sort of relief or happiness, standing there looking into her room. But all he felt was irritation, and even anger, because he couldn't form a satisfactory mental picture of her. He knew her eyes were brown and he knew how her smile flashed and he knew the color of her hair. And he even remembered the feel of her, the passion and strength

315

in her hard young body. Yet he could not bring it all together in his mind, could not conjure her there in the darkness.

Frustrated, he went back to his martinis, surprised at how many of them one could get away with when he was alone and not all that concerned about stumbling over the furniture or dropping off asleep every now and then, sometimes for hours. Drunk as he was, he still could not avoid his dreams, which came at him like starving rats off and on throughout the seemingly endless night. In one of the dreams he was hunting in the fog, shooting frantically up into the trees at some small black squirrels. Over and over he pulled the shotgun's trigger, and in time a pair of them began to fall, dropping from one limb to another, like acrobats showing off. But finally there were no limbs left and the creatures fell the rest of the way, landing at his feet. And he was shocked to see that they were not squirrels after all but tiny nude women, bleeding heavily into the snow. For some reason, he kept firing at them, almost as if he believed that was the only way he could stop the terrible flowing of their blood.

And there were other dreams, real heart-sprinters, doubly frightening because he dreamed them drunk, waking into yet another dream of sorts.

Hungover, and still wearing the clothes he had worn in Colorado Springs, he let the executor and his used-furniture buyers in at noon the next day and nodded an indifferent acceptance of the higher offer. The executor asked him if he wasn't feeling well and he said that it was the Valley smog, that at home in Seattle he was more accustomed to breathing water. The man nodded politely, evidently not expecting levity from such a wretch.

But finally the three of them left and Crow got himself together, bathing and shaving and changing his clothes. He ate a hurried breakfast on his way to the Strip and then he drove slowly up and down it for hours, not really expecting to see the girl, but hoping to anyway, for he was convinced by now that a good part of his misery was due to his feeling that he had failed Reno. While he couldn't do anything about his main problem—the slaughter—he figured he could at least try to find the girl and help her, keep her from drifting into the street life of Hollywood and Venice—keep her, that is, from a life of prostitution and drugs. Why, with the money he was soon to have, he could buy her a small used car and even drive with her to Nevada, get her safely back into the hands of her mother. And that was all he wanted, he told himself. Just to help the girl, to get her back on her feet again, at her own home.

After leaving the Strip, he drove out to Venice and prowled the oceanwalk until dark. And he wasn't particularly disappointed at not having found her, for this was only the first day, and both of those places she had mentioned—as goals of a sort—were like cities in themselves, places where even long-legged, copper-haired girls would not stand out. So he would simply go home and do his martinis and then come back the next day, almost like reporting for work. And that is what he did. But by the third day, hungover once again, sitting on a bench at the oceanwalk, he felt a growing sense of hopelessness and despair. Even as his skin tanned, his spirit seemed to grow paler and weaker, especially as he sat there watching the Southern California passing parade: the golden girls in string bikinis and the musclemen in leopard briefs, the bikers in Wehrmacht helmets and chainmail and the laidback blacks in cornrows and Day-Glo, the dopers in their sad rags leaning against the wind of their habits and the old folks too, hiding under muu-muus and pink cotton-candy hair. They came on skateboards and roller skates and on foot, wearing stereo headphones and holding transistor radios to their ears and sometimes listening to nothing in particular. And almost all had a certain glazed look in their eyes, a kind of private rapture, as if they were dreaming even now in the brilliant noon sunshine, perhaps even dreaming the dreams of a Teller or a Barbara Queen. Crow watched them as his arms tanned and his heart paled, and in time he began to wonder what he was doing there, what he was looking for. And he was never really sure—not until he finally saw her, about a quarter-mile down the oceanwalk, coming toward him with her long and easy stride, smoking a cigarette and wearing Jennifer's six-hundred-dollar jacket as jauntily as she swung her old cardboard suitcase. And it was a stunning discovery for Crow, the sudden realization that the last thing in the world he wanted was to help her return home, to help her get away from him.

As she came closer, he got up on shaky legs and walked toward

317

her. And for just a moment, when she first saw him, her smile flashed and there was joy in her eyes. Then she took it all away.

"What the hell do *you* want?"

He reached for her suitcase. "Let me carry that."

She switched it to her other hand. "You came all this way to carry my suitcase?"

"Not exactly."

"Jesus, Crow, you look terrible."

"I haven't been sleeping so good."

She looked at him. "Oh really? Why not? Jennifer been keeping you too busy?"

He told her that Jennifer was in Santa Barbara and had left Colorado right after she did. The girl smiled at that.

"Did she miss her jacket?"

"And her money too."

"I had my reasons."

"No, you didn't. It wasn't like you thought."

"Like hell it wasn't."

Crow decided that was an argument that would keep. He asked her how her trip had gone and she told him that a couple of "real nice mom-and-pop truckers" had picked her up in Colorado Springs and had taken her all the way to Palmdale, where she had stayed with them, in their house, an extra day.

"I just arrived here," she said. "And you still haven't told me what you want."

Crow took a deep breath. "Well, originally I figured I'd just sort of rescue you. You know, take you back to your mother in Nevada."

She gave him a pitying look. "Is that a fact?"

"But watching you come toward me now—" He couldn't believe what he was saying. "Watching you, I realized that wasn't what I wanted. What I really want is to take you back to Seattle. To live with me."

She gave him a wary glance, on guard against his trickery. But when his expression didn't change, she suddenly looked wounded. And she turned and ran from him, out across the strip of lawn and onto the beach, where he finally caught up with her. He took the suitcase away from her and dropped it onto the sand. He took her

318

in his arms and tried to kiss her, but she kept turning her face from him.

"*Lying bastard!*" she cried.

"It's daytime, Reno. It's day, and I ain't running anywhere."

"*Liar!*"

"It's not a lie."

"Oh yes it is! You know it is!"

He told her to look at him and when she did so, the pain and rage in her eyes slowly turned into wonderment.

"Are you *crying?*" she asked.

"Just a little."

And it was then she let him kiss her, then that she kissed him back, deeply, hugging him so tightly his back hurt. Finally she pulled away and looked up at him.

"Seattle?"

"Sure. My apartment's big enough. And if you wanted, you could go to school there. Even college. Use that one-forty I.Q. of yours."

"What about Jennifer?"

"What about her? She doesn't figure in."

"Honest?"

"Honest."

The girl just stood there looking up at him and Crow had the feeling that if they didn't do something soon, they were both going to explode.

"You got your old Datsun here?" she asked.

"You bet I do."

He picked up the suitcase and took her by the hand and together they started running down the beach toward the parking lot.